W. Davenport Adams

The Treasury of Modern Anecdote

Being a Selection from the Witty and Humorous Sayings of the last....

W. Davenport Adams

The Treasury of Modern Anecdote
Being a Selection from the Witty and Humorous Sayings of the last....

ISBN/EAN: 9783337113070

Printed in Europe, USA, Canada, Australia, Japan

Cover: Foto ©Andreas Hilbeck / pixelio.de

More available books at **www.hansebooks.com**

THE TREASURY

OF

MODERN ANECDOTE

BEING A

SELECTION FROM THE WITTY AND HUMOROUS SAYINGS
OF THE LAST HUNDRED YEARS.

Edited with Notes and Introduction

BY

W. DAVENPORT ADAMS,

AUTHOR OF THE "DICTIONARY OF ENGLISH LITERATURE," ETC.

EDINBURGH:
THE EDINBURGH PUBLISHING COMPANY.
LONDON: SIMPKIN, MARSHALL, & CO.

1881.

PREFACE.

THE present collection of Anecdotes differs from its predecessors in several particulars.

To begin with, it is strictly a Treasury of Modern Anecdote. It does not profess to dish up for the delectation of present-day readers stories which have been familiar to them all their lives, and which are, in fact, the commonplaces of ordinary conversation. There is a certain sprinkling of old favourites,—of time-honoured tales which no one likes to see omitted from any collection, however fresh it be in aim and character. But these are anecdotes of the perennial kind,—anecdotes which, the more they are known the better they are liked—which are so excellent in themselves that they never pall upon the taste. For the most part, however, the Anecdotes in this collection are emphatically modern, — modern in so far that they are drawn from modern sources, and refer to modern people. They do not, for the most part, go farther back than Walpole's "Letters," and they come down as far as the latest stories and reminiscences, such as those of Crabb Robinson and J. R. Planchè. It has seemed to the editor and to the publishers that the public is tired of the old stories that generally do duty in such collections, and that it is ready to welcome a work which shall put before it the cream of the spoken wit and humour of the last hundred years.

Again: the Anecdotes in this volume are, as far as can possibly be ascertained, authentic. The object of the editor and publishers has been to avoid as much as possible the old indefinite stories about "a lawyer," or "a doctor," or "a certain judge," and to confine this work chiefly to anecdotes for which some authority can be given, and which can be attributed with reasonable safety to particular individuals. It is not pretended that every authority given in this book is the ultimate or original authority, but an endeavour has honestly been made, in the majority of cases, to get at the origin of the anecdote, and to be sure that the witty and humorous saying quoted has been ascribed to the proper person. It is possible that, in this way, certain of our readers may notice the absence of pet anecdotes which have been attributed to different persons, and which, in the absence of sufficient evidence for identification, have been deliberately omitted from this volume. On the other hand, they will find many anecdotes apportioned for the first time to the individuals with whom they are actually connected. They will find the stories not only modern, but authentic.

Another feature of the work is the classification to which the Anecdotes have been subjected, those on "Men of Letters," or "Men of Society," or "Lawyers," or "Actors," and so on, having been grouped together on a plan which will be appreciated by the reader.

Further than this, the Anecdotes relating to particular individuals have been brought together and carefully arranged after a system which, it is hoped, will be equally useful and agreeable.

Where anecdotes have been fathered upon more than one individual on equally good authority, mention has been made of the fact; and notes have been appended in those cases where additional explanations appeared necessary. A full index has also been added.

W. D. A.

INTRODUCTION.

THE entertaining nature of a Book of Anecdotes will be freely con-
ceded. It will be acknowledged that, for whiling away a dull
afternoon or a spare half-hour, few things more suitable could be de-
vised. It is at once amusing and fragmentary; and whilst its inherent
fun excites the fancy and relieves the mind, the brevity of the matter
allows it to be taken up again and again without any weariness being felt.
A photograph album, we all know, is sometimes made to do duty on
these occasions, but the superiority of a Book of Anecdotes will readily
be allowed. The former palls upon the taste jaded by pictures of people
either unknown, or else too familiarly known; whilst an anecdote, even
if old, is, if good, perennially new, and, if it is wholly new as well as
good, it is welcomed as a "thing of beauty," and mentally recorded as a
"joy for ever." A Book of Anecdotes has, however, a further ground of
superiority over most other forms of parlour amusement. It is as useful
as it is entertaining. A poor observer is he who regards a good authentic
anecdote as being entertaining merely. To be sure, the first duty of
an anecdote is to amuse, but this is by no means all it does. A witty
or a humorous saying is not only interesting in itself; it is interesting
in reference to the circumstances that called it forth, and to the man
who uttered it. It may shed light upon the character or the life of that
man, and it may, by so doing, illustrate the history of the world. It
enlightens for us not only individual character, but human nature.

A

Elaborate histories are all very well, and profound essays are all very well; but if you want to get at the heart of a man, a woman, a people, or an event, is not a thoroughly authentic anecdote much more to the point? Does it not tell more, in the compass of a half-a-dozen lines or sentences, than the history in so many chapters, or the essay in so many pages or paragraphs?

An anecdote is valuable in two ways—in relation to the individual as a member of a class, and in relation to the individual *as* an individual. In the present volume, the anecdotes are so arranged that they may be regarded from both points of view—the men of society being grouped together, and the men of letters, and so on. Unfortunately, this classification does not altogether satisfy; as, for example, in the case of Sydney Smith, who was at once a man of society, a man of letters, and a clergyman; of Sheridan, who was a man of society, a man of letters, and a politician; of Theodore Hook, who was a man of society and a journalist; of Jekyll, who was a man of society and a barrister. In such cases, we have endeavoured to determine in which of these characters each of those we have named was most a wit or a humorist, and have ranged him accordingly under the heading to which he seemed most obviously to belong. The final decision was of the less importance that very few of the best wits and humorists were distinctly "shoppy" in their sayings. Unquestionably, however, there is a wit and there is a humour which pertains specially to special classes and professions, and the peculiar manner of which is very clearly discernible. There is a lightness and flippancy about society talk which cannot but be reflected in the recorded anecdotes of the men who frequented society. There is a sort of frivolity and vapidity, for example, about the witticisms of Luttrell and of Jekyll, of Selwyn, D'Orsay, and Alvanley, which at once stamp them as the production of members of the "fashionable" world. It is noticeable, again, in the jokes narrated of famous men of letters, that their wit and humour is decidedly tinctured by the nature of their occupation. They deal largely in quotations, and in literary allusions generally; their repartees have an unmistakeable flavour of the study and the desk. With lawyers there is just that quickness and that recklessness of retort which you would naturally expect from men whose chief stock-in-trade has so often been their readiness and unscrupulousness of wit. The sayings of academic humorists have an obviously academic tinge; the epigrams of a Parr, a Porson, and a Davidson, are the evident product of the scholarly life. And so with doctors and divines, with statesmen and with politicians, with business men, with tradesmen, and with women generally: there is a peculiarity, or rather a class character, about the anecdotes narrated of them, which, though not always obtrusive and easy of detection, is nevertheless observable by the attentive reader. A man is very much what his surroundings make him, and according to the atmosphere in which he lives will be the general nature of his outcome.

We say "the general nature," because, when all is said and done, class training and class association are not everything. If wits and humorists can be divided into classes, they can be still further subdivided according to their personal idiosyncrasy. Take the men of society, for example. The distinctive peculiarity of Sydney Smith was the exuberant character of his humour,—the enormous amount of fun which his ever-working fancy was able to accumulate round whatever subject he took up. Here was a humorist in the true sense of the term, who, hitting on a comical idea, dwelt upon it and expanded it until it was scarcely capable of any further expansion at his hands or at anybody else's. In Hook, again, we have a wit pure and simple, whose distinctive peculiarity consisted in rapidity and pungency of repartee,—generally in the way of pun, often in the way of felicitous quotation. This was very much the case with Luttrell and with Jekyll. Alvanley was more particularly a type of the young nobleman of fashion, whose wit was to a great extent impertinence tempered by urbanity. Selwyn's wit, again, was that of an originally morbid fancy modified by the pressure of society. Lord Dudley's was almost wholly part and

parcel of his uncommon personality, though we cannot help thinking that
much of his absent-mindedness was purposely assumed, for the sake of
the results which it produced. Among men of letters, again, we have
the biting sarcasm of Jerrold and the humorous *bonhomie* of Charles
Lamb. Both were slaves of the pen ; yet how different were their modes
of thought, how distinct their manner of expression! There is, in the
same way, quite a different flavour about the *bons mots* of a Sheridan and
those of, say, a Thackeray. The former are delightfully brilliant and laughable; in the latter there is always something more than the mere wit or
humour in which they are enshrined. Equally characteristic of the men
are the anecdotes recorded of Curran and of Erskine, of Lord Eldon, Lord
Norbury, and the old Scotch judges who have been so graphically described to us by Cockburn. You can tell a Curran saying directly you
hear it or see it; it is hardly necessary for it to be authenticated; it
bears the head-mark of the author. So, too, with Lord Eldon, whose
sayings are almost as individual as those of the great lexicographer himself. Among actors, one at once thinks of the admirably and prolifically
witty Foote, whom no one could ever take at a disadvantage. Among
divines, one thinks at once of Whately—surely the most epigrammatic
of all clerics, past and present. Among foreigners, again, who but recalls
to mind the numerous and pungent sayings of a Talleyrand—the French
Douglas Jerrold, with even more than the neatness of his British proto-
type,—the wit, *par excellence*, of France, unless you think he is run close
by Chamfort and by Rivarol. It is not necessary, however, to run
through the whole list of wits and humorists. It is sufficiently clear
that if there is a certain family likeness among the anecdotes of certain
classes, there is also a large measure of individuality in the stories related
about particular persons. Those persons are members of classes, we
confess; but they are nevertheless themselves. Neither they nor their
wit and humour are wholly absorbed in the various categories with
which they are connected.

Hitherto we have had to do with the wit and humour of classes and of individuals. A word or two may be said about the wit and humour of particular nationalities. That there are decided distinctions between these is universally noticeable and admitted. A German is all humour, and very ponderous with it all; a Frenchman is all wit, and as light and lively as the life he lives. The one is typified in Jean Paul, the other in Voltaire. The wit and humour of Englishmen is more varied and less easily characterized. Every one, on the other hand, knows how pawky is the ordinary Scotchman, how sly the ordinary Irishman,—the Sawny in the one case being as familiar and unperishable as is the Pat in the other. These national distinctions have always been instituted; and though you meet with Scotchmen who are not pawky, and Irishmen who are not sly, still the descriptions hold as good now as they ever did. What is so unprofitable about the matter is the abundance of anecdotes founded on these descriptions, and on no other basis. What an amount of slyness is fathered on the Irishman, and what an amount of pawkiness on the Scotchman—neither of them in any way deserved. In like manner, how constantly are the classes of society assailed! What jokes there are about doctors and their patients, about clergymen and their congregations, about lawyers and their clients! How similar is the point in all, and how dismal is the general effect!

This is not the kind of thing which the genuine anecdote lover at all cares about. He does not want this sort of manufactured, traditional material. He wants authentic matter. That is the whole secret of the value and usefulness of anecdotes,—that they should be, as far as possible, genuine and traceable. If they are not that, they are useless. They may excite a careless or an ignorant laugh, but that is all. What is wanted is, that they should be traceable to a source, and that source a genuine one. It is on this principle that the present Collection has been compiled, and it is hoped that it will, on this account, appeal powerfully to the taste and judgment of the true *connoisseur* of anecdote. Here, at any rate, is pabulum not only for amusement but for use; here is matter provocative not only of entertainment, but of insight into the characters of individuals, of classes, and of society and the world in general.

A word or two, finally, as to the sources of Modern Anecdote. These are chiefly to be found in the autobiographies, diaries, and reminiscences of the last hundred years. Of course the biography of that period is prolific in material, and in material of a thoroughly trustworthy and useful character. Still, the autobiographer and diarist is the most trustworthy and useful of all chroniclers, because he generally relates what he has heard with his own ears, and not merely what has come through an indefinite number of channels. Thus, whilst we have not neglected the various *Lives* of the most noted wits and humorists of recent times, we have drawn particularly upon such books as Walpole's *Correspondence*, Miss Berry's *Diary*, Raikes's *Diary*, Moore's *Diary*, Gronow's *Reminiscences*, Greville's *Diary*, Crabb Robinson's *Diary*, and to come farther down, J. C. Young's *Diary*, J. R. Planché's *Recollections*, and a hundred others, whose names will be found duly recorded in the work—all or most of them professing to record things at first hand, and affording the best available proofs of authenticity. In works such as these the reader will find more to enlighten him on the subject of the men, women, and manners of the last century than he will discover in any essay or history extant.   W. D. A.

TREASURY OF MODERN ANECDOTE.

ABOUT MEN OF SOCIETY.

A RASH YOUNG MAN.

LADY HOLLAND'S biography of her father, Sydney Smith,[1] naturally teems with anecdotes in illustration of his exuberant humorousness. From these we select a few of the most characteristic. For example:—Some one mentioned that a young Scotchman was about to marry an Irish widow, double his age, and of considerable dimensions. "Going to marry her!" exclaimed Sydney Smith, bursting out laughing. "Going to marry her! Impossible! You mean a part of her. He could not marry her all himself. It would be a case, not of bigamy, but of trigamy. The neighbourhood or the magistrates should interfere. There is enough of her to furnish wives for a whole parish. One man marry her! It is monstrous. You might people a colony with her; or give an assembly with her; or perhaps take your morning's walk round her, always provided there were frequent resting-places, and you were in rude health. I once was rash enough to try walking round her before breakfast, but only got half-way, and gave it up exhausted. Or you might read the Riot Act and disperse her; in short, you might do anything but marry her."

A CHARMING COMPLIMENT.

Again: on examining some new flowers in a garden, a beautiful girl, who was one of the party, exclaimed to the Canon, "Oh, Mr Sydney, this pea will never come to perfection." "Permit me, then," said he, gently taking her hand, and walking towards the plant, "to lead perfection to the pea."

---

[1] Canon of St Paul's; preacher and essayist; b. 1771, d. 1845.

THE NAKED TRUTH.

An argument arose (writes Lady Holland) in which my father observed how many of the most eminent men of the world had been diminutive in person; and after naming several among the ancients, he added, "Why look, there is Jeffrey; and there is my little friend [Lord John Russell], who has not body enough to cover his mind decently with—his intellect is improperly exposed."

JUST AS SOON.

Writes Lady Holland again:—We were all assembled to look at a turtle that had been sent to the house of a friend, when a child of the party stooped down, and began eagerly stroking the head of the turtle. "Why are you doing that, B——?" said my father. "Oh, to please the turtle." "Why, child, you might as well stroke the dome of St Paul's to please the Dean and Chapter."

POACHING AND SOCINIANISM.

Some one naming a certain person as not very orthodox, "Oh," said Sydney Smith, "accuse a man of being a Socinian, and it is all over with him; for the country gentlemen all think it has something to do with poaching."

HIS WAY OF PUTTING IT.

Sydney Smith proposed that Government should pay the Catholic priests of Ireland. "They would not take it," said a Dr Doyle. "Do you mean to say," said the Canon, "that if every priest in Ireland received to-morrow morning a post letter with a hundred pounds, first quarter of their year's income, that they would refuse it?" "Ah, Mr Smith," said Dr Doyle, "you've such a way of putting things!"

THAT IS THE QUESTION.

A Mr P—— said to Sydney Smith, "I always write best with an amanuensis." "Oh! but are you quite sure that he puts down what you dictate, my dear P——?"

THE ONLY TRUE ONES.

Mrs Marcet one day expressed to Sydney Smith her admiration of a ham of his. "Oh," said he, "our hams are the only true hams; yours are Shems and Japhets."

AN INFALLIBLE REMEDY.

Mrs Marcet, complaining to Sydney Smith that she could not sleep: "I can furnish you," he said, "with a perfect soporific. I have published two volumes of sermons; take them to bed with you. I recommended them once to Blanco White,[1] and before the third page he was fast asleep."

"PROVIDED."

We were on a visit (says Lady Holland) to Bishopthorpe;[2] our father had recently preached a visitation sermon, in which, amongst other things, he had recommended the clergy not to devote too much time to shooting and hunting. The archbishop, who rode beautifully in his youth, and knew full well my father's deficiences in that respect, said, smiling and evidently much amused: "I hear, Mr Smith, you do not approve of much riding for the clergy." "Why, my lord," said my father, bowing with assumed gravity, "perhaps there is not much objection, provided they do not ride too well, and stick out their toes professionally."

A LESSON ON HAND-SHAKING.

Meeting a young lady, and shaking hands with her—"I must," said Sydney Smith, "give you a lesson in shaking hands, I see. There is nothing more characteristic than shakes of the hand. I have classified them. Lister, when he was here, illustrated some of them. Ask Mrs Sydney to show you his sketches of them when you go in. There is the *high official*,—the body erect, and a rapid short shake, near the chin. There is the *mortmain*,—the flat hand introduced into your palm, and hardly conscious of its contiguity. The *digital*,—one finger held out, much used by the high clergy. There is the *shakus rusticus*, where your hand is seized in an iron grasp, betokening rude health, warm heart, and distance from the metropolis; but producing a strong sense of relief on your part when you find your hand released, and your fingers unbroken. The next to this is the *retentive shake*,—one which, beginning with vigour, pauses as it were to take breath, but without relinquishing its prey, and before you are aware begins again, till you feel anxious as to the result, and have no shake left in you. There are other varieties, but this is enough for one lesson."

---

[1] Author of a famous sonnet on "Night."　　　[2] Residence of the Archbishop of York.

SHUT UP.

One day, during a visit to the Archbishop of York, a Mr M——, a Catholic gentleman, was looking out of the window of the room in which he and Sydney Smith were sitting. "Ah! I see," said the worthy Canon, laughing, "you think you will get out, but you are quite mistaken; this is the wing where the Archbishop shuts up the Catholics; the other wing is full of Dissenters."

A BISHOP FLIRTING.

Some one (says Lady Holland) asked if a certain bishop was going to marry. "Perhaps he may," said my father; "yet how can a bishop marry? How can he flirt? The most he can say is, ' I will see you in the vestry after service.'"

AN ETERNAL FRIENDSHIP.

Most London dinners (writes Sydney Smith) evaporate in whispers to one's next-door neighbour. I make it a rule never to speak a word to mine, but fire across the table, though I broke it once when I heard a lady who sat next me, in a low, sweet voice, say, "No gravy, sir." I had never seen her before, but I turned suddenly round and said, "Madam, I have been looking for a person who disliked gravy all my life; let us swear eternal friendship." She looked astonished, but took the oath, and what is better, kept it.

AN AMERICAN FUNCTIONARY.

An American once said to Sydney Smith, "You are so funny, Mr Smith; do you know you remind me of our great joker, Dr Chamberlayne?" "I am much honoured," replied the Canon, "but I was not aware you had such a functionary in the United States."

AN EXTREME PROCEEDING.

Nothing (writes Sydney Smith) amuses me more than to observe the utter want of perception of a joke in some minds. Mrs Jackson called the other day, and spoke of the oppressive heat of last week. "Heat, ma'am!" I said; "it was so dreadful here, that I found there was nothing left for it but to take off my flesh and sit in my bones." "Take off your flesh and sit in your bones, sir! Oh, Mr Smith! how could you do that?" she exclaimed, with the greatest gravity. "Nothing more easy, ma'am; come and see next time." But she ordered her carriage, and evidently thought it a very unorthodox proceeding.

NOT AT ALL SENTIMENTAL.

A lady once asked Sydney Smith for a motto for her dog Spot. He proposed, "Out, damned Spot!"[1] but, strange to say (he says), she did not think it sentimental enough.

AN AWKWARD POSITION.

Sydney Smith records the following:—The oddest instance of absence of mind happened to me once in forgetting my own name. I knocked at a door in London; asked, "Is Mr B—— at home?" "Yes, sir; pray what name shall I say?" I looked in the man's face astonished;—what name? what name? Ay, that was the question; what is my name? I believe the man thought me mad; but it is literally true, that, during the space of two or three minutes, I had no more idea who I was than if I had never existed. I did not know if I was a Dissenter or a layman. I felt as dull as Sternhold and Hopkins.[2] At last, to my great relief, it flashed across me that I was Sydney Smith.

HE SAW IT AT LAST.

A joke (says Sydney Smith) goes a great way in the country. I have known one last pretty well for seven years. I remember making a joke after a meeting of the clergy in Yorkshire, where there was a Rev. Mr Buckle, who never spoke when I gave his health, saying that he was a buckle without a tongue. Most persons within hearing laughed, but my next-door neighbour sat unmoved and sunk in thought. At last, a quarter of an hour after we had all done, he suddenly nudged me, exclaiming, "I see *now* what you meant, Mr Smith; you meant a joke." "Yes, sir," I said, "I believe I did." Upon which he began laughing so heartily that I thought he would choke, and was obliged to pat him on the back.

A FEARFUL PASSION.

A certain young lady, walking one day round the grounds at Combe House, exclaimed: "Oh, why do you chain up that fine Newfoundland dog, Mr Smith?" "Because it has a passion for breakfasting on parish boys." "Parish boys?" she exclaimed, "does he really eat boys, Mr Smith?" "Yes, he devours them, buttons and all." Her face of horror (says the Canon) made me die of laughing.

---

1 *Macbeth*, act v. scene i. 　　　2 Authors of the "poetical" version of The Psalms.

AN ACCURATE MEASUREMENT.

Sydney Smith used to say:—I got into dreadful disgrace with Sir G[eorge] B[eaumont][1] who, standing before a picture at Bowood, exclaimed, turning to me, "Immense breadth of light and shade!" I innocently said, "Yes; about an inch and a half." He gave me a look that ought to have killed me.

BREAD FROM SAWDUST.

Talking (says Moore)[2] of the bread they were then (1833) about to make from sawdust, Sydney Smith said people would soon have sprigs coming out of them. Young ladies, in dressing for a ball would say, "Mamma, I'm beginning to sprout."

SEVERE!

Moore writes:—In talking of the fun he had had in the early times of the *Edinburgh Review*, Sydney Smith mentioned an article on Ritson,[3] which he and Brougham had written together; and one instance of their joint composition which he gave me was as follows:—"We take for granted (wrote Brougham) that Mr Ritson supposed Providence to have had some share in producing him—though for what inscrutable purposes (added Sydney) we profess ourselves unable to conjecture."

A MAXIM.

Lord John [Russell] mentioned to-day (writes Moore) that Sydney Smith told him he had had an intention once of writing a book of maxims, but never got further than the following:—"That generally towards the age of forty, women get tired of being virtuous, and men of being honest."

AN AWKWARD UNDERSTANDING.

Sydney Smith said of some one:—He has no command over his understanding; it is always getting between his legs and tripping him up.

VERY MERCURIAL.

Moore records in his *Diary* on one occasion:—Sydney Smith very comical about the remedy that Lady [Holland] is going to use for the bookworm, which is making great ravages in the library. She is about to have them washed

---

1 The Sir George Beaumont to whom Wordsworth addressed an *Epistle* (1811).
2 In his *Diary*, published in 1852-6 by Lord John Russell.
3 Joseph Ritson, the antiquary.

by some mercurial preparation; and Smith says it is Davy's[1] opinion that the air will become charged with mercury, and that the whole family will be salivated. "I shall see Allen,"[2] says Smith, "with his tongue hanging out, speechless, and shall take the opportunity to stick a few principles into him."

A TRUE DISSENTER.

On another occasion Moore says:—Called with [Smith] at Newton's to see my picture, [when he] said in his gravest manner to Newton, "Couldn't you contrive to throw into his face a stronger expression of hostility to the church establishment?"

REES AND RES.

Moore writes again:—Sydney, at dinner, and after, in full force . . . describing a dinner at Longman's; Rees[3] carving—*plerumque secat res.*

A LARGE CLERGYMAN.

Yet another entry by Moore:—Company at the Longmans. . . . Came away earlyish. The road up to Longman's being rather awkward, we [Moore and Sydney Smith] had desired the hackney coachman to wait for us at the bottom. "It would never do," said S., "when your memoirs came to be written, to have it said, 'He went out to dine at the house of the respectable publishers, Longman & Co., and, being overturned on his way back, was crushed to death by a large clergyman.'"

LAMARTINE.

Moore again:—S. Smith amusing before dinner. His magnanimity, as he called it, in avowing that he had never before heard of Lamartine (of whom Miss Berry[4] and I were speaking). "Was it another name for the famous blacking man?" "Yes." "Oh, then, he's Martin here, La-Martine in France, and Martin Luther in Germany."

CATCHING FIRE.

Moore once more:—Breakfasted at Rogers's: [Sydney] Smith full of comicality and fancy. . . . In talking of the stories about dram-drinkers catching fire, pursued the idea in every possible shape. The inconvenience of a man coming too near the candle when he was speaking: "Sir, your observation

---

[1] Sir Humphrey Davy.
[2] A contributor to the *Edinburgh Review.*
[3] One of the firm of Longman & Co.
[4] The well-known diarist and woman of fashion.

has caught fire." Then imagined a parson breaking out into a blaze in the pulpit; the engines called to put him out; no water to be had, the man at the water works being an Unitarian or an Atheist.

A FAT OLD CROW.

Sydney [Smith] at breakfast (writes Moore) actually made me cry with laughing. . . . In talking of the intelligence and concert which birds have among each other, cranes and crows, &c., showing that they must have some means of communicating thoughts, he said, "I daresay they make the same remark of us. That fat old crow there (meaning himself), what a prodigious noise he is making! I have no doubt he has some power of communicating," &c., &c. After pursuing this idea comically for some time, he added, "But we have the advantage of them; they can't put us into pies as we do them; legs sticking up out of the crust," &c., &c.

A TEA TEST.

In talking of the remarkable fact that women in general bear pain much better than men, I said (remarks Moore) that, allowing everything that could be claimed for the superior patience and self-command of women, still the main solution of their enduring pain better than men was their having less physical sensibility. This theory of mine was immediately exclaimed against . . . as disparaging, ungenerous, unfounded, &c., &c. I offered to put it to the test by bringing in a hot tea-pot, which I would answer for the ladies of the party being able to hold for a much longer period than the men. This set Sydney [Smith] off most comically, upon my cruelty to the female part of the creation, and the practice I had in such experiments. "He has been all his life," he said, "trying the sex with hot tea-pots; the burning ploughshare was nothing to it. I think I hear his terrific tone in a *tête-à-tête*, 'Bring a tea-pot.'"

A SAUCY SUGGESTION.

R. H. Barham[1] writes in his diary:—Dined with Smith. He told me of the motto he had proposed for **Bishop Burgess's arms,** in allusion to his brother, the well-known fish-sauce projector:—

" *Gravi* jamdudum *saucia* curâ !"

---

[1] Author of the *Ingoldsby Legends.* His *Diary* is included in his *Life* by his son (1870).

COUSINS.

The following quaint answer (says Barham) was returned by Sydney Smith to an invitation to dinner:—" Dear Longman, I can't accept your invitation, for my house is full of country cousins. I wish they were once removed.— Yours, Sydney Smith."

ADVICE TO A BISHOP.

Barham has recorded the advice which Sydney Smith is said to have given to the Bishop of New Zealand prior to his departure;—recommending him to have regard to the minor as well as the more important duties of his station—to be given to hospitality—and, in order to meet the tastes of his native guests, never to be without a smoked little boy in the bacon rack, and a cold clergyman on the sideboard; " and as for yourself, my lord," he concluded, " all I can say is, that when your new parishioners *do* eat you, I sincerely hope you will disagree with them."

AS A CUCUMBER.

At a certain party at which Sydney Smith was present, one of the company (says Barham) having said that he was about to " drop in" at Lady Blessington's, a young gentleman, a perfect stranger to him, said, with the most "gallant modesty,"—"Oh, then, you can take me with you; I want very much to know her; you can introduce me." While the other was standing aghast at the impudence of the proposal, and muttering something about being but a slight acquaintance himself, and not knowing very well how he could take such a liberty, &c., Sydney Smith observed, " Pray oblige our young friend; you can do it easily enough by introducing him in a capacity very desirable at this close season of the year. Say you are bringing with you the cool of the evening."

NOT AT ALL.

At one time (says Rogers),[1] when I gave a dinner, I used to have candles placed all round the dining-room, and high up, in order to show off the pictures. I asked Sydney Smith how he liked the plan. " Not at all," he replied; "above there is a blaze of light, and below, nothing but darkness and gnashing of teeth."

---

[1] In his *Table Talk*, published by Dyce in 1856.

JUST SO.

Rogers says that when Sydney Smith's physicians advised him to take a walk upon an empty stomach, he asked, "Upon whose?"

PROOF POSITIVE.

The same authority declares that Sydney Smith said:—"The Bishop of —— is so like Judas, that I now firmly believe in the Apostolical Succession."

NOT TALKING FAIR.

Sydney Smith, an enormous talker, complains (writes Lord Cockburn[1]) of Macaulay never letting him get in a word. Smith once said to him, "Now, Macaulay, when I am gone you'll be sorry that you never heard me speak."[2]

A TREAT.

On another occasion (says Lord Cockburn) Smith said that he had found Macaulay in bed from illness, and that he was therefore more agreeable than he had ever seen him. "There were some glorious flashes of silence."

AUDI ALTERAM PARTEM.

Bishop Bloomfield had accepted an invitation to dinner at a house where Sydney Smith was also to be present. The non-arrival of his lordship (says Mark Boyd[3]) delayed the dinner, when at last a note reached the host to say that the bishop, as he was entering London House, had been bitten by a dog, so that he must be excused. The note was read to the assembled guests, when the Dean remarked that he should very much like to hear the dog's account of the affair.[4]

ONE FOR THE BISHOP AND CO.

When the question of putting down wooden pavement around St Paul's was first mooted, the Bishop [Bloomfield] summoned the authorities of the cathedral to meet him. Sydney Smith (says Boyd) arrived early; but when some little impatience was expressed at the non-arrival of the prelate and other dignitaries, the worthy Dean remarked that, as the question of blockheads had to be discussed, they had no other course left to them than to wait.

---

1 In the *Memorials of his Time.*
2 Smith is described by Lady Holland as saying, "Oh yes, we both talk a great deal, but I don't believe Macaulay ever did hear my voice. Sometimes, when I have told a good story, I have thought to myself, 'Poor Macaulay! he will be very sorry some day to have missed hearing that.'"
3 In his *Reminiscences.*
4 This reminds us of a passage in Goldsmith's "Elegy on the Death of a Mad Dog"— "The dog it was that died."

DISPERSING A DUCHESS.

Lady Chatterton[1] says of Sydney Smith on one occasion:—He seemed to suffer extremely from the heat, and said he should go to no more evening parties, for the night before he had seriously meditated sending for the police to disperse the Duchess of A——. "She was standing in a doorway," he added, "and it was impossible to get my own large person through. Heigho! how convenient it would be if one could sit in one's skeleton in this kind of weather."

BEWARE!

The same lady writes of Sydney Smith *in loco:*—He said that he called yesterday on Lady S——, who was getting some new furniture, and he told her to beware of modern furniture, for that when he went a day or two before to visit some friends whose house was just newly furnished, he had three chairs killed under him before he left the house.

A DOUBLE CALENDAR.

Fanny Kemble says[2] that when Miss Callender, afterwards Mrs Sheridan, published a novel, the hero of which commits forgery,—that wicked wit, Sydney Smith, said he knew she was a Callender, but did not know till then that she was a Newgate Calendar.

ALMOST INCREDIBLE.

Greville[3] writes in his diary:—Dined with Moore. . . . He told a good story of Sydney Smith and Leslie the professor. Leslie had written upon the North Pole; something he had said had been attacked in the *Edinburgh Review* in a way that displeased him. He called on Jeffrey just as he was getting on horse-back, and in a great hurry Leslie began with a grave complaint on the subject, which Jeffrey interrupted with, "O damn the North Pole!" Leslie went off in high dudgeon, and soon after met Sydney, who, seeing him disturbed, asked what was the matter. He told him what he had been to Jeffrey about, and that he had in a very unpleasant way said, "Damn the North Pole." "It was very bad," said Sydney; "but, do you know, I am not surprised at it, for I have heard him speak very disrespectfully of *The Equator.*"[4]

---

[1] See her *Life*, by her husband.   [2] In her *Records of a Girlhood*.
[3] Charles Greville, for many years clerk to the Privy Council.
[4] This story is told by Lady Holland also. See her *Memoirs of* her father, where Leslie's name, however, is not given.

B

A GOOD REPROOF.

According to Lord Houghton, Sydney Smith once checked the old-fashioned freedom of speech in Lord Melbourne, by suggesting that they should assume everybody and everything to be damned, and come to the subject.

A TREASURE.

Mrs Marcet writes thus in Lady Holland's Life of Sydney Smith:—I was coming downstairs [one] morning when Mr Smith suddenly said to Bunch [the name of one of his servants], who was passing,—" Bunch, do you like roast duck or boiled chicken?" Bunch had probably never tasted either the one or the other in her life, but answered, without a moment's hesitation, "Roast duck, please, sir," and disappeared. I laughed. "You may laugh," said he, "but you have no idea of the labour it has cost me to give her that decision of character. The Yorkshire peasantry are the quickest and shrewdest in the world, but you can never get a direct answer from them; if you ask them even their own names, they always scratch their heads and say, 'A's sur ai don't knaw, sir;' but I have brought Bunch to such perfection, that she never hesitates now on any subject, however difficult. I am very strict with her. Would you like to hear her repeat her crimes? She has them by heart, and repeats them every day." "Come here, Bunch!" calling out to her, "come and repeat your crimes to Mrs Marcet;" and Bunch, a clean, fair, squat, tidy little girl about ten or twelve years of age, quite as a matter of course, as grave as a judge, without the least hesitation, and with a loud voice, began to repeat— "Plate-snatching, gravy-spilling, door-slamming, blue-bottle fly-catching, and curtsey-bobbing." "Explain to Mrs Marcet what blue-bottle fly-catching is." "Standing with my mouth open and not attending, sir." "And what is curtsey-bobbing?" "Curtseying to the centre of the earth, please, sir." "Good girl! now you may go. She makes a capital waiter, I assure you; on *state* occasions Jack Robinson, my carpenter, takes off his apron and waits too, and does pretty well, but he sometimes naturally makes a mistake, and sticks a gimlet into the bread instead of a fork."

A RENCONTRE.

A gentleman named Anderson went to dine with a Dr Hall on one occasion. The doctor was dressing when Anderson arrived. In the drawing-room he found a gentleman waiting, with whom he at once entered into conversation, under the idea that he was familiar with Brighton; but he soon undeceived him. "No, I never was in Brighton till to-day; but nevertheless, I have made acquaintance with a great local power." "Who may that be?" asked Anderson.

" *Who* he is, I know not ; but I am certain *what* he is. It is that distinguished functionary, the Master of the Ceremonies. It could be no one else. It was a gentleman attired point device, walking down the parade like Agag, 'delicately.' He pointed out his toes like a dancing-master, but carried his head high, like a potentate. As he passed the stand of flies he nodded approval, as if he owned them all. As he approached the little goat-carriages, he looked askance over the edge of his starched neckcloth, and blandly smiled encouragement. Sure that, in following him, I was treading in the steps of greatness, I went on to the pier, and there I was confirmed in my conviction of his eminence; for I observed him look first over the right side and then over the left, with an expression of serene satisfaction spreading over his countenance, which said as plainly as if he had spoken to the sea aloud, 'That is right. You are low-tide at present; but, never mind, in a couple of hours I shall make you high-tide again.'" At that instant (says J. C. Young[1]) Hall entered and begged to introduce to James Anderson the "Rev. Sydney Smith."

A PUNNING SERIES.

Lord William Lennox,[2] writing of Theodore Hook,[3] says:—I once drove with him to Epsom. During the whole journey he kept up a regular running fire of pun, anecdote, and improviso. "'*Hawes,* surgeon,'" said he; "that reminds me of two lines I made on a saw-bones of that name, during the severe frost of 1814 :—

> ' Perpetual freezings and perpetual thaws,
> Though bad for *hips*, are good for *Hawes*.'"

As we reached Vauxhall Bridge, I remarked, "I wonder if this bridge pays?" " Go over it, and you will be *tolled*," was the reply. "So," said he, addressing the gatekeeper, who was very hoarse, "you haven't recovered your voice yet." "No, sir," the man answered, "I've caught a *fresh* cold." "But why did you catch a *fresh* one ? Why didn't you have it *cured ?*" On we went, from subject to subject, from pun to pun. The sign of the "Three Ravens" suggested the reflection, "The owner must be *ravin'* mad." Soon afterwards, we discerned a party of labourers employed in sinking a well. "What are you about?" inquired Hook. "Boring for water, sir," replied a gaping clod. "Water's a *bore* at any time. Besides, you are quite wrong; remember the old proverb, 'Leave *well* alone.'" "Did you see in the paper this morning that the Exeter Theatre is burnt down?" I asked. "Oh, yes, quite dramatic— *Enter* a fire. *Exit* a theatre."

---

1 See J. C. Young's *Diary,* published with that of his father, Charles Mayne Young.
2 The author of several volumes of *Recollections.*
3 Journalist and novelist; *b.* 1788, *d.* 1841.

SOMEBODY.

Lord William Lennox records a number of anecdotes about Hook. He says in one place :—One day Hook observed a pompous gentleman walking in very grand style along the Strand. Instantly leaving his companion, he went up to him and said, "I beg your pardon, sir; but may I ask, are you any one in particular?" bowing respectfully, and passing on before the astonished magnifico could collect himself to give a practical or other answer to the query.[1]

NOT ONE.

Again :—One evening at Brighton, when Hook sat down to the pianoforte, he was given, as a subject, King William IV. "The king? That won't do; he's no *subject*," was his ready response.

A GOOD REASON.

"You're master of this house, I think," said Hook, as he drove up to a rural inn door. "I am, sir," responded Boniface. "I thought so," continued Hook, "for your wife's been dead these six months."

MAKING A BUTT OF HIM.

A young gentleman was asked to sing at a party where Hook was, but he assured the company that he could not sing, and added, that they only wished to make a *butt* of him. "Oh, no," said the wit, "all we want is to get a *stave* out of you."

VERY LIKE.

Two silly brothers, who were very much about town in Hook's time, took pains by dressing alike to deceive their friends as to their identity. Some one was expatiating upon these modern Dromios, at which Hook grew impatient. "Well," said his friend, "we will admit that they resemble each other wonderfully. They are as like as two peas." "They are," retorted Theodore, "and quite as *green*."

QUITE RIGHT.

An illiterate vendor of beer wrote over his door, "*Bear* sold here." "Quite right," said Hook; "he means to apprise us that the article is his own *Bruin*."

[1] J. C. Young has a more elaborate version of this story.

A POWERFUL LIQUID.

An advertisement of Gowland's Lotion gave Hook an opportunity of saying, "I wonder they don't wash Mount Etna with it, in the hopes of preventing an *eruption*."

"ON, STANLEY, ON!"

"You know everything," said Cannon;[1] "what's going on?" "I am," responded Hook, suiting the action to the word.

BREAD AND WINE.

Lord William Lennox and Hook once stopped to lunch at Epsom, when the landlord produced an excellent bottle of old port. "There's food and drink in this wine," exclaimed Hook. The landlord looked surprised. "Port wine, with a *crust*."

A GUESS.

An intimate friend of W. H. Harrison's[2] told him of a dinner at John Murray's (the elder), when Sir David Brewster gave some account relating to the prismatic colours of mother-of-pearl. "Mither of parl!" said Hogg, the poet; "Murray, what's mither of parl?" "Oh, I don't know," replied Murray; "there's Hook; he knows everything: ask him." "Well, Hogg," said the novelist, "I don't know, unless it's the *Venerable Bede*."

THREE WORDS.

The following anecdote of Theodore Hook was told by John Wilson Croker:—One day, when a large party had assembled previous to dinner at the marine residence of the latter, among the guests was a pious elderly lady, who was a perfect specimen of what Sydney Smith terms the "lemon-squeezers of society, who act on you as a wet blanket, see a cloud in sunshine, the nails of a coffin in the ribbons of a bride, extinguish all hope—people whose very look sets your teeth on edge." For a considerable time this spinster had, by her acid remarks, damped even the spirit of Hook, and had completely, to adopt a vulgar phrase, "shut him up." At length she approached him, and having given a lecture on temperance that would have gladdened the heart of George Cruikshank, drew forth from her pocket a packet of tracts. "Pray accept this," she said; "it is called 'Three Words to a Drunkard.'" "'Three Words to a Drunkard,'" echoed the author of "Sayings and Doings;" "I see—'Pass the bottle!'"

---

[1] A fashionable clergyman in his day, of whom some anecdotes are recorded elsewhere in this volume.

[2] The *Reminiscences* of this writer were published in the *University Magazine*.

CELLAR AND SELLER.

Moore writes in his diary:—Rogers told me some amusing things, one of which was Theodore Hook's saying to some man, with whom a bibliopolist dined the other day and got extremely drunk, "Why, you appear to me to have emptied your *wine*-cellar into your *book*-seller."

AN IMPROMPTU.

Planché writes[1]:—I had often met Hook in society without being introduced to him; but our acquaintance and intimacy dated simultaneously from the evening of a dinner at Horace Twiss's, in Park Place, St James's. . . . It was a very merry party. Mr John Murray (the great Murray of Albemarle Street), James Smith,[2] and two or three others, remained till very late in the dining-room, some of us singing and giving recitations. Hook being pressed to sing another of his wonderful extemporary songs, consented, with a declaration that the subject should be **John Murray**. Murray vehemently objected, and a ludicrous contention took place, during which Hook dodged him round the table, placing chairs in his path, which was sufficiently devious without them, and singing all the while a sort of recitative, of which I remember only the commencement:—

> " My friend, John Murray, I see, has arrived at the head of the table;
> And the wonder is, at this time of night, that John Murray should be able.
> He's an excellent hand at a dinner, and not a bad one at a lunch;
> But the devil of John Murray is, that he never will pass the punch."

PARLIAMENTARY.

The town (says Lord Albemarle[3]) was at one time running after a foreigner who played, or pretended to play, tunes on his chin. . . . The then chairman of " Ways and Means" in the House of Commons was Mr Grant, who, to distinguish him from two other members of the same surname, and from a remarkable protuberance of his lower jaw, was popularly called " Chin Grant." I was present one evening when, in some most amusing verses, Theodore Hook descanted upon what he called the Swiss and Scotch chin-men. Both, he said, had one object in view—the " Ways and Means;" but they differed in the attainment of their end. The foreigner depended solely on the *chin*, the Scotchman on the *eyes* and *nose* (Ayes and Noes).

---

[1] In his *Recollections*.
[2] Co-author, with his brother Horace, of *Rejected Addresses* and *Horace in London*.
[3] See his *Fifty Years of My Life*.

A BASHFUL MAN.

Westmacott (says Chorley[1]) told a Hookism at Lady Blessington's worthy of being kept. He was at some large party or other where the lady of the house was more than usually coarsely anxious to get him to make sport for her guests. A ring formed round him of people only wanting a word's encouragement to burst out into a violent laugh. "Do, Mr Hook; *do* favour us!" said the lady for the hundredth time. "Indeed, madam, I can't; I can't, indeed. I am like that little bird, the canary; can't lay my eggs when any one is looking at me."

A BRUTAL JEST.

Hook (says the same authority) was dining at Powell's one day, and the talk fell upon *feu* Jack Reeve. . . . "Yes," said Theodore, when they were speaking of his funeral; "I was out that day; I met him in his private box, going to the pit."

WHERE, INDEED?

Apropos of cutlets (said Hook of himself) I once called upon an old lady, who pressed me so urgently to stay and dine with her that, as I had no engagement, I could not refuse. On sitting down, the servant uncovered two chops, and my old friend said, "Mr Hook, you see your dinner?" "Thank you, ma'am," said I; "but where's yours?"[2]

A SHADE ABOVE.

Barham diarizes:—Dined at Sir Andrew Barnard's. . . . Hook made but one pun; on Walpole's remarking that, of two pictures mentioned, one was "a shade above the other in point of merit," he replied: "I presume you mean to say it was a *shade over* (*chef d'œuvre*)."

VINGT-UN.

Elsewhere Barham says:—Hook spoke in the course of the evening of his two eldest daughters, of whom Mary, the senior, had just turned twenty-one. The name of the second was Louisa, and he designated them accordingly as "Vingt-un" and "Loo!"

---

[1] In his *Life*, edited by Hewlett.   [2] Recorded by Planché.

VINGT-UN AND OVER.

Barham again records:—In the course of the evening, Hook, looking at my son, said to me. "How do these fellows make us feel! It was but the other day that chap was standing at my knee, listening to my stories with ears, eyes, and mouth wide open, and now he is a man, I suppose?" "Yes," I said, "he is three or four-and-twenty." "Ah, I see—*Vingt-un* overdrawn!"

A CHARACTERISTIC STORY.

Hook (says Barham) told us an amusing story of his going down to Worcester, to see his brother the Dean, with Henry Higginson (his companion in many of his frolics). They arrived separately at the coach, and taking their places in the inside, opposite to each other, pretended to be strangers. After some time, they begin to hoax their fellow-travellers—the one affecting to see a great many things not to be seen, the other confirming it and admiring them. "What a beautiful house that on the hill!" cried Higginson, when no house was near the spot; "it must command a most magnificent prospect from the elevation on which it stands." "Why, yes," returned Hook, "the view must be extensive enough, but I cannot think these windows in good taste. To run out bay windows in a Gothic front, in my opinion, ruins the effect of the whole building." "Ah, that is the new proprietor's doings," was the reply; "they were not there when the marquis had possession." Here one of their companions interfered. He had been stretching his neck for some time, in the vain hope of getting a glimpse of the mansion in question, and now asked: "Pray, sir, what house do you mean? I don't see any house." "That, sir, with the turrets and large bay windows, on the hill," said Hook, with profound gravity, pointing to a thick wood. "Dear me," returned the old gentleman, bobbing about to catch the desired object, "I can't see it for those confounded trees!" The old gentleman, luckily for them, proved an indefatigable asker of questions, and the answers he received, of course, added much to his stock of authentic information. "Pray, sir, do you happen to know to whom that house belongs?" inquired he, pointing to a magnificent mansion and handsome park in the distance. "That, sir," replied Hook, "is Womberly Hall, the seat of Sir Abraham Hume, which he won at billiards from the Bishop of Bath and Wells." "You don't say so!" cried the old gentleman, in pious horror, and taking out his pocket-book begged his informant to repeat the name of the seat, which he readily did; and it was entered accordingly, the old gentleman shaking his head gravely the while, and bewailing the profligacy of an age in which dignitaries of the Church practised gambling to so alarming an extent. The frequency of the remarks, however, made by the associates on objects which the eyesight of no one else was good enough to take in, began at length to excite some suspicion; and Hook's breaking suddenly into a rapturous exclamation at "the magnificent burst of the ocean!" in the midst of an inland country, a Wiltshire farmer, who had been for some time staring alternately at them and the window, thrust out his head, and after reconnoitring for a couple of minutes, drew it in again, and, looking full in the face of the sea-gazer, exclaimed, with considerable emphasis, "Well, now then, I'm d——d if I think you can see the ocean, as you call it, for all you pretends!" and continued very sulky all the rest of the way.

MORE MYSTIFICATION.

Barham's Diary also yields the following:—Called on Hook. In the course of conversation he gave me an account of his going to Lord Melville's trial with a friend. They went early, and were engaged in conversation when the peers began to enter. At this moment, a country-looking lady, whom he afterwards found to be a resident at Pye, in Sussex, touched his arm, and said, "I beg your pardon, sir, but pray who are those gentlemen in red now coming in?" "Those, ma'am," returned Theodore, "are the barons of England. In these cases the junior peers always come first." "Thank you, sir; much obliged to you. Louisa, my dear (turning to a girl about fourteen), tell Jane (about ten) those are the barons of England, and the juniors—that's the youngest, you know—always goes first. Tell her to be sure and remember that when we get home." "Dear me, ma!" said Louisa, "can that gentleman be one of the *youngest?* I am sure he looks very old." Human nature, added Hook, could not stand this. Any one, though with no more mischief in him than a dove, must have been excited to a hoax. "And pray, sir," continued the lady, "what gentlemen are these?" pointing to the bishops, who came next in order, in the dress which they wore on state occasions, viz., the rocket and lawn sleeves over their doctor's robes. "Gentlemen, madam!" said Hook, "these are not gentlemen; these are ladies—elderly ladies—the dowager peeresses in their own right." The fair enquirer fixed a penetrating glance upon his countenance, saying, as plainly as an eye can say, "Are you quizzing me, or no?" Not a muscle moved, till at last, tolerably well satisfied with her scrutiny, she turned round and whispered, "Louisa, dear, the gentleman *says* that these are elderly ladies, and dowager peeresses in their own right. Tell Jane not to forget that." All went smoothly till the speaker of the House of Commons attracted her attention by the rich embroidery of his robes. "Pray, sir," said she, "and who is that fine-looking person opposite?" "That, madam," was the answer, "is Cardinal Wolsey!" "No, sir," cried the lady, drawing herself up, and casting at her informant a look of angry disdain, "we knows a little better than that.   Cardinal Wolsey has been dead many a good year!"   "No such thing, my dear madam, I assure you," replied Hook, with a gravity that must have been almost preternatural; "it has been, I know, so reported in the country, but without the least foundation.   In fact, those rascally newspapers will say anything."   The good old gentlewoman appeared thunderstruck, opened her eyes to their full extent, and gasped like a dying carp; *vox faucibus hæsit.*   Seizing a daughter with each hand, she hurried without another word from the spot.

WHETHER OR NO.

The last time (says Barham, jun.) that Theodore Hook dined at Amen Corner, he was unusually late, and dinner was served before he made his appearance.   Mr Barham apologized for having sat down without him, observing that he had quite given him up, and had supposed "that the weather had deterred him."   "Oh," replied Hook, "I had determined to come, *weather or no !*"

A STINGY HOST.

J. C. Young is responsible for the following:—One lovely summer's day [Theodore Hook] was strolling in company with Mr B——, in the garden of the Star and Garter at Richmond, when his friend was accosted by two gentlemen, one of whom was a noble lord, equally remarkable for his colossal fortune, occasional munificence, and general parsimony.   While the three conversed together, Hook slowly walked aside.   The noble peer observing him, asked B—— who was his friend.   "Oh! that is Theodore Hook," was his reply.   On hearing the well-known name, my lord exclaimed, "You don't say so!   What good fortune!   He is a man of all others whom I desire to know.   Pray introduce me to him."   The introduction takes place, and the marquis tells Hook that he and his friend, Lord ——, are just going to lunch, and if he and B—— will join them in a *partie carrée*, he shall be delighted.   Hook, never insensible to the attractions of the table, and persuaded, from the high rank and great wealth of the inviter, that he should fare sumptuously, yielded a cordial and gratified acceptance, and adjourned to the apartment occupied by his recent acquaintance.   On entering the room the bell is rung, and on the waiter making his appearance, the host takes him aside and gives him certain instructions, about the nature of which the two just invited guests have no doubts.   Two additional napkins are laid, two additional chairs are set, two additional wine-glasses grace the board, two pickle-stands—one with red cabbage, the other with pickled onions—take their place in the centre of the table.   Hook is rather disconcerted at the sight of merely one small sherry-glass being allotted to each person, but comforts himself with the reflection that the champagne-glasses will be introduced after a few preliminary glasses of Amontillado. At last the banquet is set, the covers are taken off two willow-pattern dishes, one containing four goodly loin chops, the other four fine mealy potatoes, and a pint decanter of sherry crowns the meal. "Well," thought Hook, "I am not certain that this simple kind of repast is not the best for lunch, and I like the fashion of having one's chop hot and hot, and a change of wines, instead of being confined to one!" In a few minutes every knife and fork is laid down, every chop and potato has been despatched, and just as Hook is expecting a fresh relay of wine and viand, to his unutterable disgust his entertainer addresses him in the following language:—"My dear Mr Hook! I hope you will forgive me, but I have so very often heard of your marvellous talent, that I am naturally impatient for an exhibition of it. Would you favour us with a song?" "Oh!" said the man appealed to, "with pleasure!" To the indescribable astonishment of all present he begins to sing "God save the King." As he delivered each line his host looked to his intimate friend for something like sympathy—"What on earth can the man mean by singing us the National Anthem?" However his motive was soon explained, for on coming to the following lines—

" Happy and glorious,
Long to reign over us,"

he thus rendered them, delivering the words as if under the influence of *too much liquor*—

" Happ-y and glo-ri-ous,
A pint—between four of us."

This, I think (adds Young) was a case of " *Chop with Worcester sauce*," versus " *Cheek with Fulham sauce.*"

SOME ONE TO MEET HIM.

Lord Dudley[1] (writes Sydney Smith) was one of the most absent men, I think, I ever met in society. One day he met me in the street, and invited me to meet myself. "Dine with me to-day; dine with me, and I will get Sydney Smith to meet you." I admitted the temptation he held out to me, but said I was engaged to meet him elsewhere.

A VILLAIN.

Another time (says Sydney Smith of Lord Dudley) on meeting me, he turned back, put his arm through mine, muttering, "I don't mind walking with him a little way; I'll walk with him as far as the end of the street." As

---

1 John William Ward, Earl of Dudley, politician; b. 1781, d. 1833.

we proceeded together, W—— passed. "That is the villain," exclaimed he, "who helped me yesterday to asparagus, and gave me no toast."

"HEAR! HEAR!"

Yet another story of Lord Dudley, as told by Sydney Smith :—He very nearly upset my gravity once in the pulpit. He was sitting immediately under me, apparently very attentive, when suddenly he took up his stick, as if he had been in the House of Commons, and tapping on the ground with it, cried out in a low but very audible whisper, "Hear! hear! hear!"[1]

DUDLEY *v.* WARD.

A good deal of talk (says Moore in his Diary) about Lord Dudley: his two voices, squeak and bass, seem, as one has said, "like Lord Dudley conversing with Lord Ward."[2]

AN ADVANTAGE.

Rogers mentioned to Moore a clever thing said by Lord Dudley, on some Vienna lady remarking impudently to him, "What wretchedly bad French you all speak in London!" "It is true, madam," he answered, "we have not enjoyed the advantage of having the French twice in our capital."[3]

QUANTUM MUTATUS!

Lord Dudley (says Lord Albemarle) was a frequent guest at the Brighton Pavilion. His knowledge of good living led him easily to detect a great falling off in the royal *cuisine* since the death of George IV. Sitting next King William, he exclaimed in his deep bass, "What a change, to be sure!—cold *pâtés* and hot champagne."

POLITE.

The King and Queen, William and Charlotte, when Duke and Duchess of Clarence, once dined with Lord Dudley, who handed her Royal Highness into dinner. Scarcely seated, he began to soliloquise aloud : "What bores these Royalties are! Ought I to drink wine with her as I would with any other woman?" and in the same tone continued, "May I have the honour of a glass

---

[1] Mr Bernal Osborne told the Rev. J. C. Young a very similar story about that clergyman's father, the actor, Charles Mayne Young; how, at the close of a preacher's long and eloquent outburst, "the habits of the actor's former life betrayed themselves, and he uttered, in a deep under tone, the old familiar ' Bravo !'"

[2] His lordship's full title was " Earl of Dudley and Ward." [3] See " Tit for Tat" (p. 43).

of wine with your Royal Highness?" Towards the end of the dinner he asked her again. "With great pleasure, Lord Dudley," she replied, smiling; "but I have had one glass with you already." "The brute! and so she has!" was the rejoinder. This is also told by Lord Albemarle.

ONE AT ALL EVENTS.

Lord Dudley was introduced at an evening party to Lady N——, whom he was requested to hand down to supper. Her ladyship (says Archdeacon Sinclair)[1] availed herself of the opportunity to present her two daughters, after which ceremony she overheard him, as they went downstairs, muttering to himself in his usual undertone: "The fair one is plain; the dark one is not amiss; but the fair one is exceedingly plain." "I am glad, my lord," says Lady N——, with good-humoured readiness, "that, at all events, the dark one pleases you."

A BORE.

The same authority says that a gentleman from Staffordshire prevailed on Lord Dudley to present him at Court. They got on very well as far as St James Street, where they were stopped nearly half-an-hour by the line of carriages. His lordship then forgot himself, and, after a long pause, began: "Now, this tiresome country squire will be expecting me to ask him to dinner. Shall I ask him, or shall I not? No; I think he would be a bore." The individual so unexpectedly blackballed was at first confounded; but, recollecting his companion's infirmity, commenced in turn an audible soliloquy: "Now, this tiresome old peer will, of course, be asking me to dine with him to-day. Shall I go, or shall I not go? No; I think it would be a bore." This impromptu was well taken; and the invitation was given in earnest, and accepted.[2]

SOME KITCHEN GIRL.

At a dinner (says Sinclair) given by Lord Wilton, who had one of the best cooks in London, Lord Dudley tasted some dish of which he did not approve, and, forgetting where he was, began apologising to the company for the badness of the entertainment. "The fact is," said he, "that my head cook was taken ill, and some kitchen girl, I suppose, has been employed to dress the dinner."[3]

---

[1] See his *Old Times and Distant Places.*

[2] This story is told more briefly by Moore, and more fully by Gronow, who, however, somewhat alters the circumstances.

[3] Moore tells something very similar about a certain Dean Ogle.

A VERY PRETTY WOMAN, BUT——.

Lord Dudley (says Gronow) was once paying a morning visit to the beautiful Lady M——. He sat an unconscionably long time, and the lady, after giving him some friendly hints, took up her work and tried to make conversation. Lord Dudley broke a long fit of silence by muttering, "A very pretty woman, this Lady M——! She stays a devilish long time—I wish she'd go." He thought Lady M—— was paying him a visit in his own house.

CRUEL.

Rogers's well-known epigram on Mr Ward (afterwards Lord Dudley)—

> " They say Ward has no heart, but I deny it;
> He has a heart, and gets his speeches by it—"

was provoked (says Gronow) by a remark made at table by Mr Ward. On Rogers observing that his carriage had broken down, and that he had been obliged to come in a hackney coach, Mr Ward grumbled out in a very audible whisper, "In a hearse, I should think;" alluding to the poet's corpse-like appearance. This remark Rogers never forgave.

QUITE "CHEZ LUI."

Lord Dudley, receiving a visit from the poet Rogers at Paris, proposed that they should go together to the Catacombs. It has often been remarked (says Sinclair) that, with his fine bald head, wrinkled skin, and sunk cheeks, he was more like a death's head than any man that was ever seen alive. Accordingly, when the poet had spent an hour or two in the abodes of mortality, and was about to make his exit, the keeper, startled by his death-like appearance, tried to stop him, crying out: "Hulloa! Get you back; you have no right to come out." Rogers afterwards complained to Lord Dudley that he had cruelly deserted him in this emergency. "My dear Rogers," replied the earl, "I did not like to interfere; you looked so much at home."

STILL THEY SAY SO.

—— (says Raikes in his Diary) is a good-natured, was a very good-looking man, not overflowing with intellect, but still far from deserving the sarcastic comment of the late Lord Dudley. It was at a time when poor Dudley's mind was on the wane, when his caustic humour would still find vent through the cloud which was gradually overshading his masterly intellect; he was sitting in his room, unheeding those around him, and soliloquising aloud, as was so often his custom. His favourite Newfoundland dog was at his side, who seemed to engross the whole of his attention. At length, patting his head, he exclaimed, "Fido mio, they say dogs have no souls. Humph! And *still* they say —— has a soul!"

SUBSTANTIAL DARKNESS.

Many of Luttrell's [1] best remarks are to be found recorded in Moore's Diary. At one place Moore says:—I was mentioning that some one had said of Sharpe's very dark complexion, that he looked as if the dye of his old trade (hat-making) had got engrained into his face. "Yes," said Luttrell, "darkness that may be *felt !*" [2]

CAUSE AND EFFECT.

Moore told Luttrell of some one saying Miss ——'s father and mother were "afraid to let her off the premises." "For fear, I suppose," said Luttrell, "that she should come to the *conclusion.*"

AILING.

Moore writes in one of the entries in his Diary:—William, our servant, ill from the fright of the pony kicking last night. On my saying that I thought the strong beer at Bowood might have something to do with it, Luttrell said, "Yes, he's *ale*ing, I suppose."

ASHES.

In talking of a club, of which a certain Ashe was the founder, somebody said that a son of Ashe was at present chairman of it. "Still in its *ashes* live their wonted fires," said Luttrell.

INSTINCT INDEED!

Apropos of some stories of instinct in animals, carrier pigeons, etc.: "I am told," says Luttrell, "a man who buys a flock of Welsh sheep never sees them again; they are all off to Carnarvonshire that night."

---

1 Henry Luttrell, *b.* 1770, *d.* 1851; author of *Advice to Julia* (1820), and other poems.
2 Recorded by Greville also.

THE REVERSE.

Luttrell told a party of friends that, on some one saying to Sir F. Gould, "I am told you eat three eggs every day at breakfast:"—"No;" answered Gould, "on the contrary." Some of those present asked "what was the contrary of eating three eggs?" "Laying three eggs, I suppose," said Luttrell.

CLASSICAL.

Another entry in Moore's Diary :—Talked of the dull audience I had the other night at Bowood: told [Luttrell] I was fool enough to fancy at first that Mrs F. was crying, and that I found she was only putting up her hands to settle her spectacles. "Ay," he said, "you thought it was *nocte pluit totâ*, instead of which it was *redeunt spectacula.*"

VERY CATCHING.

When Head was describing the use of the lasso in catching men as well as animals, Luttrell said the first syllable of it had caught many a man.

A DINER-OUT.

Sydney Smith talking of the bad effects of late hours, and saying of some distinguished diner-out, that there would be on his tomb: "He dined late," —"and died early," rejoined Luttrell.

FULL STOP.

In saying something about O'Connell (I forget what), Luttrell (says Moore) applied the line : "Through all the compass of the notes he ran," and then added, after a pause, "The diapason closing full in *Dan.*"[1]

MAKING ROOM.

Talking of Lady Holland's crowded dinners, and her bidding people constantly "to make room," Luttrell said, "It must certainly be *made*, for it does not *exist.*"

ENGLISH CLIMATE.

This was Luttrell's idea of the English climate :—"On a fine day, like looking up a chimney ; on a rainy day, like looking down it."

---

[1] See Dryden's "Song for St Cecilia's Day."

SPEAKING BY HEART.

This was Luttrell's version of the joke about Lord Dudley's speaking by heart :—[1]

> " In vain my affections the ladies are seeking,
> If I give up my heart, there's an end to my speaking."

A REMINDER.

I think (says Sydney Smith) it was Luttrell who used to say, " ——'s face always reminded him of boiled butter and near relations."

AS FAR AS POSSIBLE.

Sydney Smith also records the following:—" Was not —— very disagreeable?" "Why, he was as disagreeable as the occasion would permit," Luttrell said.

MONKEYS.

And this:—Luttrell used to say, "I hate the sight of monkeys; they remind me so of poor relations."

MIXING WITH BISHOPS.

Luttrell (says Planché) rarely recounted anything he had heard or seen, but charmed you by the sparkle of his language and the felicity of his epithets. One evening at a party, having accepted a verbal invitation to dinner, under the idea that his son, who was present, would also be asked, and finding subsequently that he was not, he said, "Then who is going to dine there?" "I really don't know, but I believe the Bishop of —— for one." "The Bishop of ——!" exclaimed Luttrell. "Mercy upon me! I don't mix well with the Dean, and I shall positively effervesce with the Bishop."

THE LAST STRAW.

On one occasion the late Lady Holland took Luttrell a drive in her carriage over a rough road, and as she was very nervous, she insisted on being driven at a foot's pace. This ordeal lasted some hours, and when he was at last released, poor Luttrell, perfectly exasperated, rushed into the nearest club-house, and exclaimed, clenching his teeth and hands, "The very funerals passed us!"

---

1 See Rogers's epigram on page 30. It was written, he himself admitted, " with some little assistance from Richard Sharp."

C

A PREFERENCE.

Some of the best sayings of that famous wit and man of fashion, Jekyll, have been recorded for us by the poet Moore. For example, the latter writes in his Diary:—Bankes's "Civil History of Rome," which I have looked over, but a dull book. Jekyll said the other day to a man who professed to like Bankes's book, "I suppose you would rather have his Rome (room) than his company."

HIS RIGHT.

Moore writes elsewhere:—Luttrell mentioned a good pun of Jekyll's. Being asked why he no longer spoke to a lawyer of the name of Peat, Jekyll said, "I choose to give up his acquaintance; I have common of Turbary, and have a right to cut Peat."

"TO THE GREEKS."

Moore is further responsible for this:—Mentioned Jekyll's saying quietly to himself, when some one mentioned that —— is gone to Greece, "To the Greeks foolishness."

"RUAT CŒLUM," &c.

In another passage, Moore says:—Bobus (Smith[1]) gave a new and better reading of Jekyll's joke respecting the day the ceiling fell down during dinner at Lansdowne House; Jekyll himself having escaped dining there by an engagement to meet the judges. "I had been asked," he said, "to *Ruat Cœlum*, but dined instead with *Fiat Justitia*."

TURNING ON THE MUSIC.

Again:—Jekyll said that, when the great water works were established at Chelsea, there was a proposal for having there also a great organ, from which families might be supplied with sacred music, according as they wished, by turning the cock off or on; but one objection, he said, was, that upon a thaw occurring after a long frost, you might have "Judas Maccabæus" bursting out at Charing Cross, and there would be no getting him under.

TRUE PIETY.

Jekyll said that Kenyon[2] died of eating apple pie-crust at breakfast, to save the expense of muffins, and that Lord Ellenborough, who succeeded to the Chief-Justiceship in consequence, always bowed with great reverence to apple-pie; "which," said Jekyll, "we used to call apple pie-ty."

---

1 Robert Smith, brother of the famous Canon of St Paul's.   2 The judge.

GOOD FOR SOMETHING.

When it was mentioned that the Russians, during their stay in England, eat up great quantities of tallow candles, Jekyll said that it was a species of food "bad for the liver, but good for the lights."

A CONTRADICTION.

Upon hearing that Logier taught thorough-bass in three lessons, Jekyll said it contradicted the old saying, "*Nemo repentè fuit* turpissimus."

WHERE THE WISE MEN CAME FROM.

I think (says Sydney Smith) it was Jekyll that used to say that "the further he went west, the more convinced he felt that the wise men *did* come from the east." [1]

"A SHUTTLECOCK."

I remember (says Rogers) that when Lady Cork gave a party at which she wore a most enormous plume, Jekyll said, "She was exactly a shuttlecock,—all *cork* and feathers."

THE CORK AND THE BOTTLE.

The Earl of Albemarle says he remembers meeting, at General Phipps's, George Colman, the author of "Broad Grins;" James Smith, one of the authors of the "Rejected Addresses;" and Jekyll, *nonpareil* of the punsters. The only lady in the company was the Dowager Lady Cork. "Mr Colman," said Lady Cork, "you are so agreeable that you shall drink a glass of champagne with me." "Your Ladyship's wishes are laws to me," answered Colman, "but really champagne does not agree with me." Upon which Jekyll called out, "Faith, Colman, you seem more attached to the *Cork* than the bottle."

APPROPRIATE TO THE OCCASION.

Crabb Robinson writes:—I heard the other day of Jekyll making the following pun. He said, "Erskine[2] used to hesitate very much, and could not speak very well after dinner. I dined with him once at the Fishmongers' Company. He made such a sad work of speechifying that I asked him whether it was in honour of the Company that he *floundered* so."

---

[1] Also ascribed to Sergeant Davy.
[2] The orator and wit. See the Chapter on Lawyers.

A DIFFERENT MATTER.

Lord Eldon writes:—I met Jekyll in the street the day after his retirement [from the office of Master in Chancery]; when, according to his usual manner, he addressed me in a joke :—"Yesterday, Lord Chancellor, I was your Master ; to-day I am my own master."

TIRING.

Bored (says Jeaffreson [1]) with the long-winded speech of a prosy serjeant, Jekyll wrote on a slip of paper, which was in due course passed along the barristers' benches in the court where he was sitting—

> The serjeants are a grateful race ;
> Their dress and language show it ;
> Their purple garments come from *Tyre*,
> Their arguments go to it.

TOO TOUGH.

When Garrow (says the same authority) by a more skilful than successful cross-examination, was endeavouring to lure a witness (an unmarried lady of advanced years) into an acknowledgment that payment of certain money in dispute had been tendered, Jekyll threw him this couplet—

> Garrow, forbear ; that tough old jade
> Will never prove a *tender maid*. [2]

ALL LEAN TOGETHER.

Again : when Lord Eldon and Sir Arthur Pigott each made a stand in court for his favourite pronunciation of the word "lien,"—Lord Eldon calling the word *lion*, and Sir Arthur maintaining that it was to be pronounced like *lean*,—Jekyll, with an allusion to the parsimonious arrangements of the Chancellor's kitchen, perpetrated the following *jeu d'esprit* :—

> Sir Arthur, Sir Arthur, why, what do you mean
> By saying the Chancellor's *lion* is *lean?*
> D'ye think that his kitchen's so bad as all that,
> That nothing within it can ever get fat?

NOTHING TURNED.

"In Lord Kenyon's house," a wit exclaimed, "all the year through there is Lent in the kitchen and Passion Week in the parlour." Another caustic

---

1 In *A Book about Lawyers.* Jekyll, we may remark, was much less of a lawyer than of a man of fashion, and hence his appearance in this chapter.

2 Related also by J. C. Young. It has been attributed to Erskine.

quidnunc remarked, "In his Lordship's kitchen the fire is dull, but the spits are always bright." Whereupon Jekyll interposed with an assumption of testiness: "Spits! in the name of common sense, I order you not to talk about his spits, for nothing turns upon them."

WHY NOT?

One of Jekyll's best displays of brilliant impudence was perpetrated on a Welsh judge, who was notorious alike for his greed of office and his want of personal cleanliness. "My dear sir," Jekyll observed, in his most amiable manner, to this most unamiable personage, "You have asked the minister for almost everything else, why *don't* you ask him for a piece of soap and a nail-brush?"

A HINT.

Mr Thomas Raikes, who published a diary, was pitted with small-pox even to the tip of his nose. It seems (says Frederick Locker) that he wrote an anonymous and rather offensive letter to Count D'Orsay, and as an additional insult he secured the envelope with a red wafer and stamped it with a thimble. D'Orsay guessed who was the sender, and soon after, happening to meet Raikes, he mildly counselled him thus: "The next time, *mon cher*, you write anyone an anonymous letter, and would rather not be found out, do not seal it with the tip of your nose." [1]

"ONE GREY HAIR."

Count D'Orsay (says J. C. Young) was at a party one night at which Professor O[wen] was. The latter crept quietly behind the chair, and plucked a hair from his head, and holding up his spoil in triumph, cried out to the company, "Look, ladies and gentlemen, one grey hair." D'Orsay remained unmoved. Later in the evening, *he* went behind the grey-haired geologist, twitched out a hair from his head, held it to the candles, and exclaimed, "Ladies, look here. Here is, positively, one black hair."

MUCH MORE CONVENIENT.

Chorley tells us in his Diary that he has heard Count D'Orsay[2] tell, how, when he was in England for the first time (very young, very handsome, and not abashed), he was placed at some dinner-party next the late Lady Holland. That singular woman chanced that day to be in one of her imperious humours.

---

[1] Also told by Gronow.

[2] See Lady Blessington's *Life and Letters;* also Charles Mathews's *Life*.

She dropped her napkin; the Count picked it up gallantly; then her fan, then her spoon, then her glass; and as often her neighbour stooped and restored the lost article. At last, however, the patience of the youth gave way, and on her dropping her napkin again, he turned and called one of the footmen behind him. "Put my *couvert* on the floor," said he; "I will finish my dinner there; it will be so much more convenient to my Lady Holland."

FOR THE RETURN JOURNEY.

Lord Alvanley (says Rogers) on returning home, after his duel with young O'Connell, gave a guinea to the hackney coachman who had driven him out and brought him back. The man, surprised at the largeness of the sum, said, "My Lord, I only took you to ——." Alvanley interrupted him: "My friend, the guinea is for bringing me back, not for taking me out."[1]

A PAIR.

Some reformer (says Greville) was clamouring for the expulsion of the bishops from the House of Lords, but said he would not have them all go; he would leave two. "To keep up the breed, I suppose," said Alvanley.[2]

A GOOD PROTECTION.

Moore tells what he calls "a good story" of B. Craven and Lord Alvanley, when an accident happened to their carriage. The former, getting out to thrash the footman, saw he was an old fellow, and said, "Your *age* protects you;" while Alvanley, who had advanced towards the postillion with the same intention, seeing he was an athletic young fellow, turned from him, saying, in his waggish way, "Your *youth* protects you."

NOT TO BE DONE.

At a fête at Hatfield House, *tableaux vivants* were among the chief amusements, and scenes from *Ivanhoe* were among the selections. All the parts were filled up but that of Isaac of York. Lady Salisbury (says Barham) begged Lord Alvanley "to make the set complete by doing the Jew." "Anything in my power your Ladyship may command," replied Alvanley, "but though no man in England has tried oftener, I never could *do* a Jew in my life."

---

1 This story is also told by Raikes in his *Diary.*
2 "Attributed to Alvanley," says Greville.

A CYNICAL REJOINDER.

Miss Mitford writes to one of her correspondents :—Our king [William IV.] is *ultra*-popular. Have you heard Lord Alvanley's *bon mot* concerning him? He was standing at the window at White's, when the king, with a thousand of his loving subjects at his heels, was walking up St James's Street. A friend said to him, "What are you staring at, Alvanley?" "I'm waiting to see his Majesty's pockets picked," was the reply.

A BAD JUDGE.

One of the gay men of the day, named Judge, being incarcerated in the Bench, some one (says Gronow) observed he believed it was the first instance of a Judge reaching the Bench without being previously called to the bar; to which Alvanley replied, "Many a bad judge has been taken from the bench and placed at the bar."

BOUND IN CALF.

When Sir Lumley Skeffington, who had been a lion in his day—and whose spectacle, the "Sleeping Beauty," produced at a great expense on the stage, had made him looked up to as deserving all the blandishments of fashionable life—reappeared some years after his complete downfall and seclusion in the Bench, he fancied that by a very gay external appearance he would recover his lost position; but (says Gronow) he found his old friends very shy of him. Alvanley being asked, on one occasion, who that smart-looking individual was, answered, "It is a second edition of the 'Sleeping Beauty,' bound in calf, richly gilt, and illustrated by many cuts."

FOUR-AND-TWENTY.

Lord Chesterfield[1] (Walpole tells us) was told that the Viscontina, a vocalist, said she was but four-and-twenty. He answered, "I suppose she means four-and-twenty stone."

STRUCK BY HER.

Being told of the quarrel in Spitalfields, and even that Mrs F. struck Miss P., Chesterfield said, "I always thought Mrs F. a *striking* beauty."[2]

A MATCH.

It was Lord Chesterfield (records Rogers) who said, on occasion of a certain marriage, that "Nobody's son had married Everybody's daughter."

[1] The statesman, and author of *Letters to his Son*, &c.; b. 1694, d. 1773.
[2] This is described by Walpole as Chesterfield's "last" *bon mot*.

A GOOD DESCRIPTION.

According to Rogers, Lord Chesterfield remarked of two persons dancing a minuet, that "they looked as if they were hired to do it, and were doubtful of being paid."

A DISTINGUISHED RELATIVE.

It is said that Chesterfield was once chosen, or volunteered, to conquer the king's (George **II.**) repugnance to an important appointment. On his producing the commission and mentioning the name, the king angrily refused, and said, "I would rather have the devil." "With all my heart," replied the Earl; "I only beg leave to put your Majesty in mind that the commission is addressed *to our right trusty and well beloved cousin.*" The king laughed, and said, "My Lord, do as you please."

BREVITY AND WIT.

Sir Thomas Robinson (says M. Dutens), very tall and thin, one day challenged Lord Chesterfield to make some verses on him. Lord Chesterfield wrote immediately—

> "Unlike my subject now shall be my song,
> It shall be witty, and it shan't be long."

DEPENDS ON THE PART.

Walpole writes to a correspondent :—Have you heard [Selwyn's[1]] incomparable reply to Lord George Gordon, who asked him if he would choose him again for Luggershall? He replied, "His constituents would not." "Oh, yes, if you would recommend me, they would choose me if I came from the coast of Africa." "That is according to what part of the coast you came from : they would certainly if you came from the Gold Coast." Walpole adds : Now, is not this true inspiration as well as true wit? Had one asked him in which of the four quarters of the world Guinea is situated, could he have told?

CHEAP DIGNITIES.

George Selwyn (says Walpole) said a good thing the other day on cheap dignity. He was asked who was playing at tennis. He replied : "Nobody but three markers and a *Regent*"—(meaning Lord Sandwich).

---

1 George Augustus Selwyn, wit and man of fashion, *b.* **1719** ; *d.* **1791.** See the *Life* by **Jesse.**

A PLEASURE EITHER WAY.

George Selwyn, as everybody knows, delighted in seeing executions; he never missed *being in at a death* at Tyburn. When Lord Holland (the father of Charles Fox) was confined to bed by a dangerous illness, he was informed by his servant that Mr Selwyn had recently called to inquire for him. "On his next visit," said Lord Holland, "be sure you let him in, whether I am alive or a corpse; for, if I am alive, *I* shall have great pleasure in seeing *him;* and if I am a corpse, he will have great pleasure in seeing *me.*" The late Lord Holland (says Rogers) told me this.

REPARATION.

During the period which followed the Rebellion in 1746, Selwyn (says Raikes) had attended the execution of Lord Balmerino at the Tower, and when reproached with cruelty in witnessing the death of one whom he had personally known, he exculpated himself by pleading his foible, and adding, that if he had erred in going to see Lord Balmerino's head cut off, he had afterwards made every reparation in his power, by going the next day to see the head sewn on again, previous to the interment.

HOW HE WOULD TAKE IT.

Mr Hayward records some of Selwyn's best-known witticisms. For example : When a subscription was proposed for Fox, and some one was observing that it would require some delicacy, and was wondering how Fox would take it—"Take it ?" said Selwyn; "why, *quarterly,* to be sure !"

FAST, NOT FEAST.

Again : when one of the Foxey family crossed the Channel to avoid his creditors, Selwyn said, "It is a *pass over* which will not be much relished by the Jews."

ABOUT GUMS.

When Fox was boasting of having prevailed on the French court to give up the gum trade, Selwyn said, "As you have permitted the French to draw your *teeth,* they would be fools, indeed, to quarrel with you about your *gums.*"

UNDER THE SUN.

When Walpole, in allusion to the sameness of the system of politics continued in the reign of George III., observed, "But there is nothing new under the sun." "No," said Selwyn, "nor under the *grandson.*"

A HAILING THE POST.

One night at White's, observing the Postmaster-General, Sir Everard Fawkener, losing a large sum of money at piquet, Selwyn, pointing to the successful player, remarked, "See how he is robbing the mail!"

RAISING THE BILLS.

On another occasion, in 1756, observing Mr Ponsonby, the Speaker of the Irish House of Commons, tossing about bank-bills at a hazard-table at New-castle, "Look," said Selwyn, "how easily the Speaker passes the *money-bills.*"

A GOOD EXCHANGE.

The beautiful Lady Coventry was exhibiting to Selwyn a splendid new dress, covered with large silver spangles the size of a shilling, and inquired of him whether he admired her taste—"Why," he said, "you will be *change for a guinea.*"

PRELIMINARIES.

A namesake of Charles Fox having been hung at Tyburn, Fox inquired of Selwyn whether he had attended the execution. "No, I make a point of never frequenting *rehearsals.*"

A PERMANENT RECOVERY.

A fellow-passenger with Selwyn in a coach, imagining from his appearance that he was suffering from illness, kept wearying him with good-natured in-quiries as to the state of his health. At length, to the repeated questions of "How are you now, sir?" Selwyn replied—"Very well, I thank you, and I mean to continue so for the rest of the journey."

A GARB OF WOE.

Selwyn was one day walking with Lord Pembroke, when they were be-sieged by a number of young chimney-sweepers, who kept plaguing them for money. At length Selwyn made them a low bow: "I have often heard," he said, "of the sovereignty of the people; I suppose your Highnesses are in court mourning."

AT BATH.

A gentleman, on being twice cut by Selwyn in London, came up and re-minded him that they had been acquainted in Bath. "I remember it very well; and, when we next meet at Bath, I shall be happy to be acquainted with you again."

A SUITABLE APPOINTMENT.

On hearing that C—— (a new man) wanted to be made Earl of Ormond, Selwyn said—"It would be very proper, as no doubt there have been many Butlers in the family."

TIT FOR TAT.

The French (says Mr Hayward) have not forgiven, nor are soon likely to forgive, our neutrality during their worst hour of trial. "To be sure," observed a distinguished Frenchman to an accomplished and ready-witted Englishwoman of rank, "it was foolish in us to hope better things from a nation of shopkeepers." "These popular sayings," was the well-merited retort, "are frequently destitute of any solid foundation; *we* were in the habit of calling *you* a nation of soldiers."[1]

VERY DULL.

Apropos (says Fanny Kemble) of poor old Lady Cork's infirmity with regard to the property of others (a well-known incapacity for discriminating between *meum* and *tuum*). It was Lady Cork who had originated the idea that, after all, heaven would perhaps turn out very dull to her *when she got there; sitting on damp clouds and singing "God save the King,"* being her idea of the principal amusements there. With reference to Lady Cork's theory, Lady Harriet (D'Orsay) said, "I suppose it would be rather tiresome for her, poor thing! for you know she hates music, and there would be nothing to steal *but one another's wings.*"

SETTLED ELSEWHERE.

Lord Campbell declared that the Earl of Buchan, elder brother of Thomas and Henry Erskine, respectively Lord Chancellor of England and Lord Advocate of Scotland, might, by his talents, have made a considerable figure in the world, had it not been for his morbid vanity. Observing to the Duchess of Gordon, "We inherit all our cleverness from our mother;" she answered, "I fear that, as is usually the case with the mother's fortune, it has all been settled on the younger children."

A NIGGARDLY HEIRESS.

The first Lady Rolle, a wealthy heiress, exhibited (says Lord Teignmouth) a rare union of munificence and parsimony, endowing almshouses to the amount of £10,000, and at the same time sparing in trifles. The anecdote

---

[1] See "An Advantage" (p. 28).

has been oft repeated of her husband observing when, proud of her skill as a whip, she boasted she could drive over a sixpence : "No, my dear, you would stop to pick it up."

A NATURAL MISTAKE.

Lady Davy, Sir Humphry's wife, was a brunette of the brunettes. Sydney Smith (says J. C. Young) used to say that she was as brown as dry toast; and that if she had been in the ark and had descended from it to bathe, the sea would inevitably have been converted from salt water into toast and water. She resided for a considerable time in Rome, and, though well-up in the antiquities and classical localities, never could acquire a decent knowledge of the Italian language. She was always eager to show attention to her country-women, and became their recognised cicerone. She was about to take a drive on the Campagna one day with Lady ——, in an open barouche, habited in a rather flimsy mantle. Finding that the air was much colder than she had expected to find it, she sent for her maid, and telling her to bring her her biggest and warmest cloak, thus expressed herself: "*Portati mi il mio Cloaca Maxima.*"

"NOT MUCH."

Mr Hayward says he heard Lady Davy, at Mrs Damer's in Tilney Street, tell a story of her riding on a donkey near Naples, when the wind blew so hard as to carry off garment after garment, till, she said, "I had nothing left but my *seat*"—which (adds Mr Hayward) was not much.

EVERYBODY'S.

My Lady Townshend (says Walpole[1] in one of his Letters) told me last night that she had seen a new fat player, who looked like everybody's husband. I replied, "I could easily believe that, from seeing so many women who looked like everybody's wives."

CANTING AND RECANTING.

Here (says Walpole) is another *bon mot* of my Lady Townshend. We were talking of the Methodists. Somebody said, "Pray, madam, is it true that Whitfield has recanted?" "No, sir, he has only *canted*."

---

[1] Horace, Earl of Oxford, b. 1717, d. 1797; author of *The Castle of Otranto*, &c., &c. See his *Memoirs, Journals, and Letters.*

A PREFERENCE.

At the Polish ball (says Haydon[1]) the Lord Mayor said to Lady Douglas, who squints, "Which do you prefer, my lady, Gog or Magog?" "Of the three," said Lady Douglas, "I prefer your Lordship!"

NOT THE MAN, BUT THE ANIMAL.

Lord Andover, a very fat man, was greatly plagued at a fancy bazaar to buy some trifle or other from the ladies' stalls. At length (says Haydon) he rather rudely said, "I am like the Prodigal Son, persecuted by ladies." "No, no," retorted Mrs ——, "say, rather, the fatted calf."

HER ACQUAINTANCE.

The Duchess of York (1833), in her morning walks at Oatlands, often visited the farmyard, and amused herself (says Raikes) with noticing the different animals and their families, among which was a sow that had lately farrowed some beautiful pigs. A few days afterwards, at dinner, some person asked her if she would eat some roasted pig. Her answer was: "No, I thank you; I never eat my acquaintance."

THE CIVIL THING.

Raikes writes in his Diary:—The Dowager-Duchess of Richmond is given over. I remember a story of her long ago, which, at the time, was often repeated. She went one Sunday with her daughter to the Chapel Royal at St James's, but being late, they could find no places; after looking about some time, and seeing the case was hopeless, she said to her daughter, "Come away, Louisa; at any rate, we have done the *civil* thing."

THE REASON WHY.

At dinner at Lady Sandwich's, they told (says Raikes) an anecdote of ——, the Irish barrister, and Lord ——, to whom the former, complaining that his whiskers had grown quite white, while his hair still remained brown, the other replied, "It is no wonder; your jaws have been constantly at work for the last thirty years, while your head has remained idle."[2]

---

[1] The painter, whose *Autobiography and Diary* was edited by his son. See *Life* by Tom Taylor.

[2] An old joke. In *Delitiæ Delitiarum* (1637) there is an epigram, by Macentinus, with exactly the same point, thus freely translated in *The Spirit of the Public Journals* (1806):—

> Black locks hath Gabriel, beard that's white;
> The reason, sir, is plain:
> Gabriel works hard from morn to night,
> More with his jaw than brain.

HONOUR AND TRICKS.

Lord de Ross's methods of aiding his skill at whist were (says Hayward) only available for one hand in four,—when he dealt. He then contrived to turn an honour by what is called *sauter de coup*, and having marked the higher honours with his nail, he could see to whom they fell. During the outburst of scandalous comment which followed his exposure, one of the "bitter fools" of society, who had never been admitted to his intimacy, drawled out at Crockford's: "I would leave my card at his house, but I fear he would mark it." The retort was ready: "That would depend upon whether he regarded it as a *high* honour."

SHE WANTED TO KNOW.

Lady Greenwich (says Walpole), in a conversation with Lady Tweeddale, named the Saxons. "The Saxons, my dear!" cried the Marchioness, "who were they?"—"Lord, madam, did your ladyship never read the History of England?"—"No, my dear; pray, who wrote it?"[1]

HISTORICAL.

The authoress of "**The Wild Irish Girl**," Lady Morgan, justly proud of her gifted sister Olivia, was in the habit (says Lord Albemarle) of addressing every new comer with, "I must make you acquainted with my Livy." She once used this form of words to a gentleman who had just been worsted in an encounter of wits with the lady in question. "Yes, ma'am," was the reply; "I happen to know your *Livy*, and I would to heaven your *Livy* was *Tacitus*."

THE SUN AND THE SON.

Mr Hayward tells the following story:—"Why did you cut me at the morning party at Strawberry Hill?" asked a younger son of a young lady on her preferment. "The *sun* was in my eyes, and I did not see you." "Yes, the eldest *son*."

MISUNDERSTOOD.

" Qu'est ce que c'est que votre 'compound householder,' dont M. Gladstone parle si souvent?" inquired (says Mr Hayward) a foreign lady of distinction. " Madame, c'est le mari de la femme incomprise," was the reply.

---

[1] This is a fit pendant to the maid-servant's exclamation in the play: "Shikspur! Who wrote Shikspur?"

A VALU-ABLE VALET.

When the news of Colonel Kelly's horrible death became known,[1] all the dandies (says Gronow) were anxious to secure the services of his valet, who possessed the mystery of the inimitable blacking. Brummell lost no time in discovering his place of residence, and asked what wages he required; the servant answered, his late master gave him £150 a-year, but it was not enough for his talents, and he should require £200; upon which Brummell said, "Well, if you will make it guineas, *I* shall be happy to attend upon *you.*"

DULY HONOURED.

It happened (says the same authority) that Lord William L., a man of fashion, but, like other of the great men of the day, an issuer of paper money discounted at high rates by the usurers, was thrown off his horse. Mr and Mrs King[2] immediately quitted the carriage, and placed the noble lord within. On this circumstance being mentioned in the clubs, Brummell said it was only "a Bill *Jewly* (duly) taken up and honoured."

LED CAPTIVE.

When (says Haydon) the beautiful Mrs —— was, one evening, coming out of the House of Lords, —— said, "She looks like a Babylonish beauty." "Egad," said his friend, "it's a kind of Babylonish captivity I should be very proud of."

CONSTRICTOR AND CONTRADICTOR.

A wit, when asked if he had visited the new boa constrictor in the Zoological Gardens, replied, "No; but I have been spending all the morning with the bore contradictor," meaning Hallam.[3] The story is told by Lady Chatterton.

A SUGGESTION.

Lord Surrey (*circa* 1785) rarely made use of water for purposes of bodily refreshment and comfort. Nor (says Wraxall[4]) did he change his linen more frequently than he washed himself. Complaining one day to Dudley North that he was a martyr to the rheumatism, and had ineffectually tried every remedy for its relief—"Pray, my lord," said he, "did you ever try a clean shirt?"

---

1 He was burnt to death in trying to rescue his favourite boots from a fire.
2 King was a Jew money-lender.   3 The historian.
4 Sir Nathaniel Wraxall, in his *Memoirs.*

ON TICK.

Fox, whose pecuniary embarrassments were universally recognised, being attacked by a severe indisposition, which confined him to his apartment, Dudley frequently visited him. In the course of conversation (says Wraxall), Fox, alluding to his complaints, remarked that he was compelled to observe much regularity in his diet and hours; adding, "I live by rule, like clockwork." "Yes," replied Dudley, "I suppose you mean that you go *tick, tick, tick.*"

"I SWEAR!"

Walpole, in one of his letters to Sir Horace Mann, says:—Your friend St Leger had a cause the other day for ducking a sharper, and was going to swear: the Judge said to him, "I see, sir, you are very ready to take an oath." "Yes, my lord," replied St Leger, "my father was a judge."

"HOLLOW, HOLLOW, HOLLOW."

[At a ball at M. de Guines'], Harry Conway the younger was so surprised at the agility of Mrs Hobart's bulk, that (according to Walpole) he said he was sure she must be hollow.

A CONTRADICTORY RELIGION.

I must tell you (says Walpole to Sir Horace Mann) a *bon mot* of Winnington. I was at dinner with him and Lord Lincoln and Lord Stafford last week, and it happened to be a *maigre* day of which Stafford was talking, though, you may believe, without any scruples. "Why!" said Winnington, "what a religion is yours! They let you eat nothing, and yet make you swallow everything!"

PROFESSIONAL.

Barham tells the story of Lord Middleton, out hunting, calling to Gunter, the confectioner, to "hold hard," and not ride over the hounds. "My horse is so hot, my lord, that I don't know what to do with him." "Ice him, Gunter; ice him."

A CLEVER CHIEL.

Hook (says Jerdan) had placed some crape round the print of Peel, for some vote he disapproved of. At dinner, some one appealed to him to take it off; he consented, and, amidst a dead silence, a voice which had been scarcely heard during dinner exclaimed, "Nothing like a Tory for getting a brother

Tory out of *his crape* (his scrape)." "Who's the chiel?" asked Allan Cunningham. "Lord W. Lennox," I responded. "Happy idea," said Croker; "a glass of wine, Lord William."

WAITING ON HIS MAJESTY.

One one occasion (says Lord William Lennox) George the Fourth received a reply to an invitation to dinner, in which the writer expressed his sense of the "honour he would have in waiting upon his Majesty at dinner." "Waiting upon me at dinner," said the modern Sardanapalus; "then I hope he will bring his napkin."

HERO AND ZERO.

It is told of Queen Caroline (says Jerdan[1]) that when her bitterness against her husband was at its height, she exclaimed, "Je suis la fille d'un Hèro, la femme d'un Zèro."

A ROYAL JOKE.

A witticism of William IV. is thus recorded by Lord William Lennox. At a dinner given by the Sailor-King to the Jockey Club in 1836, the Marquis of Westminster, grandfather of the present Duke, bored the Royal host and fellow-guests by reiterating his panegyrics upon the speed and stoutness of his celebrated horse Touchstone. "I will name an animal to beat him," said the good-natured King, "and he will do it by a neck." According to the then prevailing custom at Jockey Club dinners, ink, pen, and paper were brought with a view to the conclusion of a match, and his Majesty wrote down his champion, which proved to be the giraffe.

A SCRIPTURAL REMINISCENCE.

When witnessing a debate in the House of Lords, the Duke of Sussex, who sat quite near to Moore, the poet, said in his high squeaking voice, "Did you hear that —— —— speak last night? I think we might have brought him up with another prophet: 'And he said, saddle me the ass, and they saddled *him.*'"

VERY LIKE IT.

The Duke of Cumberland was so delighted with a speech of Archbishop Howley's, that when entertaining a small party, of whom one (says Lord Teignmouth) was my informer, at his own table with the repetition of it, he

---

[1] In his *Autobiography.* Jerdan was long editor of the *Literary Gazette.*

emphasized his sentences by the interlarding of such expressions as at length to elicit from the Duchess the observation, "Why, my dear, the Archbishop did not swear;" when he replied, evidently unwilling to concede his position, "Well, if he did not say that, he said something very much like it."

TOO MUCH FOR HIM.

Sir A. C—— once telling long rhodomontade stories about America at Lord Barrymore's table, B. (winking at the rest of the company), asked him, "Did you ever meet any of the Chick-chows, Sir Arthur?" "Oh, several; a very civil race." "The Cherry-chows?" "Oh, very much among them: they were particularly kind to our men." "And pray, did you know anything of the Totteroddy bow-bows?" This (says Moore) was too much for poor Sir A., who then, for the first time, perceived that Barrymore had been quizzing him.

A SPIT-FUL JUDGE.

Like many other counsel, not of the highest class, George Fergusson, afterwards Lord Hermand, owed his professional practice chiefly to the fervour of his zeal. His eagerness (says Lord Cockburn) made him froth and sputter so much in his argumentation, that there is a story to the effect that when he was once pleading in the House of Lords, the Duke of Gloucester, who was about fifty feet from the bar, rose and said, with pretended gravity, "I shall be much obliged to the learned gentleman if he will be so good as to refrain from spitting in my face."

PRONUNCIATION.

An amusing occurrence during the trial of Planché v. Braham is worth mentioning, as a similar retort has been put into the mouth of Claude Melnotte in the "Lady of Lyons." Mr Adolphus, who was the leading counsel for the defendant, in his cross-examination of Mr Berkeley, quoted a passage from Shakespeare, and sneeringly asked him if he recognised these words? "Certainly not, as you pronounce them," answered Mr Berkeley, contemptuously, raising a general laugh at the expense of the learned gentleman. The Mr Berkeley in question was the Hon. H. Fitzhardinge Berkeley, and the story is told by Mr Planché.

WHAT HE COULD DO.

The greatest treat I saw (says A. Gibson Hunter[1]) was Sir John Lade, the famous whip, in his barouche and four. Tommy Onslow, now Lord Cranley,

---

[1] In Archibald Constable's *Correspondence.*

is on the whole reckoned the best whip of the two. The following lines on his lordship are good :—

> "What can Tommy Onslow do?
> Why? he can drive a phaeton and two;
> Can Tommy Onslow do no more?
> Yes, he can drive a phaeton and four."

STILL!

Moore says that Lord Maynard was the person who said of the House of Commons, "Is that going on still?"

UNDER.

The following is Scrope Davies' epitaph on Lord L——, as preserved by Moore:—

> " Here lies L's body, from his soul asunder;
> He once was on the turf, and now is *under*."

A FOOLISH STUDY.

Writing in 1780, Horace Walpole says:—After Sir Paul Methuen had quitted court, the late Queen, who thought she had that foolish talent of playing off people, frequently saw him when she dined abroad. Once that she dined with my mother at Chelsea, Sir Paul was there. The Queen's constant topic for teazing Sir Paul was his passion for romances, and he was weary of it. "Well, Sir Paul, what romance are you reading now?" "None, madam! I have gone through them all." " Well! what are you reading then?" "I have got into a very foolish study, madam : the History of the Kings and Queens of England."

FRENCH OF STRATFORD.

On one occasion (says Gronow) Lord Westmoreland, who was Lord Privy Seal, being asked what office he held, replied, " *Le Chancelier est le grand sceau* (sot); *moi je suis le petit sceau d'Angleterre.*" On another occasion, he wished to say, "I would if I could, but I can't," and he rendered it, " *Je voudrais se je coudrais, mais je ne connais pas.*"

HEAVEN FORBID!

Whoever the following story may be fathered on (says Sir Jonah Barrington), Sir John Hamilton was certainly its parent. The Duke of Rutland, at one of his levees, being at a loss (as probably most kings, princes, and viceroys occasionally are) for something to say to every person he was bound in etiquette to notice, remarked to Sir John Hamilton that there was "a prospect of an excellent crop. The timely rain," observed the Duke, "will bring everything above ground." "God forbid, your Excellency!" exclaimed the courtier. His Excellency stared, whilst Sir John continued, sighing heavily as he spoke:—"Yes, God forbid! for I have *three wives* under it."

WOODEN WALLS.

At one of those large convivial parties which distinguished the table of Major Hobart, when he was secretary in Ireland, amongst the usual loyal toasts (says Barrington) "The wooden walls of England" being given, Sir John Hamilton, in his turn, gave "The wooden walls of Ireland!" This toast being quite new to us all, he was asked for an explanation; upon which, filling a bumper, he very gravely stood up, and, bowing to the Marquess of Waterford and several county gentlemen, who commanded county regiments, he said—"My lords and gentlemen! I have the pleasure of giving you 'The wooden walls of Ireland'—*the colonels of militia!*"

UNDER HIS HAND.

The same authority says:—Sir Richard Musgrave, although he understood *drawing the long bow* as well as most people, never patronised it in any other individual. Sir John Hamilton did not spare the exercise of this accomplishment in telling a story, one day, in the presence of Sir Richard, who declared his incredulity rather abruptly, as indeed was his constant manner. Sir John was much nettled at the mode in which the other dissented, more particularly as there were some strangers present. He asseverated the truth on his *word:* Sir Richard, however, repeating his disbelief, Sir John Hamilton furiously exclaimed—"You say you don't believe my word!" "I *can't* believe it," replied Sir Richard. "Well, then," said Sir John, "if you won't believe my *word*, by G—d I'll give it you under my *hand*," clenching at the same moment his great fist. The witticism raised a general laugh, in which the parties themselves joined, and in a moment all was good-humour.

A PLEASANT EXCHANGE.

Lady Charlotte Lindsay (according to Lord Houghton [1]) used to say that she had sprained her ankle so often, and had been so often told that it was worse than breaking her leg, that she had come to look on a broken leg as a positive advantage.

---

[1] In *Monographs, Personal and Social.* "Lady Charlotte," says Lord Houghton, "was of the noble family of which Lord North is the political representative, and whom nature favoured rather in their talents than in their external appearance."

GONE OFF.

In Lady Lindsay's later days (according to the same authority), when once complimented on looking very well, she replied, "I dare say it's true; the bloom of ugliness is past."

A NEW ORDER.

On the elevation of some childless personage to the peerage, Lady Charlotte remarked that he was of the new order, which seemed the popular one—not the Barons, but the Barrens.

A NEW ADJECTIVE.

One day coming late to dinner in the country, Lady Charlotte excused herself on account of the "macadamnable" state of the roads.

THAT WAS ALL.

Harriet Lady Ashburton [1] said of a certain individual that he had only two ideas, and they were his legs; and they were spindle-shanked. [2]

NOT EVEN THAT.

Of another person Lady Ashburton said, that he had nothing truly human about him; he couldn't even yawn like a man.

A DISAGREEABLE SIMILE.

Of another individual Lady Ashburton said, that talking to him was like playing long whist.

FOR LACK OF FOOD.

When some one said of a gentleman, "Don't speak so hard of him, he lives on your good graces," Lady Ashburton remarked, "That accounts for him being so thin."

---

[1] Died 1857.   [2] Lord Houghton's *Monographs.*

ABOUT LAWYERS AND THE LAW.

ONLY ONE.

PHILLIPS'S "Life of Curran" is full of anecdotes of that witty lawyer. We select the following :—When Curran was at college, the Rev. Dr Hailes, one of the fellows, during a public examination, continually pronounced the word *nimirum* with a wrong quantity ; it was naturally enough the subject of conversation, and his reverence was rather unceremoniously handled by some of the academic critics. Curran affected to become his advocate. "The Doctor is not to blame," said he; "there was only one man in all Rome who understood the word, and Horace[1] tells us so—

　　　'Septimius, Claudi, *nimirum* intelligit *unus*.'"

THE BITER BIT.

At another time, when an insect of very *high birth,* but of very democratic habits, was caught upon Curran's coat, about the appearance of which he was never very solicitous, his friend Egan, observing it, maliciously exclaimed from Virgil—"Eh! Curran :

　　　'Cujum pecus? an Meliboei?'"[2]

at the same time turning with a triumphant jocoseness to the spectators. But Curran, in the coolest manner taking up the line, immediately retorted—

　　　"'Non, verum *Ægonis,*—nuper mihi tradidit *Ægon.*'"

HE MAY!

Phillips says:—I remember Curran once—in an action for breach of promise of marriage, in which he was counsel for the defendant, a young clergyman—thus appealing to the jury:—"Gentlemen, I entreat of you not to ruin this young man by a vindictive verdict; for, *though* he has talents, and is in the church, *he may rise !*"

AS IT GOES.

Curran's *bon mot* upon a brother barrister of the name of Going certainly deserves a place. This gentleman fully verified the old adage that a story

---

　　[1] Epist. I., ix. 1.　　　　　　　　　[2] Bucol. III. 1.

never loses in the telling; he took care continually to add to every anecdote
all the graces which could be derived from his own embellishment. An instance of this was one day remarked to Curran, who scarcely knew one of his
own stories, it had so grown by the carriage. "I see," said he, "the proverb is quite applicable—' *Vires acquiret eundo*'—it gathers by *Going.*"

A SUITABLE MOTTO.

Lundy Foot, the celebrated tobacconist, applied to Curran for a motto
when he first established his carriage: "Give me one, my dear Curran," said
he, "of a serious cast, because I am afraid the people will laugh at a tobacconist setting up a carriage; and, for the scholarship's sake, let it be in Latin."
"I have just hit on it," said Curran; "it is only two words, and it will at
once explain your profession, your elevation, and your contempt for their
ridicule, and it has the advantage of being in two languages, Latin or
English, just as the reader chooses. Put up '*Quid rides*' upon your
carriage."

A BAD ENDORSEMENT.

[Curran] having one day a violent argument with a country schoolmaster
on some classical subject, the pedagogue, who had the worst of it, said, in a
towering passion, that he would lose no more time, and must go back to his
scholars. "Do, my dear doctor," said Curran; "but *don't endorse my sins
upon their backs.*"

NO CHANGE.

Curran was told that a very stingy and slovenly barrister had started for
the Continent with a shirt and a guinea. "He'll not change either till he
comes back," said he.

FOR SELF AND FELLOWS.

A very stupid foreman once asked a judge how they were to ignore a bill.
"Why, sir," said Curran, "when you mean to find a true one, just write
Ignoramus for self and fellows on the back of it."

SLACK.

Curran, examining a country squire, who disputed a collier's bill—"Did he
not give you the *coals*, friend?" "He did, sir; but—" "But what?—on
your oath wasn't your payment *slack?*"

A LEGAL JOKE.

Curran was just rising to cross-examine a witness before a judge who could not comprehend any jest that was not written in *black letter*. Before he said a single word, the witness began to laugh. "What are you laughing at, my friend—what are you laughing at? Let me tell you that a laugh without a joke is like—is like—" "Like what, Mr Curran?" asked the judge, imagining he was nonplussed. "Just exactly, my lord, like a *contingent remainder* without any particular *estate* to support it."

NOTHING IN IT.

[Phillips records] Curran's retort upon an Irish judge, [who was] quite as remarkable for his good humour and raillery as for his legal researches. [The advocate] was addressing a jury on one of the state trials in 1803 with his usual animation. The judge, whose political bias, if any judge can have one, was certainly supposed not to be favourable to the prisoner, shook his head in doubt or denial of one of the advocate's arguments. "I see, gentlemen," said Mr Curran, "I see the motion of his lordship's head; common observers might imagine that implied a difference of opinion, but they would be mistaken; it is merely accidental. Believe me, gentlemen, if you remain here many days, you will yourselves perceive, that when his lordship shakes his head, there's *nothing in it!*"

HIS ELDEST.

Sir Boyle Roche[1] was very proud of his alliance with the family of Sir John Cane, and boasted that Sir John had given him his eldest daughter. "If he had had an older one, he'd have given her to you, Sir Boyle," said Curran.

THE WILL FOR THE DEED.

Sir Boyle Roche seems to have had a rival in one of the judges of the King's Bench, who, in an argument on the construction of a will, sagely declared, "It appeared to him that the testator meant to keep a life-interest in the estate to himself." "Very true, my lord," said Curran gravely; "testators generally do secure a life-interest for themselves, but in this case, I rather think your lordship *takes the will for the deed.*"

HIS SOFTEST PART.

A Limerick banker, remarkable for his sagacity, had an iron leg. "His leg," said Curran, "is the softest part about him."

---

[1] The famous Irish worthy, of whom some stories are recounted on another page.

A SENSITIVE DUELLIST.

In the very outset of his professional career, Curran was employed at Cork to prosecute an officer of the name of St Ledger for an assault upon a Roman Catholic clergyman. St Ledger, justly or unjustly, was suspected by Curran to be a mere political creature of Lord Doneraile, and to have acted in complete subserviency to the religious prejudices of his patron. On this theme he expatiated with such personal bitterness and such effect, that St Ledger sent him a message the next day. They met, and Curran not returning his fire, the affair was concluded. "It was not necessary," said Curran, "for me to fire at him; he died in three weeks after the duel, *of the report of his own pistol.*"

A JEST ON A CHEST.

John Egan, chairman of Kilmainham, was an immense-sized man, as brawny, and almost as black, as a coal porter. "Did you ever see," said he, striking his bosom triumphantly, "did you ever see such a *chest* as that?" "A *trunk*, you mean, my dear Egan," answered Curran, good-humouredly, who was a mere pigmy in comparison.

LOSING TALLOW.

In an election for the borough of Tallogh, Egan was an unsuccessful candidate; he, however, appealed from the decision, and the appeal came, of course, before the Committee of the House of Commons. It was in the heat of a very warm summer; Egan was struggling through the crowd, his handkerchief in one hand, his wig in the other, and his whole countenance raging like the dog-star, when he met Curran. "I'm sorry for you, my dear fellow," said Curran. "Sorry! why so, Jack? why so? I'm perfectly at my ease." "Alas, Egan! 'tis but too visible to every one that you're losing *tallow* (*Tallogh*) fast."

A FAIR OFFER.

During the temporary separation of Lord Avoumore and Curran, Egan espoused the judge's imaginary quarrel so bitterly that a duel was the consequence. The [parties] met, and on the ground Egan complained that the disparity in their sizes gave his antagonist a manifest advantage. "I might as well fire at a razor's edge as at him," said Egan, "and he may hit me as easily as a turf-stack." "I'll tell you what, Mr Egan," replied Curran; "I wish to take no advantage of you—let my size be *chalked* out upon your side, and I am quite content that every shot which hits outside that mark should *go for nothing.*"

HATING THE SIGHT OF IT.

Those who voted for the Union [between England and Ireland] Curran held almost in abhorrence. He was one day setting his watch at the Post Office, which was then opposite the late Parliament House, when a noble member of the House of Lords said to him, "Curran, what do they mean to do with that useless building? For my part, I am sure I hate even the sight of it." "I do not wonder at it, my lord," replied Curran contemptuously; "I never yet heard of a murderer who was not afraid of a ghost."

LOOKING FOR BULLS.

Curran happened one day to have for his companion in a stage-coach a very vulgar and revolting old woman, who seemed to have been encrusted with a prejudice against Ireland and all its inhabitants. Curran sat chafing in silence in his corner. At last, suddenly, a number of cows, with their tails and heads up in the air, kept rushing up and down the road in alarming proximity to the coach windows. The old woman manifestly was but ill at ease. At last, unable to restrain her terror, she faltered out, "Oh, dear; oh, dear, sir! what can the cows mean?" "Faith, my good woman," replied Curran, "as there's an Irishman in the coach, I shouldn't wonder if they were on the outlook for *a bull!*"

TRYING TO CATCH IT.

One morning (says Phillips of himself and Curran), we met an Irish gentleman, who certainly most patriotically preserved his native pronunciation. He had acquired a singular habit of lolling out his tongue. "What can he possibly mean by it?" said I to Curran. "I think it's clear enough," said he, "the man's trying to catch the English accent!"

NOT THAT.

Curran's notice was once attracted by a lady whose chin certainly called loudly for a razor. "In the name of wonder," he exclaimed, "who can she be?" [Phillips] told him it was reported that she was a Roman lady, of an ancient Italian family. "Well," said he, "it may be; but she manifestly is not one of the Barberinis."

HIS OWN FAMILIAR.

Passing a person whom he much disliked, Curran said, "Observe that solemn blockhead—that pompous lump of dulness. Now, if you breakfasted and dined with that fellow for a hundred years, you could not be intimate with him; he would not even be seen to smile, lest anybody might suppose he was too familiar with himself!"

REMARKABLE.

The late Sir Thomas Furton, who was a respectable speaker, but certainly nothing more, affected once to discuss the subject of eloquence with Curran, assuming an equality by no means palatable to the latter. Happening to mention, as a peculiarity of his, that he could not speak above a quarter of an hour without requiring something to moisten his lips, Sir Thomas, pursuing his comparisons, declared *he* had the advantage in that respect. "I spoke," said he, "the other night in the Commons for five hours, on the Nabob of Oude, and never felt in the least thirsty." "It is very remarkable, indeed," replied Curran, "for every one agrees that was the *driest* speech of the session."

AN INDIVIDUAL!

Curran used to relate a ludicrous encounter between himself and a fishwoman on the quay at Cork. This lady, whose tongue would have put Billingsgate to the blush, was incited one day to assail him, which she did with very little reluctance. "I thought myself a match for her," said he, "and valorously took up the gauntlet. But such a virago never skinned an eel. My whole vocabulary made not the least impression. On the contrary, she was manifestly becoming more vigorous every moment, and I had nothing for it but to beat a retreat. This, however, was to be done with dignity; so, drawing myself up disdainfully, I said, 'Madam, I scorn all further discourse with such an *individual*.' She did not understand the word, and thought it, no doubt, the very hyperbole of opprobrium. 'Individual, you wagabone!' she screamed; 'what do you mean by that?—I'm no more an individual than your mother was!' Never was victory more complete. The whole sisterhood did homage to me, and I left the quay of Cork covered with glory."

HOAXING A JUDGE.

As a judge, Lord Avonmore had one great fault: he was apt to take up a first impression of a cause, and it was very difficult afterwards to obliterate it. The advocate, therefore, had not only to struggle against the real obstacles presented to him by the case itself, but also with the imaginary ones, created by the hasty anticipation of the judge. Curran was one day most seriously annoyed by this habit of Lord Avonmore, and he took the following whimsical method of correcting it. The reader must remember that the object of the narrator was, by a tedious and malicious procrastination, to irritate his hearer into the vice which he was so anxious to eradicate. They were to dine together at the house of a common friend, and a large party was assembled, many of whom witnessed the occurrences of the morning. Curran, contrary to all his usual habits, was late for dinner, and at length arrived in the most admirably affected agitation. "Why, Mr Curran, you have kept us a full hour waiting dinner for you," grumbled out Lord Avonmore. "Oh, my dear lord, I regret it much ; you must know it is not my custom, but— I've just been witness to a most melancholy occurrence." "My God ! you seem terribly moved by it—take a glass of wine. What was it ?—what was it ?" "I will tell you, my lord, the moment I can collect myself. I had been detained at Court—in the Court of Chancery—your lordship knows the Chancellor sits late." "I do, I do—but go on." "Well, my lord, I was hurrying here as fast as ever I could—I did not even change my dress—I hope I shall be ex- cused for coming in my boots?" "Poh, poh—never mind your boots: the point—come at once to the point of the story." "Oh—I will, my good lord, in a moment. I walked here—I would not even wait to get the carriage ready—it would have taken time, you know. Now there is a market exactly in the road by which I had to pass—your lordship may perhaps recollect the market—do you ?" "To be sure I do—go on, Curran—go on with the story." "I am very glad your lordship remembers the market, for I totally forget the name of it—the name — the name —" "What the devil signifies the name of it, sir ?—it's the Castle Market." "Your lordship is perfectly right—it is called the Castle Market. Well, I was passing through that very identical Castle Market, when I observed a butcher preparing to kill a calf. He had a huge knife in his hand—it was as sharp as a razor. The calf was standing beside him—he drew the knife to plunge it into the animal. Just as he was in the act of doing so, a little boy about four years old—his only son —the loveliest little baby I ever saw, ran suddenly across his path, and he killed—oh, my God ! he killed—" "The child ! the child ! the child !" vociferated Lord Avonmore. "No, my lord—the calf," continued Curran, very coolly ; "he killed the calf, but—*your lordship is in the habit of antici- pating.*"

NOT YET.

Curran often raised a laugh at Lord Norbury's expense. The laws, at that period, made capital punishment so general that nearly all crimes were punishable with death by the rope. It was remarked Lord Norbury never hesitated to condemn the convicted prisoner to the gallows. Dining in com- pany with Curran, who was carving some corned beef, Lord Norbury inquired, "Is that hung beef, Mr Curran ?" "Not yet, my lord," was the reply ; "you have not *tried* it."

DAY AND KNIGHT.

One of the causes of great interest in which Curran acted as counsel was the prosecution of Sir Henry Hayes for carrying off Miss Pike, a quaker young lady ; she was rescued, and for two years the perpetrator of this outrage was not amenable. When arrested and bills of indictment found, Curran appeared for the prosecution, and made a masterly speech. The case enlisted the feelings of the people against the prisoner, and a woman, rushing up to Curran on his way to Court, exclaimed, "More power to you, counsellor, that you may gain the day." "If I gain the day," replied Curran, "you will lose the K(night)."

HALTING.

Macnally[1] walked with a limp, one leg being shorter than the other. When the barristers were enrolling their names in the Volunteer corps, Macnally asked Curran if he should give in his name to join. "If you enlist," said Curran, "you will shortly be tried, and perhaps shot for disobedience of orders." "Why?" asked Macnally, rather indignantly. "Because, when ordered to march, you will certainly halt," was the reply.

A HIGH AUTHORITY.

In Curran's "Life" by his son occur several anecdotes of his wit not to be found elsewhere. For example:—Mr Curran was engaged in a legal argument —behind him stood his colleague, a gentleman whose person was remarkably tall and slender, and who had originally designed to take orders. The judge observing that the case under discussion involved a question of ecclesiastical law, "Then," said Mr Curran, "I can refer your lordship to a high authority behind me, who was once intended for the *church*, though" (in a whisper to a friend beside him) "in my opinion he was fitter for the *steeple*."

NAILING HIM.

Again:—An officer of one of the courts, named Halfpenny, having frequently interrupted Mr Curran, the judge peremptorily ordered him to be silent, and sit down. "I thank your lordship," said the counsel, "for having at length nailed that rap to the counter."

AN AVANT-COURIER.

A deceased judge had a defect in one of his limbs, from which, when he walked, one foot described almost a circle round the other. Mr Curran being asked how his lordship still contrived to walk so fast, answered, "Don't you see that one leg goes before like a tipstaff, and clears the way for the other?"

---

[1] The Irish barrister.

COMMON PROPERTY.

A miniature painter, upon his cross-examination by Mr Curran, was made to confess that he had carried his improper freedoms with a particular lady so far as to attempt to put his arm round her waist. "Then, sir," said the counsel, "I suppose you took that *waist* for *common?*"

HOW MANY?

"No man," said a wealthy but weak-headed barrister, "should be admitted to the bar who has not an independent landed property." "May I ask you, sir," said Mr Curran, "how many acres make a *wise-acre?*"

THE HALL-MARK.

"Would you not have known this boy to be my son, from his resemblance to me?" asked a gentleman. Mr Curran answered, "Yes, sir; the maker's name is stamped on the *blade.*"

ALWAYS PLAINTIVE.

Chief-Justice Carleton (says Sir Jonah Barrington) was a very lugubrious personage. He never ceased complaining of his bad state of health (or rather of his hypochondriasm), and frequently introduced Lady Carleton into his "Book of Lamentations:" thence it was remarked by Curran to be very extraordinary that the Chief-Justice should appear as plaintiff (*plaintive*) in every cause that happened to come before him!

NOTHING TO TRY.

One *Nisi Prius* day, Lord Carleton came into Court, looking unusually gloomy. He apologised to the bar for being necessitated to adjourn the Court and dismiss the jury for that day, "though," proceeded his lordship, "I am aware that an important issue stands for trial; but the fact is, I have met with a domestic misfortune, which has altogether deranged my nerves!—Poor Lady Carleton" (in a low tone to the bar) "has most unfortunately *miscarried*, and—" "Oh, then, my lord!" exclaimed Curran, "there was no necessity for your lordship to make any apology, since it now appears that your lordship has *no issue* to try." The Chief-Justice faintly smiled, and thanked the bar for their consideration.

DYING BY JURY.

Curran (says Crabb Robinson) told an anecdote of an Irish Parliament-man, who was boasting in the House of Commons of his attachment to the trial by jury. "Mr Speaker, with the trial by jury I have lived, and, by the blessing of God, with the trial by jury I will die!" Curran sat near him, and whispered audibly, "What, Jack! do you mean to be hanged?"

IN CONSULTATION.

Lord Clare (says Mr Hayward) had a favourite dog which was permitted to follow him to the bench. One day, during an argument of Curran's, the Chancellor turned aside, and began to fondle the dog, with the obvious view of intimating inattention or disregard. The counsel stopped; the judge looked up: "I beg pardon," continued Curran, "I thought your lordships had been in consultation."

A GOOD COMMENCEMENT.

When Lord Erskine[1] heard that somebody had died worth two hundred thousand pounds, he observed, "Well, that's a very pretty sum to begin the next world with." Rogers tells this story, as well as the two following.

A SOPORIFIC.

"A friend of mine," said Erskine, "was suffering from a continual wakefulness, and various methods were tried to send him to sleep, but in vain. At last his physicians resorted to an experiment which succeeded perfectly: they dressed him in a watchman's coat, put a lantern into his hand, placed him in a sentry-box, and—he was asleep in ten minutes."

TERRI-BLY RUDE.

In talking of Erskine's *jeux d'esprit*, Lord Lansdowne mentioned to Moore four lines he once wrote upon an inn window, on a great attorney, named Terry; thereby losing, as he said, a great number of briefs. Among the inscriptions on the window was one, written by the attorney himself, announcing that on such a day Mr Terry had arrived here from Tenterden, and it was under this that Erskine wrote—

> "What can it matter how or when
> Terry arrives from Tenterden;
> For when he's crost the Stygian ferry
> Who'll ever ask—What's come of Terry?"

1 Thomas Erskine, Lord Chancellor; b. 1750, d. 1823.

THE DIFFERENCE.

Lord Campbell[1] has several stories about Lord Erskine :—On the trial of an action to recover the value of a quantity of whalebone, the defence turning on the quality of the article, a witness was called, of impenetrable stupidity, who could not distinguish between the two well-known descriptions of this commodity—the "long" and the "thick." [He] still confounding *thick* whalebone with *long*, Erskine exclaimed, in seeming despair, "Why, man, you do not seem to know the difference between what is *thick* and what is *long!* Now, I tell you the difference. You are *thick*-headed, and you are not *long*-headed."

A CHANGE.

Lord Erskine (continues Campbell) had a kindness for his countryman Park, afterwards a judge of the Court of Common Pleas, but occasionally quizzed him ; and he wrote upon him the following lines, which, with a little alteration, might have been applied to himself :—

"James Allan Park
Came naked stark
From Scotland ;
But now wears clo'es,
And lives with beaux
In England."

ILLUMINATION.

On the long, lanky visage of Mr Justice Ashurst, before whom he daily practised, Erskine penned the following couplet :—

"Judge Ashurst, with his *lantern jaws*
Throws *light* upon the English laws."

PLEASURE AND PAIN.

Being much indisposed during dinner at Sir Ralph Payne's, in Grafton Street, Lord Erskine retired to another apartment, and reclined for some time on a sofa. In the course of the evening, being somewhat recovered, he rejoined the festive circle ; and Lady Payne inquiring how he found himself, he presented to her the following couplet:—

" 'Tis true I am ill, but I need not complain,
For he never knew *pleasure* who never knew *Payne.*"

RHYME AND REASON.

One day in 1807, when engaged to dine on turtle with the Lord Mayor, Lord Erskine was obliged to sit late on the woolsack. Plumer pleading at

[1] *Lives of the Lord Chancellors.*

the bar with great turbulence and tediousness, the Chancellor (says Campbell) was secretly very impatient and angry, but was observed to be writing diligently.   Lord Holland, who was very familiar with him, and suspected from his manner that there was something unusual in his occupation, asked for a sight of his note-book.   Being produced, it was found to contain the following lines addressed to Plumer :—

> "Oh that thy cursed balderdash
> Were swiftly turned to callipash !
> Thy bands so stiff, and snug toupee,
> Corrected were to callipee,
> That since I can nor dine nor sup,
> I might arise and eat thee up !"

AN EXCELLENT EXAMPLE.

Another story of Lord Erskine :—A junior barrister, joining the circuit, had the misfortune to have his trunk cut off from the back of his post-chaise, on which the jocund leader (Erskine) comforted him by saying, " Young gentleman ! henceforth imitate the elephant, wisest of animals, who always carries his trunk before him."[1]

IN QUOQUE.

Crossing Hampstead Heath, Lord Erskine saw a ruffianly driver most unmercifully pummelling a miserable bare-boned pack-horse; and, remonstrating with him, received this answer, "Why, it's my own; mayn't I use it as I please?"   As the fellow spoke, he discharged a fresh shower of blows on the raw back of his beast.   Erskine, much irritated by this brutality, laid two or three sharp strokes of his walking-stick over the shoulders of the cowardly offender, who, crouching and grumbling, asked him what business he had to touch him with his stick?   "Why," replied Erskine, "my stick is my own; mayn't I use it as I please?"

EMBLEMATICAL.

Being counsel for a person who, whilst travelling in a stage-coach which started from the " Swan with Two Necks," in Lad Lane, had been upset and had his arm broken, Lord Erskine thus, with much gravity, began :—" Gentlemen of the jury, the plaintiff in this case is Mr Beverley, a respectable merchant of Liverpool, and the defendant is Mr Nelson, proprietor of the 'Swan with Two Necks'—a sign emblematical, I suppose, of the number of necks people ought to possess who ride in his vehicles."

---

[1] He made the same joke on another occasion, in reference to a keeper of wild beasts called Pollio, who had lost a portmanteau in a similar manner.

E

THE GREAT SEAL.

When Lord Erskine was Chancellor, being asked by the Secretary of the Treasury whether he would attend the grand ministerial fish dinner to be given at Greenwich at the end of the session, he answered:—"To be sure I will; what would your fish dinner be without the *Great Seal?*"[1]

WORSE STILL.

[Erskine's] friend, Mr Maylem, of Ramsgate, having observed that his physician had ordered him not to bathe, "Oh, then," said Erskine, "you are *Malum prohibitum.*" "My wife, however," resumed the other, "does bathe." "Worse still," rejoined Erskine, "for she is *Malum in se.*"

A GENEROUS SUBSCRIPTION.

The late worthy Sir John Sinclair having proposed that a testimonial should be presented to himself by the British nation, for his eminent public services, in answer to one of his circulars Lord Erskine wrote on the first page of a letter, in a flowing hand, these words:—"MY DEAR SIR JOHN,—I am certain there are few in this kingdom who set a higher value on your public services than myself; and I have the honour to subscribe"—then, on turning over the leaf, was to be found—"myself, your most obedient faithful servant, ERSKINE."

UNLESS.

One of Erskine's smartest puns (says Jeaffreson) referred to a question of evidence. "A case," he observes, in a speech made during later years, "being laid before me by my veteran friend, the Duke of Queensberry—better known as 'old Q'—as to whether he could sue a tradesman for breach of contract about the painting of his house; and the evidence being totally insufficient to support the case, I wrote thus:—'I am of opinion that this action will not *lie* unless the witnesses *do.*'"[2]

A BORE.

Mr O'Flannagan relates many anecdotes of Plunket:—Some mutual acquaintance, who was not remarkable for his brilliancy, was spoken of as having foretold an event. "I always knew he was a *bore*," remarked Plunket, "but did not know he was an *augur.*"

---

1 J. C. Young has a different version of this story.

2 It is worthy of notice that this witticism was but a revival (with a modification) of the pun attributed to Lord Chancellor Hatton in Bacon's "Apophthegms."

TWO CONUNDRUMS.

Again:—One of the officials of the Court of Chancery, named Moore, was noted for his peculiar writing—his *caligraphy,* as he called it; while one of the most eminent practitioners, seldom absent during the sittings, was a dandy solicitor named Morris. One day, while several of the king's counsel were waiting for the Lord Chancellor's coming, Bushe[1] asked Plunket, "Why should this Court remind them of Chester?" "I give it up," replied Plunket. "Don't you see," rejoined Bushe, "we are near *Penman Moore* (Penman-Maur)?" "I was stupid, indeed," said Plunket; "and ask you in return why it reminds us of North Wales?" Bushe was unable to solve the riddle; so, pointing to the dandy solicitor, Plunket jocosely said, "Why, there's *Beau Morris.*"

AN EARLY RISER.

Once more:—On a learned serjeant, more remarkable for late sitting than early rising, having been appointed a judge of the Common Pleas, when that Court, unlike its present position, had little business, "It's the very Court for him," said Plunket; "it will be *up* every day before himself."

A VERY BAD QUARREL.

At a dinner-party given by the Archbishop of Dublin, Dr Magee, a young Fellow of College wished to attract observation by narrating a difference of opinion between two celebrated men of science, Dr Brinkley,[2] the great astronomer, and Dr Pond.[3] The gentleman, being asked to mention the cause of controversy, replied: "Brinkley says that the parallax of a lyrae is three seconds, and Pond contends that it is only two. Each maintains his own opinion with the most obstinate pertinacity; and, in short, I do not know how it will end, the quarrel is so keen between them." "Upon my word, sir," said Plunket, with a grave comic face, which to those who knew him portended a joke, "it must be a very bad quarrel when the seconds cannot agree."

A GREAT BORE.

A somewhat solemn dinner-party was ranged at opposite sides of the well-furnished table at Holland House. Statesmen and literary celebrities mingled with beauties without wit, and wits without beauty, in the select coterie. Hume[4] was there, and full of dry statistics, pouring tables of figures into the

---

1 Sir Charles Kendal Bushe, Chief-Justice of Ireland; *d.* 1843.
2 Astronomer-Royal (1767-1836).   3 Bishop of Cloyne (1763-1835).
4 Joseph Hume, M.P. (1777-1855).

unwilling ears of his next neighbour, and his hard Scotch voice could be heard for a considerable distance. "Don't you think Mr Hume a great bore?" inquired a fair daughter of the aristocracy, who sat next to Plunket. "Indeed I do, Lady ——," was the reply ; "a great Caledonian boar."

CONCEITED.

Moore writes in his Diary :—Corry described a merry day with Plunket and Bushe at the Pigeon House; their endeavours to out-pun each other : "Well that's as bad as his; isn't it?" "No, no! mine was the worst; I appeal to all around." Con Lyne was one of the party, and on his undertaking to recite something, Plunket said, "Come, come, Lyne, stand up while you do it, and nobody can say you're *Con seated* (conceited)."

A SLIGHT ALTERATION.

Con Lyne (says Mr O'Flannagan) was a very social and convivial Irish barrister, who loved the report of a champagne flask better than a Report of Law. "Any relation," asked a stranger, "to Con of the Hundred Battles?" "No," replied Lord Plunket, "but he is Con of the Hundred Bottles."

NEITHER ONE NOR THE OTHER.

On the formation of the Grenville administration, Charles Kendal Bushe, who had the reputation of a waverer, apologized one day for his absence from Court, on the ground that he was "cabinet making." The Chancellor (says Phillips) maliciously disclosed the excuse on his return. "Oh, indeed, my lord, that is an occupation in which my friend would distance me, as I never was either a *turner* or a *joiner*."

NOT OVERTAXED.

On being told that his successors in the Court of Common Pleas had little or nothing to do, "Well, well," said [Plunket], "they're equal to it."

NOT SO SICK AS ALL THAT.

Everybody (says Phillips) knew how acutely Plunket felt his forced resignation of the Chancellorship, and his being superseded by Lord Campbell. A violent tempest arose on the day of his expected arrival, and a friend remarking to him how sick of his promotion the passage must have made him : "Yes," said Plunket, ruefully, "but it won't make him throw up the seals."

REAL AND PERSONAL.

Lord Albemarle tells the following story :—"One of my aides-de-camp," said Lord Wellesley to Plunket on one occasion, "has written a personal narrative of his travels,—pray, Chief-Justice, what is your definition of 'personal?'" "My lord," replied Plunket, "we lawyers always consider *personal* as opposed to *real*." Lord Albemarle was himself the aide-de-camp referred to, and was present when the witticism was uttered.

THE REVERSE.

On Plunket once applying the common expression to accommodation bills of exchange, that they were *mere kites*, the judge (an English Chancellor) said "he never heard that expression applied before to any but the kites of boys." "Oh," replied Plunket, "that's the difference between kites in England and in Ireland. In England the wind raises the kite, but in Ireland the kite raises the wind."

ALL HIS EYE.

Moore records :—Walked Corry over to Bowood. In looking at the cascade, he mentioned what Plunket said, when some one, praising his waterfall, exclaimed, "Why, it's quite a cataract." "Oh, that's all my eye," said Plunket.

HIS PREFERENCE.

Bushe, during a visit to a certain neighbourhood, regularly attended the theatre, and being intimate with the company, they requested his opinion as to their respective merits. "My good friends," said he, "comparisons at best are but invidious. Besides, how can I give a preference where all are perfect?" Nothing, however, would satisfy them. "We are unanimous," they replied; "all jealousy is out of the question, and your opinion we must have." "Well, well," gravely replied Bushe, "I give it most reluctantly. I protest to you I prefer the prompter, for I heard the most and saw the least of him." This, as well as anecdotes immediately following, is told by Phillips.

BOUND TO SUPPORT HIM.

When the Ecclesiastical Board was established in Dublin, the commissioners met to choose its officers. Amongst those members who attended, there were two eminent and truly grateful prelates, upon whom the individual merits of the candidates were pressed. The candid answer was, that "owing their mitres to the minister, they felt bound to support his nominees!"   On this somewhat startling announcement, Bushe quietly wrote across to Lord Plunket, "It is he that hath made us, and not we ourselves; we are his people, and the sheep of his pasture."

BUT FOR THAT.

One day after Mr Plunket had concluded a most able argument, Bushe's neighbour said to him, "Well, I declare, if it wasn't *for the eloquence*, I'd as soon listen to M——."   "No doubt," said Bushe, "just as our countryman, in his eulogium on whisky, declared, 'Upon my conscience, if it wasn't *for the malt and the hops*, I'd as soon drink ditch-water as porter.'"

AN IMPROMPTU.

On a Leinster circuit, the bar were once prevented by a violent storm from crossing a ferry called Ballinlaw.   Amongst its members there was a Mr Cæsar Colclough, whose usual travelling appendages consisted of a pair of saddle-bags.   Magnanimously heedless of danger, he flung the luggage into the boat, and ordered that it should proceed.   Bushe, somewhat disconcerted, penned his revenge in the following impromptu :—

> "While meaner souls the tempest keeps in awe,
> Intrepid Colclough, crossing Ballinlaw,
> Shouts to the boatman, shivering in his rags,
> 'You carry Cæsar—and— *his saddle-bags.*'"

A TOUR DESCRIBED.

One of the Chief-Justice's brethren, a rigid teetotaller, amused himself during a long vacation by making a tour in Germany.   Bushe described it as a *traverse absque hoc(k !)*

UNQUESTIONABLY A DRAWBACK.

A relative of Bushe's, not remarkable for his Hindoo ablutions, once applied to him for a remedy for a sore throat.   "Why," said Bushe, gravely, "fill a pail with water, as warm as you can bear it, till it reaches up to your knees; then take a pint of oatmeal, and scrub your legs with it for a quarter of an hour."   "Why, hang it! man," interrupted the other, "this is nothing more than washing one's feet."   "Certainly, my dear Ned," said he; "I do admit it is open to that objection."

HILLS AND BUSHES.

There was a barrister named Hillas on the Connaught circuit who had much criminal business. One day, during the assizes of Sligo, he happened to go into the Civil Court, when the prisoners in the dock began one and all to call out, "Mr Hillas, Mr Hillas." Bushe, who presided, immediately exclaimed, "Pray, send for Mr Hillas. Indeed, he should be here. 'Hillas, Hillas, omne *nemus* resonat.'"

ANOTHER IMPROMPTU.

There is an impromptu of Bushe's upon two political agitators of the day who had declined an appeal to arms, one on account of his wife, the other from the affection in which he held his daughter :—

> "Two heroes of Erin, abhorrent of slaughter,
> Improved on the Hebrew command—
> One honoured his wife, and the other his daughter,
> That 'their' days might be long in 'the land.'"[1]

ELEVATING THE HOST.

One more *mot* of Bushe's cannot be omitted. Although attached to what was called the Tory party, and, in virtue of that attachment, their Solicitor-General, he was more than suspected of entertaining Liberal opinions, particularly on the Roman Catholic question. During the reign of the Duke of Richmond, politics ran high, and it is needless to specify the banner of his Grace. The duke, however, as a convivial spirit, much cultivated—as who would not?—the society of his accomplished Solicitor-General. Dining one day with a right-trusty Orangeman and "something more," the Charter toast, as a matter of course, was given. Bushe seemed to hang fire. The duke vociferated, "Come, come, Mr Solicitor, do justice for once to the 'immortal memory.'" Hours passed on, and the master of the revels did it such ample and such repeated justice, that at last he tumbled from his chair. The duke immediately raised and re-installed him. "Well, my lord duke," said Bushe, "this is indeed retribution. Attached to the Catholics you may declare me to be—but, at all events, I never assisted at the *elevation of the Host.*"

A QUID PRO QUO.

A cause of much celebrity was tried at some county assizes. Chief Baron O'Grady (says Lord Albemarle) was the presiding judge. Bushe, then a

---

[1] We give this on Phillips's authority. It is, however, claimed for Moore, the poet, in whose *Memoirs* it is given, with slight variations. The challenger in the duel was Sir C. Saxton; the two "agitators" were Lord Kenmare and O'Connell.

king's counsel, who held a brief for the defence, was pleading the cause of his client with much eloquence, when a donkey in the Court set up a loud bray. "One at a time, brother Bushe!" called out his lordship. Peals of laughter filled the Court. The counsel bore the interruption as best he could. The judge was proceeding to sum up with his usual ability of speech : the donkey again began to bray. "I beg your lordship's pardon," said Bushe, putting his hand to his ear; "but there is such an echo in the Court that I can't hear a word you say."

A HIT AT THE DOCTORS.

Lord Eldon[1] jocularly complained of the longevity of his incumbents. Being strongly pressed (says Campbell) by George III. to confer a living upon the son of a Court physician, he answered, "I shall be able more speedily to comply with your Majesty's wishes if your Majesty would be pleased to order your physicians to prescribe for my incumbents."

A HIT AT A BISHOP.

The following hit at a bishop (which Lord Eldon was ever fond of) his lordship himself related :—" Lord Donoughmore came to me on the woolsack upon a day in which something was to pass on the Catholic question, and an eminent prelate, it was understood, was to vote with Donoughmore. Entering into conversation with me, Lord Donoughmore said, 'What say you to us now? We have got a great card to-night.' I said, 'What card do you mean? I know the king is not with you; there is no queen ; there is only another great card.' 'What !' said Donoughmore, 'the right reverend prelate a knave !' 'You have called him so,' said I ; 'I have not.'"

KNEE AND *NE*.

Lord Eldon (says Campbell) long retained the relish he had acquired at University College for bad puns. When suffering from the gout in both feet, where, though painful, it is not dangerous, he said, "He did not much mind gout below the *knee*—provided it were '*ne* plus ultra.'"

GREAT SNORING.

According to the same authority, Lord Eldon caused a loud laugh while the old Duke of Norfolk was fast asleep in the House of Lords, and amusing their

---

[1] Lord Chancellor; *b.* 1781, *d.* 1838.

lordships with "that tuneful nightingale, his nose," by announcing from
the woolsack, with solemn emphasis, that the Commons had sent up a bill
for "enclosing and dividing Great Snoring in the county of Norfolk!"

REGULAR EXERCISE.

Lord Eldon, in allusion to Lord Stowell's love of good things, which induced him to dine in the Temple Hall at five, by way of a whet for an eight
o'clock dinner at the west end of the town, would say, "My brother takes
regular exercise twice a-day—*in eating.*"[1]

ON KEEPING BOOKS.

Unconscious (says Lord Campbell of Lord Eldon) of the joke which I have
often heard circulated against himself—that when Chancellor he greatly aug-
mented his own library by borrowing books quoted at the bar, and forgetting
to return them—he would say of such borrowers, "Though backward in
accounting, they are well practised in *book-keeping.*"

NO UNDERSTANDING.

A counsel at the Chancery bar, by way of denying collusion, suspected to
exist between him and the counsel representing another party, having said,
"My lord, I assure your lordship there is no *understanding* between us,"
Lord Eldon said, "I once heard a squire in the House of Commons say of
himself and another squire, "We have never, through life, had but *one idea
between us;*' but I tremble for the suitors when I am told that two eminent
practitioners at my bar have *no understanding* between them!"

THEY WERE SO POSITIVE.

Lord Eldon was rather a strict preserver of his game, although always
disposed to act good-humouredly to trespassers when he personally came in
contact with them. "One day," he said [on one occasion], "as I was with
my dog and gun on my grounds in my usual shooting attire, I heard two
reports in an adjoining field, and saw what appeared to be, as in fact they
afterwards proved, two gentlemen. I accosted them with—'Gentlemen, I
apprehend you have not Lord Eldon's permission to shoot on his grounds?'
to which one of them replied, 'Oh, permission is not necessary in our case.'
'May I venture to ask why, gentlemen?' I said. 'Because we flushed our

---

[1] Lord Stowell, it would seem, had his revenge, in saying of Lord Eldon, "My brother
will drink any *given* quantity of wine;" and, when asked what the Chancellor killed when
he went out shooting, "He kills—*time.*"

birds on other ground, and the *law* entitles us to follow our game anywhere; if you ask your master, Lord Eldon, he'll tell you that is the *law*.' Whereupon I said, ' I don't think it will be necessary to trouble him on that account, since, to tell you the truth, I am Lord Eldon myself!' They instantly sought to apologise; but I added, ' Come, gentlemen, our meeting has begun in good humour, and so let it end. Pursue your pleasure on my grounds—only next time don't be quite so positive in your *law*.'"

"OLD BAGS."

Lord Eldon when out shooting one day required a half-pay captain (who was trespassing) to show his certificate. " Who are you?" said the trespasser; " I suppose, one of old Bags' keepers." " No," replied the Chancellor with a smile, " I am old Bags himself;" and they parted good friends.

X'S NOT Y'S.

Moore records the following:—Old Bond (the clergyman) having said, in conversing with Lord E[ldon], " You are now then, my lord, one of the Ex's." " Yes, Mr Bond," answered Lord E[ldon], "and, in this last instance, I must confess the X's were not Y's" (wise).

EATEN AND EATABLE.

In the early days of his married life, whilst playing the part of an Oxford Don, Lord Eldon was required (says Jeaffreson) to decide in an action brought by two undergraduates against the cook of University College. The plaintiffs declared that the cook had "sent to their rooms an apple-pie *that could not be eaten.*" The defendant pleaded that he had a remarkably fine fillet of veal in the kitchen. Having set aside this plea on grounds obvious to the legal mind, and not otherwise than manifest to unlearned laymen, Mr John Scott ordered the apple-pie to be brought into Court; but the messenger despatched to do the judge's bidding returned with the astounding intelligence, that during the progress of the litigation, a party of undergraduates had actually devoured the pie—fruit and crust; nothing but the pan was left. Judgment: —" The charge here is, that the cook has sent up an apple-pie that cannot be eaten. Now, that cannot be said to have been uneatable which has been eaten; and as this apple-pie has been eaten, it was eatable. Let the cook be absolved."

MOST UNLIKELY.

In 1829, when Lyndhurst was occupying the woolsack for the first time, and Eldon was longing to recover the seals, the latter (says Jeaffreson) presented a petition from the Tailors' Company at Glasgow against Catholic Relief. "What!" asked Lord Lyndhurst from the woolsack, in a low voice, "do the *tailors* trouble themselves about such *measures?*" Whereto, with unaccustomed quickness, the old Tory of the Tories retorted, "No wonder! You can't suppose that *tailors* like *turncoats.*"

THE VERY LEAST.

Lord Campbell notes some good anecdotes of Thurlow.[1] He says that judge's habit of profane swearing he could not always control, even when on the bench. Yet some supposed that, in reality, he had a great deal of good humour under an ostentatiously rough exterior. It is related that once, at the adjournment of the Court for the long vacation, he was withdrawing without taking the usual leave of the bar, when a young barrister exclaimed in a stage whisper, "He might at least have said d—n you." The Chancellor, hearing the remark, returned and politely made his bow.

TAKING HIM DOWN.

Lord Thurlow was induced to dine with George Johnstone, who, being the most ridiculous toady of great men, and aspiring to what he thought genteel manners, said to him, " I am afraid, my lord, the port wine is not so good as I could wish;" upon which Thurlow growled out, " I have tasted better."

DITTO.

On one occasion one of the caterers for company for Lord Thurlow's amusement thought he had secured a great card, when he took Sir —— ——, an F.R.S., a solemn conceited pedant of great pretension on very moderate foundation, to call upon him. In mentioning the circumstance afterwards, Lord Thurlow merely observed, "A gentleman did me the honour to call upon me to-day; *indeed, I believe he was a knight!*"

HARD ON THE SOLICITOR.

A solicitor once had to prove a death before Lord Thurlow, and being told, upon every statement he made, "Sir, that is no proof," at last exclaimed, much vexed, "My, lord, it is very hard that you will not believe me. I knew him well to his last hour; I saw him dead and in his coffin, my lord. My lord, he was my client." *Lord Chancellor:* "Good G—d, sir! why did

---

[1] Lord Chancellor ; b. 1732, d. 1806.

you not tell me that before? I should not have doubted the fact one moment; for I think nothing can be so likely to kill a man as to have you for his attorney."[1]

BAD REASONS.

Lord Eldon writes:—After dinner, one day when nobody was present but Lord Kenyon and myself, Lord Thurlow said, "Taffy, I decided a cause this morning, and I saw from Scott's face that he doubted whether I was right." Thurlow then stated his view of the case, and Kenyon instantly said, "Your decision was quite right." "What say you to that?" asked the Chancellor. I said, "I did not presume to form a case on which they were both agreed. But I think a fact has not been mentioned, which may be material." I was about to state the fact, and my reasons. Kenyon, however, broke in upon me, and with some warmth stated that I was always so obstinate there was no dealing with me. "Nay," interposed Thurlow, "that's not fair. You, Taffy, are obstinate, and give no reasons. You, Jack, are obstinate, too; but then you give your reasons, and d—d bad ones they are!"

NOT BAD.

Thurlow having heard that Kenyon had said to a party who had threatened to appeal from his decision, by filing a bill in Chancery, "Go into Chancery, then; *abi in malam rem!*" The next time he met the testy Chief-Justice, he said, "Taffy, when did you first think the Court of Chancery was such a *mala res?* I remember when you made a very *good thing* of it."

NIPPED IN THE BUD.

I have been told (says Lord Campbell) by an old gentleman, who was standing behind the woolsack at the time that Sir Hay Campbell, then Lord Advocate, arguing a Scotch appeal at the bar in a very tedious manner, said, "I will noo, my lords, proceed to my seevent pownt." "I'll be d—d if you do," cried Thurlow, so as to be heard by all present; "this house is adjourned till Monday next," and off he scampered.

HE WISHED HE WAS.

From another valet Lord Thurlow received a still more cutting retort. Having scolded this meek man for some time without receiving any answer, he concluded by saying, "I wish you were in hell." The terrified valet at last exclaimed, "I wish I was, my lord! I wish I was!"

---

[1] This brutal jest is said to have ruined the business of the unfortunate victim of it.

A POLITE VARIATION.

Lord Thurlow having once got into a dispute with a bishop respecting a living of which the Great Seal had the alternate presentation, the bishop's secretary called upon him, and said, "My lord of —— sends his compliments to your lordship, and believes that the next turn to present to —— belongs to his lordship." *Chancellor:* "Give my compliments to his lordship, and tell him that I will see him d—d first before he shall present." *Secretary:* "This, my lord, is a very unpleasant message to deliver to a bishop." *Chancellor:* "You are right; it is so; therefore tell the bishop that I will be d—d first before he shall present."

A DEFENDER OF THE FAITH.

Crabb Robinson writes:—When, in 1788, Beaufoy made his famous attempt to obtain the repeal of the Corporation and Test Act, a deputation waited on the Lord Chancellor Thurlow to obtain his support. The Chancellor heard them very civilly, and then said, "Gentlemen, I'm against you, by G—d. I am for the Established Church, d—m me! Not that I have any more regard for the Established Church than any other church, but because it *is* established. And if you can get your religion established, I'll be for that too!"

A COMPANY.

You remember (says Sydney Smith) Thurlow's answer to some one complaining of the injustice of a company. "Why, you never expected justice from a company, did you? They have neither a soul to save, nor a body to kick."

A CURIOUS COINCIDENCE.

In his undergraduate days at Cambridge, Lord Thurlow is said to have worried the tutors of Caius with a series of disorderly pranks and impudent escapades; but on one occasion he unquestionably displayed at the University the quick wit that in after-life rescued him from many an embarrassing position. "Sir," observed a tutor, giving the unruly undergraduate a look of disapproval, "I never come to the window without seeing you idling in the court." "Sir," replied young Thurlow, imitating the Don's tone, "I never come into the court without seeing you idling at the window."[1]

---

[1] Mr Frederick Locker tells very much the same story of "a certain friend" of his—now "champion of our Lyrical Light Weights."

NOT RETURNABLE.

On a motion once before [Lord Norbury], a sheriff's officer, who had the hardihood to serve a process in Connemara, Dick Martin's territory, where the king's writ *did not run*, swore that the natives made him eat and swallow both copy and original. Norbury, affecting great disgust, exclaimed, "Jackson, Jackson, I hope it's not made returnable into this Court."

SHAKE-SPEARE.

In all his leisure hours, Norbury was on horseback, and almost as frolicsome as if he was on the bench. Meeting one day a barrister of the name of Speare, he immediately joined him, "I protest, Speare, that's a very fine horse." "He's a very fine trotter, my lord; and I have been ordered to ride him for the sake of the exercise." "What's his name?" "He has no name, my lord," said Speare. "Well, then, in honour of his paces and his rider—call him *Shake-Speare.*" This and the above are told by Phillips.

A BIBLICAL CITATION.

Lord Norbury (says O'Flannagan) had a testy neighbour in the country near Phibsborough, whose cattle often roamed on his lordship's grounds; but when the cows of his lordship returned their visit, he was threatened with an action for damage done. To this he replied somewhat irreverently, "Forgive us our trespasses, as we forgive them that trespass against us."

A GOOD NAME.

On another occasion a Mr Pepper being thrown from his horse, Lord Norbury inquired "if the horse had any name?" "Yes," said the owner, "we call him Castor." "And a very good name for him," replied his lordship; "but henceforth you may call him Pepper-Caster."

A FOOLISH TAILOR.

Lord Norbury, walking to Court one morning, saw a crowd on the quay, near the Four Courts. He inquired the cause, and was informed "a tailor had just been rescued from attempting suicide by drowning." "What a fool," responded the Chief-Justice, "to leave his hot goose for a cold duck."

MINDING THE SCRIPTURE.

The son of a peer having been accused of arson, of which offence he was generally believed guilty, but acquitted on a point of insufficiency of evidence to sustain the indictment, was tried before Lord Norbury. The young gentleman met the judge next at the Lord-Lieutenant's levee in the Castle. Instead of avoiding the Chief-Justice, the scion of aristocracy boldly said, " I have recently married, and have come here to enable me to present my bride at the Drawing-Room." "Quite right to mind the Scripture. Better marry than burn," retorted Lord Norbury.

SHOOTING HAIRS.

A gentleman having boasted in his presence of having shot seventy hares before breakfast, Lord Norbury caused a laugh by observing, very drily, "I dare say you fired at a wig."

AN EXPLANATION.

[Sir Boyle Roche] (says Phillips) was the droll of the House of Commons, and was continually perpetrating bulls, which Curran used to insist were the result of preparation. His celebrated one, confounding ages past and present, deserves a record. "Mr Speaker," said he, "I don't see why we should put ourselves out of the way to benefit posterity. What has posterity ever done for us?" When the roar which followed had subsided, Sir Boyle entered upon a lucid explanation. "By posterity, sir, I do not mean our ancestors, but those who were to come immediately after them."

WILLING.

On another occasion (says the same authority) Sir Boyle Roche announced that "he for one was quite prepared to give up, not merely a part, but the whole of the constitution, to preserve the remainder."

A SUGGESTION.

Indignant at receiving small bottles from his wine-merchant, Sir Boyle Roche took occasion to suggest to Parliament that for the future, by law, "every quart bottle should hold a quart."

A FLATTERING REQUEST.

One of Sir Boyle Roche's invitations to an Irish nobleman was amusingly equivocal. "I hope, my lord, if ever you come within a mile of my house, you'll stay there all night."

THE VERY REVERSE.

Sir Boyle Roche's rebuke to his shoemaker, when he had the gout, was not wanting in natural humour. "Oh! you're a precious blockhead to do directly the reverse of what I desired you. I told you to make one of the shoes *larger* than the other, and, instead of that, you have made one of them *smaller* than the other! The very opposite!"

AN ENEMY OF THEIRS.

Curran by no means liked Sir Boyle. Having said one night that he needed no aid from anyone, and could be "the guardian of his own honour"—"Indeed!" exclaimed Sir Boyle; "why, I always thought the right honourable member was an enemy to sinecures."

THE AFFIRMATIVE.

Moore speaks of Sir Boyle Roche saying energetically in the House, "Mr Speaker, I'll answer boldly in the affirmative, No!"

MIXED METAPHOR.

Speaking of the invasion then expected from France, Sir Boyle Roche styled the Marsellaise the "Marshal-law men, who, if they came, would cut us into mince-meat, and throw our bleeding heads on the table to stare us in the face; but the best way to avoid danger was to meet it plump."

HE WOULD LAY IT DOWN.

According to Rogers the poet, Lord Ellenborough[1] had infinite wit. When the Income-tax was imposed, he said that Lord Kenyon (who was not very nice in his habits) intended, in consequence of it, to lay down—his pocket—handkerchief.

QUITE RIGHT.

A lawyer one day pleading before him, and using several times the expression, "My unfortunate client," Lord Ellenborough suddenly interrupted him: "There, sir, the Court is with you."[2]

---

[1] Edward Law, Lord Ellenborough, **Lord Chief-Justice**; *b.* 1748, *d.* 1818.

[2] "This," says Sydney Smith, "was perhaps irresistible; but yet, how wicked! how cruel! it deserves a thousand years' punishment, at least."—*Life*, by Lady Holland.

OUT OF THE QUESTION.

Moore records what Lord Ellenborough said to —— the barrister, upon his asking, in the midst of a most boring harangue, "Is it the pleasure of the Court that I should proceed with my statement?" "Pleasure, Mr ——, has been out of the question for a long time; but you may proceed."

MOST UNNATURAL.

Moore also records the story of Lord Ellenborough's saying to a witness, "Why, you are an industrious fellow; you must have taken pains with yourself; no man was ever *naturally* so stupid."

TAKING HIM DOWN.

Jekyll, in talking of figurative oratory, mentioned in Moore's hearing this story of the barrister before Lord Ellenborough:—"My lord, I appear before you in the character of an advocate from the city of London; my lord, the city of London herself appears before you as a suppliant for justice. My lord, it is written in the book of nature—" "What book?" says Lord E. "The book of nature." "Name the page," says Lord E., holding his pen uplifted, as if to note the page down.

ASKING HIMSELF.

Moore further records the story of Lord W—— saying in one of his speeches, "I ask myself so and so," and repeating the words, "I ask myself." "Yes," said Lord Ellenborough, "and a d—d foolish answer you'll get."

ENCROACHING.

When (says Sydney Smith) I hear the rustics yawn audibly at my sermons, it reminds me of that observation of Lord Ellenborough's, who, on seeing Lord —— gape during his own long and dull speech, said, "Well, I must own there is some taste in that, but is not Lord —— rather encroaching on our privileges?"[1]

A MATTER OF SCIENCE.

Notwithstanding (says Jeaffreson) his high reputation for wit, Lord Ellenborough would deign to use the oldest jests. To silence a wearisome talker, he would pelt him with puns from Joe Miller; but though his missiles were of

[1] This story is also told by Moore.

F

the cheapest kind, and picked from public ground, he hurled them with a force and precision that drew the applause of bystanders. Thus of Mr Caldecott, who over and over again, with dull verbosity, had said that certain limestone quarries, like lead and copper mines, "were not rateable, because the limestone could only be reached by boring, which was matter of science," he gravely inquired: "Would you, Mr Caldecott, have us to believe that *every* kind of boring is matter of science?"

NOTHING GAINED.

Very pungent, too, was Lord Ellenborough's ejaculation at a Cabinet dinner, when he heard that Lord Kenyon was about to close his penurious old age by dying. "Die!—why should he die? What would he get by that?" interposed Lord Ellenborough.

A SAVING.

Having jested about Kenyon's parsimony as the old man lay *in extremis*, Ellenborough placed another joke of the same kind upon his coffin. Hearing that, through the blunder of an illiterate undertaker, the motto on Kenyon's hatchment in Lincoln's Inn Fields had been painted "*Mors Janua Vita,*" instead of "*Mors Janua Vitæ,*" he exclaimed, "Bless you! there's no mistake. Kenyon's will directed that it should be 'Vita,' so that his estate might be saved the expense of a diphthong."

NO ONE.

To the surgeon in the witness-box who said, "I employ myself as a surgeon," Lord Ellenborough retorted, "But does anybody else employ you as a surgeon?"

IN DISGUISE.

The demand to be examined on affirmation being preferred by a Quaker witness, whose dress was so much like the costume of an ordinary conformist that the officer of the Court had begun to administer the usual oath, Lord Ellenborough inquired of the "Friend," "Do you really mean to impose upon the Court by appearing here in the disguise of a reasonable being?"

A PROPER YOUNG MAN.

Lord Campbell records the following of Sir Nicholas Bacon, Lord Keeper of the Great Seal[1]:—Being asked his opinion, by the Earl of Leicester, concerning

---

[1] Born 1510, died 1579.

two persons of whom the Queen seemed to think well, "By my troth, my lord," said he, "the one is a grave councillor; the other is a proper young man, *and so will he be as long as he lives.*"[1]

"LICENSE, THEY CRY."

At a time when there was a great clamour about monopolies created by a licence to make a particular manufacture, with a prohibition to all others to do the like, being asked by Queen Elizabeth what he thought of these mono- poly licences, Sir Nicholas Bacon answered, "Madam, will you have me speak the truth? *Licentiâ omnes deteriores sumus:* we are all the worse for licences."

"HOG" AND "BACON."

Once going the Northern Circuit as judge, before he had the Great Seal, Sir Nicholas Bacon was about to pass sentence on a thief convicted before him, when the prisoner, after various pleas had been overruled, asked for mercy on account of kindred. "Prithee," said my lord judge, "how comes this about?" "Why, if it please you, my lord, your name is *Bacon,* and mine is *Hog,* and in all ages *Hog* and *Bacon* have been so near kindred that they are not to be separated." "Ay, but," replied the judge, "you and I cannot be kindred except you be hanged, for *Hog* is not *Bacon* until it be well *hanged.*"

A DIFFICULT MATTER.

Lord Campbell tells this story about Henry Erskine[2]:—Having been speak- ing in the Outer House, at the bar of Lord Swinton, a very good, but a very slow and deaf judge, Erskine was called away to the bar of Lord Braxfield, who was Lord Ordinary for the week. On his coming up, Lord Braxfield said to him, "Well, Dean, what is this you've been talking so loudly about to my Lord Swinton?" "About a cask of whisky, my lord" (replied Harry); "but I found it no easy matter to make it run in his lordship's head."

NOT HIS OWN STYLE.

Andrew Balfour, one of the commissaries of Edinburgh, was a man of much pomposity of manner, appearance, and expression. Harry Erskine met him one morning coming into the Court, and observing that he was lame, said to

---

[1] Campbell adds: "This sarcasm (indifferent as it is) was stolen from Sir Thomas More, who, when his wife at last had a son who turned out rather silly, observed to her that she had so long prayed for a *boy,* he was afraid her son would continue a *boy* as long as he lived.

[2] Lord Advocate; *b.* 1746, *d.* 1817.

him, "What has happened, Commissary? I am sorry to see you limping." "I was visiting my brother in Fife," said the commissary, "and I fell over his stile, and had nearly broken my leg." "It was lucky, Commissary" (replied Harry), "it was not your own stile, for you would then have broken your neck."

VERY POOR.

Henry Erskine's brother, the Earl of Buchan, who aimed at being a jester as well as a philosopher and a poet, one day, putting his head below the lock of the parlour door, exclaimed, "See, Harry, here's 'Locke on the Human Understanding.'" "Rather a poor edition, my lord," replied Harry.

ABANDONED HABITS.

Henry Erskine succeeding Dundas as Lord Advocate, that good-humoured politician offered to lend him his embroidered official gown, as he would not want it long. "No," said he in the same spirit, "I will not assume the abandoned habits of my predecessors."

THE BEST OF IT.

Robert Smith (brother of Sydney Smith, and familiarly called "Bobus") was a lawyer and an ex-advocate general, and happened on one occasion, says Mr Hayward, to be engaged in argument with an excellent physician touching the merits of their respective professions. "You must admit," urged Dr ——, "that your profession does not make angels of men." "No," was the retort; "there you have the best of it; yours certainly gives them the first chance."

A USEFUL SUBORDINATE.

Macaulay writes of Robert Smith :—Bobus was very amusing. He is a great authority on Indian matters. We talked of the insects and the snakes, and he said a thing which reminded me of his brother Sydney : "Always, sir, manage to have at your table some fleshy, blooming young writer or cadet, just come out, that the mosquitoes may stick to him, and leave the rest of the company alone."

A WORD AND A BLOW.

Talking of Kean (records Moore), I mentioned his having told me that he had eked out his means of living, before he emerged from obscurity, by teaching dancing, fencing, elocution, and boxing. "Elocution and boxing!" (repeated Bobus Smith)—"a word and a blow."

A FREE TRANSLATION.

According to Barham, Sydney Smith said his brother Robert had, in George III.'s time, translated the motto, "*Libertas sub rege pio*"—"The pious king has got liberty under."

HARDLY!

When the Munster Circuit met in Limerick, the bar (says O'Flannagan) were usually entertained by a hospitable gentleman, named Flatly, who occupied a handsome suburban residence near Castle Connell. Lysaght being at one of these parties, where everything was arranged with exquisite taste, said to their host, "I really feel surprised that you are allowed to remain a bachelor, and so near a city celebrated for the beauty of the fair daughters. Why is this?" The host coloured, and said "he often wished to change his solitary condition, but could not muster sufficient courage to pop the question." "I tell you this," said Lysaght, "depend upon it, if you ask any girl *boldly*, she never will refuse you *Flatly!*"

BREECHLOADERS.

J. C. Young has left behind him several anecdotes of Hicks, the barrister. For example :—I walked with Hicks to see the sport [at a shooting party]. At one moment during the *battue*, Mr H——, in firing at a hare, very nearly peppered Hicks. The shot did actually rattle against his coat-tails. He supposed himself that he was hit, and, springing off the ground a good ten or twelve inches, and clapping his hands behind him to ascertain that he was unharmed, said, with a tremulous voice, "I say—I say—this comes of firing with *breech*-loaders."

BEST *V.* WALL.

Hicks, at church at Bodmin, heard the rector publish the banns of marriage between Job Wall and Mary Best. He wrote these lines off-hand, and sent them (says Young) to the officiating clergyman:—

> "Job, wanting a partner, thought he'd be blest,
> If, of all womankind, he selected the Best ;
> For, said he, of all evils that compass the globe,
> A bad wife would most try the patience of Job.
> The Best, then, he chose, and made bone of his bone,
> Though 'twas clear to his friends she'd be Best left alone ;
> For, though Best of her sex, she's the weakest of all,
> If 'tis true that the weakest must go to the Wall."

LOT AND SALTER.

On another similar occasion, Mr Lot, the hatter of Bodmin, was married to a Miss Salter; when [Hicks] wrote the following lines :—

> "Because on her way she chose to halt,
> Lot's wife, in the Scriptures, was turn'd into salt;
> But, though in her course she ne'er did falter,
> This young Lot's wife, strange to say, was Salter."

PICKLE AND SALTER.

Hicks was in Court at Bodmin Assizes, when a Mr Bickle was tried for a breach of promise of marriage to a Miss Salter. A certain eminent counsel who was engaged in the suit, threw across the table to Hicks these lines on a slip of paper—

> "Oh! Mr Bickle
> You're in a pickle
> For being fickle!"

Hicks threw back the paper with this answer—

> "'Tis true he did falter
> In going to the altar,
> But he's not in a pickle,
> For he did not get *Salter*."

THE THREE BALLS.

A gentleman of very great talent, but of rather extravagant habits, was going to a dance; and knowing Hicks to have a very handsome pin, which had been presented to him, he asked him if he would lend it him. "What for?" said Hicks. "Well, if you must know, I want to take it to the ball." "Pooh, pooh! Don't tell me. You want to take it to the three balls," was the answer.

THAT WAS ALL.

A mirth-loving judge, Justice Powell, could be as thoroughly humorous in private life as he was fearless and just upon the bench. When Fowler, Bishop of Gloucester—a thorough believer in what is nowadays called spirit-ualism—was persecuting his acquaintance with silly stories about ghosts, Powell gave him a telling reproof for his credulity, by describing a horrible apparition which was represented as having disturbed the narrator's rest on the previous night. At the hour of midnight, as the clocks were striking twelve, the Judge was roused from his first slumber by a hideous sound. Starting up, he saw at the foot of his uncompanioned bed a figure—dark, gloomy, terrible—holding before its grim and repulsive visage a lamp that shed an uncertain light. "May Heaven have mercy upon us!" ejaculated the Bishop at this portion of the story. The Judge continued his story: "Be calm, my lord Bishop; be calm. The awful part of this mysterious interview has still to be told. Nerving myself to fashion the words of enquiry, I addressed the nocturnal visitor thus—'Strange being, why hast thou come at this still hour to perturb a sinful mortal?' You understand, my Lord, I said this in hollow tones—in what I may almost term a sepulchral voice." "Ay—ay," responded the Bishop, with intense excitement; "go on—I implore you to go on. What did *it* answer?" "It answered, in a voice not greatly different from the voice of a human creature—'Please, sir, *I am the watchman on beat, and your street door is open.*'"[1]

THE BENEFIT OF THE ACT.

Peter Burrowes and John Parsons were (says Phillips) the first Irish Commissioners of Insolvency, and the appointments were understood to have come just in time. Kites—in matter-of-fact England called, prosaically, accommodation bills—had flown between them; so long, indeed, that the flight grew somewhat feeble. The retrieved associates, on their way to Court for the first time, indulged, as was natural, in mutual congratulations. "What a lucky hit!" said Peter; "who could have expected it?" "Everybody, Peter; what else had we before us but the benefit of the act?"

NEVER.

There was (says the above authority) a grave literal meaning about Parsons' *notabilia*, which at once affiliated them. One instance occurs in his answer to a Crown solicitor on circuit. The man had an awful halt in his gait, and limped hastily up to Parsons in the street with "Pray, Mr Parsons, did you see Mr MacNally" [who was also lame] "walking this way?" "Upon my word, sir," was the answer, "I never saw him walking any other way."

HIS DUE.

There is a terseness in the following (says Phillips) which seems to me inimitable. Norbury was travelling with [Parsons]: they passed a gibbet. "Parsons," said Norbury, with a chuckle, "where would *you* be now if every one had his due?" "Alone in my carriage," replied Parsons.

---

[1] Jeaffreson's *Book about Lawyers.*

THE POSITION OF RUNNER.

Lysaght, the Irish barrister, once met Mr La Touche, the Dublin banker, and knowing the extreme particularity of this descendant of the Huguenots respecting the character of his bank officials, startled the staid banker by saying, "When a situation among the officers of the house on Corkhill was vacant, he, Mr Lysaght, would be ready to fill it." "You, my dear Lysaght," said the banker, "what situation in my establishment could possibly suit you?" "Not only one, but two," replied the wit. "Pray, what are they?" asked the banker. "If you make me cashier for one day, I'll become runner the next," was the wit's reply.

GRAVITY AND LEVITY.

Capable of anything (says Phillips), Jeremiah Keller achieved nothing. An independent spirit more than counteracted his superior powers. He was ignorant of the mean and manifold arts by which blockheads distanced him. At last, worn out by hope deferred, in an evil hour [he] sought refuge in society. The bottle became a substitute for the brief; and all that remains of talents sadly sacrificed are the random sallies which sprang from its inspiration. Bitterly conscious must he have been, when, seeing Mayne—the dull and solemn Mayne, who never earned a laugh—taking his seat upon the bench—he was overheard muttering to himself, "What is Newton worth, when there's Mayne risen by his gravity, and here's Keller sunk by his levity!"

CLAUSE AND CLAWS.

There was a luckless attorney in the city of Cork, who happened to have a malformation of the hands. He and Keller differed at sessions on the construction of an Act of Parliament. Both were warm and pertinacious. At length the attorney sent for the statute, and, spreading his unfortunate fingers over a section, exclaimed in triumph, "I knew I was right—the barrister's beaten—here's the clause for you." "You are right for once," cried Jerry, "they're a great deal liker claws than hands!"

PRESERVES AND PICKLES.

There was a Sir Judkin Fitzgerald, who, being Sheriff of Tipperary, had, it was said, during the Rebellion of 1798, practised great cruelties. Among other things, he was reported to have dipped the cat-o'-nine-tails in brine before a flogging! By way of excuse to Keller, he boasted that, by his firmness, he had "preserved the country." "No," said Jerry, "but you pickled it."

THE THING BORN.

Keller and some of his companions were one evening enjoying themselves rather freely at the lodging of a friend with whom they had dined, when an intimation was given them that the lady of the house had just been unexpectedly confined. The host considerately proposed an adjournment of the sitting to an hotel opposite. "Oh, certainly," said Keller, "*pro re natâ.*"

DARING.

Judge Doherty possessed much ready wit, and a few of his *bon mots* (says O'Flannagan) are worth recording. At one of the viceregal balls a brother judge, having imbibed somewhat too much of the juice of the grape, was not very steady on his legs. Next morning the Chief-Justice was asked, "Is it true, Judge —— danced at the Castle ball last night?" "Well," replied Doherty, "I certainly can say I saw him in a reel."

THE WORST OF IT.

One rough March day the Chief-Justice was alighting from his carriage at the entrance to the Four Courts, as his official came puffing and blowing, from the effects of the gale. "You seem quite out of breath," said the Chief-Justice, as he shook hands with his official. "Yes," replied the other, "as I came along the quays the wind was cutting my face." "Upon my word," gravely replied the Chief-Justice, "I think the wind had the worst of it."

NOT SINCE THEN.

Dr Thorpe, who married the Countess of Pomfret, told Harrison a story of a young lady at a ball at the Castle in Dublin whose style of dress displayed her charms with a liberality which attracted the attention of a gentleman, who, turning to Chief-Justice Doherty, said, "Doherty, did you ever see anything like that since you were born?" "I can't say since I was born," said the judge; "but certainly not since I was weaned." [1]

AN HONEST BOY.

A boy was charged before Chief-Baron O'Grady with a larceny of pantaloons. The case being clearly proved, the prisoner received an excellent character for honesty. The Chief-Baron's charge to the jury (says O'Flannagan) was pithy. "Gentlemen, the prisoner was an honest boy, but he stole the breeches."

---

[1] This is told somewhat differently by J. C. Young.

ONE FOR THE SHERIFF.

At the assizes in Tralee, great noise prevailing in the Court-house, annoyed the Chief-Baron (O'Grady). The crier called "Silence!" in vain. Observing the High Sheriff intently reading a book, instead of preserving due decorum, the Chief-Baron called aloud—"Mr Sheriff, I tell you that if you allow this noise to continue, you'll never be able to finish your novel in quiet."

WELL PHRASED.

A case being left to arbitration, the counsel named on each side were in no great repute as lawyers, so the Chief-Baron (O'Grady) said : "You leave this to two indifferent lawyers, with liberty, if they disagree, to call in an odd one."

STICKY TURNIPS.

Mr Darby O'Grady, Chief Baron O'Grady's brother, caught a boy stealing his turnips. The Chief-Baron, being in the neighbourhood, the despoiled owner of the turnips asked his learned brother "if the boy could be prosecuted under the Timber Acts." "No," replied the Chief-Baron ; then he added, "unless, indeed, the turnips are sticky !"

LAYING TWO.

Some one in the presence of Jonathan Henn proposed the riddle, "Why should the captain of a ship never be at a loss for an egg?" The riddle was a new one to all present, and Henn was the only person who solved it. "Because he can always lay-to (lay two). He was asked, "How came you, Jonathan, to guess that?" To which (says O'Flannagan) he promptly replied, "Who had a better right to guess it than a Henn?"

A SITTING HEN.

Henn made many puns on his name. When late in life he was asked "If he took much walking exercise?" "I did formerly," he replied, "but now I am chiefly a sitting hen."

DOMY-SILLY-AIRY.

Moore mentions Twiss as having quoted a joke of his own, saying, of the man who remained so long swung from the dome of St Paul's, while taking a panorama of London, "It was a *domy-silly-airy* visit;" a domiciliary visit.

ALL HEART.

According to Fanny Kemble, Horace Twiss was one of the readiest and most amusing talkers in the world; and when he began to make his way in

London society, which he eventually did very successfully, ill-natured persons considered his first step in the right direction to have been a repartee made in the crushroom of the opera, while standing close to Lady L——, who was waiting for her carriage. A man he was with saying, "Look at that fat Lady L——; isn't she like a great white cabbage?" "Yes," answered Horace, in a discreetly loud tone, "she *is* like one—all heart, I believe." The white-heart cabbage turned affably to the rising barrister, begged him to see her to her carriage, and gave him the *entrée* of H[olland] House.

PLEASE DON'T.

Mr Jeaffreson speaks of the pain endured by Lord Mansfield whenever a barrister pronounced a Latin word with a false quantity. "My Lords," said the Scotch advocate Crosby, at the bar of the House of Lords, "I have the honour to appear before your lordships as counsel for the curātors." "Ugh," groaned the Westminster-Oxford Lord, softening his reproof by an allusion to his Scotch nationality, "Curātors, Mr Crosby, curātors: I wish *our* countrymen would pay a little more attention to prosody." "My lord," replied Mr Crosby, with delightful readiness and composure, "I can assure you that *our* countrymen are very proud of your Lordship, as the greatest senātor and orātor of the present age." The barrister who made Baron Alderson shudder under his robes by applying for a *"nolle prosēqui"* was not equally quick at self defence, when that judge interposed: "Stop, sir—consider that this is the last day of term, and don't make things unnecessarily long."

VERY TOUGH.

On one occasion, Lord Mansfield covered his retreat from an untenable position with a sparkling pleasantry. An old witness named *Elm* having given his evidence with remarkable clearness, although he was more than eighty years of age, Lord Mansfield examined him as to his habitual mode of living, and found he had been through life an early riser and a singularly temperate man. "Aye," remarked the Chief-Justice, in a tone of approval, "I have always found that without temperance and early habits longevity is never attained." The next witness, the elder brother of this model of temperance, was then called, and he almost surpassed his brother as an intelligent and clear-headed utterer of evidence. "I suppose," observed Lord Mansfield, "that you also are an early riser?" "No, my Lord," answered the veteran stoutly; "I like my bed at all hours, and special-*lie* I like it of a morning." "Ah; but, like your brother, you are a very temperate man?" quickly asked the judge, looking out anxiously for the safety of the more important part of his theory. "My Lord," responded this ancient Elm, disdaining to plead guilty to a charge of habitual sobriety, "I am a very old man, and my memory is as clear as a bell, but I can't remember the night when I've gone to bed without being more or less drunk." "Ah, my Lord," Mr Dunning exclaimed, "this old man's case supports a theory upheld by many persons — that habitual intemperance is favourable to longevity." "No, no," replied the Chief-Justice, with a smile, "this old man and his brother merely teach us what every carpenter knows—that Elm, whether it be wet or dry, is a very tough wood."   ●

THE JUDGE AND THE SAILOR.

Lord Mansfield was presiding at a trial consequent upon a collision of two ships at sea, when a common sailor, whilst giving testimony, said : "At the time I was standing abaft the binnacle ;" whereupon his Lordship, with a proper desire to master the facts of the case, observed, "Stay, stay a minute, witness : you say that at the time in question you were *standing abaft the binnacle ;* now tell me, where is 'abaft the binnacle ?'" This was too much for the gravity of "the old salt," who, immediately before climbing into the witness-box, had taken a copious draught of neat rum.   Removing his eyes from the bench, and turning round upon the crowded Court with an expression of intense amusement, he exclaimed at the top of his voice, "He's a pretty fellow for a judge ! Bless my jolly old eyes !—[the reader may substitute a familiar form of 'imprecation on eyesight']—you have got a pretty sort of a land lubber for a judge ! He wants me to tell him where *abaft the binnacle* is!" Not less amused than the witness, Lord Mansfield rejoined, "Well, my friend, you must fit me for my office by telling me where *abaft the binnacle* is; you've already shown me the meaning of *half seas over !*"

THE SIDE OF MERCY.

Baron Alderson being asked by the chaplain of the High-Sheriff at the assizes over which he was to preside, how long he would like him to preach, replied, "About half-an-hour, with a leaning to mercy." This and the following story are told by J. C. Young.

THE K-NAVY.

The late Bishop of Exeter and Baron Alderson were sitting next each other at a public dinner. After the usual toasts had been drunk, the health of "The Navy" was proposed. Lord Campbell, expecting to have to return thanks for "The Bar," and not having heard the toast distinctly, and sup- posing the time for giving it had arrived, got up. On which (says J. C.

Young) the late Bishop of Exeter whispered to Baron Alderson, "What is Campbell about? What is he returning thanks for the navy for?" "Oh," answered the witty judge, "he has made a mistake. He thinks the word is spelt with a K."

FOR OUTWARD APPLICATION ONLY.

I was once (says W. H. Harrison) at an anniversary festival of the Literary Fund, when a clumsy waiter upset a glass of champagne over me, and I sat for some time in an unenviable state of sloppiness, to which Sir F. P——,[1] who sat next to me, tried to reconcile me by saying, "Never mind, H——; it has only been administered as a lotion instead of a draught."

AN EPISCOPAL BOA-CONSTRICTOR.

On another occasion (says the same authority) on which, at a public dinner, a very distinguished writer was replied to by an eloquent prelate,[2] Sir F—— said to me that the bishop reminded him of the dealing of a boa-constrictor with a rabbit; he first oiled his antagonist all over, and then swallowed him at a mouthful.

A HIGH POSITION.

Between sixty-five and seventy years from the present time, when Sir Frederick Pollock was a boy in St Paul's School, he drew upon himself the displeasure of Dr Roberts, the somewhat irascible head master of the school, who frankly told Sir Frederick's father, "Sir, you'll live to see that boy of yours hanged." Years afterwards, when the boy of whom this dismal prophecy was made had distinguished himself at Cambridge and the bar, Dr Roberts, meeting Sir Frederick's mother in society, overwhelmed her with congratulations upon her son's success, and fortunately oblivious of his former misunderstanding with his former pupil, concluded his polite speeches by saying, "Ah, madam! I always said he'd fill an *elevated* situation."

FRESH AND STALE.

Jerdan says that when Elliston was in treaty to become lessee of Drury Lane Theatre, he gave way to more than his usual excitement, and consulting his legal adviser, Mr Fladgate, at all hours, in no very proper state, Fladgate exclaimed to him, "Hang it, sir, there is no getting through any business with you, who come to me fresh drunk every night, and stale drunk every morning."

---

[1] Sir Frederick Pollock; *b.* 1783, *d.* 1870. [2] Probably the late Bishop Wilberforce.

WHICH?

One of the best things attributed to Sir Christopher Hatton [1] is a pun. In a case concerning the limits of certain land, the counsel on one side having remarked with explanatory emphasis, "We lie on this side, my lord," the Lord Chancellor leaned backwards, and drily observed, "If you lie on both sides, which am I to believe?"

A STANDING JEST.

They were wont (says Bacon) to call referring to the Master in Chancery *committing.* My Lord Keeper Egerton, when he was Master of the Rolls,[2] was wont to ask, "What the cause had done that it should be committed?"[3]

BOTH HIS HANDS.

My Lord Chancellor Ellesmere, when he had read a petition which he disliked, would say, "What, would you have my hand to this now?" And the party answering "Yes," he would say farther, "Well, you shall; nay, you shall have both my hands to it." And so would (says Bacon), with both his hands, tear it in pieces.

AN UPRIGHT JUDGE.

L'Estrange records that, when a stone was hurled by a convict from the dock at Charles I.'s Chief-Justice Richardson, and passed just over the head of the judge, who happened to be sitting at his ease and lolling on his elbow, the learned man smiled, and observed to those who congratulated him on his escape, "You see now, if I had been an *upright judge,* I had been slain."

A SMART RETORT.

Speaking of Lord Commissioner Maynard, Lord Campbell says : "From the mouth of this dull blackletter lawyer came two of the most felicitous sayings in the English language, envied by Congreve and Sheridan." For example :— Jeffreys having once rudely taunted him with having grown so old as to forget his law, "True, Sir George," replied he, "I have forgotten more law than you ever learned."[4]

---

[1] Lord Chancellor; *d.* 1591. See p. 94.   [2] Afterwards Lord Ellesmere; *d.* 1617.

[3] "This, it seems," says Campbell, "was a standing equity jest."

[4] And Jeaffreson describes him as adding, "But allow me to say, I have not forgotten much."

A CLEVER REPLY.

When the Prince of Orange first took up his quarters at Whitehall, on James's flight, different public bodies presented addresses to him, and Lord Commissioner Maynard came at the end of the men of the gown. The Prince took notice of his great age, and observed that he must have outlived all the lawyers of his time. "If your Highness," said he, "had not come over to our aid, I should have outlived the law itself."[1]

HIS MAJESTY'S.

Cockburn tells some good stories of Lord Eskgrove.[2] He says:—As usual then with stronger heads than his, everything was connected by his terror with republican horrors. I heard him, in condemning a tailor to death for murdering a soldier by stabbing him, aggravate the offence thus—"And not only did you murder him, whereby he was bereaved of his life, but you did thrust, or push, or pierce, or project, or propel the lethal weapon through the belly-band of his regimental breeches, which were his Majesty's !"

UNSEASONABLE BRUTALITY.

Lord Eskgrove (says Cockburn) had to condemn two or three persons to die who had broken into a house at Luss, and assaulted Sir James Colquhoun and others, and robbed them of a large sum of money. He first, as was his almost constant practice, explained the nature of the various crimes: assault, robbery, and hame-suchen, of which last he gave the etymology; and he then reminded them that they attacked the house and the persons in it, and robbed them, and then came to this climax—"All this you did, and, G—— preserve us! joost when they were sitten doon to their denner !"

EXTREMELY.

A very common arrangement of Lord Eskgrove's logic to juries was this— "And so, gentlemen, having shown you that the pannell's argument is utterly impossibill, I shall now proceed for to show you that it is extremely improbabill."

---

[1] Sir John Maywood; born in 1602, lived till 1690.
[2] David Rae, Lord Eskgrove, succeeded Braxfield as head of the Scotch Criminal Court. Cockburn describes him as "a very considerable lawyer, in mere knowledge probably Braxfield's superior; but he had nothing of Braxfield's grasp or reasoning, and a more ludicrous personage did not exist."

TO WHOM DID HE ALLUDE?

Lord Hermand [1] (says Cockburn) sometimes made little ceremony in disdaining the authority of an Act of Parliament, when he and it happened to differ. He once got rid of one which Lord Meadowbank (the first), whom he did not particularly like, was for enforcing, because the Legislature had made it law, by saying, in his snorting, contemptuous way, and with an emphasis on every syllable: "But there we're told that there's a statute against all this. A statute! What's a statute? Words. Mere words! And am I to be tied down by words? No, my Lords; I go by the law of *right reason.*" Lord Holland noticed this in the House of Peers as a strange speech for a judge. Lord Gilkes could not resist the pleasure of reading Holland's remark to Hermand, who was generally too impetuous to remember his own words. He entirely agreed with Lord Holland, and was indignant at the Court suffering "from the rashness of fools." "Well, my Lord, but who could Lord Holland be alluding to?" "Alluding to? who *can it* be but that creature Meadowbank?"

SOME COMFORT.

Cockburn writes to Lord Braxfield: [2] Almost the only story of him I ever heard that had some fun in it without immodesty, was when a butler gave up his place because his Lordship's wife was always scolding him. "Lord!" he exclaimed; "ye've little to complain o': ye may be thankfu' ye're no married to her."

A MISTAKE.

Macaulay writes: Lord Aberdeen told us some droll stories of the old Scotch judges. Lord Braxfield, at whist, exclaimed to a lady with whom he was playing: "What are ye doing, ye damned auld ——;" and then recollecting himself, "Your pardon's begged, madam: I took ye for my ain wife."

FOR ONCE.

In a note to a passage in one of the Waverley Novels, Scott tells a story of an old Scotch judge, who, as an enthusiastic chess-player, was much mortified by the success of an ancient friend, who invariably beat him when they tried their powers at the beloved game. After a time, the humiliated chess-player

---

[1] Another Scotch law lord.

[2] Judge in the Scotch Court of Session. Cockburn describes him elsewhere as "The giant of the bench." "In every matter depending on natural ability and practical sense, he was very great. . . . Thousands of his sayings have been preserved, and the staple of them is indecency."

had his day of triumph. His conqueror happened to commit murder, and it became the Judge's not altogether painful duty to pass upon him the sentence of the law. Having in due form, and with suitable solemnity commended his soul to the divine mercy, he, after a brief pause, assumed his ordinary colloquial tone of voice, and nodding humorously to his old friend, observed —"And noo, Jammie, I think ye'll aloo that I hae checkmated you for ance."

METAPHORICALLY SPEAKING.

According to Mr Hayward, a quondam leader of the Western Circuit and Vinerian Professor (Philip Williams), in a law lecture at Oxford, spoke thus : "The student, launched on an ocean of law, skips like a squirrel from twig to twig, vainly endeavouring to collect the scattered members of Hippolytus."

NOT SO BAD AS THAT.

Walking with Kane one day, we (says Phillips) met a mutual friend whose coat was much torn near the breast. Kane at once cried out, "Rents are enormous." "Well," replied the wearer of the coat, "you cannot say it is *rent in arrear.*"

HE DIDN'T DRINK THEM!

Sir Toby Butler, [Irish] Solicitor-General in 1689, was pledged "not to drink a drop of liquor" until he made his argument in a case of vast importance, and acquitted himself so ably that bench and bar complimented him for his able speech ; yet (says O'Flannagan) when the attorney expressed his conviction the success was owing to abstemiousness: "Not so fast, my friend," replied the jolly old toper, "perhaps it was the other way." "Why, Sir Toby," exclaimed the attorney, "surely you have not broken your pledge ?" "What was that ?" demanded Sir Toby. "You pledged your word you would not *drink a drop* of liquor until you concluded your argument." "Nor have I," answered the barrister, "I did not *drink a drop,* but I soaked two fresh penny loaves in two bottles of claret, and I *ate them !*"

ACCORDINGLY.

I remember (says O'Flannagan) the late George Bennett, Crown prosecutor on the Munster Circuit, used sometimes to raise a laugh at a medical witness in a case of death by his interrogation, "Well, doctor, you attended the deceased ?" "Yes." "And he died accordingly."

G

GETTING SCARCE.

Lord Chancellor Norbury on one occasion addressed himself to Mr Garrat O'Farrell, a jolly Irish barrister, who always carried a parcel of coarse national humour about with him. Independent in mind and property, he generally said whatever came uppermost. "Mr Garrat O'Farrell," said the Chancellor solemnly, "I believe your name and family were very respectable and numerous in county Wicklow. I think I was introduced to several of them during my late tour there." "Yes, my lord, said O'Farrell, "we *were* very numerous; but so many of us have been lately hanged for sheep-stealing, that the name is getting rather scarce in that county."

OBDURATE INDEED.

Egan, the Irish barrister, was never remarkable (says Barrington) for the correctness of his English. In speaking to some motion that was pending, he used the word *obdurate* frequently. I happened to laugh; Egan turned round, and then addressing himself to the Chief-Baron, "I suppose, my lord," said he, ironically, "the gentleman laughs at my happening to pronounce the word *obdurate* wrong." "No, my lord," replied I, "I only laughed because he pronounced it right." I never heard him utter the word *obdurate* afterwards.

QUID PRO QUO.

A very able barrister, named Collins, had the reputation of occasionally involving his adversary in a legal net, and, by his superior subtlety, gaining his cause. On appearing in Court in a case with the eminent barrister, Mr Pigot, Q.C., there arose a question as to who should be leader, Mr Collins being the senior in standing at the bar, Mr Pigot being one of the Queen's Counsel. "I yield," said Mr Collins; "my friend holds the honours." "Faith if he does, Stephen," observed Mr Herrick, "'tis you have all the tricks."

MUCH BETTER.

There is (says Phillips) a celebrated reply in circulation of Mr Dunning[1] to a remark of Lord Mansfield, who curtly exclaimed at one of his legal positions, "O, if that be law, Mr Dunning, I may burn my law books!" "Better read them, my lord," was the sarcastic and appropriate rejoinder.

WHAT A HAND!

When walking one day with a friend in Dublin, Burgh, the barrister, passed the mansion of a nobleman whose family acquired notoriety by a propensity

---

[1] Afterwards Lord Ashburton (1731-1783).

for taking the goods of others—in short, confounding *meum* and *tuum*. The knocker on the hall door was a large iron hand. Burgh (says O'Flannagan) at once uttered this impromptu :—

"Could man Promethean fire command,
  To warm with life that iron hand,
  And touch it with a sense of feeling,
  Lord ! what a hand 'twould be for stealing."

TRUMPET-TONGUED.

"I spoke to them trumpet-tongued," said Chief-Baron Wolfe to a friend, after a fine speech to a Cork jury. "You did, I heard you; but it was a penny trumpet, Stephen," replied Harry Cooper.

SO SELFISH !

Lord Campbell tells how, at the opening period of his professional career, soon after the publication of his "*Nisi Prius* Reports," he, on circuit, successfully defended a prisoner charged with a criminal offence ; and how, whilst the success of his advocacy was still quickening his pulses, he discovered that his late client, with whom he had held a confidential conversation, had contrived to relieve him of his pocket-book, full of bank notes. As soon as the presiding judge, Lord Chief-Baron Macdonald heard of the mishap of the reporting barrister, he exclaimed, "What ! Does Mr Campbell think that no one is entitled to *take notes* in Court except himself ?"

DEAL, NOT LEAD.

One of the best "legal" puns on record is unanimously attributed by the gossipers of Westminster Hall to Lord Chelmsford. As Sir Frederick Thesiger he was engaged in the conduct of a case, and objected to the irregularity of a learned sergeant, who, in examining his witnesses, repeatedly put leading questions. "I have a right," maintained the sergeant, doggedly, "to *deal* with my witnesses as I please." "To that I offer no objection," retorted Sir Frederick. "You may *deal* as you like, but you shan't *lead*."

ANYTHING.

Of the same brilliant conversationalist, Mr Grantley Berkeley has recorded a good story.[1] Walking down St James's Street, Lord Chelmsford was accosted by a stranger, who exclaimed, "Mr Birch, I believe." "If you believe that, sir, you'll believe anything," replied the ex-Chancellor, as he passed on.

---

[1] In *My Life and Recollections.*

MAKING HIS LIVING.

Joseph Gillon was a Writer to the Signet. Calling on him one day in his writing office, Sir Walter Scott said, "Why, Joseph, this place is as hot as an oven." "Well," quoth Gillon, "and isn't it here that I make my bread? This story is told by Lockhart.

THE DIFFERENCE.

Barham records that when Judge Littledale took leave on his retirement, Sir J. Campbell, the Attorney-General, addressed him in the name of the bar, and both appeared to be much affected during his speech. In his account of it at the Garrick, Murphy remarked that "Sir John cried a little *dale* and that Littledale cried a great *dale*."

POOR MR SMITH !

Mr Jeaffreson tells the story of the cruel answer given by a great lawyer to a country attorney, who, through fussy anxiety for a client's interests, committed a grave breach of professional etiquette. Let this attorney be called Mr Smith, and let it be known that Mr Smith, having come up to London from a secluded district of a remote county, was present at a consultation of counsellors learned in the law, upon his client's case. At this interview, the leading counsel in the cause, the Attorney-General of the time, was present, and delivered his final opinion with characteristic clearness and precision. The consultation over, the county attorney retreated to the Hummons Hotel, Covent Garden, and instead of sleeping over the statements made at the conference, passed a wretched and wakeful night, harassed by distressing fears, and agitated by a conviction that the Attorney-General had overlooked the most important point of the case. Early next day, Mr Smith, without appointment, was at the great counsellor's chambers, and by vehement importunity, as well as a liberal donation to the clerk, succeeded in forcing his way to the advocate's presence. "Well, Mis-ter Smith," observed the Attorney-General to his visitor, turning away from one of his devilling juniors, who chanced to be closeted with him at the moment of the intrusion, "what may you want to say? Be quick, for I am pressed for time." Notwithstanding the urgency of his engagements, he spoke with a slowness which, no less than the suspicious rattle of his voice, indicated the fervour of displeasure. "Sir Causticus Witherett, I trust you will excuse my troubling you; but, sir, after our yesterday's interview, I went to my hotel, the Hummons, in Covent Garden, and I have spent the evening and all the night turning over my client's case in my mind ; and the more I turn the matter over in my mind, the more reason I see to fear that you have not given one point due consideration." A pause, during which Sir Causticus Witherett steadily eyed his visitor, who began to feel strangely embarrassed under this searching scrutiny; and then—"State the point, Mis-ter Smith, but be brief." Having heard the point stated, Sir Causticus Witherett inquired, "Is that all you wish to say?" "All, sir—all," replied Mr Smith; adding nervously, "and I trust you will excuse me troubling you about the matter; but, sir, I could not sleep a wink last night; all through the night I was turning the matter over in my mind." A glimpse of silence. Sir Causticus rose, and, standing over his victim, made this final speech:—"Mis-ter Smith, if you take my advice, given with sincere commiseration for your state, you will without delay return to the tranquil village in which you habitually reside. In the quietude of your accustomed scenes you will have leisure to *turn this matter over in what you are pleased to call your mind,* and I am willing to hope that *your mind* will recover its usual serenity. Mr Smith, I wish you a very good morning."

EXTREMELY UNPLEASANT.

The late Judge Williams (says W. H. Harrison) had once a clerk who, the judge found on going to chambers one morning, had hanged himself behind the door. The alleged cause of the act was domestic infelicity. It happened that the clerk who succeeded the unfortunate man in his office asked leave to go out of town on a matter of moment. "It is very inconvenient," said the judge, "and, besides, you have been with me but a few weeks. Is your business in the country of so very pressing a nature?" "Why, yes, my lord," was the reply, "I am going to be married." "Oh, then," was the rejoinder, "go by all means; but mind, when you come back, don't hang yourself behind my door, because it is extremely unpleasant to come to chambers and find persons hanging behind one's door."

AN UNELIGIBLE CONFESSOR.

When near his end Lord Northington was reminded of the propriety of his receiving the consolations of religion, and he readily agreed that a divine should be sent for, but when (says Campbell) the Right Rev. Dr ——, with whom he had formerly been intimate, was proposed, he said, "No! that won't do. I cannot well confess to him, for the greatest sin I shall have to answer for was making him a bishop!"

ONE FOR THE JUDGE.

A story is told of Judge Fortescue-Aland (subsequently Lord Fortescue) and a counsel. Sir John Fortescue-Aland was disfigured by a nose which was purple, and hideously misshapen by morbid growth. Having checked a ready counsel with the needlessly harsh observation, "Brother, brother, you are handling the case in a very lame manner," the angry advocate gave vent to his annoyance by saying with a perfect appearance of *sang-froid*, "Pardon me, my lord; have patience with me, and I will do my best to make the case as plain as—as—the nose on your lordship's face."

IT DOTH REVIVE AGAIN.

Lord Campbell is said to have affected, and perhaps felt, a great contempt for puisne judges, who, he maintained, when sitting *in banco* always followed the lead of their superior on the bench; and he is said (remarks Harrison) to have embodied this feeling in the following lines—

> "A woman with a settlement
> Married a man with none;
> The question was—he being dead,
> If that she had was gone?

> "Quoth Sir John Pratt, 'The settlement
> Suspended did remain,
> The husband living; but, he dead,
> It doth revive again.'

> *Chorus of Puisne Judges.*
> 'The husband living; but, he dead,
> It doth revive again.'"

TAKING STEPS.

In talking of Miss Gayton, the pretty little dancer, marrying Murray, a clergyman, Joy (says Moore) applied two lines well, saying they might now, in their different capacities,

> "Teach men for heaven or money's sake,
> What *steps* they were through life to take."

A CRUEL MIMIC.

Alike commendable for its subtlety and inoffensive humour, was the pleasantry with which young Philip Yorke (afterwards Lord Hardwicke) answered Sir Lyttleton Powys's banter on the Western Circuit. An amiable and upright, but far from brilliant judge, Sir Lyttleton had a few pet phrases —amongst them "I humbly conceive," and "Look, do you see,"—which he sprinkled over his judgments and colloquial talk with ridiculous profuseness. Surprised at Yorke's sudden rise into lucrative practice, this most gentleman-like worthy was pleased to account for the unusual success by maintaining that young Mr Yorke must have written a law book which had brought him early into favour with the inferior branch of the profession. "Mr Yorke," said the venerable justice, whilst the barristers were sitting over their wine at a "judge's dinner," "I cannot well account for your having so much business, considering the short time you have been at bar: I humbly conceive you must have published something; for, look you, do you see, there is scarcely a cause in Court but you are employed in it, on one side or the other. I should therefore be glad to know, Mr Yorke, do you see, whether this be the case." Playfully denying that he possessed any celebrity as a writer on legal matters, Yorke, with an assumption of candour, admitted that he had some thoughts of lightening the labours of law students by turning Coke upon Littleton into verse. Indeed, he confessed he had already begun the work of versification. Not seeing the nature of the reply, Sir Lyttleton Powys treated the droll fancy as a serious project, and insisted that the author should give a specimen of the style of his contemplated work. Whereupon the young barrister—not pausing to remind a company of lawyers of the words of the original: "Tenant in fee simple is he which hath lands or tenements to hold to him and to his heirs for ever"—recited the lines—

> "He that holdeth his lands in fee,
> Need neither to quake nor to quiver,
> *I humbly conceive: for look, do you see,*
> They are his and his heirs for ever."

The mimicry of the voice being not less perfect than the verbal imitation, Yorke's hearers (says Jeaffreson) were convulsed with laughter.

THE MEMBER FOR BARKSHIRE.

Judge Haliburton was dining one day with the Leander Club at the Star and Garter at Putney. It was a fine day in summer, and the window towards the river immediately over the towpath was open. The Justice (says Harrison) was returning thanks for the toast of his health; and, being interrupted by the loud barking of a dog, paused, and said that when the member for *Bark*-shire had finished his speech, he (the Justice) would finish his.

A *NOLLE PROSEQUI.*

According to Trevelyan, Macaulay told a story about one of the French "prophets" of the seventeenth century, who came into the Court of Queen's Bench, and announced that the Holy Ghost had sent him to command Lord Holt[1] to enter a *nolle prosequi*. "If," said Lord Holt, "the Holy Ghost had wanted a *nolle prosequi* he would have bade you apply to the Attorney-General. The Holy Ghost knows that I cannot enter a *nolle prosequi*. But there is one thing which I can do. I can lay a lying knave by the heels," and thereupon he committed him to prison.

---

[1] Lord Chief-Justice; *b.* 1642, *d.* 1709.

A RETORT COURTEOUS.

In an action brought to recover damages done to a carriage, a learned counsel repeatedly called the vehicle in question a broug-ham, pronouncing both syllables of the word *brougham*. Whereupon Lord Campbell, with considerable pomposity, observed, "*Broom* is the more usual pronunciation; a carriage of the description you mean is generally and not incorrectly called a *broom;* that pronunciation is open to no grave objection, and it has the great advantage of saving the time consumed by uttering an extra syllable.' Half-an-hour later in the same trial Lord Campbell, alluding to a decision given in a similar action, said, "In that case the carriage which had sustained injury was an *omnibus*—" "Pardon me, my lord," interposed the Queen's counsel, with such promptitude that his lordship was startled into silence, "a carriage of the kind to which you draw attention is usually termed a ''buss ;' that pronunciation is open to no grave objection, and it has the great advantage of saving the time consumed by uttering two extra syllables." The interruption was followed by a roar of laughter, in which Lord Campbell joined more heartily than any one else.

VERY TIRED, TOO.

O'Flannagan writes of Holmes, the Irish barrister :—He made us laugh very much one day in the Queen's Bench. I was waiting for some case in which I was counsel, when the crier called "Pluck and Diggers," and in came James Scott, Q.C., very red and heated, and, throwing his bag on the table within the bar, he said, "My lords, I beg to assure your lordships I feel so exhausted I am quite unable to argue this case. I have been speaking for three hours in the Court of Exchequer, and I am quite tired ; and pray excuse me, my lords, I must get some refreshment." The Chief-Justice bowed, and said, "Certainly, Mr Scott." So that gentleman left the Court. "Mr Holmes, you are in this case," said the Chief-Justice; "we'll be happy to hear you." "Really, my lord, I am very tired too," said Mr Holmes. "Surely," said the Chief-Justice, "you have not been speaking for three hours in the Court of Exchequer ? What has tired you ?" "Listening to Mr Scott," was Holmes' sarcastic reply.

JOINING THE ARMY.

Some *bon mots* of Phil. O'Connell are preserved. A friend of his was engaged to be married to the third daughter of Dr Foot. At this time the friend was expecting a commission in the line. The late Judge Berwick asked Phil. O'Connell, "Is it true our friend is joining the army ?" "Quite true, judge," replied Phil. "He is attached to the 3d Foot."

HE WANTED ELEVEN.

Curran used to tell a story of poor Lord Avonmore, who was at that time the plain, untitled, struggling Barry Yelverton. "I wish, mother," said Barry, "I had *eleven* shirts." "*Eleven*, Barry! why *eleven?*" "Because, mother, I am of opinion that a gentleman, to be *comfortable*, ought to have *the dozen.*"

AN ELOQUENT REPLY.

Lord Avonmore (says O'Flannagan) was frequently lost in reverie, and quite oblivious of what was passing around him. Both he and Curran were at a dinner-party, and Curran, who sat next to the Chief-Baron, observing him quite abstracted when the toast—"Our Absent Friends"—was drunk, nudged him. "My lord," he said, "our host has just proposed your health, which has been received in very cordial terms; surely you will respond." "Thank you, Curran, really I was not aware of it," replied the Chief-Baron ; and up he got, and, to the surprise of many and the amusement of more, made an eloquent speech in reply to a toast which was not given.

IF HE CHOSE.

Phillips says that had Goold, the barrister, been contented with the world's estimate of him as he really was, all would have admitted him to be an eminent man. But he sharpened censure, and excited ridicule, by aspiring to be what no man ever was—in every art, trade, science, profession, accomplishment, and pursuit under the sun, a *ne plus ultra*. The pitch to which he carried this foible was incredible. Expatiating one day on the risk he ran from a sudden rise of the tide when riding on the North Strand, near Dublin, he assured his hearer, "had he not been the very best horseman in existence, he must inevitably have been drowned : in short, never was human being in such danger." "My dear Tom," his friend replied, "there was one undoubtedly in still greater, for a poor man was actually drowned there on that morning." "By heaven! sir," bellowed Goold, "I might have been drowned *if I chose.*"

A DISTINGUISHED PATRIOT.

Shiel, though a very epigrammatic speaker, was not (says O'Flannagan) remarkable for witty sayings. One of the best I have heard was in reference to a gentleman connected with trade. During O'Connell's agitation several of the distilleries and breweries in Ireland vied with each other for popular favour, and either the proprietors themselves, or persons in their employment, attended public meetings, and made eloquent speeches in support of the

people's rights.   It was often, as the late General Barry observed, "froth at
top and beer at the bottom."   While a gentleman in the great distillery
establishment of Sir John Power, of Dublin, was haranguing a Catholic
meeting, some one asked Shiel "Who is this?"   "Oh," replied Shiel, "he
is a patriot to a distillery."

A SQUINTING JUDGE.

The unfortunate obliquity of Sir John Trevor's vision is perceptible (says
Lord Campbell) in the portraits and prints we have of him, and made the
wags assert that "Justice was blind, but at the Rolls Equity was now seen to
squint."

THE SAME.

While Sir John Trevor was in the chair, as Speaker, two members in
different parts of the House were often equally confident (says Campbell) of
having "caught his eye."

A LEGAL JOKE.

When, some years ago, the practice of having daily prayers in our churches
was still a novelty, Sir George Rose's [1] own clergyman called upon him and
asked him his opinion as to its adoption.   Sir George replied, "I see no objection whatever, but I hope that in my own particular case *service at the house
will be deemed good service.*" [2]

ANOTHER.

When a singularly matter-of-fact gentleman had related a story in which
the listeners had failed after all their efforts to discover the faintest spark of
humour, Sir George accounted for the circumstance at once.   "Don't you
see?" he said; "he has *tried a joke*, but *reserved the point!*"

A THIRD.

The late Sir John Rolt, meeting Sir George Rose one day in the later years
of his life, remarked to him, "I am very glad, Sir George, to see you looking so
well; you do not look a day older than when you used to come among us."
Sir George pointed to his hair, and said, "this *d——d poll* may not disclose
the fact; but" (opening his mouth, and pointing to a certain gap in his front

---

[1] The distinguished lawyer and scholar.
[2] *Macmillan's Magazine*, vol. xxix., from which we extract most of the following anecdotes
of Sir George.

teeth) "*this indenture witnesseth.*" It may be added (says our authority) for the instruction of the laity, that a *deed poll* was a kind of deed properly distinguished from an indenture.

CENTURY AND SENTRY.

Sir George Rose's doctor assuring him that he would live to be a hundred, he promptly replied, "Then I suppose my coffin may be called a 'cent'ry box.'"

BY HONOURS.

When Sir George Rose was appointed one of the four judges of the now extinct Court of Review, he came to Lincoln's Inn with his colleagues to be sworn in. Some friend congratulating him on his access of dignity, he observed, "Yes! here we are, you see—*four by honours !*"

THE FIRST ON RECORD.

In some case that was being heard before Sir George Rose, it appeared that a picture of "Elijah fed by the Ravens" had been given as part of some security. He handed down a note to one of the counsel in the case : "This is, so far as I am aware, the first instance on record of an *accommodation bill.*"

HIS RIGHT EYE.

A friend meeting Sir George Rose one day in Lincoln's Inn Fields, with his left eye greatly swollen and inflamed, remonstrated with him, adding that he was surprised Lady Rose should have let him go out of doors in such a condition. "Ah!" replied Sir George, "I am out *jure mariti*" (my right eye).

NOT A GOOD LIVING.

Dining, on one occasion, with the late Lord Langdale, his host was speaking of the very diminutive church in Langdale, of which his lordship was patron. "It is not bigger," said Lord Langdale, "than this dining-room.". "No," returned Sir George, "*and the living not half so good.*"

A POSY AND A POSER.

On one occasion, when a new sergeant had been created, and it became his duty, according to custom, to present rings to the judges, inscribed with the usual brief "posy" in Latin, Sir George Rose indicated his appreciation of the then existing company of sergeants by suggesting for the motto in question, "Scilicet" (silly set).

THAT WAS ALL.

When Sir George Rose was dining one day with some friends, the out-door servants had been enlisted into the service of the dining-room; and it chanced that one of them, in carrying out a tray of glass, as he left the room stumbled and fell with a heavy crash. "What is that?" exclaimed Sir George's next-door neighbour, in great alarm. "Oh, nothing," he replied; "only the coachman gone out with his *break.*"

VERY DIFFERENT.

Sir George Rose was at a funeral on a bitterly cold day in winter, and his companion in a mourning coach called his attention to the poor men in scarves, and bearing staves, who were trudging along by the side of the carriage. "Poor fellows!" said his companion, "they look as if they were frozen!" "Frozen!" returned Sir George; "my dear friend, they are *mutes*, not *liquids.*"

GONE TO GRAVES' END.

As a companion to the above "improvement" of a funeral, may be quoted Sir George Rose's remark on an acquaintance who had died of dropsy—"He has gone to *Gravesend by water.*"

A CHARMING PAIR.

Sir George Rose, being introduced one day to two charming young ladies, whose names were Mary and Louisa, instantly added, with a bow, "Ah, yes! *Marie-Louise*—sweetest pear I know"—a compliment almost worthy of being coupled with that most beautiful one of Sydney Smith, suggested by the sweet pea.[1]

TEMPLE AND MITRE.

A report having originated that Archdeacon Robinson, Master of the Temple, was to be elevated to the episcopal bench, Sir George Rose said, "Well, if he must leave the Temple, I hope it will be by *Mitre Court.*"

THE SACRED WAY.

On another occasion, when Sir George met his old friend the Archdeacon, walking, apparently deep in thought, in the neighbourhood of the Temple, he inquired playfully, "Well, Master, and what are you dreaming about?" "Oh," said the Archdeacon, quoting the first lines of the familiar satire of Horace, "I was *nescio quid meditans nugarum.*" "But then, with you, dear friend," was the singularly felicitous reply, "it is always in the *Via Sacra.*"

---

[1] See page 7.

AT THE BOTTOM.

It was James **Smith,** of *Rejected Addresses* celebrity, himself an attorney, whose cruel reflection on his own calling provoked a famous retort from Sir George Rose. James Smith had written thus—or "to this defect," for there is more than one version of the lines:—

> " In Craven Street, Strand, ten attorneys are found;
> And down at the bottom the barges abound.
> Fly, Honesty, fly, to some safer retreat;
> For there's craft in the river, and craft in the street!"

To which Sir George replied, impromptu:—

> " Why should Honesty fly to some safer retreat?
> From barges and lawyers, 'od rot 'em?
> The lawyers are *just* at the top of the street,
> And the barges are just at the bottom."

I DOUBT.

The same originator of happy sayings pointed (says Jeaffreson) to Eldon's characteristic weakness in the lines:—

> " Mr Leach made a speech,
> Pithy, clear, and strong;
> Mr Hart, on the other part,
> Was prosy, dull, and long;
> Mr Parker made that darker
> Which was dark enough without;
> Mr Bell spoke so well,
> That the Chancellor said, 'I doubt.'"[1]

Far from being offended by this allusion to his notorious mental infirmity, Lord Eldon, shortly after the verses had floated into circulation, concluded one of his decisions by saying, with a significant smile, "And here the Chancellor does *not* doubt."

---

[1] Another version runs:—

> " Mr Leach made a speech,
> Angry, neat, and wrong;
> Mr Hart, on the other part,
> Was right, but dull and long;
> Mr Parker made that darker
> Which was dark enough without;
> Mr Cook quoted his book,
> And the Chancellor said, 'I doubt.'"

These lines were written, at the request of a law reporter, as the summary of speeches made in a case before Lord Eldon.

'BUS AND BUSS.

At a legal dinner given at **Greenwich many years** ago, the late Mr **Justice** Barley, who was in **the chair, informed the** assembled guests, when the decanter had begun **to circulate after** dinner, that as it was most important to **ensure** the safety of so eminent a company as that **present,** he had ordered a handsome and roomy omnibus, which would be at the door at ten o'clock, to **convey** them back to town.   Sir George at once rose, and said:—

> " The Grecian of old bade his comrades entwine
> The myrtle of Venus with Bacchus's vine;
> Which our excellent chairman interpreteth thus—
> Begin with a bumper, **and end** with a bus(s)."

BEAMS AND BEAMES.

When Mr Beames, the reporter, defended himself against the *friction* of passing barristers by a wooden **bar, the flimsiness** of which was pointed out to Sir George **(then Mr Rose), the** wit replied—

> " Yes, the partition is certainly thin,
> Yet thick enough, truly, the Beames within."

NOT UPSET.

Lord William Lennox records what he calls an **admirable saying** of one of the wittiest men of our age, perhaps of any age, who, when Sir **John Paul's** bank stopped payment, was met coming out of it by a friend.   "**So Sir John has** failed?" said the friend.   "Yes," replied the lawyer, "**and I've been** victimised."   "Really!" continued **the** other, "**the** news **must have quite upset you.**"   "Not at all; **I was not upset, although** I lost my balance."

A HAPPY REBUKE.

There is one great **drawback to the lovers** of music, which is **the** introduction **of stalls, where** the majority **congregate,** not **to** listen **to** the opera, but **to their own insipid** conversation.   **Never (says Lord** William Lennox) was there **a happier rebuke than that made by a popular** member of the legal profession **to a gentleman who kept up a running fire** of small talk with his neighbour.   "**Sir,**" said he, "**what an impudent fellow** that Rubini must be!" "Really," **responded the other,** "**I was not aware** of that."   "Were you not?   Why, the fellow has **the impudence to spoil your** conversation by his singing."

THE ONLY ONE LEFT.

Lord William Lennox tells the following story of the late Earl of Carlisle, one of the most popular noblemen that ever ruled over Ireland, and whose good-nature was proverbial. A returned convict, who had been exemplary in his conduct during the time he was undergoing his punishment for a robbery of plate, applied to the noble lord, who was at that period Viceroy of Ireland, to take him back into his Lordship's service. Lord Carlisle hesitated, but afterwards determined to give the reformed culprit a chance, and communicated his intention to a gentleman well known about the Irish Court, and upon whom the mantle of the witty Lord Norbury seemed to have fallen. "Take him back?" said the friend; "if you do, I think you will be the only spoon left in the Castle."

HE AND HIS NAME.

A friend of Jerdan's once said to him :—I was one day in Gray's Inn Hall, where, in vacation, the Court of Exchequer sat in Equity, and Chief-Baron Richards was hearing causes in one corner, the rest of the hall occupied by loungers and waiters on the cause-paper. An attorney came to me, and, pointing to Chief-Baron Richards, said : "Pray, sir, is that Baron *Wood?*" "*Yes,* sir," I said, "but his name is Richards."

A BUTTRESS OF THE CHURCH.

On one occasion (says Lord Campbell) when Lord Eldon's merits were discussed among some lawyers, a warm partisan of the Chancellor extolled him as "a pillar of the Church." "No," retorted another, "he may be one of its *buttresses,* but certainly not one of its *pillars,* for he is never seen inside its walls."

A BAD JUDGE.

Mark Boyd says :—I recollect a humorous M.P. pointing out to me a retired West India judge not very remarkable for sagacity on the bench. There was a ball at Government House, and the judge began to criticise the waltzing of a witty member of the West India bar. "Ah, my friend, you are a bad waltzer !" "Ah, but you are a bad judge."

CROWN AND HALF-CROWN.

A friend told Mr O'Flannagan the following anecdote of the Masters in Chancery, Thomas Goold and Isaac Burke Bethel, an old member of the bar, who was ever ready to accept any meals he could get, or take any fee that was offered. On one occasion, when engaged in a prosecution, he said very pompously, "I appear for the Crown, my lord." "Oftener for the *half-crown*," whispered a wit, who knew Burke Bethel's line of practice.

NOR SO GREEN.

Soon after Canning's statue was put up in Palace Yard, in all its verdant freshness—the carbonate of copper was not yet blackened by the smoke of London—Justice Gazelee (better known as Starelee, who tried the case of Bardell *v.* Pickwick) was walking away from Westminster Hall with Curwood, when the judge, looking at the statue (the size of which is heroic, if not colossal), said : "I don't think that is very like Canning ; he was not so large a man." "No, my Lord," said Curwood, "nor so green." This story was told to Jerdan by a friend.

HE WAS MISSING.

An eminent judge used to say that, in his opinion, the very best thing ever said by a witness to a counsel was the reply given to Missing, the barrister, at the time leader of his circuit. He was defending a prisoner charged with stealing a donkey. The prosecutor had left the animal tied up to a gate, and when he returned it was gone. Missing (says Boyd) was very severe in his examination of the witness. "Do you mean to say, witness, the donkey was stolen from that gate ?" "I mean to say, sir," giving the judge, and then the jury, a sly look, at the same time pointing to the counsel, "the ass was Missing !"

A DISTINCTION.

Moore relates that it was said of Lords Eldon and Leach, that "one was *Oyer sans terminer*, and the other *Terminer sans oyer.*"

AN ERUPTION.

Luttrell told once, in Moore's hearing, of a good phrase of an attorney's in speaking of a reconciliation that had taken place between two persons whom he wished to set by the ears: "I am sorry to tell you, sir, that a compromise has *broken out* between the parties."

About Men of Letters.

UN ANGLAIS TIMIDE.

THE poet Bowles,[1] it is well known, was a timid—a painfully timid person. [On one occasion], Bowood (Lord Lansdowne's place) was full of guests, and Moore, Rogers, and Milman being among the number, Mr and Mrs Bowles were invited to meet them. Bowles (says J. C. Young) was no sooner dressed, than, on entering the drawing-room, he walked up to Lady Lansdowne and made some complaint or other to her, which caused her at once to leave the room. He forthwith followed her. In a few minutes they both returned. As Lady Lansdowne passed me, she said, "Bless the dear man, there is no pleasing him." I did not know to what she alluded, until Bowles came up to me with a face of blank dismay, and asked me if I were going to sleep there. On my telling him that I was not, he exclaimed, "I wish I were going home too. I shan't sleep a wink here. I was shown into a bed-room to dress in, in which I was intended to pass the night; but it was on the ground floor, where there was nothing whatever to prevent thieves from getting in and cutting my throat! I remonstrated with Lady Lansdowne, and the dear lady, by way of rendering me easier in my mind, has transferred me to a room so high, that, in case of fire, I shall be burnt to a cinder before I can be rescued!"

A "NASTY OLD CLERGYMAN."

Many are the stories told of Bowles' nervousness. Here is another, related also by J. C. Young:—Bowles was invited by the late excellent Dr Law, Bishop of Bath and Wells, to stay at Banwell. As usual, the first thing he did when he went to his room to dress for dinner was to inspect his quarters, and see if he could detect any assailable point from which danger might be expected. He crept about suspiciously, looked to the fastenings of the windows, tested the working of the door-locks, peeped into the closets, and then into a small adjoining dressing-room, in which there was a tent-bed, unmade. From that fact, and the absence of wash-stand, towel-horse, &c., &c. he con-

---

[1] William Lisle Bowles (1762-1850), whose sonnets were once popular, and are said to have inspired Coleridge.

H

cluded it was to be unoccupied. Out of this dressing-room (if I remember rightly what I was told by one of the Bishop's sons) there was a door of outlet to a back stair. The idea of sleeping alone in a room so exposed to nocturnal assault on two sides so appalled poor Bowles, that, when a maid-servant brought him up his hot water, he took her by the hand, and told her that, if she would consent to occupy the vacant bed in the adjoining room, he would give her a sovereign. Conceiving that he meant to insult her, she bounced out of the room, and told the Bishop that he must get somebody else to wait on the nasty old clergyman who had just come, as he had made improper advances to her. The Bishop insisted on knowing what he had said; and on hearing his *ipsissima verba*, told her that she had quite misconceived him, for all that he wanted was the protection of some one within ready call. "I wish," he added, "that you and the under-housemaid would oblige me by taking up your quarters together in the room next to my timid guest. You can place the bed against the door ; and as it opens in on your side, you will be safe from any intrusion on his part, if you are silly enough to fear it; and I shall have the satisfaction of knowing that if my friend should be taken ill in the night he will have some one near him." It so happened that the Bishop forgot to tell Bowles of the considerate arrangement made for him ; so that, on retiring at night to his chamber, still believing the dressing-room to be empty, he locked, not only the door by which he entered his own room, but that of the smaller room. In the middle of the night he fancied he heard footsteps in the direction of the back stairs. It then occurred to him that he had neglected to lock the *outer* door of the little room, which communicated with them. He jumped out of bed to rectify his oversight, and unlocked the door of the dressing-room. On trying to push it open, he felt a powerful resisting body opposed to him (viz., the maids' bed), and as he pushed he distinctly heard whisperings. This at once confirmed him in his conviction that there were thieves in the house. He ran back to the other door, bawling out "Murder ! thieves !" with such stentorian energy, that the Bishop and all his family were roused out of their beds (not frightened, for the Laws are all remarkably fearless) ; and it was long before their visitor could be reconciled to his position, and induced to go again to bed.

ONE AND ONE MAKE TWO.

Yet another anecdote of Bowles from the same source:—He went once to dine and sleep at the Rev. William Money's, at Whetham. Mrs Bowles' toilet was soon made : she was in the drawing-room as soon as Mrs Money herself; but Mr Bowles not having come down when the dinner-bell rang, his wife requested they would not wait for her husband, but go at once into dinner. Soup and fish had been served, when a servant tapped at the door with a message, desiring Mrs Bowles to step up to her husband, as she was wanted. On going to him, she found him in a state of boiling indignation, with no trousers on, with one leg in a black silk stocking, and the other bare. "Here, madam," he cried out, "has that idiot of a maid of yours put me up only one silk stocking for my two legs: the consequence is, I can't go downstairs to dinner, or have any dinner at all, unless some is sent up to me here." "Oh, my dear," said his amiable wife, "you need not stand on much ceremony with such old friends as the Moneys. Put on again the stockings which you have taken off, and come down in them. I will explain matters to the company." He took the hint, and was in the act of peeling off the black silk stocking from his leg, when he discovered that he had put the two on the same leg, utterly unconscious of what he had done.

"MAN WANTS," &c.

Moore writes in his Diary:—Dined at Joy's chambers in the Temple. Company: Bowles, Corry, Locke, and a General Brackenbury. Joy's dandy dinner of mutton chops, brought in one by one, "like angels' visits, few and far between," highly amusing, except that we were all in a state of starvation. "Joy," says Bowles, in a sort of reverie, "I want—I want—" "What do you want, my dear Bowles?" "D—n it, I want something to eat."

WHAT'S IN A NAME!

Mark Boyd tells the following about Thomas Campbell[1]:—The poet was dining with my brother and myself, when a witty and humorous friend, whose hospitality in the neighbourhood of Harrow for many years is still remembered by a large circle of friends, was of the party, and drew out the Bard of Hope very successfully. The poet had just returned from Algiers, and was full to overflow with anecdotes connected with his residence in Northern Africa. He gave us a most animated description, which did not suffer in illustration from his having imbibed a bottle and a-half of claret. "Oh," said the poet, "I can never forget my visit to the desert; oh, dear me, no! An impression was made on my mind there that can never be erased. Yes, it is quite true; her image is before me now—one of Nature's gentlewomen. Oh, that poor and exquisitely beautiful Arab girl! it grieves me to the heart to think what will be her fate. The chisel of Canova never produced anything to bear a comparison with that angelic young Arab." His pathos had now reached a serious point, as the tears trickled down his cheeks; but he so far rallied as to be able to tell us, that if he had ever intended to marry a second time, that Arab

---

[1] Born 1777, died 1844.

girl should have been his wife. On hearing this, we reminded him that there were always two interested in a marriage-contract, and that possibly, on his popping the question to this captivating and enchanting girl of the desert, she might have replied in the words of the Shunamite woman: "I dwell among my own people." "That is quite true," said the poet; "and it might have been the answer." Our friend—the same who plotted and carried out the Waterloo Bridge "trot out"—took up the question, and, addressing the poet, said, "Supposing you *had* married this lovely maiden of the desert, what would you have called your eldest son?" "How can I answer such a question? But, on second thoughts, I daresay," looking round the table, "it is something good—I really do not know what I should have called him." "Well, I shall tell you what, in my opinion, you should have called the boy —'Sandy Campbell.'" "Ah," said Campbell, "good, very good. You will be the death of me. In the meantime, here's to you in a bumper of claret."

HE HAD ONE MERIT.

At a literary dinner (says Trevelyan) Campbell asked leave to propose a toast, and gave the health of Napoleon Bonaparte. The war was at its height, and the very mention of Napoleon's name, except in conjunction with some uncomplimentary epithet, was in most circles regarded as an outrage. A storm of groans broke out, and Campbell with difficulty could get a few sentences heard. "Gentlemen," he said, "you must not mistake me. I admit that the French emperor is a tyrant. I admit that he is a monster. I admit that he is the sworn foe of our own nation, and, if you will, of the human race. But, gentlemen, we must be just to our great enemy. We must not forget that *he once shot a bookseller.*" The guests, of whom two out of every three lived by their pens, burst into a roar of laughter, and Campbell sat down in triumph.

HER LOVELY OFFSPRING!

One day (says Jerdan) Campbell was so smitten by a beautiful child in St James's Park, that he put an advertisement in the newspaper to discover its residence, the result of which was excessively ludicrous. For some wags of the Hook & Co. clique, aware of the circumstances, answered the appeal, and, not knowing what address to give, took the last name in the Directory, a Z——, No. — Sloane Street. Thither Campbell hurried the next forenoon in full dress, and was shown up to the drawing-room, where he found a middle-aged lady waiting to learn his errand. It was not long in being explained, and the indignant Miss Z——, on being asked to bring in her lovely offspring to gratify the longings of the poet, rushed to the bell, and rang violently for her servant to show the insolent stranger to the door!

A BAD LISTENER.

Says Moore in his Diary:—Shee told me a *bon mot* of Rogers's the other day. On somebody remarking that Payne Knight had got very deaf, "It is from want of practice," says R.; Knight being a very bad listener.

HIS THEOFFY.

Moore speaks of some ludicrous verses as being quoted at a certain dinner; among others, the following by Rogers, on "Theophilus:"—

> "When I'm drinking my tea
> I think of my *The*,
> When I'm drinking my coffee
> I think of my *Offee;*
> So, whether I'm drinking my tea or my coffee,
> I'm always a thinking of thee, my Theoffy."

NOT SAFE.

Speaking (says L'Estrange) of Moore's taste for biography, and the number of memoirs he had composed, Rogers one day cynically observed, "Why, it is not safe to die while Moore's alive!"[1]

QUITE UNIVERSAL.

Lord Lansdowne (says the same authority) once spoke to Rogers in congratulatory terms about the marriage of a common friend. "I do not think it so desirable," observed Rogers. "No!" replied Lord Lansdowne; "why not? His friends approve of it!" "Happy man!" returned Rogers, "to satisfy all the world. His friends are pleased, and his enemies are delighted!"

QUITE THE REVERSE.

Lady Chatterton says that Lady Davy one day said to Rogers, "Oh, Mr Rogers, I hear that you have been abusing me to people." He replied, "I! my dear Lady Davy? On the contrary, I pass my life in defending you."[2]

HARD ON THE POET.

Barry Cornwall writes:—I never heard Rogers volunteer an opinion about Campbell, except after his death, when he had been to see the poet's statue. "It is the first time," said he, "that I have seen him stand straight for many years."

---

[1] Moore wrote biographies of Sheridan, Byron, and **Lord Edward Fitzgerald.**

[2] According to Mr Hayward, what Lady Davy said was—"Now, Mr Rogers, I am sure you are talking about me." To which Rogers replied, "I pass my life in defending you."

ALL FOR HERSELF.

One day (says Hayward), while Rogers was on bad terms with Ward [Lord Dudley], Lady D[avy] said to him, "Have you seen Ward lately?" "*What* Ward?" "Why, our Ward, of course." "*Our* Ward!—you may keep him all to yourself."[1]

AT BATH!

Rogers tells this story of himself:—A man stopped me one day in Piccadilly, and said, "How do you do, Mr Rogers?" I didn't know him. "You don't remember me, Mr Rogers? I had the pleasure of seeing you at Bath." I said, "Delighted to see you again—at Bath."[2]

NOT CONTENT.

"Is that the contents you are looking at?" inquired (says Mr Hayward) an anxious author, who saw Rogers's eye fixed on a table or list at the commencement of a presentation copy of a new work. "No," said Rogers, pointing to the list of subscribers, "the *dis*contents."

WELL DONE.

Rogers (says the same authority) was known to have spoken highly of the picture (by Landseer) of a Newfoundland dog, entitled, "Portrait of a Distinguished Member of the Humane Society." On Landseer expressing his gratification, Rogers said: "Yes, I thought the ring of the dog's collar well painted."

TOO BAD A BARGAIN.

When a late member for a western county and his wife were stopped by banditti in Italy, Rogers used to say, "The banditti wanted to carry off P——— into the mountains; but she flung her arms round his neck, and, rather than take her with them, they let him go."

HE NEVER LIKED WALKING ALONE.

One evening, when, leaning on the arm of a friend, Rogers was about to walk home from an evening party, a pretentious gentleman made a desperate

---

[1] It was Ward, according to Mr Hayward, who, alluding to Rogers's cadaverous countenance, once asked him why he did not set up a hearse, now that he could afford it. It was the same sympathising companion who, when Rogers repeated the couplet—

> "The robin, with his furtive glance,
> Comes and looks up at me askance,"

struck in with, "If it had been a carrion crow, he would have looked you full in the face."
[2] This is told of Selwyn. See p. 42.

attempt to fasten on them, and prefaced the meditated intrusion by saying that he never liked walking alone. "I should have thought, sir," said Rogers, "that no one was so well satisfied with your company as yourself."

CONVINCED OF THAT.

One summer day, at a dinner party at Holland House, the guests—among whom were Sir Philip Francis, suspected of the authorship of the letters signed "Junius," and Rogers—were, previous to the dinner bell, sauntering in the open conservatory and terrace below; and on one of the promenades the Junius secret became the subject of conversation, and Lord H[olland] suggested to the bold banker [Rogers] that it would be an excellent opportunity to put the interrogatories flatly to the suspected man. But (says Jerdan) Francis happened to overhear the plot, and in a few minutes after, as Rogers was sidling towards him, he threw himself into an attitude of open defiance, and exclaimed, "By heaven, sir! if you dare to ask me any questions, regardless of where we are, I will fell you to the earth!" The little poet quickly enough shrank back appalled; but when playfully asked after dinner (in the absence of Francis) if he had discovered the author, replied, "I cannot say whether or not Francis is Junius, but he has quite convinced me he is Brutus!"

BETTER THAN NOTHING.

At an evening party many years since at Lady Jersey's, everyone (says Gronow) was praising the Duke of B——, who had just come in, and who had lately attained his majority. There was a perfect chorus of admiration, to this effect: "Everything is in his favour; he has good looks, considerable abilities, and a hundred thousand a-year." Rogers, who had been carefully examining the "young ruler," listened to these encomiums for some time in silence, and at last remarked, with an air of great exultation, and in his most venomous manner, "Thank God, he has got bad teeth!"

HIS STORY AND MY STORY.

At a large dinner-party at Jerdan's, one of the guests (says Planché) indulged in some wonderful accounts of his shooting. The number of birds he had killed, and the distance at which he had brought them down, were extraordinary. Hood[1] quietly remarked—

> " What he hit is history,
> What he missed is mystery." [2]

---

[1] The poet; *b.* 1798, *d.* 1845.　　　　[2] See Moore's *Diary.*

AN OLD PROVERB.

At the same house (says Planchè) on another occasion, when Power the actor was present, Hood was asked to propose his health. After enumerating the various talents that popular comedian possessed, he requested the company to observe that such a combination was a remarkable illustration of the old proverb, "It never rains but it *Powers*."

"A PENNYWORTH OF BREAD," ETC.

In his last illness, reduced as he was to a skeleton, Hood noticed a very large mustard poultice which Mrs Hood was making for him, and exclaimed, "O Mary! Mary!—that will be a great deal of mustard to a very little meat!"

DISAGREEABLE.

Shortly before his death, being visited by a clergyman whose features as well as language were more lugubrious than consoling, Hood looked up at him compassionately, and said, "My dear sir! I'm afraid your religion doesn't agree with you."

FILLED UP.

When the water broke into the Thames tunnel, during the progress of the work, Hood said to Planchè, "They've been labouring at that affair for a long time, and now the Thames has filled up their leisure." On Planchè repeating this to Charles Kemble, he said, "Well, Planchè, I can't see anything in that so—" laughable, he would have added ; but he began to laugh before he could finish the sentence.

"UNANEALED."

[Lord] Byron[1] (says Lord W. Lennox) was so jealous of Miss O'Neil's reputation interfering with that of his favourite Edmund Kean, that in order to guard himself against the risk of becoming a convert, he refused to go and see her act. Tom Moore endeavoured sometimes to persuade him into witnessing at least one of her performances, but his answer was, "No, I'm resolved to continue *un-O'Neiled*."

HOW TO TURN HIM.

Crabb Robinson records the following about Byron :—At Finch's, he repeated a retort uttered in his (Finch's) house by Lord Byron. Ward[2] had been a Whig, and became ministerial. "I wonder what could make me turn

---

1 Born 1788, died 1824.   2 Afterwards Lord Dudley. See pp. 27-31.

Whig again," said Ward. "That I can tell you," said Byron. "They have only to *re-Ward* you."

AN IMPROMPTU.

J. C. Young writes in his Diary :—The only instance I can recall in which [Coleridge[1]] said anything calculated to elicit a smile, during the two or three weeks I was with him, was when he, Wordsworth, and I were floating down the Rhine together in a boat we had hired conjointly. The day was remarkably sultry ; we had all three taken a considerable walk before our dinner, and what with fatigue, heat, and the exhaustion consequent on garrulity, Coleridge complained grievously of thirst. When he heard there was no house near at hand, and saw a leathern flask slung over my shoulder, he asked me what it contained. On my telling him it was Hochheimer, he shook his head, and swore he would as soon take vinegar. After a while, however, finding his thirst increasing, he exclaimed, "I find I must—conquering dislike—eat humble pie, and beg for a draught." He had no sooner rinsed his mouth with the obnoxious fluid, than he spat it out, and vented his disgust in the following impromptu :—

> "In Spain, that land of monks and apes,
> The thing called wine doth come from *grapes;*
> But, on the noble river Rhine,
> The thing called *gripes* doth come from wine."

"A SORRY *BRINGING-UP.*"

A writer in *Macmillan's Magazine* records a curiously-unfeeling remark made by Coleridge to a sea-sick schoolmaster, with whom he was making the trip to Margate in the ante-steamboat days by the old Margate Hoy. Coleridge watched his friend's efforts over the side, and at length said, "Why, Robinson, I didn't expect this from you; I thought you brought up nothing but young gentlemen !"

A BIBLICAL TOAST.

Allen (writes Moore) told me some anecdotes of Burns [the poet] :[2] his saying at some public dinner, during the feverish times of Jacobinism, on being asked for a toast, "I'll give you a Bible toast : the last verse of the last chapter of the last Book of Kings."[3]

---

[1] Samuel Taylor Coleridge, the poet; b. 1772, d. 1824.   [2] Born 1759, died 1796.

[3] 2 Kings xxv. 30: "And his allowance was a continual allowance given him of the king, a daily rate for every day, all the days of his life." The meaning of Mr Allen evidently was that Burns wished to see an end of kings ; but it is curious that this last verse should be susceptible of a totally different interpretation.—*Earl Russell.*

A HIGH TORY TOAST.

On another occasion (says Moore), having to give a toast before some high Tories, Burns said to the chairman, "You agree that lords should have their privileges?" "Yes, certainly." "Well, then, I'll give you the privileges of the Lords of the Creation."

ROAKE OR VARTY?

As an example of the playfulness of Leigh Hunt's[1] fancy, take (says Planchè) the following:—I was on my way to the theatre one morning with Charles Mathews, [sen.], in his carriage. We had not spoken for some minutes, when, as we were passing a wholesale stationer's at the west end of the Strand, Mathews, in his whimsical way, suddenly said to me, "Which would you rather be? Roake or Varty?"—such being the names painted over the shop windows. I laughed at the absurdity of the question, and declined hazarding an opinion, as I had not the advantage of knowing either of the persons mentioned. On my return home in the evening, I found Hunt at tea with my family, and told him the ridiculous question that had been put to me. "Now, do you know," he said, "I consider that anything but a ridiculous question. I should say it was an exceedingly serious one, and which might have very alarming, nay fatal, consequences under certain mental or physical conditions. You might have been impressed by the notion that it was absolutely necessary for you to come to some decision on the question, and so absorbed in its consideration that you could think of nothing else. All business, public or private, would be neglected. Perpetually pondering on one problem, which daily became more difficult of solution, would result in monomania. Your health undermined, your brain overwrought, in the last moments of fleeting existence, only a few seconds left you in which to make your selection, you might rashly utter 'Roake!' Then, suddenly repenting, gasp out 'Var,' and die before you could say 'ty.'"

A FILLIP.

Croly[2] (says W. H. Harrison) said very smart things, and with surprising readiness. I was at his table one day when one of the guests inquired the name of a pyramidal dish of barley. "Sugar," some one replied. "A pyramid à *Macedoine*." "For what use?" rejoined the other. "To give a *Philip* to the appetite," said Croly.

---

[1] The poet and prose writer; *b.* 1784, *d.* 1859.
[2] The Rev. George Croly, author of *Pride shall have a Fall*, &c.; *b.* 1780, *d.* 1860.

VERY MISLEADING.

Croly (says the same authority) once asked me if I had read a certain book. I said, "Yes, I had reviewed it." "What!" he exclaimed, "do you read the books you review?" "Yes," I replied, "as a rule, I do." "That's wrong," replied the Doctor; "it creates a prejudice."[1]

LUMINOUS v. VOLUMINOUS.

Rogers relates that during Hastings' trial, Sheridan,[2] having observed Gibbon among the audience, took occasion to mention "the luminous author of *The Decline and Fall.*" After he had finished, one of his friends reproached him with flattering Gibbon. "Why, what did I say of him?" asked Sheridan. "You called him the luminous author," &c. "Luminous! Oh, I meant—*vo*luminous."

OPERATIONS.

Rogers also tells us that during Sheridan's last illness, the medical attendants, apprehending that they would be obliged to perform an operation on him, asked him "if he had ever undergone one." "Never," replied Sheridan, "except when sitting for my picture, or having my hair cut."

A WITTY TOAST.

When the Duke of York was obliged to retreat before the French, Sheridan (says Rogers) gave as a toast—"The Duke of York and his brave followers."

NO JOKE.

Moore notes in his Diary:—Sheridan's answer to Lord Lauderdale excellent. On the latter saying he would repeat some good thing I had mentioned to him: "Pray don't, my dear Lauderdale; a joke in your mouth is no laughing matter."

A SPEAKING SILENCE.

Another note from Moore's Diary:—Adair told to-day of Sheridan's saying, "By the silence that prevails, I conclude Lauderdale has been cutting a joke."

NON SATIS.

Moore writes elsewhere:—[Charles] Sheridan told me that his father, being a good deal plagued by an old maiden relation of his always going out to walk with him, said one day that the weather was bad and rainy; to which

---

[1] This saying is attributed to Sydney Smith by Lady Holland.
[2] The dramatist and orator; *b.* 1751, *d.* 1816.

the old lady answered, that, on the contrary, it had cleared up. "Yes," said Sheridan, "it has cleared up enough for *one*, but not for *two*."

WHY NOT?

The Rev. Ozias Linley[1] records how some one expressed surprise that Sheridan, a proprietor of **Drury Lane, should have** been seen taking tea and **muffins in** a coffee-house while the **theatre** was in flames. "**And** why not?" asked Sheridan; "is it not allowable to toast a muffin at one's own fire?"

PROFITS *V.* WORTH.

"I'll stake the profits of my last book **on** that point," said "Monk" Lewis[2] at the close of a **warm** discussion. "No," answered Sheridan, "I can't afford so much, but I am **ready to bet the worth of it.**"

AN UNGRATEFUL FELLOW.

Cumberland,[3] jealous of Sheridan's reputation as a dramatist, said **he** went to hear the "**School for Scandal,**" but could not conceive what it was the world was laughing at. "Did he not laugh?" says Sheridan. "No." "Well, then, that was very ungrateful in Mr Cumberland, for *I* laughed at his last tragedy till I was ready to split my sides."

ALL TO NO PURPOSE.

Says Jerdan in his *Recollections :*—When Thomas Sheridan was **in a ner-vous** debilitated condition, **and** dining with his father at Peter Moore's, the servant, in passing by **the** fireplace, knocked **down** the plate-warmer, and made such a clatter as caused the invalid to start and **tremble.** Moore, provoked by the accident, rebuked **the man,** and added, "**I suppose** you have broken all the **plates?**" "No, sir," said the **servant,** "not one!" "Not one!" exclaimed Sheridan; "then, d—n it, you have **made all this noise for** nothing!"

DRIPPING.

Jerdan also says that when Coleridge's **tragedy of** "Remorse" was first produced, Sheridan had his jest upon the **cavern** scene, **where** the percolating of the water is described. "**Drip, drip,** drip," said the satirist; "nothing but dripping."

---

[1] In Archdeacon's Sinclair's *Old Times and Distant Places.*
[2] Author of *The Monk, The Bravo of Venice*, &c.; b. 1775, d. 1818.
[3] **Richard** Cumberland, author of *The West Indian*, and other plays; b. **1732, d. 1811.**

"TO LET—UNFURNISHED."

Lady Chatterton writes in her Diary:—We had a pleasant dinner at Captain Blackwood's [now Lord Dufferin]. His charming wife told me some amusing stories about her family [the Sheridans]. Her father, Tom Sheridan, reproached his father [the dramatist] one day for being a party man. "What do you get for it?" said he; "for my part, I think I shall put a ticket on my head, 'To let.'" "Do so, my dear boy," said his father, "only, add 'unfurnished.'"

THE "ANGRY SCHOOLBOY."

Although (says Mark Boyd) Mr Pitt rarely lost his temper, it is said that on one occasion he was seriously angry with Sheridan, whom he told to his face that he would be much better occupied at home correcting his plays. "Probably I should," said Richard Brinsley, "and the first I shall endeavour to correct will be the 'Angry Schoolboy.'"

A HAPPY RETORT.

I was much amused one evening (says Archdeacon Sinclair) with the graphic account [Dr Chalmers] gave me of what he saw and heard, when, as a young man, he stood among the mob in front of the hustings at Covent Garden, to hear Sheridan badgered as candidate for Westminster. "His readiness in reply," said the Doctor, "was marvellous." An ugly fellow, raised on the shoulders of the mob, addressed him: "Mr Sheridan, unless you mend your ways, I shall withdraw my countenance from you." "I am glad to hear it," said Sheridan, "for an uglier countenance I never saw." [1]

RATHER!

Sir Ralph Payne (says Sir Nathaniel Wraxall) was reported not always to treat his wife with kindness. Sheridan, calling on her one morning, found her in tears, which she placed, however, to the account of her monkey, who had expired only an hour or two before, and for whose loss she expressed deep regret. "Pray write me an epitaph for him," added she: "his name was *Ned*." Sheridan instantly penned these lines:—

> "Alas! poor Ned,
> My monkey, is dead!
> I had rather by half
> It had been Sir Ralph."

---

[1] This is also told of Charles Yorke and a member of the University of Cambridge.

HOW DID HE LOSE HER?

At the time when Bath was a fashionable place during the winter, it was frequented (says Raikes) by many gamblers, and there was constant high-play at the rooms. Amongst these was a Major Brereton, who had obtained great celebrity by his constant devotion to the passion. Sheridan, who had often seen him here, meeting him again after a long absence, said to him, "How are you, major? how have you been going on of late?" "I have had a great misfortune," replied the major, "since we met; I have lost Mrs Brereton." "Aye,' said the wit, "how did you lose her, at hazard or at quinze?"

HIS CHIEF SOURCE OF PRIDE.

George IV. (says Raikes) was not only a man of refined manners and classical taste, but he was endowed by nature with a very good understanding; still there is no doubt that for several years before his death, whether from early indulgence in luxury, or from a malady inherent in his family, his mind would occasionally wander, and many anecdotes have been current of the unfortunate impressions under which he laboured. After the glorious termination of the long Continental War in 1815, by the battle of Waterloo, it would not perhaps be unpardonable vanity in him to have thought that the English nation had mainly contributed to this great event; but he certainly at times in conversation arrogated to himself, personally, the glory of subduing Napoleon's power, and giving peace to the world. It was upon one of these assumptions being reported to the sarcastic Sheridan, that he archly remarked, "That is all well enough, but what he particularly piques himself upon is the last productive harvest."

AN EXCELLENT MEMORY.

Planché tells the following anecdote about Sheridan Knowles, the dramatist.[1] He says:—Walking one day with a brother dramatist, Mr Bayle Bernard, in Regent's Quadrant, Knowles was accosted by a gentleman in these terms:— "You're a pretty fellow, Knowles! After fixing your own day and hour to dine with us, you never make your appearance, and from that time to this not a word have we heard from you!" "I couldn't help it, upon my honour," replied Knowles; "and I've been so busy ever since, I haven't had a moment to write or call. How are you all at home?" "Oh, quite well, thank you; but come now, will you name another day, and keep your word?" "I will —sure I will." "Well, what day? Shall we say Thursday next?" "Thursday? Yes, by all means—Thursday be it." "At six?" "At six. I'll be there punctually. My love to 'em all." "Thank ye. Remember, now.

---

[1] Born 1784, died 1862.

Six, next Thursday." "All right, my dear fellow; I'll be with you." The friend departed; and Knowles, relinking his arm in that of Bayle Bernard, said, "Who's that chap?"—not having the least idea of the name or residence of the man he had promised to dine with on the following Thursday, or the interesting "family at home," to whom he had sent his love.

"MOST UNPARDONABLE."

Upon one occasion when Sheridan Knowles was acting in the country, he received (says Planché) an anxious letter from Mrs Knowles, informing him that the money—£200—which he had promised to send up on a certain day had never reached her. Knowles immediately wrote a furious letter to Sir Francis Freeling, at that time at the head of the Post Office, beginning, "Sir," and informing him that on such a day, at such an hour, he himself put a letter into the Post Office at such a place, containing the sum of £200 in bank-notes, and that it had never been delivered to Mrs Knowles; that it was a most unpardonable piece of negligence, if not worse, of the Post Office authorities, and that he demanded an immediate inquiry into the matter, the delivery of the money to his wife, and an apology for the anxiety and trouble its detention had caused them. By return of post he received a most courteous letter from Sir Francis, saying that he was perfectly correct in stating that on such a day and at such an hour he posted a letter at ——, containing bank-notes to the amount of £200; but that, unfortunately, he had omitted not only his signature inside, but the *address outside*, having actually sealed up the notes in an envelope containing the words, "I send you the money," and posted it without a direction! The consequence was that it was opened at the chief office in London, and detained till some inquiry was made about it.

STILL UNDECIDED.

One day, also in the country, Sheridan Knowles said to Abbot, with whom he had been acting there, "My dear fellow, I'm off to-morrow. Can I take any letters for you?" "You're very kind," answered Abbot; "but where are you going to?" "I haven't made up my mind."

HIS NAMESAKE.

On another occasion, seeing O. Smith, the popular melodramatic actor, on the opposite side of the Strand, Sheridan Knowles rushed across the road, seized him by the hand, and inquired eagerly after his health. Smith, who only knew him by sight, said, "I think, Mr Knowles, you are mistaken; I am O. Smith!" "My dear fellow," cried Knowles, "I beg you ten thousand pardons—I took you for your namesake, T. P. Cooke!"

PERHAPS!

Planché relates of Poole, the dramatist,[1] that, dining one day where the host became exceedingly excited and angry at not being able to find any stuffing in a roasted leg of pork, Poole quietly suggested, "Perhaps it is in *the other leg.*"

A CITY KNIGHT.

Dining in Poole's company, on another occasion, the conversation (says Planché) turned on the comedy of "The School for Scandal." A city knight who was present inquired, "Who wrote 'The School for Scandal'?" Poole, with the greatest *sang-froid*, and a glance of infinite contempt, replied, "Miss Chambers, the banker's daughter." "Ah, indeed," said Sir J——; "clever girl! *very* clever girl!" Almost immediately afterwards, Poole said, "Pray, Sir J——, are you a knight bachelor or a knight errant?" "Well, now—I really can't say—I don't think I ever was asked that question. I'll make it a point to inquire." It was as good as a play to watch Poole's countenance, but I confess (says Planché) his audacity made me shiver.

AN ANTI-CLIMAX.

At the dinner which followed a state procession of Her Majesty in London (1837), one of the guests (says Barham), moved by enthusiasm and loyalty, to say nothing of champagne, rose to propose the health of the Queen. "We have heard to-day," he commenced, "many hurrahs"— "Yes," interrupted Poole, "and we have seen to-day many *hussars!*"

PRIEST AND CLERKS.

The following capital pun has been very generally attributed to James Smith: —An actor named Priest was playing at one of the principal theatres. Some one remarked at the Garrick Club that there were a great many men in the pit. "Probably clerks who have taken Priest's orders." The pun (says Mr Hayward) is perfect; but the real proprietor is Mr Poole, one of the best punsters as well as one of the cleverest comic writers of the day.

ON HIMSELF.

Dear, good-tempered, clever, generous, eccentric, Sam Beazley! He died (writes Planché) in Tonbridge Castle, where he resided for the few last years

---

[1] Best known, perhaps, as the author of a travestie of *Hamlet.*

of his life, having a professional appointment in connection with the South-Eastern Railway.[1] Many years before, he wrote his own epitaph :

> " Here lies Samuel Beazley,
>   Who lived hard, and died easily."

HIS ULTIMATUM.

Alas ! (continues Planché) the latter declaration was not prophetic. Beazley suffered considerably a short time before his decease,[2] and his usual spirits occasionally forsaking him, he one day wrote so melancholy a letter, that the friend to whom it was addressed, observed, in his reply, that it was " Like the first chapter of Jeremiah." " You are mistaken, my dear fellow," retorted the wit; " it is the last chapter of Samuel."

GLEAMS OF WIT.

Beazley's pleasant sayings would fill a volume. The wit was not, perhaps, particularly pungent, but it was always playful. Building a staircase for Sir Henry Meux, he called it making a new " Gradus ad Parnassum," because it was steps for the *muses*. And when the question arose how the title of Herold's charming opera, " Le Prè aux Clercs," should be rendered into English, he quietly suggested " Parson's Green."

WITH ALL HIS HEART.

Colman[3] (says Macready) was put into a state of extreme perturbation once on the occasion of a very indifferent player, who was the hero of a private theatre in the Tottenham Court Road, appearing as Mortimer at the Haymarket Theatre. On tenterhooks during the whole play, when in the last scene Falkner, the representative of Mortimer, exclaimed in his delirium, " Where is my honour now ? " Colman could not restrain himself, but called out, " I wish your honour was in Tottenham Court Road again with all my heart ! "

UNKIND.

Jerdan relates that as George Colman was walking up the Haymarket one day, with his handkerchief hanging out of his pocket, a good-natured fellow gave him the hint, " You'll lose your handkerchief, sir." " Not," retorted George, " if you'll pass on."

---

[1] He was architect as well as playwright. [2] He died in 1851.
[3] The dramatist; b. 1762, d. 1836.

I

KEEP IT!

The bitter dispute between Colman and his brother-in-law and partner was wont (says the same authority) to explode in violent altercations. In one of these Mr Morris accused him of "taking away his name;" and the following dialogue ensued:—*C.* "How did I take away your name?" *M.* "By villifying me with other odious epithets." *C.* "What?" *M.* "You called me a scoundrel, sir." *C.*, with a forced grin, "Keep your name!"

WHY, INDEED?

Planché says of Richard Peake, the dramatist,[1] that his humour consisted in a grotesque combination of ideas. As, for example:—Calling with him one summer day on a mutual friend, the fireplace in the drawing-room was found to be ornamented with a mass of long slips of white paper falling over the bright bars of the stove. Peake's first question was—" What do you keep your maccaroni in the grate for?"

A USEFUL NIGGER.

At a party at Beazley's, the latter's black servant entered to make up the fire. Peake whispered to Planché—"Beazley's nigger has been scratching his head, and got a scuttle of coals out."

DANGEROUS EXPOSURE!

According to Moore, Kenny[2] said that Anthony Pasquin (who was a very dirty fellow) " died of a cold caught by washing his face."

WHAT, NEVER?

There was a good story told of Frank Talfourd, a worthy son of a most worthy sire,[3] which proves his readiness at repartee. One day in winter, snow on the ground, thermometer below freezing point, young Talfourd was met by a friend in Russell Square, who thus accosted him : " Why, I see you never wear (*were*) a great-coat?" " I never *was*," he quaintly replied.

---

[1] Author of *Amateurs and Action, A Hundred Pound Note*, and other farces and dramas. He was also for a long time treasurer of the Lyceum Theatre. " He was not," says Planché, "a wit in the true sense of the term, but there was some good fun in a few of his farces."

[2] The dramatist; *d.* 1849.

[3] His father was Sergeant Talfourd, the author of " Ion," and the biographer of Lamb. Frank himself was a writer of light pieces for the stage ; some of his burlesques were admirable.

AN ANTICIPATION FULFILLED.

The best anecdote of Dr Johnson, not to be found in Boswell,[1] was related to me (says Archdeacon Sinclair) by Dr Chalmers. "Dr Johnson," he said, "on his arrival at St Andrews, was taken by the College authorities to see the ruins. He afterwards dined with them in the College Hall; but he had not got over his indignation at the vandalism which had wantonly destroyed some of the oldest and finest remains of ecclesiastical architecture in Scotland. He was so rude and overbearing that at last the conversation dropped. After a pause, one of the younger and more adventurous professors addressed him: 'Dr Johnson, I hope that you have not been *disappointed* in your visit to Scotland?' 'Sir,' replied the Doctor, 'I came here to see savage men and savage manners, and I have not been disappointed.'"

BY DEGREES.

J. C. Young says:—When Dr Johnson, in his tour to the Hebrides, visited St Andrews, he was shown over the old library. The then librarian had been exhibiting some of his rare literary treasures. "Have you got," asked Johnson, "such and such a book?" "No, sir, we have not. It is a very expensive book, and, I fear, beyond the means at our command." "Oh?" said he, "you'll get it by degrees"—alluding to the habit which then prevailed of selling degrees.

ONLY THAT, AND NOTHING MORE!

On one occasion (says Mark Boyd) Lord Stowell, then William Scott, of University College, Oxford, entertained [Dr] Johnson [to dinner]. [After dinner], the party adjourned to the College Garden, and Johnson observed Scott pitching snails, which had come out after rain on the walks, into his neighbour's garden. "Hallo, Scott!" exclaimed Johnson; "do unto thy neighbour as you would be done by." "But, my dear Doctor," said Scott, "he is a Dissenter." "A Dissenter!" ejaculated Johnson; "then pitch away."

HE MIGHT HAVE BEEN WORSE!

About the time of the trial of O'Quigley, who was hanged at Maidstone for treason, in 1798, some articles appeared in the *Morning Chronicle*, apparently reflecting on Fox. Dr Parr[2] (says Jerdan) read them, and was much displeased. He attributed them to Macintosh (not then Sir James), because they contained some literary criticism or remark which Parr thought he had communicated

[1] Boswell's "Life" is so familiar to every one, that it is unnecessary to quote from it.
[2] The famous scholar; *b.* 1747, *d.* 1825.

to Macintosh exclusively. In point of fact he was wrong, as it turned out in the sequel that Macintosh had nothing to do with them; but while in the state of wrath which his belief that Macintosh was the author occasioned, he (Dr Parr) and Macintosh dined together at the table of Sir William Milner, in Manchester Street, Manchester Square. In the course of conversation after dinner, Macintosh observed that "O'Quigley was one of the greatest villains that ever was hanged." Dr Parr had been watching for an opening, and immediately said, "No, Jemmy! bad as he was, he might have been a great deal worse. He was an Irishman; he might have been a Scotchman! He was a priest; he might have been a lawyer! He stuck to his principles—(giving a violent rap on the table)—he might have betrayed them!"

HE DOESN'T MEAN IT!

Procter's biography of Charles Lamb[1] is a mine of authentic stories about that delightful humorist, and we shall be indebted to it for the next few anecdotes. For example:—One evening Coleridge had consumed the whole time in talking of some "regenerated" orthodoxy. Leigh Hunt, who was one of the listeners, on leaving the house, expressed his surprise at the prodigality and intensity of Coleridge's religious expressions. Lamb tranquillized him by "Ne-ne-never mind what Coleridge says; he's full of fun."

HIS DAILY WORK.

"Charles," said Coleridge to Lamb, "I think you have heard me preach?" "I n-n-never heard you do anything else," replied Lamb.

A PREFERENCE.

A Mrs K——, when one day conversing with Charles Lamb, after expressing her love for her young children, added tenderly, "And how do *you* like babies, Mr Lamb?" His answer, immediate, almost precipitate, was, "Boi-boi-boiled, ma'am."

A COOL CUSTOMER.

The second son of George the Second, it was said, had a very cold and ungenial manner. Lamb stammered out in his defence that "This was very natural in the Duke of Cu-Cum-ber-land."

---

[1] Born 1775, died 1834.

NO DOUBT!

Procter writes of Lamb:—I once said something in his presence, which I thought possessed smartness. He commended me with a stammer: "Very well, my dear boy, very well; Ben (taking a pinch of snuff) Ben Jonson has said worse things than that—and—and—b-b-better."[1]

QUITE FULL.

Once, whilst Lamb was waiting in the Highgate stage, a woman came to the door and inquired in a stern voice, "Are you quite full inside?" "Yes, ma'am," said Charles, in meek reply, "quite; that plateful of Mrs Gillman's pudding has quite filled us."

IN A PARLOUR.

What (says Procter) do you think of Charles Lamb (it was after supper) saying to his company, among whom was Wordsworth and his train—"We sit ve-ve-ve-e-ery silent here. Like a company in a parlour—all silent and all damned."

A REMINISCENCE.

Hood tempting Lamb to dine with him, said, "We have a hare." "And many friends?" inquired Lamb.[2]

DRAWING THE LINE.

It being suggested to Lamb that he would not sit down to a meal with the Italian witnesses at the Queen's trial, Lamb rejected the imputation, asserting that he would sit with anything, except a hen or a tailor.

LEGAL.

A person sending an unnecessarily large sum with a lawyer's brief, Lamb said it was "a fee simple."

A TRADE-MARK.

On being asked by a schoolmistress for some sign indicative of her calling, Lamb recommended "The Murder of the Innocents."

---

[1] "This," says Procter, "is given in Mr Thomas Moore's Autobiography. I suppose I must have repeated it to him, and he forgot the precise words."

[2] The allusion is to a well-known fable by the poet Gay. One of the famous family to which J. C. Hare belonged was said to be so popular that he was called the Hare with many friends.

A NOBLE RESOLVE.

A fine sonnet of Lamb's ("The Gipsy's Malison") being refused publication, he exclaimed, "Hang the age! I'll write for Antiquity."

RELATIONS.

On two Prussians of the same name being accused of the same crime, it was remarked as curious that they were not in any way related to each other. "A mistake," said Lamb, "they are cozens german."

A THREAT.

Of a man too prodigal of lampoons and verbal jokes, Lamb said, threateningly. "I'll Lamb-pun him."

A HAPPY FATHER.

Crabb Robinson[1] writes in his Diary :—I called on the Lambs. . . . Lamb said, "If you will quote any of my jokes, quote this, which is really a good one. Hume and his wife and several of their children were with me. Hume repeated the old saying, "One fool makes many." "Ay, Mr Hume," said I. pointing to the company, "you have a fine family."

PAYNE-FULL.

Crabb Robinson writes again :—Took tea with Lamb. Hessey gave an account of De Quincey's description of his own bodily sufferings. "He should have employed as his publishers," said Lamb, "Pain and Fuss" (Payne and Foss).

RETICUL-OUS.

Crabb Robinson records:—Punsters being abused, and the old joke repeated that he who puns will pick a pocket, some one said, "Punsters themselves have no pockets." "No," said Lamb, "they carry only a ridicule."

A WITTY CITATION.

Crabb Robinson writes elsewhere :—Went with Lamb to Richman's . . . Richman produced one of Chatterton's forgeries. In one manuscript there were seventeen different kinds of e's. "Oh," said Lamb, "that must have been written by one of the

'Mob of gentlemen who write with *ease.*'"

---

[1] A great friend of Lamb's, and a constant visitor at his house.

ANOTHER.

Called on Charles Lamb. I was speaking (says Crabb Robinson) of my first brief, when he asked, "Did you not exclaim—
    'Thou great first cause, least understood?'"[1]

A VENTURE.

Moore records in his Diary:—Kenny to-day mentioned Charles Lamb's being once bored by a lady praising to him "such a charming man!" etc., etc., ending with "I know him, bless him !" on which Lamb said, "Well, I don't, but d—n him, at a hazard."

A COMPENSATION.

Charles Lamb (says Moore) was sitting next some chattering woman at dinner. Observing he didn't attend to her, "You don't seem," said the lady, "to be at all the better for what I have been saying to you." "No, ma'am," he answered, "but this gentleman at the other side of me must, for it all came in at one ear and went out at the other."

FOR THEM !

Leigh Hunt says, that to a person abusing Voltaire, and indiscreetly opposing his character to that of Jesus Christ, Lamb said admirably (though he by no means overrated Voltaire, nor wanted reverence in the other quarter), that "Voltaire was a very good Jesus Christ—for the French."

A VALUABLE HOLDING.

Lamb (writes Leigh Hunt) said once to a brother whist-player [Martin Burney], whose hand was more clever than clean, and who had enough in him to afford the joke, "M., if dirt were trumps, what hands you would hold !"

"WHEN GREEK," ETC.

L'Estrange narrates that Elliston, the actor, a self-educated man, was playing cribbage one evening with Lamb, and on drawing out his first card, exclaimed, "When Greek meets Greek, then comes the tug of war." "Yes," replied Lamb, "and when you meet Greek, you don't understand it."

---

[1] This story is also told by Moore, who, however, misquotes the line from Milton as "Thou first *best* cause," etc.

TRULY DISMAL.

Barry Cornwall told J. T. Fields that when he and Charles Lamb were once making up a dinner-party together, Charles asked him not to invite a certain lugubrious friend of theirs, "Because," said Lamb, "he would cast a damper even over a funeral."

A WALK HOME.

At a friend's house (says Frederick Locker) Charles Lamb was presented with a cheese; it was a very ripe, not to say a very lively, cheese, and, as Lamb was leaving, his friend offered him a piece of paper in which to wrap it, so that he might convey it more conveniently. "Thank you," said Charles, "but would not several yards of twine be better, and then, you know, I could *lead* it home?"

A QUAINT LITTLE BOY.

Some amusing stories of Macaulay's[1] childhood are related in the biography by Mr G. O. Trevelyan. For example, we learn that, on one occasion, his father took the boy on a visit to Lady Waldegrave at Strawberry Hill. After some time had been spent among the wonders of the Oxford collection, a servant who was waiting upon the company in the great gallery spilt some hot coffee over his legs. The hostess was all kindness and compassion, and when, after a while, she asked how he was feeling, the little fellow looked up in her face, and replied: "Thank you, madam, the agony is abated."

SENTENTIOUS, TRULY!

Mr Trevelyan tells us that Mrs Macaulay once explained to her son that he must learn to study without the solace of bread and butter; to which he replied: "Yes, mamma, industry shall be my bread, and attention my butter."

RIGHTEOUS INDIGNATION.

At one period of his boyhood (says the same authority) Macaulay's fancy was much exercised with the threats and terrors of the law. He had a little plot of ground at the back of the house, marked out as his own by a row of oyster-shells which a maid one day threw away as rubbish. He went straight to the drawing-room, where his mother was entertaining some visitors, walked into the circle, and said very solemnly: "Cursed be Sally: for it is written, Cursed is he that removeth his neighbour's land-mark.'"

---

[1] Born 1800, died 1859.

THE PERSON WHO SHAVED HIM.

Macaulay, it appears, was unhandy to a degree quite unexampled in the experience of all who knew him. After he had sailed for India (says his biographer), there were found in his chambers between fifty and sixty strops, hacked into strips and splinters, and razors without beginning or end. About the same period he hurt his hand, and was reduced to send for a barber. After the operation, he asked what was to pay. "Oh, sir," said the man, "whatever you usually give the person who shaves you." "In that case," said Macaulay, "I should give you a great gash on each cheek."

NOT BETTY MARTIN!

Lady Chatterton says that Rogers happened to ask Macaulay what he thought of Miss Harriet Martineau's wonderful cures by mesmerism. He said, with one of his rare smiles, "Oh, it's all my eye, and Hetty Martineau!"

"MINE OYSTER."

J. T. Fields narrates the following anecdote of Thackeray[1]:—In London he had been very curious in his inquiries about American oysters, as marvellous stories, which he did not believe, had been told him of their great size. We apologised [at dinner]—although we had taken care that the largest specimens to be procured should startle his unwonted vision when he came to the table —for what we called the extreme *smallness* of the oysters, promising that we would do better next time. Six bloated Falstaffian bivalves lay before him in their shells. I noticed that he gazed at them anxiously with fork upraised; then he whispered to me, with a look of anguish, "How shall I do it?" I described to him the simple process by which the freeborn citizens of America were accustomed to accomplish such a task. He seemed satisfied that the thing was feasible, selected the smallest one of the half-dozen (rejecting a large one "because" he said, "it resembled the High Priest's servant's ear that Peter cut off"), and then bowed his head as if he were saying grace. All eyes were upon him to watch the effect of a new sensation in the person of a great British author. Opening his mouth very wide, he struggled for a moment, and then all was over. I shall never forget the comic look of despair he cast upon the other five over-occupied shells. I broke the perfect stillness by asking him how he felt. "Profoundly grateful," he gasped, "and as if I had swallowed a little baby."

---

[1] Born 1811, died 1863.

MUTUAL FRIENDS.

Hicks[1] and Thackeray (says J. C. Young), walking together, stopped opposite a doorway, over which was inscribed in gold letters these words: "Mutual Loan Office." They both seemed equally puzzled. "What on earth can that mean?" asked Hicks. "I don't know," answered Thackeray; "unless it mean, that two men who have nothing, agree to lend it to each other."

"NONE BUT HIMSELF," ETC.

Hicks (says the same authority) was talking to Thackeray of a certain gentleman's strange addiction to beer. "It's a great pity," said Hicks, "that he does not keep a check-rein on himself, for he is a marvellous fellow otherwise—I mean, for talent. I hardly know his equal." "No," retorted Thackeray, "he is a remarkable man. Take him for half-and-half, we ne'er shall look upon his like again."

A GREAT MAN.

Mrs Kemble told J. C. Young of an excellent remark made to her by Washington Irving.[2] The merits of a certain American diplomatist being on the *tapis*, he said, in allusion to his pomposity, "Ah, he is a great man; and, in his own estimation, a very great man—a man of great weight. When he goes to the West, the East tips up."

A SNOW-FALL.

According to W. H. Harrison, Joseph Snow, at one time Clerk to the Literary Fund and afterwards editor of a Welsh newspaper, had one answer to any witticism perpetrated on his name: "He could not see the drift of it."

AMONG THE FLATS.

Mark Boyd writes:—Mr MacCulloch, the eminent political economist,[3] in dining with us a few days after [an aeronautical friend had made an ascent], was most anxious to learn where he had descended on this occasion. The answer was, "Among the flats of Essex." "A most appropriate locality," exclaimed my distinguished countryman, "and one which shows how true it is that 'birds of a feather flock together.'"

---

[1] A barrister, of whom some anecdotes will be found recorded on pp. 85, 86.
[2] The American essayist; b. 1783, d. 1859.
[3] John Ramsay MacCulloch; b. 1789, d. 1864.

A SEQUITUR.

Moore writes in his Diary :—In talking of Frere,[1] Smith told a *mot* of his I have not heard before. Madame de —— having said, in her intense style, "I should like to be married in *English*, in a language in which vows are so faithfully kept." Some one asked Frere, "What language, I wonder, was *she* married in ?" "*Broken* English, I suppose," answered Frere.

TOO LATE FOR HIM.

Barham's reply to Mr Hodson, his tutor, afterwards Principal of Brase. nose, will convey some notion of the hours he was wont to keep at college. This gentleman sent for him on one occasion to demand an explanation of his continued absence from morning chapel. "The fact is, sir," urged his pupil, "you are too late for me." "Too late !" repeated the tutor, in aston- ishment. "Yes, sir—too late. I cannot sit up till seven o'clock in the morning. I am a man of regular habits, and unless I get to bed by four or five at the latest, I am fit for nothing next day." Barham tells this story himself.[2]

HIS BIRTHRIGHT.

Jerdan, the editor of the *Literary Gazette*, was very ready in repartee. His friend W. H. Harrison writes :—I was dining once with him and Crofton Croker, shortly after the death of the Earl of Moira, when Croker remarked that the Earl, with all his talents and accomplishments, would "leave no wake upon the stream of time." "Nonsense, Crofty," said Jerdan, "every dead Irishman has a wake !"

THE ODD TRICK.

Jerdan told Lord William Lennox that when Thomas Campbell published his domestic tale of "Theodric," the conversation turned upon it. "I think," said a wag, "it is selling prodigiously, and that the author will gain a large sum on *the odd trick* (Theodric), without counting the honours." I rather fancy (says Lord William) the wag referred to was Jerdan himself.

THE SECOND JAMES.

The two following (says Mr Hayward) are among the best of James Smith's[3] good things:—A gentleman with the same Christian and surname took lodgings

---

[1] John Hookham Frere, diplomatist and author ; *b.* 1769, *d.* 1846.

[2] See his *Life* by his son. Barham is still best known by his pseudonym of Thomas Ingoldsby, the fictitious author of the "Ingoldsby Legends."

[3] One of the authors of *Rejected Addresses*, and a facile epigrammatist; *b.* 1775, *d.* 1839.

in the same house. The consequence was eternal confusion of calls and letters. Indeed, the postman had no alternative but to share the letters equally between the two. "This is intolerable, sir," said our friend, "and you must quit." "Why am I to quit more than you?" "Because you are James the Second, and must *abdicate.*"

THE OTHER EXTREME.

Mr Bentley proposed to establish a periodical publication, to be called "The Wits' Miscellany." Smith objected that the title promised too much. Shortly afterwards the publisher came to tell him that he had profited by the hint, and resolved on calling it "Bentley's Miscellany." "Isn't that going a little too far the other way?" was the remark.[1]

STRICTLY PROPER.

In a letter, dated May 21, 1836, James Smith wrote to a lady friend:— "Our dinner party yesterday at H——'s chambers in the Temple was very lively. An opportunity for a *bon mot* occurred, which I had not sufficient virtue to resist. Lord L—— mentioned that an old lady, an acquaintance of his, kept her books in detached bookcases—the male authors in one, and the female in another. I said, 'I suppose her reason was, she did not wish to add to her library.'" The joke (says Mr Hayward) was made by Lord L——; the story, an invented pleasantry, illustrative of Madame Genlis' prudery, having been related by another of the company.

THE WORLD AND THE POLES.

Those (says Lord William Lennox) who liked a witty remark, or a pungent epigram, would join the table at which James Smith sat, and any commonplace remark of the day was immediately committed by him into verse. I remember once asking him if he was going to the ball at the Mansion House, got up in aid of the unfortunate Polish refugees. "No," said he. Then, calling for a sheet of paper and a pencil, he wrote the following lines:—

> "Aloft, in rotatory motions hurled,
> The poles are called on to support the world.
> In these our days a different law controls:
> The world is called on to support the Poles."

[1] This is also attributed to Douglas Jerrold.

MANTON AND EGG.

When asked (says the same authority) " Whose are the best guns, Manton's or Egg's?" Smith replied, " Egg's—for poaching," and in a second produced the following epigram :—

> " Two of a trade can ne'er agree,
>   Each worries each, if able ;
> In Manton and in Egg we see
>   This proverb proved no fable.

> " Each famed for guns, whose loud report
>   Confirms the fact I'm broaching ;
> Manton's the best for lawful sport,
>   But Egg's the best for poaching."

"THE CAUSE."

John Heneage Jesse (writes J. C. Young in his Diary) gave me a curious instance of [James Smith's] ready wit. When he was preparing for the press his " Gleanings in Natural History," James Smith one day unexpectedly burst in upon him. The moment he saw him, he said, " My dear Smith, you have come to me in the nick of time as my good genius, to extricate me from a difficulty. You must know that to each of my chapters I have put an appropriate heading : I mean by that, that each chapter has prefixed to it a quotation from some well-known author, suited to the subject treated of, with one exception. I have been cudgelling my brains for a motto for my chapter on ' Crows and Rooks,' and cannot think of one. Can you?" " Certainly," he said, with felicitous promptitude, " here is one from Shakspeare for you !—

> ' The cause (caws), my soul, the cause (caws).'"

RIVERS AND THEIR GENDERS.

Young says elsewhere :—After dinner [at Jesse's, with Smith as a companion], " By the bye," said I, " if I recollect rightly, in Latin the names of rivers are generally masculine." " I forget," said Smith, " but that can't be the invariable rule in English, for the two great American rivers must be feminine—Miss-souri and Miss-sisippi."[1]

---

[1] Smith afterwards versified this joke as follows:—

> " In England rivers all are males—
>   For instance, Father Thames;
> Whoever in Columbia sails
>   Finds them ma'amselles or dames.
> Yes, there the softer sex presides,
>   Aquatic, I assure ye;
> For Mrs Sippy rolls her tides
>   Responsive to Miss Souri."

INCONCEIVABLE.

The late Mr Nightingale (says J. C. Young) was telling Horace Smith[1] of his having given a late Royal Duke an account of an accident he had met with when he had been run away with, and of the Duke's exclaiming aloud to himself, when he heard he had jumped out of the carriage, "Fool! fool!" "Now," said the narrator to his auditor, "it's all very well for him to call me a fool; but I can't conceive why he should. Can you?" "No," replied the wag, as if reflecting, "No, I can't; because he could not suppose you ignorant of the fact."

A NIGGER RISING.

The Earl of Albemarle records the following:—At a dinner of the Duke of St Albans', some one was predicting that negro emancipation would be followed by a general massacre of the white population. At this moment a sudden gust of wind filled the room with soot. "Your worst fears are verified," said Horace [Smith], turning to the speaker; "behold an insurrection of the blacks!"

INEVITABLE.

Blanchard Jerrold's memoir of his father is full of admirable anecdotes of the great wit. For instance:—Douglas Jerrold[2] regarded the adapter as somebody who managed to cozen a reputation for originality from the foreigner. Discussing one day with Mr Planchè this vexed question, this gentleman insisted upon claiming some of his characters as strictly original creations. "Do you remember my Baroness in *Ask no Questions?*" said Mr Planchè. "Yes, indeed, I don't think I ever saw a piece of yours without being struck by your barrenness," was the retort. This closed the discussion with a hearty laugh.

A RETROGRADE MOVEMENT.

Off the Swan at Battersea some mismanagement of a boat occurred, during which (his son tells us) Jerrold fell backwards into the water. He was taken into the boat with much difficulty, conveyed ashore, and put to bed in the Swan Inn. On the following day he repeated a conversation he had had with the Swan chambermaid. *Jerrold:* "I suppose these accidents happen frequently off here." *Servant:* "O yes, sir, frequently; but it's not the season yet." *Jerrold:* "Ah! I suppose it's all owing to a backward spring!"

---

[1] Brother of James Smith, and one of the authors of *Rejected Addresses.*
[2] Humorist and dramatist; b. 1803, d. 1857.

A BAD LOCALITY.

On a certain day Jerrold met Mr Alfred Bunn[1] in Jermyn Street. "What!" said Mr Bunn, "I suppose you're strolling about, picking up character." "Well, not exactly," was the reply, "though there's plenty lost here, I'm told."

DECIDEDLY WOODEN.

When Morris had the Haymarket Theatre, Jerrold, on a certain occasion, had occasion to find fault with the strength, or rather the want of strength, of the company. Morris expostulated, and said, "Why, there's V——; he was bred on these boards!" *Reply:* "He looks as though he had been cut out of them."

WHY NOT?

"Do you know," said a friend to Jerrold, "that Jones has left the stage, and turned wine-merchant?" *Reply:* "O yes; and I am told that his wine off the stage is better than his whine on it."

NO DOUBT ABOUT IT.

Douglas Jerrold (says his son) was always nervous during the first representation of his pieces. On one of these first nights a very successful transplanter from the French rallied the nervous dramatist. "I," said the soothing gentleman, "I never feel nervous on the first night of my pieces." *Reply:* 'Ah! my boy, *you* are always certain of success. Your pieces have always been tried before."

FAMILY FEELING.

Returning to London on one occasion, Jerrold was recognised in the railway carriage by a gentleman who wished—seeing the enthusiasm with which Jerrold pointed to the beauties of the landscape—to ingratiate himself by the assumption of an equal enthusiasm. But the counterfeit was plain and revolting. "I take a book," said the stranger, "retire into some unfrequented field, gaze on God's heaven, then study. If there are animals in the field so much the better; the cow approaches, and looks down at me, and I look up at her." "With a filial smile?" asked the stranger's annoyed listener.

NOT TOO OLD.

Jerrold orders a bottle of old port. "Not *elder* port," he adds.

---

[1] The well-known impresario.

THE BETTER OF THE TWO.

A friend—let us say Barlow—was describing to Jerrold the story of his courtship and marriage—how his wife had been brought up in a convent, and was on the point of taking the veil when his **presence** burst upon her en-**raptured** sight. [Jerrold] listened to the end of the story, and by way of **comment said,** "Ah! she evidently thought Barlow better than nun."

A LIBERAL SUBSCRIPTION.

A friend of Jerrold's drops into the club, and walks across the smoking-**room** to Douglas Jerrold's chair. The friend wants to enlist Mr Jerrold's sympathies in behalf of a mutual acquaintance who **is** in want of a **round** sum **of money.** But this **mutual** friend has already sent his hat about **among** his literary brethren **on more than one occasion.** Mr ——'s hat was becoming an institution, **and friends** were grieved at the **indelicacy of the proceeding.** On the occasion to **which we** now refer, the **bearer of the hat was received by** Jerrold **with** evident dissatisfaction. "**Well,**" said Douglas Jerrold, "how much does —— **want this time?**" "**Why, just a** four and two noughts will, I think, **put him straight,**" the **bearer of the hat** replied. *Jerrold:* "Well, put **me down for one of the** noughts."

A PIOUS ASPIRATION.

An old gentleman, whom (says Blanchard Jerrold) I will call Prosy Very, was in the habit of meeting Jerrold and pouring long pointless stories into his patient ears. On one occasion Prosy related a long limp account of **a** stupid practical joke, concluding with the information that the effect of the **joke was so** potent, "he really thought **he** would have died with laughter." *Jerrold:* "I wish to heaven you had."

THAT'S ALL.

A stormy discussion takes place, during which a gentleman rises **to settle** the matter in dispute. Waving his hands majestically over the excited dis-putants, he begins: "Gentlemen, all I want is common sense—." "Exactly," Douglas Jerrold interrupts ; "that is what you *do* **want.**" The discussion is **lost in** a burst of laughter.

A HITCH SOMEWHERE.

The **talk at** a **club lightly passes** to the writings of a certain Scot. **A mem-**ber holds that the Scot's name should be handed down to a grateful posterity. *Douglas Jerrold:* "I **quite agree** with you **that he** should have an **itch in the** Temple of Fame."

A TRUE FRIEND.

Brown drops in. Brown is said by all his friends to be the toady of Jones. The appearance of **Jones in** a room is the proof that Brown is in the passage. When Jones has the influenza, Brown dutifully catches a cold in the head. Douglas Jerrold to Brown : "Have you heard the rumour that's flying about town ?" "No." "Well, they say Jones pays the dog-tax for you."

A VERY DIFFERENT MATTER.

Douglas Jerrold is seriously disappointed with a certain book written by one of his friends, and has expressed his disappointment. *Friend :* "I hear you said —— was the worst book I ever wrote." *Jerrold :* "No, I didn't. I said it was the worst book anybody ever wrote."

SHEEPISH.

A supper of sheep's heads is proposed, and presently served. One gentleman present is particularly enthusiastic on the excellence of the dish, and, as he throws down his knife and fork, exclaims, "Well, sheep's head for ever, say I !" *Jerrold :* "There's egotism !"

QUERY?

When some member of the Museum Club, hearing an air mentioned, exclaimed, "That always carries me away when I hear it." "Can nobody whistle it ?" asked Douglas Jerrold.

AN UNFORTUNATE OCCUR-ENCE.

Jerrold asking once about the talent of a young painter, his companion declared that the youth was mediocre. "Oh !" was the reply ; "the very worst ochre an artist can set to work with."

A MORAL SAYING.

As Jerrold was walking to the club with a friend from the theatre, some intoxicated young gentlemen reeled up to the dramatist and said, "Can you tell us the way to the Judge and Jury ?" "Keep on as you are, young gentlemen," was the reply ; "you're sure to overtake them."

A PLEASURE TO COME.

The author of an epic poem [J. A. Heraud] asked Jerrold (says the same authority) if he had ever seen his "Descent into Hell." "No," replied Jerrold, with a chuckle of delight; "but I should like to."

K

"SUCH KINDNESS!"

Quick and free (says Charles Mackay) from the slightest taint of ill-nature was Jerrold's remark about the affectionate letters written from America by an actor who had left his wife in London without money, and who had never sent her any. "What kindness!" he said aloud, with strong emphasis, when one of the letters was read aloud in the greenroom of the Haymarket. "Kindness!" ejaculated one of the actresses, indignantly, "when he never sends the poor woman a penny." "Yes," said Jerrold, "unremitting kindness!"

NONE CAME DOWN.

Of a different character (adds Mackay) was Jerrold's jest when one of the members of the "Hooks and Eyes" was expatiating on the fact that he had dined three times at the Duke of Devonshire's, and that on neither occasion had there been any fish at table. "I cannot account for it," he added. "I can," said Jerrold; "they ate it all upstairs."

ONE, BUT NOT THE OTHER.

Jerrold (says Mackay) was once asked by a literary acquaintance whether he had the courage to lend him a guinea. "Oh yes," he replied, "I've got the courage, but I haven't got the guinea."

NOBODY TO BLAME.

Mrs Cowden Clarke relates that it was while walking home together from Serle's house, one bleak night of English spring, that, in crossing West-minster Bridge, with an east wind blowing keenly through every fold of clothing we wore, Jerrold said to us, "I blame nobody, but they call this May!"

"VERY LIKE A WHALE."

Says the same authority:—When an acquaintance came up to him and said, "Why, Jerrold, I hear you said my nose was like the ace of clubs!" Jerrold returned, "No I didn't; but now I look at it, I see it is very like."

READY.

Writes J. C. Young:—My friend the late Sam Phillips, the author of *Essays from the Times*, one day met Douglas Jerrold, and told him he had seen, the day before, Payne Collier,[1] looking wonderfully young and well—quite an evergreen. "Ah," said Jerrold, "he may be evergreen, but he's never red (read)." On my repeating this to Hicks, he smiled and said, "Now that's what I call 'ready wit.'"

---

[1] Author of *The History of Dramatic Poetry*, &c.

A DEFINITION.

The following (says Crabb Robinson) is from Kenyon : " What is dogmatism ? " asked some one of Douglas Jerrold. " Puppyism full grown."

SOMETHING WANTING.

One morning (say Henry Compton's sons[1]) that famous actor and Douglas Jerrold proceeded together to view the pictures in the "Gallery of Illustration." On entering the ante-room, they found themselves opposite to a number of very long looking-glasses. Pausing before one of these, Compton remarked to Jerrold: "You've come here to admire works of art! Very well, first feast your eyes on that work of nature!"—pointing to his own figure reflected in the glass—"look at it; there's a picture for you!" "Yes," said Jerrold, regarding it intently, "very fine, very fine indeed!" Then turning to his friend: "Wants hanging, though!"

BOVINE INDIFFERENCE.

Walter Bagehot (says Mr Hutton[2]) delighted in observing and expounding the bovine slowness of rural England in acquiring a new idea. Somersetshire, he used to boast, would not subscribe £1000 " to be represented by an archangel."

A DISTINCTION.

Bagehot used to say banteringly to his mother, by way of putting her off at a time when she was anxious for him to marry, " A man's mother is his misfortune, but his wife is his fault."

TASTY SOUP.

I remember asking Bagehot (says Mr Hutton) if he had enjoyed a particular dinner which he had rather expected to enjoy, but he replied, "No, the sherry was bad; tasted as if L——— had dropped all his h's into it."

NO END TO IT.

Perhaps (says Mr Hutton) the best illustration I can give of his more sardonic humour was his remark to a friend who had a church in the grounds near his house :—"Ah, you've got a church in the grounds ! I like that. It's as well the tenants shouldn't be quite sure that the landlord's power stops with this world."

---

[1] In their *Life* of their father.   [2] See Mr Hutton's preface to Bagehot's *Essays*.

STICKING TO PORT.

W. H. Harrison writes :—Among the guests at the table of a friend was a clergyman of the old school, who, doubtless enjoying "the feast of reason and the flow of soul," was equally alive to the merits of the turtle and the port, which last was exceptionally fine. "I see," said my clerical neighbour, addressing myself, "You stick to port." "Yes," I said, "and so am safe from being half seas over."

A FELICITOUS QUOTATION.

John Hamilton Reynolds[1] (says Planchè) was specially distinguished for the aptness of his quotations. Finding him one day lunching at the "Garrick," I asked him if the beef he was eating was good. "It would have been," he answered, "if damned custom had not *brazed* it so."[2]

ANOTHER.

Planchè tells another good story of Reynolds :—He told me how that, one evening, he had attended a tea-party, and noticing a pretty, bright-looking girl, he entered into conversation with her, and elicited from her, to his great gratification, that she was very fond of poetry. "Then, of course you admire, as much as I do, Shakespeare's exquisite comedy of 'As You Like It'." "I have read it," she answered; "but I don't understand it—" "Not understand it! then I am afraid you don't understand a tree." This was infinitely beyond her, and with a look of blank astonishment, she replied, "I don't know what you mean." "Upon which," says Reynolds, "I took my leave of her 'under the shade of melancholy *bows*.'"[3]

BRED AND BREAD.

It was in the drawing-room of my uncle's house in Arlington Street (writes Lady Chatterton) that Tom Paine,[4] who had been brought there as a sort of lion, was breakfasting with my aunt one day, received a note from one of the Prince Regent's Court to the effect that the Prince was anxious to know if he (Tom Paine) had been bred to the sea. The writer had, by a slip of the pen spelt the word *bread*, upon which Tom Paine wrote in pencil on the cover :—

> "No, not bread to the sea,
> But it was bread to me
> And—bad bread it be."

---

[1] John Hamilton Reynolds, **Hood's brother-in-law**, and collaborateur in some of his works, less generally known to the public, was only inferior to his celebrated connection, as a wit, a poet, and if I may be allowed the expression, a philosophical punster.—*Planchè.*

[2] *Hamlet*, act iii., scene 4.   [3] *As You Like It*, act ii., scene 7.

[4] Author of *The Age of Reason; b.* 1737, *d.* 1809.

THE FAULT OF THE PUPPY.

"Monk" Lewis[1] (says Raikes) was sometimes invited to Oatlands, and had a turn for epigram that rather amused the Duchess of York. On one occasion I remember that Lord Erskine, after dinner, inveighed bitterly against marriage; and smarting, I suppose, under the recollection of his own unsuccessful choice, concluded by saying, that a wife was a tin canister tied to a man's tail, which very much excited the indignation of Lady Ann Culling Smith, who was of the party. Lewis took a sheet of paper, and wrote the following neat epigram on the subject, which he presented to her Royal Highness :—

> " Lord Erskine at marriage presuming to rail,
> Says a wife's a tin canister tied to one's tail,
> And the fair Lady Ann, while the subject he carries on,
> Feels hurt at his Lordship's degrading comparison.
> But wherefore degrading? if taken aright
> A tin canister's useful, and polished, and bright,
> And if dirt its original purity hide,
> 'Tis the fault of the puppy to whom it is tied." [2]

A TORY VIRGIN.

At one of Lydia White's small and agreeable dinners in Park Street, the company (most of them, except the hostess, being Whigs) were discussing, in rather a querulous strain, the desperate prospects of their party. "Yes," said Sydney Smith, "we are in a deplorable condition; we must do something to help ourselves; I think we had better sacrifice a Tory Virgin." This (says L'Estrange) was partially addressed to Lydia White, who at once catching and applying the allusion to Iphigenia, "Well, I believe there is nothing the Whigs would not do to raise the wind!"

AN EPITAPH.

Miss Mitford mentions in one of her letters an epitaph on Mr Wordsworth, which (she says) I don't quite recollect, but which was to this effect:—

> " Here lyeth W. W.,
> Who never more will trouble you, trouble you."

MOLE-CULAR FORCE.

Moore writes:—A Mr Joyce—who, they tell me, wrote the "Modern Parnassus" some years ago—made not a bad pun in the course of the night. A seat on which Mrs Mole was sitting gave way, and he said, "*Mole ruit suâ.*"

---

[1] See p. 124.   [2] These lines are also attributed to Sheridan.

NONE PLAINER.

Basil Montague (writes Miss Mitford on one occasion) said a very good thing. Talking of the Doctor [Parr]'s illegible MS., "Ay," said he, "his letters are illegible, except they contain a commission or an announcement that he is coming to see you, and then no man can write plainer."

A FAVOURITE LIE.

When Mr Blackwood[1] visited Aytoun, in Orkney, he was repeatedly taken (says Martin[2]) by his friend to view a bank which Aytoun said was "a favourite lie" of the seals. None of the phocid race, however, were ever to be seen there. At last Mr Blackwood, turning to Mrs Aytoun, said, "Apparently this is a favourite lie of William's, if not of the seals."

LINLEY MYSTIFIED.

William Linley, brother to the first Mrs Sheridan, though a man of the world, and a member of the celebrated "Beefsteak Club," the hoaxing propensities of whose members are so proverbial, was (says Barham) a man of great good-nature and still greater simplicity of mind. He always occupied a particular table at the "Garrick," and, though a general favourite, was somewhat too fond of reciting long speeches from various authors, generally Shakespeare. It was one day in this month that he had began to spout from the opening scene in "Macbeth," and would probably have gone through it (continues Barham) if I had not cut him short at the third line—

> "When the hurly-burly's done,"

with "What on earth are you talking about? Why, my dear Linley, it is astonishing that a man so well read in Shakespeare as yourself should adopt that nonsensical reading! What is '*hurly-burly*' pray? There is no such word in the language; you can't find an allusion to it in Johnson." Linley, whose veneration for Dr Johnson was only inferior to that which he entertained for the great poet himself, said, "Indeed! are you sure there is not? What can be the reason of the omission? The word, you see, is used by Shakespeare." "No such thing," was the reply; "it appears so indeed in one or two early editions, but it is evidently mistranscribed. The second folio is the best and most authentic copy, and gives the true reading, though the old nonsense is still retained upon the stage!" "Indeed, and pray what do you call the true reading?" "Why, of course, the same that is followed by Johnson and Steevens in the edition upstairs:—

> '*When the early purl is done;*'

---

[1] The late John Blackwood, publisher.
[2] In his *Life of W. Edmonstoune Aytoun*, poet, essayist, and novelist.

that is, when we have finished our 'early purl,' *i.e.*, directly after breakfast." Linley was startled, and after looking steadily at me to see if he could discover any indication of an intention to hoax him, became quite puzzled by the gravity of my countenance, and only gave vent in a hesitating tone, half-doubtful, half-indignant, to the word "Nonsense !" "Nonsense? It is as I assure you. We will send for the book, and see what Steevens says in his note upon the passage." The book was accordingly sent for, but I took good care to intercept it before it reached the hands of Linley, and taking it from the servant, pretended to read from the volume—

> " When the hurly-burly's done."

"Some copies have it ' When the *early purl* is done ;' and I am inclined to think this reading the true one, if the well-known distich be worthy of credit—

> ' Hops, reformation, turkeys, and beer
> Came to England all in one year.'

This would seem to fix the introduction of beer, and consequently of early purl, into the country to about that period of Henry VIII.'s reign when he intermarried with Anne Boleyn, the mother of Queen Elizabeth, Shakespeare's great friend and patroness, and to whom this allusion may perhaps have been intended by the poet as a delicate compliment. Purl, it is well known, was a favourite beverage at the English Court during the latter part of the sixteenth century; and from the epithet then affixed to it, 'early,' an adjunct which it still retains, was no doubt in common use for breakfast at a time when the China trade had not yet made our ancestors familiar with the produce of the tea-plant. Theobald's objection, that, whatever may have been the propriety of its introduction at the Court of Elizabeth, the mention made of it at that of Macbeth would be a gross anachronism, may be at once dismissed as futile. Does not Shakespeare, in the very next scene, talk of

> 'Cannons overcharged with double cracks ?'

and is not allusion made by him to the use of the same beverage at the Court of Denmark, at a period co-eval, or nearly so, with that under consideration—

> 'Hamlet, this purl is thine?'"

"But dear me !" broke in Linley, "that is *pearl*, not purl. I remember old Packer used to hold up a pearl, and let it drop into the cup." "Sheer misconception on the part of a very indifferent actor, my dear Linley, be assured." Here Beazley, who was present, observed, "'Early purl' is all very well, but my own opinion has always leaned to Warburton's conjecture, that a political allusion is intended. He suggests

> 'When the *Earl of Burleigh's* done ;'

that is, when we have 'done,' *i.e.*, cheated or deceived, the Earl of Burleigh, a great statesman, you know, in Elizabeth's time, and one whom, to use a cant phrase among ourselves, 'you must get up very early in the morning to take in!'" "But what had Macbeth or the witches to do with the Earl of Burleigh? Stuff! nonsense!" said Linley indignantly. And though Beazley made a good fight in defence of his version, yet his opponent would not listen to it for an instant. "No, no," he continued, "the Earl of Burleigh is all rubbish, but there may be something in the other reading." And as the book was closed directly the passage had been repeated, and was replaced immediately on the shelf, the unsuspicious critic went away thoroughly mystified, especially as Tom Hill, for whose acquaintance with Early English literature he had a great respect, confirmed the emendation with "'Early purl!' Pooh! pooh! to be sure it is 'early purl;' I've got it so in two of my old copies."

THEIR FUTURE STATE.

Lady Ruthven (wrote J. C. Young in 1872) understands the management of her estate as well as if she had had the special training of a factor, and preserves and rears her own game. By-the-bye, a well-known *littérateur* on seeing her, after breakfast, feeding her pheasants with crumbs and milk, exclaimed, "Ah! I see your ladyship is preparing them *here*, for bread-sauce *hereafter.*

MUCH MORE APPROPRIATE.

Lord William Lennox says that it was Jerdan who told him of the following repartee, made by a most brilliant wit and dramatic writer of the day. The above gentleman, upon meeting poor Sterling Coyne in the street, noticed his very untidy appearance, for he was completely covered with mud. "Why," said he in a pertinent manner, which almost excused the *im*pertinency, "you are called Sterling Coin; but I think, in your present state, *filthy lucre* would be a more appropriate appellation."

A TEST OF SANITY.

In one of [his] pleadings, when defending a client alleged to be rather imbecile, because he scribbled doggerel rhymes, Sergeant Wilde replied (says Jerdan) that the writing of doggerel was no proof of weakness of intellect, for he could quote an old friend of his who enjoyed a just celebrity in the literary world, and yet had addressed a post letter to another friend with this super-scription:—

> " This is for David Pollock, 'squire;
> In Elm Court, Temple, pray inquire
> On the ground floor, and look no higher
>   To catch him.
> He'll pay you twopence for this letter,
> He never did so for a better;
> But if he should remain your debtor,
>   Do watch him."

AN EMENDATION.

The poet Rogers remarked on one occasion:—I never derived any benefit from the strictures of a critic but once, and that was on the occasion of an alliteration which I had not premeditated. The second canto of the " Pleasures of Memory," as published in the first edition, commenced with the lines,—

> " Sweet Memory, wafted by thy gentle gale,
> Oft up the tide of Time I turn my sail."

The critic remarked on this passage that it suggested the alliteration—

> " Oft up the tide of Time I turn my *tail.*"

About Plays and Players.

IN HIS OWN HANDS.

MOORE records what Foote[1] said to a clergyman, a very dirty fellow, who was boasting of his agricultural labours: "Oh, it's easy to see, sir, you keep your glebe in your own hands."

NO WONDER.

Another witticism of Foote's, also recorded by Moore:—"Why are you for ever humming that air?" "Because it haunts me." "No wonder, for you are for ever murdering it."[2]

NO HARM IN IT.

A third witticism of Foote, also recorded by Moore:—His saying to a canting sort of lady that asked him, "Pray, Mr Foote, do you ever go to church?" "No, madam; not that I see any harm in it."

THEY STAYED DOWN.

The then Duke of Cumberland (the foolish Duke, as he was called) came one night into Foote's green-room at the Haymarket Theatre. "Well, Foote," said he, "here I am, ready, as usual, to swallow all your good things." "Upon my soul," replied Foote, "your Royal Highness must have an excellent digestion, for you never bring any up again." Rogers tells this story.

---

1 Samuel Foote, comedian; *b.* 1720, *d.* 1777.

2 Fanny Kemble writes:—My music master was a worthy old Englishman of the name of Shaw, who played on the violin, and had been at one time leader of the orchestra at Covent Garden Theatre. Indeed, it was to him that John Kemble addressed the joke (famous, because in his mouth unique) upon the subject of a song in the piece of "Cœur de Lion." This Mr Shaw was painfully endeavouring to teach my uncle, who was entirely without musical ear, and whose all but insuperable difficulty consisted in repeating a few bars of the melody supposed to be sung under his prison window by his faithful minstrel, Blondin. "Mr Kemble, Mr Kemble! you are murdering the tune, sir!" cried the exasperated musician; to which my uncle replied, "Very well, sir; and you are for ever beating it!"

WARBURTON ON SHAKESPEARE.

Thomas Green, writing in his Diary, says:—Mr Selwyn mentioned that Foote, having received much attention from the Eton boys in showing him round the College, collected them about him in the quadrangle, and said, "Now, young gentlemen, what can I do for you to show you how much I am obliged to you?" "Tell us, Mr Foote," said the leader, "the best thing you ever said." "Why," says Foote, "I once saw a little blackguard imp of a chimney-sweeper mounted on a noble steed, prancing and curveting in all the pride and magnificence of nature—There, said I, goes Warburton on Shakespeare."

SELLING THE TIMBER.

The following was told to Rogers by Murphy:—The latter, describing to Foote some remarks made by Garrick on Lacy's love of money, as a mere attempt to cover his own parsimony by throwing it on his fellow-patentee, had ended with the old question of, "Why on earth didn't Garrick take the beam out of his own eye before attacking the mote in other people's?" "He is not sure," said Foote, "of selling the timber."

SENDING ROUND THE HAT.

Rogers was fond of relating the following, which he told with infinite humour:—At the Chapter coffee-house, Foote and his friends were making a contribution for the relief of a poor fellow, a decayed player, who was nick-named the "Captain of the Four Winds," because his hat was worn into four spouts. Each person of the company dropped his mite into the hat as it was held out to him. "If Garrick hears of this," exclaimed Foote, "he will certainly send us *his* hat."

A PRECAUTION.

A story is told of a somewhat pompous announcement, at one of Foote's dinner parties, when the Drury Lane manager was among the guests, of the arrival of "Mr Garrick's servants;" whereupon, "Oh, let them wait," cried the wit, adding, in an affected undertone to his own servant, but sufficiently loud to be generally heard, "But, James, be sure you lock up the pantry."

GOING A LONG WAY.

Another story of Foote and Garrick (says Forster[1]) is of their leaving the Bedford together one night when Foote had been the entertainer, and on his

---

[1] In his *Biographical and Critical Essays.*

pulling out his purse to pay the bill, a guinea had dropped.   Impatient at
not immediately finding it, "Where on earth can it be gone to?" he said.
"Gone to the devil, I think," rejoined Garrick, who also had been seeking
for it everywhere.   "Well said, David," cried Foote; "let you alone for
making a guinea go farther than anybody else."

HARD ON GARRICK.

Says Dr Johnson :—There is a witty satirical story of Foote.   He had a
small bust of Garrick placed upon his bureau.   "You may be surprised," said
he, "that I allow him to be so near my gold ; but you will observe he has no
hands."

EQUALLY HARD.

"Pray, sir, are your puppets to be as large as life?" asked a lady of
fashion.   "Oh dear, madam, no," replied Foote; "not much above the size
of Garrick."

MUST HAVE A VENTILATOR.

One sultry summer night at the Haymarket (says Forster) the *Lying Valet*
had been put up after the *Devil upon Two Sticks* to please Garrick, and the
satisfied little manager has called in at the green-room with a triumphant,
"Well, Sam, so you are taking up, I see, with *my* farces, after all!" whereupon Foote cannot but throw in this drop of allaying Tiber : "Why, yes,
David, what could I do better?   I must have some ventilator this intolerably
hot weather."

THE MEANING OF IDEA.

One of Mrs Montagu's blue-stocking ladies fastened upon Foote at one of the
routs in Portman Square with her views of *Locke on the Understanding*, which
she protested she admired above all things ; only there was one particular
word very often repeated which she could not distinctly make out, and that
was the word (pronouncing it very long) "*ide-a ;* but I suppose it comes from
a Greek derivation."   "You are perfectly right, madam," said Foote; "it
comes from the word *idea-owski.*"   "And pray, sir, what does that mean?"
"The feminine of idiot, madam."

A GOOD REASON.

A pompous person, who had made a large fortune as a builder, was holding
forth on the mutability of the world.   "Can you account for it, sir?" said
he, turning to Foote.   "Why, not very clearly, sir," said Foote; "unless we
could suppose the world was built by contract."

TAKE CARE!

Being in company where Hugh Kelly[1] was mightily boasting of the power he had, as a reviewer, of distributing literary reputation to any extent, "Don't be too prodigal of it," Foote quietly interposed, "or you may leave none for yourself."

ALL THAT HAD HAPPENED.

Conversation turning one day on a lady having married very happily, whose previous life had been of extremely doubtful complexion, some one attributed the unexpected result to her having frankly told her husband, before marriage, all that had happened. "What candour she must have had!" was the general remark upon this—"what honesty!" "Yes," said Foote, "and what an amazing memory!"

LONG DRAWN OUT.

A stately and silly country squire was regaling a large party with the number of fashionable folk he had visited that morning. "And among the rest," he said, "I called upon my good friend the Earl of Chol-mon-dely, but he was not at home." "That is exceedingly surprising," said Foote. "What! nor none of his pe-o-ple?"

VERY SMALL.

When Foote dined in Paris with Lord Stormont, that thrifty Scotch peer, then ambassador, as usual produced his wine in the smallest of decanters, and dispensed it in the smallest of glasses, enlarging all the time on its exquisite growth and enormous age. "It is very little of its age," said Foote, holding up his diminutive glass.

HIS WEAKEST PART.

No one could so promptly overthrow an assailant; so quietly rebuke an avarice or meanness; so effectually "abate and dissolve" any ignorant affectation or pretension, as Foote. "Why do you attack my weakest part?" he asked of one who had raised a laugh against what Johnson calls his depeditation; "did I ever say anything about your head?"

TAKING HIMSELF OFF.

Whilst Foote was one night at his friend Delaval's, and when the glass had been circulating freely, one of the party would suddenly have fixed a quarrel

---

1 The dramatist; b. 1739, d. 1777.

upon Foote for his indulgence of personal satire. "Why, what would you have?" exclaimed Foote, good-humouredly putting it aside; "of course I take all my friends off, but I use them no worse than myself; I take *myself* off." "Gad so!" cried the malcontent, "that I should like to see;" upon which Foote took up his hat and left the room.

AD HOMINEM.

At one of Macklin's absurd Lectures on the Ancients, the lecturer was solemnly composing himself to begin, when a buz of laughter from where Foote stood ran through the room, and Macklin,[1] thinking to throw the laugher off his guard, and effectually for that night disarm his ridicule, turned to him with this question, in his most severe and pompous manner—"Well, sir, you seem to be very merry there; but do you know what I am going to say, now?" "No, sir," at once replied Foote; "pray, do you?"

HE KNEW THE COMPANY.

Foote was taken one day into White's Club by a friend who wanted to write a note. Standing in a room among strangers, and men he had no agreement with in politics, he appeared to feel not quite at ease; when Lord Carmarthen, wishing to relieve his embarrassment, went up to speak to him, but, himself feeling rather shy, merely said, "Mr Foote, your handkerchief is hanging out of your pocket." Whereupon Foote, looking round suspiciously, and hurriedly thrusting the handkerchief back into his pocket, replied, "Thank you, my lord, thank you: you know the company better than I do."

ON ATTORNEYS.

Foote's jokes against attorneys would fill a volume; but space may be spared for the grave communication he made to a simple country farmer who had just buried a rich relation, an attorney, and who was complaining to him of the very great expenses of a country funeral, in respect to carriages, hatbands, scarves, &c. "Why, do you bury your attorneys here?" asked Foote. "Yes, to be sure we do; how else?" "Oh! we never do that in London." "No!" said the other, much surprised; "how do you manage?" "Why, wh' the patient happens to die, we lay him out in a room overnight by himself, lock the door, throw open the sash, and in the morning he is entirely off." 'Indeed!" said the other, with amazement, "what becomes of him?" " Why, that we cannot exactly tell; all we know is, there's a strong smell of brimstone in the room the next morning."

---

[1] Charles Macklin, author of *The Man of the World.*

IN THE FIRE.

Much bored by a pompous physician at Bath, who confided to him, as a great secret, that he had a mind to publish his own poems, but had so many irons in the fire he really did not well know what to do—"Take my advice, doctor," says Foote, "and put your poems where your irons are."

NINE AND ONE.

Foote was not less distressed on another occasion by a mercantile man of his acquaintance, who had also not only written a poem, but exacted a promise that he would listen to it, and who mercilessly stopped to tax him with inattention even before advancing beyond the first pompous line—"Hear me, O Phœbus, and ye Muses nine!" "Pray, pray be attentive, Mr Foote." "I am," said Foote; "nine and one are ten; go on!"

WHICH WAS IT?

Sir George Beaumont (says Rogers) once met Quin[1] at a very small dinner-party. There was a delicious pudding, which the master of the house, pushing the dish towards Quin, begged him to taste. A gentleman had just before helped himself to an immense piece of it. "Pray," said Quin, looking first at the gentleman's plate and then at the dish, "which *is* the pudding?"

A MUDDLE.

Lord William Lennox says:—A story is told of Quin, when acting Judge Balance in the "Recruiting Officer," who thus addressed Mrs Woffington, "Sylvia, what age were you when your dear mother married?" The actress remained silent, when Quin proceeded, "I ask what age you were when your mother was born?" "I regret," replied Sylvia, "I cannot answer your question; but I can tell you how old I was when my mother died."

HE KNEW HIM PERFECTLY.

The following story (says Barham) was told me as a fact by George Raymond :—Yates (the well-known actor and manager of the Adelphi Theatre) met a friend from Bristol, in the street, whom he well recollected as having been particularly civil to his wife and himself when at that town, in which the gentleman was a merchant. Yates, who at that time lived at the Adelphi Theatre, invited his friend to dinner, and made a party, among whom were Hook and Mathews, to meet him. On reaching home he told his wife what

---

[1] James Quin ; *b.* 1693, *d.* 1766.

he had done, describing the gentleman, and calling to her mind how often they had been at his house near the cathedral. "I remember him very well," said Mrs Yates, "but I don't just now recollect his name—what is it?" "Why, that is the very question I was going to ask you," returned Yates. "I know the man as well as I know my own father, but for the life of me I can't remember his name, and I made no attempt to ascertain it, as I made sure you would recollect it!" What was to be done? All that night and the next morning they tried in vain to recover it, but the name had completely escaped them. In this dilemma Yates bethought him of giving instructions to their servant which he considered would solve the difficulty, and calling him in told him to be very careful in asking every gentleman, as he arrived, his name, and to be sure to announce it very distinctly. Six o'clock came, and with it the company in succession, Hook, Mathews, and the rest—all but the anonymous guest, whom Yates began to think, and almost to hope, would not come at all. Just, however, before the dinner was put on the table, a knock was heard, and the lad being at that moment in the kitchen, in the act of carrying up a haunch of mutton which the cook had put into his hands, a maid-servant went to the door, admitted the stranger, showed him upstairs, and opening the drawing-room door allowed him to walk in without any announcement at all. At dinner time everybody took wine with the unknown, addressing him as "Sir,"—"A glass of wine, sir?"—"Shall I have the honour, sir?" &c., but nothing transpired to let out the name, though several round-about attempts were made to get at it. The evening passed away, and the gentleman was highly delighted with the company; but about half-past ten o'clock he looked at his watch and rose abruptly, saying, "Faith, I must be off or I shall get shut out, for I am going to sleep at a friend's, in the Tower, who starts for Bristol with me in the morning. They close the gates at eleven precisely, and I shan't get in if I am a minute after, so good-bye at once. Be sure you come and see me whenever you visit Bristol." "Depend on me, my dear friend. God bless you, if you must go!" "Adieu," said the other; and Yates was congratulating himself on having got out of so awkward a scrape, when his friend popped his head back into the room, and cried hastily: "Oh, by-the-bye, my dear Yates, I forgot to tell you that I bought a pretty French clock as I came here to-day at Hawley's, but as it needs a week's regulating, I took the liberty of giving your name, and ordering them to send it here, and said that you would forward it. It is paid for." The door closed, and before Yates could get it open again, the gentleman was in the hall. "Stop!" screamed Yates over the balusters, "you had better write the address your-self, for fear of a mistake." "No, no, I can't stop, I shall be too late:—the old house, near the cathedral; good-bye!" The street door slammed behind him, and Yates went back to the company in an agony.

WITH TWO P's.

Barham records a very similar story of King the actor, who, meeting an old friend, whose name he could not recollect, took him home to dinner. By way of making the discovery, he addressed him in the evening, having previously made several ineffectual efforts :—"My dear sir, my friend here and myself have had a dispute as to how you spell your name ; indeed, we have laid a bottle of wine upon it." "Oh, with two P's," was the answer, which left them just as wise as before.

AS IT SHOULD BE.

When Compton the comedian was playing at Burton, a gentleman of the same name as that town happened to be in the company. Taking a walk with a friend one day, Henry Montague remarked some of the gentlemen of the company embarking in a small boat, to take a little excursion up the river, Mr Burton amongst the number. "Quite right," said Mr Montague, as the latter gentleman took his seat ; "just as it should be : Burton-on-Trent !"

THE MAN WHO DIDN'T LIKE TRIPE.

Like Young and others, his contemporaries, [Liston[1]] delighted in practical joking in the public streets. Walking one day through Leicester Square with Mr Miller, the theatrical bookseller of Bow Street, Liston (says Planchè) happened to mention casually that he was going to have tripe for dinner, a dish of which he was particularly fond. Miller, who hated it, said, "Tripe! Beastly stuff! How can you eat it?" This was enough for Liston. He stopped suddenly in the crowded thoroughfare in front of Leicester House, and holding Miller by the arm, exclaimed, in a loud voice, "What, sir! Do you mean to assert that you don't like tripe?" "Hush!" muttered Miller; "don't talk so loud ; people are staring at us." "I ask you, sir," continued Liston in louder tones, "do you not like tripe?" "For heaven's sake, hold your tongue!" cried Miller ; "you'll have a crowd round us." And naturally people began to stop and wonder what was the matter. This was exactly what Liston wanted, and again he shouted, "Do you mean to say you don't like tripe?" Miller, making a desperate effort, broke from him, and hurried in consternation through Cranbourne Alley, followed by Liston, bawling after him, "There he goes!—that's the man who doesn't like tripe!"—to the immense amusement of the numerous passengers, many of whom recognized the popular comedian ; but the horrified bookseller took to his heels and ran,

---

[1] John Liston, comedian; *b.* 1776, *d.* 1846.

L

as if for his life, up Long Acre to Bow Street, pursued to his doorstep by a pack of young ragamuffins, who took up the cry, "There he goes!—The man that don't like tripe!"

SO MUCH OBLIGED TO HIM.

One of the noblest tragedians on the stage, and a most perfect gentleman in private society, Young[1] (says Planché) was an irrepressible *farceur*, constantly playing, with imperturbable gravity, the most whimsical pranks in public. He undertook to drive Charles Mathews (*fils*) to Cassiobury on a visit to the Earl of Essex. Having passed through a turnpike and paid the toll, he pulled up at the next gate he came to, and, addressing himself most politely to a woman who issued from the toll-house, inquired if Mr ——, the toll-taker, whose name he saw on the board above the door, happened to be in the way. The woman answered that he was not in the house, but she would send for him, if the gentleman wished to see him particularly. "Well, I'm sorry to trouble you, madam, but I certainly should like to have a few minutes' conversation with him," rejoined Young. Upon which the woman called to a little boy, "Tommy, run and tell your father a gentleman wants to speak to him." Away ran Tommy, down a straight, long path in the grounds of a nursery-and-seedsman, the entrance to which was close to the turnpike,— Young sitting bolt upright in the tilbury, to the astonishment of Mathews, who asked him what on earth he wanted with the man. "I want to consult him on a matter of business," was the reply. After some five or six minutes, the boy, who had entered a building at the extreme end of the path, re-appeared, followed by a man pulling on his jacket as he walked, and in due time both of them stood beside the tilbury. The man touched his hat to Young. "You wished to see me, sir?" "Are you Mr ——?" "Yes, sir." "The Mr —— who is entrusted to take the toll at this gate?" "Yes, sir." "Then you are precisely the person who can give me the information I require. You see, Mr ——, I paid sixpence at the gate at ——, and the man who took it gave me this little piece of paper" (producing a ticket from his waistcoat pocket), "and assured me that if I showed it to the proper authorities at this gate I should be allowed to drive through without payment." "Why, of course," said the man, staring with amazement at Young, "that ticket clears this gate." "Then you do not require me to pay anything here?" "No! Why, any fool—" "My dear Mr ——, I'm so much obliged to you. I should have been so sorry to have done anything wrong, and therefore wished to have your opinion on the subject. A thousand

---

[1] Charles Mayne Young, tragedian; *b.* 1777, *d.* 1856.

thanks. Good morning, Mr ——." And on drove Young, followed, as the reader may easily imagine, by a volley of imprecations and epithets of anything but a flattering description, so long as he was within hearing.

AN INTIMATE CONNECTION.

Young (says Planché) was a special favourite with the late Lord Essex, and they were so much together, and on such familiar terms, that Poole, being asked what Englishmen he had seen in Paris, said, "Only Lord Young and Mr Essex."

HE WOULD NOT TAKE MUSTARD.

The following anecdote (says J. C. Young) will illustrate the elder Mathews'[1] morbid sensibility to things which most people would deem insignificant:—He had an appointment with a solicitor. They were to meet at a particular hour at a small inn in the city, where they might hope to be quiet and undisturbed. Mathews arrived at the trysting-place a few minutes too soon. On entering the coffee-room, he found its sole tenant a commercial gentleman earnestly engaged on a round of boiled beef. Mathews sat himself down by the fire and took up a newspaper, meaning to wile away the time till his friend arrived. Occasionally he glanced from the paper to the beef, and from the beef to the man, till he began to fidget and look about from the top of the right-hand page to the bottom of the left in a querulous manner. Then he turned the paper inside out, and, pretending to stop from reading, addressed the gentleman in a tone of ill-disguised indignation, and with a ghastly smile,—"I beg your pardon, sir, but I don't think you are aware that you have no mustard." The person thus addressed looked up at him with evident surprise, mentally resenting his gratuitous interference with his tastes, and coldly bowed. Mathews resumed his paper, and, curious to see if his well-meant hint would be acted on, furtively looked round the edge of his paper, and finding the plate to be still void of mustard, concluded the man was deaf. So, raising his voice to a higher key, and accosting him with sarcastic acerbity, he bawled out, with syllabic precision, "Are—you—a-ware —sir—that—you—have—been—eat-ing—boiled—beef—with-out—mustard ?" Again a stiff bow, and no reply. Once more Mathews affected to read, while he was really "nursing his wrath to keep it warm." At last, seeing the man's obstinate violation of conventionality and good taste, he jumped up, and, in the most arbitrary and defiant manner, snatched the mustard-pot out of the cruet-stand, banged it on the table, under the defaulter's nose, and shouted out, "Confound it, sir, you SHALL take mustard!" He then slapped

---

[1] Charles Mathews, comedian; b. 1776, d. 1835.

his hat on his head, and ordered the waiter to show him into a private room, vowing that he had never before been under the same roof with such a savage, and that he had been made quite sick by the revolting sight which he had seen in the coffee-room.

A HORSE CUTTING ITS THROAT.

Mathews had often told Charles Kemble of the great amusement his man-servant's peculiarities afforded him, but Kemble said he had never been able to discover anything in him but crass stupidity. "Ah," said Mathews, "you can't conceive what a luxury it is to have a man under the same roof with you, who will believe anything you tell him, however impossible it may be." One warm summer's day, Mathews had a dinner party at Highgate. There were present, among others, Broderip, Theodore Hook, General Phipps, Manners Sutton (then Speaker of the House of Commons), and Charles Kemble. Dessert was laid out on the lawn. Mathews, without hinting his intention, rang the bell in the dining-room, and on its being answered, told the man to follow him to the stables while he gave his coachman certain directions in his presence. The instant Mathews reached the stable-door, he called to the coachman (who he knew was not there), looked in, and, before the man-servant could come up, started back, and, in a voice of horror, cried out, "Good heavens! go back, go back—and tell Mr Kemble that his horse has cut his throat!" The simple goose, infected by his master's well-feigned panic, and never pausing to reflect on the absurdity of the thing, burst on to the lawn, and, with cheeks blanched with terror, roared out, "Mr Kemble, sir, you're wanted directly!" Seeing Mr Kemble in no hurry to move, he repeated his appeal with increased emphasis, "For heaven's sake, sir, come: your poor horse has cut his throat!"

HE DINED AT THREE.

Compton (says one of his sons[1]) had a remarkable knack of saying things that were not especially funny in themselves in a way that made them appear remarkably so. The utter absence of any effort to be "droll," produced an effect altogether superior to the comic remarks of the habitual joker. For instance, one day he was walking home through Kensington Gardens, and he met a friend, a clergyman who lived near him, and they fell into conversation. Presently Compton said rather abruptly, "Well, I can't stop talking any longer, as it's nearly three, and I dine at three." "Dear me," replied the clergyman, "do you, indeed?" "Yes, I do," rejoined Compton severely.

---

[1] See *ante*, p. 147.

"Yes, I do. Do you see anything objectionable in dining at three?" "Oh, not at all," answered the clergyman, a little taken aback at the seriousness of his companion's tone. "Is there anything about the hour that meets with your disapproval?" again asked Compton, if possible more gravely than before. "No, no, not at all," stammered the other, almost afraid that he had trodden on a tender corn. "*I* consider it a remarkably *good* hour," remarked Compton, almost defiantly; "don't *you?*" "Well—a—I really—" "Think it over, and let me know," exclaimed Compton impressively, as he grasped the clergyman's hand and wrung it violently. A moment more, and the comedian was striding homeward through the trees, whilst the clergyman stared blankly after him with a dim notion in his mind that he had been chaffed.

LET HIM TRY HAMLET.

Compton had a wholesome horror of amateur actors, and on one occasion, when an egotistical young gentleman button-holed him, to discant on acting, he administered an unmistakable reproof to the presumptuous one. "I am anxious to become a professional now," said the young man, "for I always get splendid notices, and all my friends think I should make a great hit." "What line?" inquired Compton. "Well," smiled the youth, "I play all the funny parts, but I don't succeed in making my audience laugh heartily. I want to make them scream as you do—to make the house ring again with laughter, in fact." "Ah," dryly responded Compton, "change your line of character a bit; try Hamlet, and let me know how you succeed!"

AN AGREEABLE LITTLE TRIFLE.

Mr Henry Irving writes of Compton:—I shall never forget the speech which he made on the first hundreth night of "Hamlet," when, after the performance, the event was celebrated by a supper given by my dear friend Mr Bateman, at which a number of our friends and associates were present. Mr Compton was then playing nightly the character of Sam Savory, in the farce of "The Fish out of Water." This farce had preceded "Hamlet" one hundred nights, and he took occasion to impress this fact upon us in the following way. We were all in high spirits. Mr Bateman's health, Mr Compton's, and my own were drunk amidst enthusiasm and jocularity. [Compton], with his peculiar gravity, ended the reply to the toast with which he was associated somewhat after this fashion : "Thank you, gentlemen, for your appreciation of my efforts in that immortal drama, 'The Fish out of Water.' I take this opportunity of thanking my friend Irving for the really indefatigable support which he has given me in that agreeable little trifle of 'Hamlet,' with which, as you know, we are in the habit of winding up the evening." The burst of laughter which greeted this I shall ever remember.

NOT THE WORD.

A brother actor, who had not exactly "taken the house by storm" at his first appearance in London, very stupidly asked Compton: "Was my acting good?" "Well," was the reply, delivered in his inimitable style; "hum! ha! *Good* is not the word!"

AN UNHEARD-OF THING.

The following *bon mot* of Compton's has been erroneously ascribed to Jerrold. Meeting a friend one day, when the weather had taken a most sudden and unaccountable turn from cold to warmth, the subject was mooted as usual, and characterised by the gentleman as being "most extraordinary." "Yes," replied Compton, "it is a most unheard-of thing; we've jumped from winter into summer without a spring."

A SLIGHT ALTERATION.

We were sitting (writes Planché) in the greenroom [at the Haymarket] one evening during the performance, chatting and laughing, [Mrs Nisbett] having a book in her hand which she had to take on to the stage with her in the next scene, when Brindal, a useful member of the company, but not particularly remarkable for wit and humour, came to the door, and, leaning against it, in a sentimental manner, drawled out—

> "If to her share some female errors fall,
> Look on her face"[1]—

He paused. She raised her beautiful eyes to him, and consciously smiled — *her* smile—in anticipation of the well-known complimentary termination of the couplet, when, with a deep sigh, he gravely added—

> "—And you'll *believe* them all!"

The rapid change of that radiant countenance—first to blank surprise and then to fury, as, suiting the action to the look, she hurled the volume in her hand at the culprit's head—was one of the most amusing sights imaginable. Concentrating the verbal expression of her indignation in the word "Wretch!" she burst into one of her glorious laughs, too infectious to be resisted even by the contrite offender, who certainly was never, to my knowledge, guilty of anything so good either before or after.

WHAT IT WANTED.

Planché writes of a whilom treasurer of Drury Lane :—He was a dry fellow, that Billy Dunn—a great character. During the many years he was treasurer

---

[1] Pope, *Rape of the Lock*, canto ii.

of Drury Lane, I don't suppose he once witnessed a performance; but regularly after the curtain had fallen on a new piece, it mattered not of what description, he would let himself through with his pass-key from the front of the house, as if he had sat it out, and on being asked his opinion, invariably answered, after a long pause and a proportionate pinch of snuff, "Wants cutting."

A DELIBERATE ANSWER.

Writing of the same individual, Planchè says:—The trouble of extracting a direct reply from him, at any time or concerning anything, was remarkable. I called one morning at the theatre, on my way to the city, to ask him a question about writing orders on some particular night. I was told he was in the treasury; accordingly ran up to it. He was alone at his desk counting cheques. "Would there be any objections, Dunn, to my sending a friend or two to the boxes on such a night?" He looked at me, but made no answer, and continued to count his cheques. I waited patiently till he had finished and replaced them in the bags. Still no answer. He turned to his books. I waited perhaps five more minutes, and then, without repeating my inquiry, or speaking another word, walked quietly out of the room and went about my other business. Returning between two and three in the afternoon, I ascertained from the hall-keeper that Mr Dunn was still in the theatre. I mounted the stairs again, entered the treasury, and found him, as before, alone. I stood perfectly silent while he looked at me, and took the customary pinch of snuff, after which he drawled out, "No, I should think not;" some four hours having elapsed since I asked him the question.

OBLEEGE AND OBLIGE.

John Kemble (says Gronow) had the honour of giving the Prince of Wales some lessons in elocution. According to the vitiated pronunciation of the day, the prince, instead of saying "oblige," would say "obleege;" upon which Kemble, with much disgust depicted upon his countenance, said—"Sir, may I beseech your Royal Highness to open your royal jaws and say 'oblige?'"

HIS HONOUR.

Lord William Lennox narrates a smart saying of Henry Harris, for many years manager of Covent Garden Theatre. An actor of the name of Faulkner, who had recently arrived from the provinces, made his appearance on the metropolitan boards as Octavio in "The Mountaineers." The anxious manager was at the wing watching the performance, and when Faulkner exclaimed, in a deep guttural tone, "Oh! where is my honour now?" replied, "I wish your honour was back at Newcastle again with all my heart."

"THEY SAY."

Mrs Powell (then Mrs Renaud), a beautiful woman, and an actress of the old school, succeeded Mrs Siddons in many of her characters. She was anxious (says Planché) to conceal her second marriage, not from any unworthy motive, but for private family reasons. An actress in the Covent Garden company, who bore by courtesy the name of one of the performers, and had become acquainted with the fact, maliciously addressed her one night in the green-room, before a numerous assemblage of actors and visitors, thus :—"Mrs Powell, everybody says you are married." "Indeed !" retorted Mrs Renaud, coldly; "everybody says you are not."

TERRI-BLE.

Miss M. Tree's *Clari* (says Lord Wm. Lennox) was perfection; and this reminds of an anecdote. Daniel Terry, the comedian, and friend of Walter Scott, was one evening in the greenroom of Covent Garden Theatre, when the question of casting this popular drama in some anticipated trip to the provinces was discussed. "I suppose," said Terry, in his harsh voice, "I must become the tender father, and study the part of Rolamo." "I hope you will," responded Harley, who happened to have paid a visit to the rival establishment, "for if you are not *clari*-fied, I know full well that Maria Tree will be *terri*-fied."

ANY SIDE-US.

Macready once told a story of George B——, the actor, who, it seems, was not popular in the profession, being considered a sort of time-server : "There goes Georgius," said some one.   "Not Georgium Sidus," replied Keeley. "Yes," added Power,[1] "Georgium *Any*-sidus."

"THE DAY OF JUDGMENT."

The following anecdote is Planché's :—An Easter piece on the subject of "Oberon" had been rushed out at Drury Lane in anticipation of Weber's opera, and, in addition to this, Bishop was engaged to write an opera in opposition to it, the libretto by George Soane being founded on the popular story of "Aladdin and the Wonderful Lamp."   It was not very favourably received, and the delicious warbling of Miss Stephens could not secure for it more than a lingering existence of a few nights.   Tom Cooke, the leader of the orchestra at Drury Lane, one of the cleverest of musicians and most amusing of men, met Braham in Bow Street, and asked him how his opera

---

[1] See p. 120.

("Oberon") was going. "Magnificently!" replied the tenor, and added, with a fit of what he used to call *enthoosemusy,* "not to speak it profanely, it will run to the Day of Judgment!" "My dear fellow," rejoined Cooke, "that's nothing! Ours has run five nights afterwards!"

UNFRIENDLY ECHOES.

An amateur named Plunkett was acting in Dublin as *Richard III.* The audience (says Macready) were in fits of laughter from the beginning to the end. When he said in Gloster's soliloquy, "Why, I can smile, and murder while I smile," the response from the pit was, "Oh, by the Powers, you can!" To his question, "Am I then a man to be beloved?" voices answered, "Indeed, then, you are not!"

A KINDLY INDIVIDUAL.

Macready writes:—I remember on one occasion acting in "Venice Preserved." A long and rather drowsy dying speech of my poor friend Jaffier was "dragging its slow length along," when one of the gallery, in a tone of great impatience, called out very loudly, "Ah, now, die at once;" to which another from the other side immediately replied, "Be quiet, you black-guard;" then, turning with a patronising tone to the lingering Jaffier, "take your time!"

LET HIM DO IT.

An actor named Beaubourg, who was extremely ugly, acted Mithridate, and in one scene Mademoiselle Le Couvreur, who represented Moncine, has to say, "Seigneur, vous changez de visage." "Laissez le faire!" cried one from the pit.

IT WAS HIGH TIME.

In the "Revue des Théâtres" (1753), De Chevrier the author introduced a danseuse; she arrived just at the moment the piece was flagging.

"Quel motif en ces lieux vous fait porter vos pas?"

demanded the performer acting the part of the critic, when she replied,

" Je viens tirer un auteur d'embarras."

"Ma foi, il était temps," shouted one from the stalls.

TIRED OF SANCHO.

In a play entitled "Sancho Panza," the Duke has to say, "I'm beginning to get tired of Sancho." "And so are we," shouted voices from the pit, which immediately put an end to the performance.

FOR THE PROVINCES.

Talma, soon after his return to Paris, where the playgoers were angry at his long absence, performed "Coriolanus" at the Théâtre Française, and when he came to the line—

> Adieu Rome ; je pars—

A sharp voice called out from the *parterre*—

> Pour les départments—

which (says Jerdan) set the house in a roar.

A HAPPY QUOTATION.

During the performance of "Andronicus," selected for the *début* of an actor from Lille, the unfortunate man, who had signally failed in the early part of the play, had to deliver the following line :—

> "Mais pour ma fuite, ami, quel parti dois-je prendre ?"

In reply a voice from the front exclaimed :—

> "L'ami, prenez la poste et retournez en Flandre,"—

a verse taken (says Lord William Lennox) from "La Fille Capitaine," in which Angélique has to say :—

> "Demain je prends la poste et je retourne en Flandre."

"NOW THEN, FANNY!"

Fanny Kemble says in her Memoirs :—When I was acting Lady Townley, in the scene where her husband complains of her late hours and she insolently retorts, "I won't come home till four to-morrow morning," and receives the startling reply with which Lord Townley leaves her, "Then, madam, you shall never come home again," I was apt to stand for a moment aghast at this threat ; and one night during this pause of breathless dismay, one of the gallery auditors, thinking, I suppose, that I was wanting in proper spirit not to make some rejoinder, exclaimed, "Now then, Fanny !" which very nearly upset the gravity produced by my father's impressive exit, both in me and in the audience.

"LE MEURT SE ROI!"

The French stage (says Dutton Cook) has a story of a *figurant* who ruined at once a new tragedy and his own prospects by an unhappy *lapsus linguæ*, the result of undue haste and nervous excitement. He had but to cry, aloud, in the crisis of the drama : "Le roi se meurt !" He was perfect at rehearsal ; he earned the applause even of the author. A brilliant future, as he deemed, was open to him. But at night he could only utter in broken tones, "Le meurt se roi !" and the tragic situation was dissolved in laughter.

"DON'T THROW HIM OVER, BUT—"

J. T. Fields describes the following little incident which, he says, Charlotte Cushman once related to him. She said a man in the gallery of a theatre (I think she was on the stage at the time) made such a disturbance that the play could not proceed. Cries of "Throw him over" arose from all parts of the house, and the noise became furious. All was tumultuous chaos, until a sweet and gentle female voice was heard in the pit, exclaiming, "No! I pray you don't throw him over! I beg of you, dear friends, don't throw him over, but—kill him where he is."

SOMEWHAT MIXED.

Among the numerous instances in which the *lapsus linguæ* of performers have convulsed the audiences with laughter, may be mentioned that which occurred to the inimitable Mrs Davenport as Mrs Heidelberg in the "Clandestine Marriage," who said "she had the keys of her pocket in the cupboard."

A LEGEND.

In our own theatre (says the same writer), there is the established legend of Delphini, the Italian clown, who, charged to exclaim, at a critical moment, "Pluck them asunder!" could produce no more intelligible speech than "Massunder em plocket!" Much mirth in the house and dismay on the stage ensued.

A VARIATION.

An item in Moore's Diary :—Told of the actor saying by mistake—

"How sharper than a serpent's *thanks* it is
To have a *toothless* child." [1]

AN ANCIENT STORY.

Another story by Moore :—I mentioned the actor who could never be got to say, "Stand by, and let the coffin pass," but instead of it always said, "Stand by, and let the parson cough."

ANOTHER VARIATION.

An actress playing the Countess in the "Stranger," when Mrs Haller inquired if she ever heard of the Countess Walburg, instead of giving the author's words, "I have heard of such a wretch at a neighbouring Court; she

---

[1] See *King Lear*, act i., scene 4.

left her husband and fled with a villain," replied, "I 'ave 'eard of sitch a wretch at a neighbouring 'ouse; she left 'er 'usband and ran away with a blackguard."

AN ACCOMMODATING MAN.

It would almost seem that there are some performers whom it is quite vain to prompt: it is safer to let them alone, doing what they list, lest bad should be made worse. Something of this kind (says Dutton Cook) happened once in the case of a certain Marcellus. Hamlet demands of Horatio concerning the ghost of "buried Denmark," "Stayed it long?" Horatio answers, "While one with moderate haste might tell a hundred." Marcellus should add, "Longer, longer." But the Marcellus of this special occasion was mute. "Longer, longer," whispered the prompter. Then out spoke Marcellus to the consternation of his associates, "Well, say two hundred!"

"THOUGHT HE WAS!"

Another disconcerted performer (says the same authority) must have been the provincial Richard III., to whom the Ratcliffe of the theatre—who ordinarily played harlequin, and could not enter without something of that tripping and twirling gait peculiar to pantomime—brought the information long before it was due, that "the Duke of Buckingham is taken!" "Not yet, you fool," whispered Richard. "Beg pardon; thought he was," cried Harlequin Ratcliffe, as, carried away by his feelings and the force of habit, he threw what tumblers call "a catherine-wheel," and made a rapid exit.

A COUPLE.

A novice who had merely to say, "Sonnez trompettes," was so nervous that he exclaimed, "Trompez sonnettes." Another, instead of saying, "C'en est fait, il est mort," blurted out, "C'en est mort, il est fait."

THE REVERSE.

An actress who was representing Agrippine had to say, "Avec Claude dans mon lit, et Rome à mes genoux!" instead of which she exclaimed, amidst a breathless silence, "Avec Rome dans mon lit, et Claude à mes genoux!"

WHAT DID HE DO?

At the Comédie Française, one of the principal artists in a tragedy stopped short after delivering the following line, "I was in Rome, where—" when, finding the prompter not at all disposed to help him out of his difficulty, he turned to him and exclaimed, with the utmost dignity, "Well, you varlet, what did I do in Rome?"

"THAT GENTLEMAN."

At Lunéville, when "La Mélanide" was performed, the actor who represented Darviam quite forgot the words at an important crisis, namely, when declaring his love, but the prompter came to his assistance, and in a loud tone repeated them. With the utmost coolness the actor turned to the actress, to whom he was paying addresses, and said, "Yes, as that gentleman has told you, &c."

THEY HAD CUT HIM OUT.

Here (says Dutton Cook) is a story of a *sotto voce* communication which must have gravely troubled its recipient. A famous Lady Macbeth, "starring" in America, had been accidentally detained on her journey to a remote theatre. She arrived in time only to change her dress rapidly, and hurry on the scene. The performers were all strangers to her. At the conclusion of her first soliloquy, a messenger should enter to announce the coming of King Duncan. But what was her amazement to hear, in answer to her demand, "What is your tidings?" not the usual reply, "The king comes here to-night," but the whisper, spoken from behind a Scotch bonnet, upheld to prevent the words reaching the ears of the audience, "Hush, I'm Macbeth. We've cut the messenger out—go on, please!"

AN UNEXPECTED ELEVATION.

A good story is told of a rich banker at Paris, who, though a sexagenarian, fancied himself a perfect Adonis, and was always behind the scenes, hanging about, and making love to Mademoiselle Saulnier, to whom the machinist of the Opera House was paying his addresses. Determined to be revenged, and profiting by the moment when his rival, in uttering soft nonsense, had inadvertently placed his foot upon a cloud, the machinist gave a whistle, which was the signal for raising the cloud, and when the curtain was drawn up, the audience (says Lord William Lennox) were not a little edified at seeing the banker, with powdered head, and gorgeously attired in evening costume, embroidered coat and waistcoat, ascending to the clouds by the side of Minerva, represented by the object of his devotion.

SHORN OF HIS TRESSES.

Upon another occasion (says the same writer), in the days of pigtails, when an elderly gentleman, with French gallantry, was stooping down to present an actress with a bouquet and kiss her hand, she was suddenly told the stage was waiting; off she ran, and appeared before the audience unconscious that her aged admirer's wig had fallen off and clung to the spangles of her dress.   Loud was the laughter of those in front, and louder still was it when the bald-headed victim appeared at the wing shorn of his capillary ornament.

A NEW READING.

Charles Kean told J. C. Young that, when he (Kean) was fulfilling an engagement at Dublin, Lord Normanby, then Lord Lieutenant, asked him to dine and accompany him to some private theatricals, in which an amateur of original powers was to play the part of Hamlet.   He was said to have thrown new light on obscure passages.   The following Charles Kean gave Young as a specimen of his inventive faculty :—

> " The spirit that I have seen
> May be a devil ; and the devil hath power
> To assume a pleasing shape ; yea, and perhaps
> Out of my weakness and my melancholy
> (As he is very potent with such spirits)
> Abuses me to damn me." [1]

As an improvement on the hackneyed traditional delivery of the last line, he rendered it thus :—

> " Out of my weakness and my melancholy
> (As he is very potent with such spirits)
> Abuses me, too,—Damn me!"

ANOTHER.

I remember on one occasion (says Lord William Lennox) being present at an amateur performance, when the " Lady of Lyons " was represented.   The gentleman who acted Claude Melnotte had evidently studied in the Edmund Kean school, and, like that celebrated tragedian, had a trick of dividing his words ; such as converting " I am your prisoner," into " I am your pris-oner." In the scene where Claude hears from Damas that Pauline is faithless, and has to say,

> " One gleam of sunshine,
> And the ice breaks, and I am lost ! Oh, Damas,"

the unfortunate amateur laid a slight stress upon the first syllable of his friend's name, and no effect was produced.   When, however, he got more impassioned and declaimed the lines, " When first I lost her, Damas," he, wishing to make a Kean hit, divided the word Dam-a, and dropping the last letter delivered it in a way that sounded very like a denunciation, which, according to the magisterial penalty for an oath, would have cost him five shillings.

[1] See *Hamlet*, act ii., scene 2.

"HE WOULD FIND IT ALL RIGHT."

[On one occasion, when "Virginius" was being performed] my unhappy temper (says Macready) was severely tried in the third act of the play, where Siccius Dentatus should be discovered on a bier with a company of soldiers mourning over it. I saw the old man, who represented the Roman Achilles, lying on the ground, and two men standing near. This was too absurd, the body having to be borne off in sight of the audience. I positively refused to go on. "Oh pray, sir," urged the manager, "go on; the men have rehearsed the scene, and you'll find it all right." In vain I represented that the men could not carry off the old man. "Oh yes, indeed, sir," reiterated the manager; "they perfectly understand it." There was nothing for it but submission. After some delay, the scene was drawn up and disclosed the scene as described. On I went, and uttered my lamentation over the prostrate veteran; but when I gave the order, "Take up the body and bear it to the camp," to my agony and horror the two men, stooping down, put an arm underneath the shoulder of the dead Dentatus, raised him to his feet, he preserving a corpse-like rigidity, his eyes closed and his head thrown back, and arm in arm the trio walked off at the opposite side of the stage, amid roars of laughter from the convulsed spectators.

STAND A LITTLE 'BACCA.

Barham tells the following anecdote of Phil Stone, the property-man of Drury Lane. "Will you be so good, sir, as to stand a little backer?" said Phil to a gentleman behind the scenes who had placed himself so forward as to be seen by the audience. "No, my fine fellow," returned the exquisite, who quite mistook his meaning; "but here is a pinch of snuff at your service."

WHICHEVER HE PLEASED.

On one occasion when Macready played Virginius, the actors at rehearsal were greatly amused when Mr Bass as Icilius replied to the playful question of Virginius—"Do you wait for me to lead Virginia in, or will you do it?" "Whichever you please, sir."

MUCH OBLIGED.

Charles Kemble used to tell a story about some poor foreigner, dancer or pantomimist in the country, who after many annual attempts to clear his expenses, came forward one evening with a face beaming with pleasure and gratitude, and addressed the audience in these words: "Dear public! moche oblige. Ver good benefice—only lose half-a-crown—I come again!"

HE WAS MACREADY.

Macready has this entry in his Diary:—In the stage-coach, Captain Bouchier . . talked much, . . . related many amusing stories about the theatre. One of Macready, who is a good actor, but he can never play without applause. He went on one night to play, and no notice was taken of him, on which he said to the manager, "I cannot get on if they do not applaud me." Upon which the manager went round and told the audience that Mr Macready could not act if they did not applaud him. When Macready reappeared, the applause was so incessant as to disconcert him, and he observed, "Why, now I cannot act there is so much applause." I told him I rather discredited the story. "In short," I observed, "perhaps I ought to apologise to you for allowing you to tell it without first giving you my name; my name is Macready."

THE REASON WHY.

Moore records the following as among other happy sarcasms of Redmond Barry on John Crompton. He said once to Corry, who was praising Crompton's performance of some particular character a night or two before, "Yes, he played that part pretty well; he hadn't time to study it !"

"SHAKES HIS HEAD."

The late Mr Charles Mathews (says Mr Walter Baynham[1]) used to relate that on one occasion, in "The Critic," the gentleman who had rehearsed Lord Burleigh's part in the morning was at night missing. "Send in anybody," said the stage manager. The "anybody" was found, dressed, and the book put into his hands. He read the stage direction, "Enter Lord Burleigh, bows to Dangle, shakes his head, and exits." "Anybody" did enter, bowed to Dangle, shook his (Dangle's) head, and made his exit.

"ST PIERRE."

An "anybody" was under similar circumstances sent on, in Knowles's play of "The Wife," to say, "St Pierre waits below." He read the words, mistook the significance of the "St," and announced, "The street-pier is a-waitin' below." He alleged, when remonstrated with, "It was not to be expected that anyone could swallow *Shakespeare* only from the mornin'."

---

[1] In *The Theatre* for 1879.

ASSOCIATION.

Mr Baynham relates how, on one occasion, Macready was victimised in "Virginius." The Numitorius couldn't remember his own name. "You will remember it, sir," said the tragedian, carefully pronouncing it for him, "by the association of ideas. Think of Numbers, the Book of Numbers." The Numitorius *did* think of it all day, and at night produced, through the "association of ideas," the following effect:—

> *Numitorius*—Where is Virginia? Wherefore do you hol'
> That maiden's hand?
> *Claudius*— Who asks the question?
> *Numitorius*—I! her uncle—Deuteronomy!"

SLIGHTLY ALTERED.

I remember (says the same authority) one unfortunate young gentleman who was to make his first appearance in "Richard III.," as one of the small noblemen who wait on Richmond. We had a very small company, and our army on the occasion was represented by one unhappy super, who stood with a banner, and the characteristic "super-shivering legs." The young gentleman had but to say:—

> "Your words are fire, my lord, and warm our men," &c.

He was not *quite* perfect at rehearsal. Night came. The scene drew. "Go on!" shouted the prompter. On the young gentleman was pushed. His cue was given. All that stage fright would permit him to think of was *one* word in the speech. That one word was—*Fire*. He looked at the shivering standard-bearer, and desperately blurted out—

> "If we'd a *fire*, my lord, we'd warm our *men*."

ABOUT STATESMEN AND POLITICIANS.

SINCERE FOR ONCE.

WALPOLE tells what he calls a very **good-humoured** story of Lord North,[1] who was quite **blind in** his old **age.** Colonel Barré made him a visit. Lord North said, " Colonel Barré, nobody will suspect us of insincerity, if we say that we should be overjoyed to *see* each other."

HE WOULD NOT HAVE HIS.

Greville records:—Tommy Townshend, a violent, foolish fellow, who was always talking strong language, said in some debate, "Nothing will satisfy me but to have the noble Lord [North]'s head; I will have his head." Lord North said, "The honourable gentleman says he will have my head. I bear him no malice in return, for though the honourable gentleman says he will have my head, I can assure him I would on no account have his."

NOT TILL THEN.

The Duke of Montrose was called the "Goose," when Lord Graham (in the Rolliad). Moore says that Lord North one night, when, as usual, asleep, was waked to be told that Lord Graham was going to speak. "No, no," said Lord North, "he'll not speak till Michaelmas."

I F !

George the Third (says Barham) scolded Lord North for never going to the concert of ancient music. "Your brother, the bishop," said the king, "never misses them, my lord." "Sir," answered the premier, "if I were as deaf as my brother, the bishop, I would never miss them either!" Barham adds: "Told me by Doctor Blombery, who was present."

A COMPLIMENT.

Lord North's figure (says Mr Hayward) was certainly ill-fitted for oratorical effect; but by dint of tact, temper, and wit, he converted even his personal

---

[1] Second Earl Guildford, and Premier; *b.* 1732, *d.* 1792. Colonel Barré died in the latter year also.

disadvantages into means of persuasion or conciliation. "One member," he once said, "who spoke of me, called me 'that thing called a minister.' To be sure," he said, patting his large form, "I am a thing; the member, therefore, when he called me a 'thing,' said what was true; and I could not be angry with him. But when he added 'that thing called a minister,' he called me that thing which of all things he himself most wished to be, and therefore I took it as a compliment."

TAKING HIS REMEDY.

With equal adroitness Lord North turned his incurable sleepiness to account. When a fiery declaimer, after calling for his head, denounced him for sleeping, he complained how cruel it was to be denied a solace which other criminals so often enjoyed—that of having a night's rest before their execution. And when a dull prosy speaker made a similar charge, he retorted that it was somewhat unjust in the gentleman to blame him for taking the remedy which he himself had been so considerate as to administer.

HIS CONSTITUENTS' LANGUAGE.

Alderman Sawbridge having accompanied the presentation of a petition from Billingsgate with an invective of more than ordinary coarseness, Lord North began his reply in the following words : "I cannot deny that the hon. alderman speaks not only the sentiments but the very language of his constituents."

A MISCONCEPTION.

Lord Shelburne[1] (says Rogers) could say the most provoking things, and yet appear quite unconscious of their being so. In one of his speeches, alluding to Lord Carlisle, he said, "The noble lord has written a comedy." "No, a tragedy." "Oh, I beg pardon; I thought it was a comedy."

A CHOICE OF EVILS.

According to Young the poet, Lord Bolingbroke's father said to him on his being made a lord, "Ah, Harry, I ever said you would be hanged, but now I find you will be beheaded."

TRUE FORBEARANCE.

Mr Hayward says that the first day Shaftesbury presided as Lord Chancellor, he gave occasion to a scene by telling the Duke of York, who had taken

---

[1] Earl of Shelburne, and Premier; *b.* 1737, *d.* 1805.

a seat on the right hand of the throne, that his proper place, as only heir presumptive, was on the left. The Duke submitted with a very bad grace, exclaiming: "My lord, you are a rascal and a villain." To which Shaftesbury calmly replied : "I am much obliged to your royal highness for not calling me likewise a coward and a Papist."

GERMAN DIGNITARIES.

One of Henry Fox's[1] jokes (says Raikes) was that played off on the late Mrs ——, who had a great fondness for making the acquaintance of foreigners. He first forged a letter of recommendation to her in favour of a German nobleman, the Baron von *Seidlitz Powdertz*, whose card was left at her door, and for whom a dinner was immediately planned by Mrs ——, and an invitation sent in form. After waiting a considerable time, no Baron appearing, the dinner was served ; but during the second course a note was brought to the lady of the house, with excuses from the Baron, who was unexpectedly prevented from coming by the sudden death of his aunt, the Duchess von *Epzom Saltz*, which she read out to the company without any suspicion of the joke, and to the entertainment of her guests, among whom was the facetious author.

GOVERNMENT POWDER.

Mr Coke (of Holkham) told Haydon a story of Charles James Fox.[2] One night at Brookes's, Fox made some remark upon Government powder, in allusion to something that had happened. Adam[3] considered it a reflection, and sent Fox a challenge. Fox went out and took his station, giving a full front. Fitzgerald, his second, said, "You must stand sideways." "Why?" said Fox, "I am as thick one way as the other." "Fire!" was given. Adam fired. Fox did not ; and so they shook hands. Adam's bullet had hit Fox below the waist, and fell into his breeches. "Adam," said Fox, "you would have killed me if it hadn't been Government powder."

TWO MAXIMS.

Moore, one day mentioning what Sheridan said to Charles Fox when he was a boy, "Never do to-day what you can put off till to-morrow," found (he says) it was not Sheridan, but the old Lord Holland, who said it to Charles Fox, adding another maxim, "Nor ever do yourself what you can get anyone else to do for you."

---

1 Brother to the Right Hon. **Charles** James Fox, and minister to the United States.
2 **Born 1749**, died 1806.   3 William Adam, lawyer and politician.

A POTATO GARDEN.

The Right Hon. John Heley Hutchinson, after having amassed a large fortune at the bar, and held a distinguished seat in the Senate, accepted the Provostship of Trinity College, and was, I believe (says Phillips) the first person promoted to that rank who had not previously obtained a fellowship. His appointment gave great offence to the University; but he little heeded the resentment which was the consequence of any pecuniary promotion; and, indeed, such was his notoriety in this respect that Lord Townshend, wearied out with his applications, is reported to have said, "By G—! if I gave Hutchinson England and Ireland for an estate, he would solicit the Isle of Man for a potato garden!"

HE WAS SO.

After Legge was appointed Bishop of Oxford, he had the folly (says Rogers) to ask two wits, Canning and Frere, to be present at his first sermon. "Well," said he to Canning,[1] "how did you like it?" "Why, I thought it rather— short." "Oh, yes, I am aware that it was short; but I was afraid of being tedious." "You *were* tedious."

A REASON.

A lady having put to Canning the silly question, "Why have they made the spaces in the iron gate at Spring Gardens so narrow?" he replied, "Oh, ma'am, because such very fat people used to go through"—a reply concerning which (says Rogers) Tom Moore said that "the person who does not relish it can have no perception of real wit."

FACTS AND FIGURES.

According to Sydney Smith, Canning said nothing was so fallacious as facts, except figures.[2]

AN IMPROMPTU.

Canning one night (says Haydon) wrote an impromptu on Phillimore and Wynn :—

> "Oh, Phillimore
> Is such a bore,
> He makes me cry.
> But tho' a bore
> Is Phillimore,
> He don't spit in my eye—"

which Wynn, in speaking, always did.

---

[1] The Right Hon. George Canning; *b.* 1770, *d.* 1827.
[2] The saying is also attributed to Benjamin Constant.

THE DERBY DILLY.

Some of O'Connell's[1] parodies and poetical applications in debate caught (says Phillips) the humour of the House of Commons, and were considered felicitous. Amongst these was his sneer at the smallness of Lord Stanley's personal adherents, after some general election :

> " Thus down thy hill, romantic Ashbourne ! glides
> The *Derby dilly*, carrying *six* insides."

THREE COLONELS.

O'Connell's celebrated parody on three very excellent, and certainly very good-humoured, members of Parliament—Colonels Sibthorp, Perceval, and Verner, was extremely ready, and produced a roar :

> " Three colonels, in three distant counties born,
> Lincoln, Armagh, and Sligo did adorn.
> The first in matchless impudence surpassed,
> The next in bigotry—in both the last :
> The force of nature could no farther go—
> To beard the third, she shaved the other two." [2]

Two of these gentlemen looked as if they never needed a razor, and the third as if he repudiated one.

TIT FOR TAT.

In a political trial O'Connell had charged upon the Attorney-General, Saurin, whom he hated, some official unfairness, of which his colleague, Bushe, chivalrously assumed the responsibility. "If there is blame in it," said he, " I alone must bear it— .

> ' Me, me, adsum qui feci, in me convertite ferrum.'"

" Finish the sentence, Mr Solicitor," exclaimed O'Connell ; "add

> ' Mea *fraus* omnis.'"

EASILY APPREHENDED.

Sir Robert Peel (says Mr Hayward) was the challenger in three affairs which ended peacefully, through no fault of his or his second's. One of these was with O'Connell. An Irish newspaper (inspired, it was said, by the Agitator) announced, first, his departure from Dublin, and next, "his arrival at Slaughter's Coffee-House, on his way to a hostile meeting with the Secretary for Ireland" (Peel). The announcement attracted the attention of the autho-

---

[1] Daniel O'Connell; *b.* 1775, *d.* 1847.
[2] The original of this is, of course, Dryden's " epigram " on Milton.

rities; O'Connell was apprehended, and the further prosecution of the affair was stopped. Shortly afterwards, O'Connell was arguing a case in the Irish Common Pleas, and on the Chief-Justice (Lord Norbury) assuming a puzzled look, paused and said: "Possibly your lordship does not *apprehend* me?" "O yes, Mr O'Connell," was the reply, "no one is more easily *apprehended* when he wishes it."

AN INTEREST IN IT.

One one occasion (says Phillips) Grattan [1] beheld the spot, near Windsor Forest, where some notorious criminal had expiated his guilt, and as yet the gibbet remained. Grattan apostrophized the "hanging wood," as George Robins once called it, and was in the frenzy of an oratorical display, when some one who was passing tapped Grattan on the shoulder, and, pointing to the tenantless gibbet, made the inquiry, "How the d—l did you contrive to get down?" Grattan readily turned the tables upon the wit. "I suppose," he said to his interrogator, "you have an interest in asking that question."

THE BEST THING FOR HIM.

On Lord Thurlow's exclaiming—"When I forget my king, may my God forget me,"—Wilkes [2] muttered—"He'll see you d—d first." Lord Russell states (says Hayward) that Burke's comment on the same occasion was—"And the best thing God can do for him."

A LEVITICAL DEGREE.

Sir Boyle Roche [3] (says Barrington) was induced by Government to fight as hard as possible for the Union;—so he did, and I really believe fancied, by degrees, that he was right. On one occasion, a general titter arose at his florid picture of the happiness which must proceed from this event. "Gentlemen (said Sir Boyle) may titther, and titther, and titther, and may think it a bad measure, but their heads at present are hot, and will so remain till they grow cool again, and so they can't decide right now; but when the *day of judgment* comes, *then* honourable gentlemen will be satisfied at this most excellent Union. Sir, there is no Levitical degrees between nations, and on this occasion I can see neither sin nor shame in *marrying our own sister.*"

A DREADFUL PICTURE.

Sir Boyle (says the same authority) was a determined enemy to the French Revolution, and seldom rose in the House for several years without volunteer-

---

[1] The famous Irish patriot; b. 1750, d. 1820.   [2] John Wilkes; b. 1727, d. 1797.
[3] See pp. 79, 80.

ing some abuse of it.   " Mr Speaker," said he, in a mood of this kind, " if we once permitted the villainous French masons to meddle with the buttresses and walls of our ancient constitution, they would never stop nor stay, sir, till they brought the foundation stones tumbling down about the ears of the nation !   There," continued Sir Boyle, placing his hand earnestly on his heart, his powdered head shaking in unison with his loyal zeal, whilst he described the probable consequences of an invasion of Ireland by the French Republicans ; " There, Mr Speaker ! if those Gallican villains should invade us, sir, 'tis on *that very table*, may-be, these honourable members might see their own destinies lying in heaps a-top of one another ! Here, perhaps, sir, the murderous *marshal-law-men* (Marseillois) would break in, cut us to mince-meat, and throw our bleeding heads upon that table to stare us in the face !"

THE TAIL END.

Sir Frederick Hood, once member for County Wexford, was making (says Barrington) a long speech in the Irish Parliament, lauding the transcendent merits of the Wexford magistracy.   As he was closing a most turgid oration by declaring "that the said magistracy ought to receive some signal mark of the Lord Lieutenant's favour,"—John Egan, who was rather mellow, and sitting behind him, jocularly whispered, "and be whipped at the cart's tail." —"And be whipped at the cart's tail !" repeated Sir Frederick, unconsciously, amidst peals of the most uncontrollable laughter.

FOR VIEWS, READ PROSPECTS.

Possessing a good share of wit and humour, Mackintosh[1] (says Earl Russell) took his part in political warfare, armed no less with the "tart reply" than with the "eloquent harangue."   I remember sitting by him when a great lawyer, disclaiming from the Treasury Bench, all participating in the opinions of the Liberal party, said, "I could see nothing to tempt me in the views of the gentlemen opposite." "For views, read prospects," whispered Mackintosh to me.

TWO BROTHERS.

Of the two brothers Grant—Lord Glenelg and Sir Robert—Robert[2] (says Lord Teignmouth) was unquestionably the more energetic and vivacious.

> " Glenelg and ——
> " He has a very good berth,
> He does nothing at all on the face of the earth ;
> But his brother Bob beyond the sea
> Is a far sprightlier chimpanzee."

So sang Theodore Hook.

---

[1] Sir James Mackintosh: b. 1765, d. 1832.   [2] Sir Robert was governor of Bombay.

"THE SPLENDID SHILLING."

Sir Robert Grant told a story well, and could pun successfully without boring. By way of instance, on the beach at Sidmouth he pronounced the six beautiful Miss Twopennys to be the "splendid shilling."

CON SPIRITO.

Lord Teignmouth says of Sir Robert Grant:—When in the House of Lords, on the occasion of a memorable dissolution of Parliament, I congratulated him, as one of the ministers, on the success of the measure, observing at the same time that I looked on them as conspirators. Drawing himself up, and looking good-humoured, as was his wont when he meditated a *bon mot*, he remarked, "If you mean that we have dissolved Parliament *con spirito*, I admit that we have."

THE FOOD OF HIS ANCESTORS.

One of Moore's anecdotes:—On one of the country gentlemen saying in Parliament, "We must return to the food of our ancestors," somebody asked, "What food does he mean?" "Thistles, I suppose," said Tierney.[1]

WHICH?

Raikes records the following joke made by Holmes in the House of Commons. When Mr Morrison, the member for Leicester, who, being a haberdasher, had made himself conspicuous by a speech on the foreign glove question, came up to him, and asked him if he could get him a *pair* for the evening. "Of what," said Holmes, "gloves or stockings?"

NOT AN OPERA BUFFO.

I must tell you (writes Walpole to Sir Horace Mann) a *bon mot* that was made the other night at the Serenata of "Peace in Europe" by Wall [the Spanish ambassador]. Grossatesta, the Modenese minister, a very low fellow, with all the jackpudding-head of an Italian, asked, "Mais qui est ce qui représente mon maître?" Wall replied, "Mais, l'abbé, ne savez vous pas que ce n'est pas un opéra boufou?"

A WORTHY REPRESENTATIVE.

Moore records what Elliot, the well-known ambassador,[2] said to Frederick of Prussia, on his sending a *roué* of a fellow as minister to England, merely to spite the English Cabinet. "Well, what do you think," asked Frederick,

---

[1] George Tierney; b. 1761, d. 1830.   [2] Ambassador at the Court of Prussia.

tauntingly, "of Monsieur ——?" "Digne représentant de votre Majesté," answered Elliot, bowing very low.

PERSONAL.

Moore also records the story of the King of Prussia (Frederick) asking, "Who is this Hyder Ali?" and Elliot (he thinks it was) answering pointedly, "Un vieux despote militaire, qui a pillé tous les voisins et qui commence à redoter."

THEY WILL SAVE THEMSELVES.

Elliot (says Wraxall) nourished all the anti-Gallican antipathies of a thorough home-bred Englishman, though his whole life had been passed on the Continent among foreigners. Being at the Comèdie Française, during "La Bataille d'Ivry," a dramatic piece, in which Henry IV., after gaining the victory, with a view to stop the effusion of blood, exclaims, "Epargnez mes sujets! sauvez les Francais!" Elliot, who was seated in the amphitheatre, rose, and, elevating his voice, cried out, "Ne vous mett ez pas en peur! ils se sauveront bien eux-mêmes."

A TURKEY MERCHANT.

When Horne Tooke[1] was at school (says Rogers), the boys asked him "What his father was?" Tooke answered, "A Turkey merchant." (He was a poulterer).

A LITTLE PATRIMONY.

At the trial oi Horne Tooke, the Attorney-General (Scott, Lord Eldon), replying to some attack of the defendant, said, "I can endure anything but an attack on my good name; it is the little patrimony I have to leave to my children, and, with God's help, I will leave it unimpaired." Here (says Hayward) he burst into tears, and the Solicitor-General (Mitford) wept with his leader. "Do you know," exclaimed Tooke in a loud aside, "what Mitford is crying for? He is crying to think of the *little* patrimony Scott's children are likely to get."

THE FRENCH OF STRATFORD AT BOW.

[Haydon] asked William Hamilton if Lord Castlereagh[2] spoke good French. Hamilton said, "No. I heard him once, at dinner, say to the Spanish ambassador, 'Votre Roi Ferdinand n'est pas en belle *ordure* (odeur) dans ce

---

[1] Author of *The Diversions of Purley.*   [2] Born 1796, died 1822.

pays-ci.'" This is as good as D'Orsay's story of Lady —— saying to him, when he had a boil on his neck, "Eh bien—aujourd 'hui comment se porte votre queue (cou)?"

DUDLEY AND WARD.

One of Lord Dudley's eccentric habits (says Sinclair) was that of speaking to himself or thinking aloud. Soon after he had succeeded to the title of Dudley and Ward,[1] a lady asked Lord Castlereagh how he accounted for the custom. "It is only Dudley speaking to Ward," was the ready answer to her inquiry.

A COMMON WANT.

One night, at the Duke of Devonshire's, the beautiful Mrs —— was en-treating Lord Melbourne[2] to grant her some favour for a friend. In her eagerness (says Haydon) she seized hold of his hand, saying, "Now *do*, my dear Lord Melbourne, *do!*" Lord Melbourne looked round merrily, and said, "Now *do*, my dear Mrs ——, *do* let go my hand; I want to scratch my nose!"

WHAT DID HE WANT?

On one occasion (says Torrens) a member of the party, whom Lord Melbourne had once described as a fellow who was "asking for everything and fit for nothing," intimated that he had a new request to make, for reasons he wanted an interview to explain. The weary dispenser of patronage showed his note to Anson, saying, "What the devil would he have now! does he want a garter for the other leg?"

BEARING HIS TESTIMONY.

Archbishop Whately (writes the Rev. H. H. Dickenson) asked me if I had ever heard this story of Lord Melbourne. Lord Melbourne was in the House one evening when —— stood up to speak on the Government side. The speech was a very indiscreet one; the speaker dashed into topics about which ministers would rather have had nothing said, and in the course of his remarks, turned towards the bench where Lord M. was sitting, saying, "The noble lord at the head of the Government is fully aware of the accuracy of what I state; the noble lord, having been present at the interview of which I speak, will bear his testimony." The only answer from the Treasury bench was a loud snore.

---

[1] See p. 28.   [2] See the *Life* by Mr Torrens.

HIS CAPITAL AND HIS CREDIT.

Sir Robert Peel (says Hayward) excelled in quiet sarcasm.   In the debate on Commercial Distress (Dec. 3, 1847), Alderman Reynolds, one of the members for Dublin, had asked : "Did not everybody know that the profit and advantage of banking consisted very much in trading on your credit in contradistinction to your capital ?"   In the course of the masterly reply with which Peel closed the debate, he said : "I have the greatest respect for bankers in general, and Irish bankers in particular, and among Irish bankers I well know the position enjoyed by the honourable gentleman.   Now, with all the respect to which he is entitled, and with all suavity and courtesy, I would tell him, that in his banking capacity I would rather have his capital than his credit."

THE CONFIDENCE OF THE CROWN.

In 1848, Feargus O'Connor[1] was charged in the House with being a Republican.   He denied it, and said he did not care whether the Queen or the Devil was on the throne.   Peel replied : "When the honourable gentleman sees the sovereign of his choice on the throne of these realms, I hope he'll enjoy, and I am sure he'll deserve, the confidence of the Crown."

NOT ALWAYS.

Shiel had learnt and forgotten the exordium of a speech which began with the word "necessity."   This word he had repeated three times, when Sir R. Peel broke in—"is not *always* the mother of invention."

NOT THE LEAST OFFENDED.

Lord Palmerston (says Mr Hayward) had humour of the genial give-and-take kind, which, for a party leader, is often more serviceable than wit.   He was told that Mr Osborne, a popular speaker, whose dash and sparkle are enhanced by good feeling and sagacity, regretted a personal conflict, which he had provoked.   "Tell him," said Lord Palmerston, "that I am not the least offended, the more particularly because I think I had the best of it."

THE LAST THING.

Mr Jeaffreson tells us that Lord Palmerston, during his last attack of gout, exclaimed, playfully, "*Die*, my dear doctor !   That's the *last* thing I think of doing."

---

[1] The Chartist, d. 1855.

CANT AND RE-CANT.

Lord John Russell (says Mr Hayward) particularly excelled in a comprehensive reply at the end of an important debate ; and one of the most telling retorts ever uttered in either House was his, when Sir Francis Burdett, after turning Tory and becoming a member of the Carlton Club, thought proper to sneer at the "cant of patriotism." "I quite agree with the honourable baronet that the cant of patriotism is a bad thing. But I can tell him a worse—the re-cant of patriotism—which I will gladly go along with him in reprobating whenever he shows me an example of it."

THE TERRIER PARTS.

As Mr Hayward says, one of the best specimens of Mr Bright's racy humour was in the speech in which he introduced the cave of Adullam, and, in allusion to the alliance between two of the principal occupants, Mr Lowe and Mr Horsman, said: "This party of two reminds me of the Scotch terrier, which was so covered with hair that you could not tell which was the head and which was the tail of it."

HE PREFERRED THE GOUT.

Lord William Lennox records the following clever saying of the late Earl of Derby. The story runs thus: The noble lord received a present of some wine, which was pronounced by the wine-merchant to be an admirable specific against gout. Not receiving a gracious acknowledgment of the gift, the donor addressed a letter of remonstrance to the head of the House of Stanley, which drew forth the following reply : "Lord Derby presents his compliments to Messrs —— —— & Co., and in reply to their letter, begs to say that he much prefers the gout to their wine."

' REPROVED BY HIS ASS.

In the debate on the Occasional Conformity and Schism Bill in the House of Lords, in December 1718, it was very warmly opposed by Bishop Atterbury, who said " he had prophesied last winter this bill would be attempted in the present session, and he was sorry to find he had proved a true prophet." Lord Coningsby rose immediately after the bishop, and remarked that " one of the right reverends had set himself forth as a prophet ; but, for his part, he did not know what prophet to liken him to, unless to that famous prophet Balaam, who was reproved by his own ass." The bishop, in reply : " Since the noble lord hath discovered in our manners such a similitude, I am well content to be compared to the prophet Balaam ; but, my lords, I am at a loss how to make out the other part of the parallel.   I am sure that I have been reproved by nobody but his lordship."

RISING TO THE OCCASION.

The witty and profligate Lord Rochester was very unfortunate when, to win a bet or stimulated by the taunts of his gay companions, he made an attempt [at oratory in the House of Lords].   He began thus:—" My Lords, I rise this time.   My Lords, I divide my discourse into four branches."   Here he faltered and paused.   " My Lords, if ever I rise again in this House, I give you leave to cut me off, root and branch, for ever."

AN *A PROPOS* STORY.

Charles Greville writes:—Payne told me a good story by the way.   A certain bishop in the House of Lords rose to speak, and announced that he should divide what he had to say into twelve parts, when the Duke of Wharton interrupted him, and begged he might be indulged for a few minutes, as he had a story to tell which he could only introduce at that moment.   A drunken fellow was passing by St Paul's at night, and heard the clock slowly chiming twelve.   He counted the strokes, and when it had finished, looked towards the clock, and said, " D—n you! why couldn't you give us all that at once?"   There was an end of the bishop's speech.

EASILY GRATIFIED.

One evening (says Mark Boyd) an English member, in his peroration, in some humorous remarks respecting Scotland, had given sad offence to Mr Dempster, M.P. for the burghs of Forfar, Perth, Dundee, Cupar, and St Andrews, who was no exception to Sydney Smith's charge against Scotchmen of not understanding a joke, for the moment he concluded, up rose the aggrieved member, and in a loud voice addressed the Speaker.   "Sir, I beg to inform the honourable member, in reply to those most illiberal remarks with which he has concluded his speech, that I am proud of having been born a Scotchman and brought up a Presbyterian," and down he sat; when his honourable opponent rose and said—" Mr Speaker, all I have to say is that I consider the honourable member very thankful for extremely small mercies."

A PROFANE BREWER.

When Sir Paul Methuen endeavoured to stop the interruptions of a tipsy brewer, called Kearsley, the latter, amidst the roars of the House, shouted, "Paul! Paul! why persecutest thou me?"

ONLY WILKES COULD DO IT.

Lord Sidmouth said that the only time his gravity was tried in the chair was when Brook Watson, getting up (on some subject connected with Nootka Sound), said—"Mr Speaker, it is impossible, at this moment, to look at the north-east without at the same time casting a glance to the south-west." The Speaker stood this pretty well; but hearing some one behind the chair say, "By G—, no one in the House but Wilkes could do that,"[1] he no longer could keep his countenance, but burst out into a most undignified laugh.

AGAINST HIM.

Moore once heard Luttrel tell the story of some Irish member (Crosbie, I believe) who, in speaking of some one in the House, said, "Sir, if I have any partiality for the hon. gentleman, it is against him."

NOT THAT.

Fox (says Rogers) was sitting at Brookes's, in a very moody humour, having lost a considerable sum at cards, and was indolently moving a pen backwards and forwards over a sheet of paper. "What is he drawing?" said some one to Hare.[2] "Anything but a draft," was the reply.

"WITH ONE ACCORD."

Luttrell (writes Moore in his Diary) told us about Hare, describing Tarleton, on some occasion when there was a mob collected round Devonshire House, saying to them, "My good fellows, if you grow riotous, I shall really be obliged to *talk to you*." "Upon which (said Hare) they dispersed immediately."

---

[1] It should be explained that Wilkes *squinted*.   [2] James Hare, *d.* 1804.

ABOUT THE CHURCH AND THE CLERGY, UNIVERSITIES AND SCHOLARS.

HE MIGHT BE BOTH.

AT one of the annual dinners of the members of the Chapel Royal, a gentleman had been plaguing Barham (of "Ingoldsby" fame) with a somewhat dry disquisition on the noble art of fencing. Wishing to relieve himself of his tormentor, the latter observed that his crippled hand had precluded him from indulging in that amusement; but, pointing to Cannon,[1] who sat opposite, he added, "That gentleman will better appreciate you; he was an enthusiastic admirer of fencing in his youth." After a few minutes the disciple of Angelo contrived to slip round the table, and commenced a similar attack upon Cannon. For some time he endured it with patience, till at length, on his friend's remarking that Sir George D—— was a great fencer, Cannon, who disliked the man, replied, "I don't know whether Sir George D—— is a great fencer, but Sir George D—— is a great fool." A little startled, the other rejoined, "Well, possibly he is; but then a man may be both." "So I see, sir!" said Cannon, turning away. The story is told by Barham's son.

PSALMS AND HYMNS.

At Hook's one day (says Jerdan) the conversation turned on the Duke of Cumberland, and a question asked who he married. "Don't you know," said Cannon; "the Princess de *Psalms* (Salms),—good enough for *Hymn* (him)."

"AND THEY SADDLED HIM."

Mr Hayward recalls to us, in one of his essays, Rowland Hill's[2] reply when, on one occasion, he read from his pulpit an anonymous letter reproaching him with driving to chapel in his carriage, and reminding him that this was not our blessed Lord's mode of travelling. He said, "I must admit that it is not. But if the writer of this letter will come here next Sunday, bridled and saddled, I shall have great pleasure in following our blessed Lord's example in that as in all other matters within my power."

---

[1] See *ante*, p. 21.
[2] The well-known Dissenting preacher. See the *Life* by Mr Charlesworth.

BIG ONES.

When preaching (says Mr Charlesworth) at St John's, Wapping, on one occasion, observing that his auditory was unusually large, and made up chiefly of seafaring persons, Rowland Hill remarked, "I am come to preach to great sinners, notorious sinners, profane sinners," and, with peculiar emphasis, exclaimed, "yea, to *Wapping* sinners."

A HAVEN OF REFUGE.

On a wet day, a number of persons took shelter in Rowland Hill's chapel during a heavy shower, while he was preaching. Hill remarked, "Many people are greatly to be blamed for making their religion a *cloak*, but I do not think that those are much better who make it an umbrella."

"NOTHING IN IT."

A lady once requested Rowland Hill to examine her son as a candidate for the ministry, remarking, "I am sure he has a talent, but it is hid in a napkin." At the close of the interview with the young man, Mr Hill said, "Well, madam, I have shaken the napkin, but I cannot find the talent."

SIMILIA SIMILIBUS.

Rowland Hill once witnessed the ordination of a minister in Scotland, and one of the elders of the Presbytery, not being able to reach his hand far enough to impose it on the head of the candidate, used the end of his cane for the purpose. "This," said Mr Hill, "did equally well; it was timber to timber."

AN UNKNOWN QUANTITY.

A rather talkative woman one day said to Rowland Hill, "I have been a good deal of late with some Papists, and they have sadly tempted me to change my religion." "Indeed, ma'am," he replied, "I was not aware until now that you had any religion to change."

GREATLY RELIEVED.

Rowland Hill once became surety for a member of his church. The man failed, and the incautious pastor had to pay £1000—the amount of the bond. The same day on which he discharged his liability, he called upon a friend, who, observing that he was unusually depressed, remarked, "Why, Mr Hill, what's the matter with you to-day? You seem altogether heavy and uncomfortable." "Heavy, sir," replied Mr Hill; "you are quite mistaken there, for I am a thousand pounds lighter than I was yesterday."

N

HIS FIRST UTTERANCE.

According to Mr L'Estrange, the Rev. W. Harness tells several little anecdotes illustrative of Paley's[1] homely manners and rough humour. For example :—At the first visitation [Paley] attended, after his preferment to the Archdeaconry [of Carlisle], he dined in company with a large assemblage of clergymen, all of whom were eager to hear his observations. He remained silent, to their great disappointment, till the second course was served. At length the great man spoke! Every ear was strained. What was his oracular utterance ? "I don't think these *puddens* are much good unless the seeds are taken out of the raisins !"

A VERY DIFFERENT MATTER.

At another banquet, shortly after Paley's preferment, he found himself exposed to an unpleasant draught of air. "Shut that window behind me," he called to one of the waiters, "and open one lower down, behind one of the curates !"

FLAT BURGLARY.

Among the Rev. Ozias Linley's most notable eccentricities was absence of mind. His brother-in-law, Sheridan, invented ludicrous instances of it, and even told them in his presence. When allusion was made to one of these (says Archdeacon Sinclair) Linley exclaimed with indignation, "That is an everlasting lie; but," he added, with returning good humour, "I will tell you something better, which really befell me." He then began : "While I was a minor canon at Norwich, I went one evening to my tobacconist's, and having filled my snuff-box, was about to leave the shop, when, I know not how it happened, but I took up the two brass candlesticks that were standing lighted on the counter, and was walking into the street with them, one in each hand, when the tobacconist recalled me to myself by exclaiming, 'Surely, Mr Linley, you do not intend to carry off my candlesticks !'"

AN ADVENTURE.

The Rev. Ozias Linley sometimes related a still more remarkable instance of his own obliviousness :—"It was my turn," he said, "as a minor canon, to preach in Norwich Cathedral, and well knowing my own infirmity, I rang the bell, and put the key of my study into my landlady's hands, requesting her to lock the door, and come again to let me out in time for the service. She raised objections, and insisted on returning the key, but somehow I remained under an impression that she had taken it with her as I desired.

---

[1] William Paley, D.D., author of the famous *Evidences;* b. 1743, d. 1805.

Accordingly I read my sermon over till the bells began to ring. I then put on my surplice, but no landlady came to release me. I read half my sermon over again, but still no landlady appeared. Looking out of the window I saw the congregation assembling, and at length the great bell began to toll, as it always did when the Dean and Chapter were about to form into procession. Still no landlady appeared. In this extremity I threw open the window, and with the help of the water-butt and water-spout, climbed down in my canonicals into the street. Happily I was so late that comparatively few of the congregation witnessed this exploit. On my return home after the service I put my hand mechanically into my pocket, and had opened the door of my lodgings before I called to mind my imaginary difficulty."

NOTHING TO PAY.

"What have I to pay?" said Mr Linley, coming to a turnpike, whip in hand, with a bridle trailing on the ground. "You have nothing to pay, sir," replied the turnpike keeper; "you must have left your horse behind you." This conjecture was correct. Linley had undertaken to do duty at a church a few miles from Norwich, and in order to relieve his horse, had dismounted to walk part of the way. The bridle had slipped off while he was in a brown study, thinking of "Plato's Dialogues" or "Hartley on Man," and he reached the turnpike quite unconscious of the loss he had sustained.[1]

MALE AND FEMALE.

Lord Teignmouth tells several amusing stories about Dr Drake of Langton. For instance :—On his first visit to his neighbours he would introduce his wife and himself, as "Duck and Drake."

SCRUTON-Y.

When Dr Drake heard of a very likely young man staying at Scruton Hall, the residence of some well-apportioned young ladies, he would circulate the report that so-and-so was "*scrutinising.*"

A GOOD GRACE.

When the good Duchess of Leeds requested Dr Drake to say the grace at the dinner-table at Hornby Castle, he simply replied, "Madam, your Grace is sufficient for me."

---

[1] A similar story is told by the Rev. J. C. Young of the poet Bowles, and Sydney Smith has a reference to such a tale as being recounted of "a clergyman."

UNBEARABLE.

A close glass bookcase once provoked from Dr Drake the remark that he never could stand "Locke on the Human Understanding."

A MEDDLER.

It was when dining with a friend in Worcester College (says Miss Whately) that a trifling incident brought out one of Whately's[1] happiest *bons mots.* There were some medlars on the table, and his host regretted that he had in vain tried to procure also some **services** (*Pyrus domestica,* a fruit which grows wild in Kent and Sussex, and is there called "checquers.") One of the company asked the difference between a "service" and a "meddler," to which Mr Whately replied, "The same kind of difference as between ' officium ' and ' officiosus.' "

PERSECUTION.

One day, when Dr Whately was conversing with a friend, something was said on the subject of religious persecution ; on which he remarked, "It is no wonder that some English people have a taste for persecuting on account of religion, since it is the first lesson that most are taught in their nurseries." His friend expressed his incredulity, and denied that *he,* at least, had been taught it. "Are you sure ?" replied Dr Whately. "What do you think of this ?—

> ' Old Daddy Longlegs *won't say his prayers,*
> Take him by the left leg, and throw him downstairs.'

If that is not religious persecution, what is ?"

DISSENT IN CHINA.

A lady from China who was dining with Archbishop Whately told him that English flowers reared in that country lose their perfume in two or three years. "Indeed !" was the immediate remark, "I had no idea the Chinese were such de-scent-ers."

THAT IS WHY.

Whately once asked a roomful of divines why white sheep eat so very much more than black sheep. It was solemnly suggested that black being a warmer colour than white, black sheep could do with less nutriment. Whately gravely shook his head, and answered, "White sheep eat more, because there are more of them."

---

1 **Richard Whately,** Archbishop of Dublin; *b.* 1787, *d.* 1863.

ONE OF THE FIRST.

"Sir, you are one of the first men of the age,"[1] said Whately to one whose conceit had offended him. "Oh, my lord," replied the other, highly delighted; "you do me too much honour." "Not at all," replied Whately; "you were born, I believe, in 1801."[2]

QUERY.

"There is nothing," said a dealer, speaking of a horse, "which he cannot draw." "Can he draw an inference?" asked Whately.

RE-TAILED.

Whately once startled his listeners by asking, "If the devil lost his tail, where would he go to find a new one?" and without waiting for others to guess, replied, "To a gin palace, for bad spirits are re-tailed there."

THE REASON.

"Why [asked Whately] does the operation of hanging kill a man?" A physiologist gravely replied, "Because inspiration is checked, circulation stopped, and blood suffuses and congests the brain." "Bosh!" cried Whately; "it is because the rope is not long enough to let his feet touch the ground."[3]

A DREADFUL ALTERNATIVE.

While at Heidelberg (says J. C. Young) I used to take daily lessons in German from a certain Dr Hühle, who had been for some years the minister of the German Lutheran chapel in the Strand. He was the dirtiest man I ever saw. I may safely add, he was the vainest. I found him, on a particular occasion, overlooking, sorting, and making selections from a large pile of sermons and manuscripts. I said to him, "Have you never published any of your many compositions?" Looking over his pipe at me, with an air of great

---

[1] The same joke occurs in Heine's *Reisebilde:*—"'I was born, signora, on New Year's Night, 1800.' 'Did I not tell you,' said the Marquis, 'that he is one of the first men of our century?'"

[2] See Fitzpatrick's *Life of Whately*, where will be found all the more familiar of his witticisms.

[3] Many of Whately's most amusing sayings were in this form of question and answer. Thus:—"What is the female of a male coach? A miscarriage." "Why has Ireland the richest capital in the world? Because its capital is always *doubling* (Dublin)." "What is the difference between an Irishman and a Scotchman on the top of a mountain in frosty weather? One is *cowld* with the *kilt*, and the other is *kilt* with the *cowld*." And so on.

importance, he thus addressed me : "Saar ! you are not de erste persone who have asked me dat question wit surbrise.　Der Herr von Nöhden, die Librarium of die Breeches Mooseum at London, von day said to me ver plain— 'Mein goote frennd, vy do you not bublish ?' I shook mein head. 'Oh,' said dat great man, 'you musht bublish ! you musht indeed ! I vill speak out ! You musht ovacooate your brain, or, by —— ! you vill bursht !"

"A LAPSY LINGO."

Barham records that [at a] dinner of the Sons of the Clergy at Merchant Tailors' Hall, Archbishop Howley,[1] a nervous man, by a ludicrous *lapsus linguæ* gave as a toast, instead of "Prosperity to the Merchant Tailors' Company," "Prosperity to the Merchant Company's Tailor !"

A PRECISE PRAYER.

The long reign of George the Third was brought to a close on the 29th of January 1820.　On the following Sunday (says Lord Cockburn) Sir Harry Moncreiff, not satisfied with merely praying for the new sovereign generally, said in plain terms, giving the very date, that there might be no mistake about it, "And oh, Lord, stablish his heart in righteousness, and in the principles of the glorious revolution of sixteen hunder and echty-echt."

TIT FOR TAT.

Lord Campbell[2] says that Sir John Trevor was so incensed by the promotion to the primacy of Tillotson,[3] whom he considered a Low Churchman, that, passing him one day near the House of Lords, he could not refrain from uttering, loud enough to be heard by the object of his spleen, "I hate a fanatic in lawn sleeves." "And I," retorted the primate, "hate a knave in any sleeves."

BISHOP BLUSTER.

Lord Teignmouth notes that Bishop Mansell, of Bristol, was the subject of the following allusion to his having purchased, with a view to pulling it down, a public-house in the town next door to his own residence, glorying in the sign of Bishop Blaize :—

> "'Two of a trade can ne'er agree,'
> No proverb e'er was juster ;
> They've ta'en down Bishop Blaize, d'ye see?
> And set up Bishop Bluster."

---

[1] Archbishop of Canterbury; b. 1765, d. 1848.
[2] The authority for this story seems to be the *Life of Jeffreys*.
[3] John Tillotson, Archbishop of Canterbury; b. 1630, d. 1694.

A MATTER OF CHOICE.

Mark Boyd writes:—Among the numerous anecdotes of my late Lincoln-shire clerical friend, the Rev. W. Wright, of Brattleby, was the following : The clergyman of a mountainous district in Yorkshire, whose parsonage was under repair, arrived at the public-house of the village to attend to his duties on the Sunday morning. The rain was descending in torrents, and, when the time had arrived for going into church, he sent the clerk to see what sort of congregation there was, who returned and reported that it consisted of Smith and Davies, the two shepherds. On hearing this the clergyman said, "You had better go and ask them whether they would prefer a sermon or a pot of beer." He came back immediately to inform him that they would much prefer the pot of beer. The pot was sent for and discussed accordingly, and the sermon put by for a "more convenient season."

A STEADY EYE.

Curran (says Phillips) used to relate with great glee a mishap which befell a Roman Catholic bishop who went up to the Castle [at Dublin] to adulate the Lord Lieutenant. It seems one of Lord Cornwallis's eyes was smaller than the other, and had acquired a quick, perpetual, oscillatory motion. The addressers, who had never seen him, had elaborated their com-pliments in the country. His excellency was on his throne in high state, when Bishop Lanigan of Kilkenny, at the head of his clergy, auspiciously commenced: "Your Excellency has always had *a steady eye* upon the interests of Ireland." The room was in a roar.

A KING.

Sheridan (says L'Estrange) was not devoid of that vanity which so often accompanies talent. On one occasion he made a very high-flown speech, in which he spoke of himself as being "descended from the loins of kings!' "That's quite true," said Dr Spry, who was sitting next Harness ; "the last time I saw his father [who was an actor], he was the King of Denmark."

PITHY AND CONCISE.

Mark Boyd says in his *Reminiscences:—*I have before me, in remembrance, that charming and aged Irish Episcopalian clergyman, the late Dr Richardson, of Confagle, in the county of Tyrone. As boys, we admired the doctor's grace much, because it was pithy and concise. My mother's usual request, "Doctor, will you say grace ?" "With pleasure, *ma'am.*" The words were then uttered rapidly, but sonorously :—"God bless us and our *mate,* Amen. At the conclusion of dinner, "Doctor, may I ask you ?" "Most *sartenly, ma'am.* 'Thank God for what we have *resaived,* Amen.'"

"THE OTHER NINE."

Doctor Hughes told Barham the following anecdote, which he heard from the "Great Unknown." A Scottish clergyman, whose name was not mentioned, had some years since been cited before the Ecclesiastical Assembly at Edinburgh, to answer to a charge brought against him of great irreverence in religious matters, and Sir Walter was employed by him to arrange his defence. The principal fact alleged against him was his having asserted, in a letter which was produced, that "he considered Pontius Pilate to be a very ill-used man, as he had done more for Christianity than all the *other nine apostles* put together." The fact was proved, and suspension followed.

NUBERE AND *BIBERE*.

Lord Eldon used to tell the following story :—A clergyman who had two small Corpus livings adjoining each other, Newbury and Bibury, and who always performed the morning service in the former and the evening in the latter, being asked in the Hall why he did not divide the duties equally between them, made answer, "I go to *nubere* in the morning, because that is the time *to marry*, and I go to *bibere* in the evening, because that is the time *to drink*."

NOTHING BETTER.

Mr Hayward says that George III. once ironically asked an eminent divine, who was just returned from Rome, whether he had converted the Pope. "No, sire ; I had nothing better to offer him."

BEYOND PURGATORY.

L'Estrange says :—The Bishop of Derry was disputing with a Roman Catholic priest about Purgatory. "Well, my lord," replied the priest in conclusion, "you may go farther and fare worse."

"IN ALL RESPECTS CONTEMPTIBLE."

Dickens writes to his friend Fields[1] :—I saw a scene of mingled comicality and seriousness at [a] funeral some weeks ago, which has choked me at dinner time ever since. C—— and I went as mourners. There was an independent clergyman present, with his bands on and a Bible under his arm, who, as soon as we were seated, addressed —— thus in a loud, emphatic voice, "Mr C——, have you seen a paragraph respecting our departed friend, which has gone the round of the morning papers ?" "Yes, sir," says C——, "I have," looking very hard at me the while, for he had told me with some

---

[1] *Yesterdays with Authors.*

pride coming down that it was his composition. "Oh!" said the clergyman. "Then, you will agree with me, Mr C——, that it was not only an insult to me, who am a servant of the Almighty, but an insult to the Almighty, whose servant I am." "How is that, sir?" said C——. "It is stated, Mr C——, in that paragraph," says the minister, "that when Mr H—— failed in business as a bookseller, he was persuaded by *me* to try the pulpit, which is false, incorrect, and unchristian, in manner blasphemous, and in all respects contemptible. Let us pray." With which, and in the same breath, I give you my word, he knelt down, as we all did, and began a very miserable jumble of an extemporary prayer. I was really penetrated with sorrow for the family, but when C—— (upon his knees, and sobbing for the loss of an old friend) whispered me, "That if that wasn't a clergyman, and it wasn't a funeral, he'd have punched his head," I felt as if nothing but convulsions could possibly relieve me.

·IT WENT, BUT WAS NOT GONE.

A late Bishop of Exeter, in the course of conversation at a dinner-party, mentioned that many years since, while trout-fishing, he lost his watch and chain, which he supposed had been pulled from his pocket by the bough of a tree. Sometime afterwards, when staying in the same neighbourhood, he took a stroll by the side of the river, and came to the secluded spot where he supposed he had lost his valuables, and there, to his surprise and delight, he found them under a bush. The anecdote, vouched for by the word of a bishop, astonished the company; but this was changed to amusement by his son's inquiring whether the watch, when found, was going. "No," replied the bishop; "the wonder was that it was not gone."

"DO RABBIT IT!"

Everyone (says J. C. Young) knows the old story of the curate, who had his Sunday dinner invariably with his rector, and who, never having had anything but rabbits served up in different ways, was asked to say grace, and delivered himself of these lines:—

> " For rabbits hot, for rabbits cold,
> For rabbits young, for rabbits old,
> For rabbits tender, for rabbits tough,
> We thank the Lord we've had enough."

A very amusing person rendered them into Latin, thus—

> " Pro conibus calidis, conibus frigidis,
> Pro conibus mollibus, conibus rigidis,
> Pro conibus senibus,
> Atque juvenibus,
> Grates aqimus fatis,
> Habuimus satis."

ORIGINAL.

A clergyman had commenced an able discourse, when one of the hearers, an accomplished but eccentric man, exclaimed, "That's Tillotson !" This (says Mark Boyd) was allowed to pass, but very soon another exclamation followed. "That's Paley." The preacher then addressed the disturber. "I tell you, sir, if there is to be a repetition of such conduct, I shall call on the church-warden to have you removed from the church." "That's your own," was the ready reply.

A WITTY PRIEST.

Yelverton, the Irish lawyer, was at Killarney with his friend, the witty Father O'Leary. Both were present at a stag-hunt, and the hunted deer approaching the Attorney-General, fell quite exhausted at his feet. "Dear Mr Yelverton," exclaimed Father O'Leary, "what wonderful instinct that stag possesses ! He comes directly to you, expecting that, in your official capacity, you'll at once issue a *nolle prosequi* in his favour."

BOTH OF THEM WERE APOSTLES.

There was an old woman living at Naples, very devout, who went to her confessor on a case of conscience. Her object (says Barham) was to learn whether San Gennaro or the Virgin Mary was the greater saint. "Why, daughter," said the padre, "that is a very nice question, and perhaps it might puzzle the Holy Father himself to decide upon it. However, for your comfort it may perhaps be satisfactory to know that both of them were Apostles."

IT WOULD NOT HAVE HAPPENED.

When Porson[1] was told that Prettyman[2] had been left a large estate by a person who had seen him only once, he said, "It would not have happened if the person had seen him twice." This and the following things are told by Maltby.

NOT A SCOTCHMAN.

A gentleman who had heard that Bentley was born in the North, said to Porson, "Wasn't he a Scotchman ?" "No, sir," replied Porson ; Bentley was a great Greek scholar."

---

[1] The famous scholar: *b.* 1759, *d.* 1808.

[2] "Then Bishop of Lincoln. A valuable estate was bequeathed to him by Marmaduke Tomline (a gentleman with whom he had no relationship or connection) on condition of his taking the name of Tomline."—*Dyce.*

APT RHYMES.

Maltby says he often heard Porson repeat the following lines, which he presumed were his own composition:—

> " *Poetis non laetamur* **tribus,**
> Pye, *Petro* Pindar, **parvo** Pybus;
> *Si ulterius ire pergis,*
> *Adde his* Sir James Bland Burgess."

HE AND HECUBA.

At some college dinner, where (says Moore), in giving toasts, the name was spoken from one end of the table, and a quotation applicable to it was to be supplied from the other, on the name of Gilbert Wakefield [the scholar] being given out, Porson, who hated him, roared forth, "What's Hecuba to him, or he to Hecuba?"[1]

SOBER AND DRUNK.

According to Moore, Porson said one night, when he was very drunk, to Dodd, who was pressing him hard in an argument, "Jemmy Dodd, I always despised you when sober, and I'll be d—d if I'll argue with you now that I'm drunk."

OUT OF HIS MOUTH.

Crabb Robinson tells some good stories of Donaldson (the scholar).[2] For instance:—Some one complaining, "You take the words out of my mouth;" Donaldson replied, "You are very hard to please; would you have liked it better if I had made you swallow them?"

A SOUND DIVINE.

At the Athenæum with Dr Donaldson, the term *sound Divine* being used, I said, "I do not know what is a sound Divine," quoting Pope,—

> "Dulness is sacred in a sound divine."

"But I do," said Donaldson; "it is a divine who is *vox et praeterea nihil.*"

A COMPLIMENT.

Lady C——, offering a wager, was asked what it should be. "A feather from one of my wings when I am an angel." "I would recommend your ladyship," said Donaldson, "to abstain from such wagers. There is a great danger, if you do not, you may be plucked."

---

[1] In allusion to his classical criticisms. [2] Born 1812, died 1861.

SUPER-FISH-ALL.

It was said at table, "If you can give me at dinner a good dish of fish after soup, I want no more." "That is not my doctrine," said Dr Donaldson. "On such a theme I am content to be held *superficial.*"

AND WAS IT?

Rogers once said to Planché—My old friend Maltby, the brother of the Bishop, was a very absent man.   One day at Paris, in the Louvre, we were looking at the pictures, when a lady entered, who spoke to me, and kept me some minutes in conversation.   On rejoining Maltby, I said, "That was Mrs ——. We have not met so long, she had almost forgotten me, and asked if my name was Rogers."   Maltby, still looking at the pictures, said, "And was it?"

A MOTTO.

Being one day at Trinity College at dinner, [Donne] was asked to write a motto for the college snuff-box, which was always circulating at the dinner-table. "Considering where we are," said Donne, "there could be nothing better than 'Quicunque vult!'"   The story is told by Crabb Robinson.

A TIMID WOOER.

Dr Haldane, a Professor of St Andrews University, was one of the most estimable of men, universally respected by all who knew him, and yet, in spite of a pleasing person, a genial manner, a good position, a good house, and a handsome competency, he was well advanced in life before he could make up his mind to marry. No misogynist was he! Womankind he loved, "not wisely, but too well;" and yet, when in their presence, his self-possession forsook him, and he became a much-oppressed and bashful man. When it was reported that he had fitted up his house afresh, at the very time when appearances were of less consequence to him, it was generally supposed, and currently reported, that he was going to change his state. There is no doubt the rumour was well founded; for, on a given day, at an hour unusually early for a call, the good doctor was seen at the house of a certain lady, for whom he had long been supposed to have a predilection, in a bran-new coat, wiping "his weel-pouthered head" with a clean white handkerchief, and betraying much excitement of manner, till the door was opened. As soon as he was shown "ben," and saw the fair one whom he sought calmly engaged in knitting stockings, and not at all disturbed by his entrance, his courage, like that of Bob Acres in the "Rivals," began to ooze out at the tips of his fingers, and he sat himself down on the edge of his chair in such a state of pitiable confu-

sion as to elicit the compassion of the lady in question. She could not understand what ailed him; but felt instinctively that the truest good-breeding
would be to take no notice of his embarrassment, and lead the conversation
herself. Thus, then, she opened fire:—"Weel, Doctor, hae ye got through
a' your papering and painting yet?" (A clearing of the throat preparatory to
speech, but not a word uttered). "I'm told your new carpets are just
beautifu'." (A further clearing of the throat, and a vigorous effort to speak,
terminating in a free use of his handkerchief). "They say the pattern o' the
dining-room chairs is something quite out o' the way. In short, that everything aboot the house is perfect." Here was a providential opening he was
not such a goose as to overlook. He "screwed his courage to the sticking
place," advanced his chair, sidled towards her, simpering the while, raised
his eyes furtively to her face, and said, with a gentle inflection of his voice,
which no ear but a wilfully deaf one could have misinterpreted, "Na! na!
Miss J—n. It's no *quite* perfect. It canna be quite that, so long as there's
ae thing wanting!" "And what can that be?" said the imperturbable spinster. Utterly thrown on his beam ends (says Young) by her wilful blindness
to his meaning, the poor man beat a hasty retreat, drew back his chair from
its dangerous proximity, caught up his hat, and, in tones of blighted hope,
gasped forth his declaration in these words—"Eh! dear! eh! Well 'am sure!
The thing wanting is, a—a—a—sideboard!"

NOT DEAD—MAY DIE.

Windham,[1] when undergraduate, hated a pun, good or bad. Reading
Demosthenes one day with great admiration, and coming to Τί εὐηχι Φίλιππος;
(Is Philip dead?) Οὐ, μὰ Δἰ (No! by Jupiter!) he was put (says Lord Eldon
into a great passion by a fellow-student saying, "No, Windham, you see he
is *not dead;* the Greek words only say he *may die.*"

THAT WAS WHAT HE SAID.

Harrison says:—I heard an anecdote at Oxford of a proctor encountering on
his rounds two undergraduates, who were without their gowns, or out of
bounds, or out of hours. He challenged one: "Your name and college?"
They were given. Turning to the other: "And pray, sir, what might your
name be?" "Julius Cæsar," was the reply. "What, sir! Do you mean to
say your name is Julius Cæsar?" "Sir, you did not ask me what it is, but
what it *might* be." The proctor, repressing a smile, turned away.

---

[1] William Windham, the politician: *b.* 1810.

HALVES AND QUARTERS.

Says the same writer:—I remember a Trinity College (Dublin) story of a student, who, having to translate Cæsar, rendered the first sentence, "Omnis Gallia divisa est in tres partes"—"All Gaul is quartered into three halves."

CASTING REFLECTIONS.

At the same time (says Harrison) I was told of one of the undergraduates of the same college amusing himself with a mirror, by throwing the reflection of the sun's rays on the heads of the dons as they crossed the quod, for which he was summoned before the authorities, who, however, were puzzled to find a name for the offence, until one of them suggested, "Casting reflections on the heads of the college."

TO THE POINT.

Lord Eldon told the following story:—The drinking cups, or glasses, at Oxford, from their shape were called *ox-eyes*. Some friends of a young student, after inducing him to fill his ox-eye much fuller and oftener than consisted with his equilibrium, took pity at last upon his helpless condition, and led or carried him to his rooms. He had just Latin enough at command to thank them at the stair-head with "Pol, me *ox-eye*—distis, amici."

AB HISS.

The Vice-Chancellor, Dr Leech of Balliol, a determined punster, having given offence to the young men by some act of discipline, when he next appeared among them he was saluted with much sibilation; whereupon, turning round, he said, "Academici laudamur ab *his!*" which (says Eldon) produced a change in his favour, and they loudly applauded him.

NE QUID NIMIS.

Smoking (says Eldon) was common in those days, and a fellow secretly indulged even in the habit of chewing tobacco. Having once inadvertently squirted near the master's niece, who was passing by, he was thus admonished, "*Ne quid nigh Miss.*"

NOT THE LION—THE BEAR.

When Professor Whewell returned to Cambridge a benedict, and his lady discovered the estimation in which he was generally held, she is reported (says Jerdan) to have exclaimed, "Why, W., how is this! When I married you I was taught to believe my husband was the Lion of Cambridge, but I find to my sorrow he is only the Bear."

HIS LAST ADVICE.

According to the Rev. J. C. Young, the Rev. John W. Burgon, of Oriel College, Oxford, was a great favourite of the late president of Magdalen [Dr Routh]. [1] On one occasion, when Dr Routh had been saying many kind and encouraging things to him, he asked him to give him some advice which might stay by him, and be of use to him in his future life. "Always verify citations," was his answer.

NOT FOR ANY MONEY.

A country rector (says L'Estrange), coming up to preach at Oxford in his turn, complained to Dr Routh, the venerable principal of Magdalen, that the remuneration was very inadequate, considering the travelling expenses, and the labour necessary for the composition of the discourse. "How much did they give you?" inquired Dr Routh. "Only five pounds," was the reply. "Only five pounds!" repeated the Doctor; "why, I would not have preached that sermon for fifty."

"CALL ME EARLY."

J. C. Young is responsible for the following :—When Tennyson entered the Oxford Theatre to receive his honorary degree of D.C.L., his locks hanging in admired disorder on his shoulders, dishevelled and unkempt, a voice from the gallery was heard crying out to him, "Did your mother call you early, dear?"

---

[1] Died December 22, 1854, in his hundredth year. "Independently of his high distinction as a scholar, he was interesting from his extensive experience of life."—*Young.*

ABOUT PEOPLE IN GENERAL.

SOLDIERS AND SAILORS.

HALF WOULD TRY.

MOORE tells the story of Frederick the Great saying to some English general (?), "Could any regiment of yours of the same number of men perform such a feat?" "I don't know, sire," was the answer, "but half the number would try."

"THE PIE'S YOURS, SIR!"

Barham, when a boy, along with a young friend called Diggle, having, in the course of one of their walks, discovered a Quakers' meeting-house, forthwith procured a penny tart of a neighbouring pastry-cook. Furnished with this, Diggle marched boldly into the building, and holding up the delicacy in the midst of the grave assembly, said with perfect solemnity, "Whoever speaks first shall have this pie." "Friend, go thy way," commenced a drab-coloured gentleman, rising; "go thy way, and—." "The pie's yours, sir!" exclaimed Master Diggle politely, and placing it before the astounded speaker hastily effected his escape. Barham tells this tale himself. [1]

"SHE DIDN'T MEAN IT."

Monk Lewis[2] (says Rogers) was a great favourite at Oatlands. One day after dinner, as the duchess was leaving the room, she whispered something into Lewis's ear. He was much affected, his eyes filling with tears. We asked him what was the matter. "Oh," replied Lewis, "the duchess spoke so *very* kindly to me!" "My dear fellow," said Colonel Armstrong, "pray don't cry; I daresay she didn't mean it."

RAPID PROMOTION.

A Colonel W—— had been dining with an old brother officer, who had but just returned from India, and whom he had not seen for some years. He

---

1 Diggles afterwards became governor of the military college at Sandhurst.
2 See p. 124.

brought him in the course of the evening to a ball at the Pavilions, the seat of General Moore. The colonel was not exactly inebriated, but somewhat elevated. With high broad shoulders, epaulettes up to his ears, a stiff military carriage, and a salute rather than a bow, he presented his friend to the General in the following coherent terms : "General Moore, let me introduce to you a friend of mine !" Then, waving his hand from one to the other, in the approved fashion, he said, "General Moore ! Captain Cox !—General Cox ! Captain Moore !" The rapidest instances of promotion and reduction (says J. C. Young) I ever heard of !

A FIG FOR HIM.

Tom Assheton Smith gave J. C. Young the following impromptu by Sir William Meadows on Lord Cornwallis being voted a plum, after the conquest of Seringapatam, while *he* only was made free of the city by the Grocers' Company.

> "From Leadenhall the *reasons* (raisins) come
>   Why Grocers made me free ;
> To you, my lord, they vote a *plum*,
>   But say *a fig* for me."[1]

HE KNEW NOTHING ABOUT THEM.

The Duke of Wellington used to say of his old aide-de-camp, Sir Colin Campbell, who died at last Lieutenant-Governor of Plymouth—a man gallant, trustworthy, and naturally intelligent—"that he knew no language except his own, and that very incorrectly." I had a French cook in Spain (says Lord William Lennox), and Colin had charge of my domestic affairs. The *batterie de cuisine* was not, as you may suppose, very perfect, and the cook came to Colin to complain. Neither understood a word of what the other was saying, but I overheard this pass between them : "*Mais, Monsieur, comment travailler ?*" "*Travel,*" replied Colin, "why, you always travel in a coach; and as for *batteries* and your *quizzing*, I know nothing about them."

COLIN AGAIN.

On another occasion (says Lord William Lennox) when we were in St Jean de Luz, I had the mayor and all the magnates to dine with me. In going away, the mayor took up an umbrella which belonged to Colin, upon which Colin seized the other end of it, and said with a low bow, "*C'est moine.*"

---

[1] "The Fig for thee, then."—*Henry V.*, act iv., scene 1.

COLIN ONCE MORE.

Again : Later in the evening, this worthy Scot wished to say, "I would if I could, but I cannot," which he thus rendered, "*Je voudrais, si je coudrais, mais je ne cannais pas.*"

COLIN, FINALLY.

At Paris, in 1815, Colin told us one morning at breakfast that he proposed dining early, so as to go to the play. We felt surprised, as he had always declined to join in any theatrical amusement. "But to-night," said he, "there's to be a grand performance. I find by the play-bills '*Relache*' is to be given at all the theatres; that must be something worth seeing." We allowed him to remain in a happy state of ignorance.

MITY AND MIGHTY.

An incident which occurred at the mess of the 1st Life-Guards many years ago, when an incautious visitor, *Bacchi plenus*, referred to the *sobriquet* that gallant corps bore. "What do you mean by cheesemongers?" asked an infuriated Irish cornet, bent on parading the libeller next morning. "Cheesemongers," replied the other with great quickness, "so called after their mity (mighty) deeds."

A SELL.

One of the most amusing men I ever met with (says Lord William Lennox) was the late Richard Armit of the 3d, now Fusilier Guards. I remember that upon one occasion he nearly involved himself in a duel. In the days I write of, when the Guards were quartered at Windsor, he dined with me at the mess of the Blues. There happened to be present a fire-eating, quarrelsome man, who had been involved in many of what were termed affairs of honour. Dick, who had all the pluck of a son of Erin, and who had listened patiently to this oracle laying down the law, thought he would cause a laugh at his expense ; so, suddenly turning to him, he quietly said, "I saw a man to-day who would give any sum of money he possessed to kick you." "Kick me !" responded the Sir Lucius O'Trigger. "Kick me ! I call upon you to name him," at the same time turning livid with rage. "Oh, bedad, I'll tell you," replied his tormentor. "I insist upon knowing," interrupted the angry man. "Well, if you wish to know, but it must not go farther—the man was —" "Who? Who?" "Ah, don't be in such a hurry ; the man was Billy Water, who goes about in a bowl, because why, he has not any legs, and, by the powers, would give all he has to be able to kick anyone."

A SOLDIER'S STORY.

Mark Boyd says :—I was accompanying my father over the field of Waterloo, when our guide, an old British soldier who had been in the battle, stopped us rather abruptly at what I should say was the north-east corner of Hougoumont. "Here, sirs, his the werry spot vere 'Is Majesty, King George IV., said the werry cleverest thing that vas hever said afore hor since by hany king, hi doesn't care a morsel vere ye picks 'im. Vell, sirs, ven King George vas hon 'is journey to 'Anover, he pay Waterloo a wisit, hand was haccompanied by 'Is Royal Highness the Duke o' Clarence hand 'Is Grace the Duke o' Wellington. Just hon this eere spot the Duke o' Wellington's oss slipped hup hon the dry tuff hand a-throwed the duke. 'Is Majesty vas for ha moment hafeared, so vas the Duke o' Clarence ; but the Duke o' Wellington vas hon 'is feet hin ha moment, hall right. Ven the king sees that, he says to 'is brother, 'Vell, Clarence, ve can say vat t'others can't, that ve seed Wellington a-floored hat Waterloo.'"

THE LATE LORD CHATHAM.

The Earl of Chatham, brother of the Rt. Hon. Wm. Pitt, was (says Raikes) an indolent man, and so remarkable for his want of punctuality that he was frequently called *the late* Lord Chatham. He commanded the unfortunate expedition to the Isle of Walcheren, while the fleet was entrusted to Admiral Sir Richard Strahan. Their inactivity on this occasion gave rise to the wellknown epigram :—

> "Lord Chatham with his sword undrawn,
> Keeps waiting for Sir Richard Strahan ;
> Sir Richard, longing to be at 'em,
> Keeps waiting, too,—for whom? Lord Chatham !"[1]

RASH *V.* CHOLERIC.

Sir Walter Scott writes :—Colonel Blair told us that at the commencement of the Battle of Waterloo there was some trouble to prevent the men from breaking their ranks. He expostulated with one man—"Why, my good fellow, you cannot propose to beat the French alone ? You had better keep your ranks." The man, who was one of the 71st, returned to his place saying, "I believe you are right, sir, but I am a man of a very hot temper."

---

[1] There are several slightly-differing versions of this epigram.

HE NEVER TOOK ANYTHING.

Theodore Hook declared that when the "skipper" of a noble schooner asked the owner whether he would like to "take the helm," he replied that "he never took anything between breakfast and dinner."

NOT A GREAT ORATOR.

I remember (says the same writer) once being at a dinner, with the late lamented Prince Consort in the chair, when a general officer got up to return thanks for the army. "May it please—may it please—your Royal—your Royal Highness—I rise—I rise to return thanks for the—for the British—British—and—your Royal—" At this moment the toast-master caught hold of the General by the skirts of his coat, and said, "Thank the gentlemen and sit down," which the gallant soldier accordingly did.

NOT EVEN HIS WIFE.

The wife of a colonel at a review in Dublin was stopped by a sentry, and on her telling him she was "the colonel's lady,"—"No matter for that, madam," said the sentry; "if you were even his wife you couldn't pass." This old anecdote is embalmed by Moore in his diary.

HE DIDN'T DRINK FAIR.

At a dinner of an Irish volunteer regiment (says Harrison) a member, appealing to the president, said: "Colonel, I wish ye'd spake to Sargeant Skurray, he won't drink fair." "Oh! Sergeant Skurray," exclaimed the colonel, "fill your glass, man, and pass the bottle!" "Oh!" was the reply, "it is not that I mane at all, at all! He's taking two for one."

TIT FOR TAT.

Dr Busby (says Gronow) was notorious for his Spartan discipline, and constantly acted up to the old adage of not sparing the rod and spoiling the boy. He was once invited, during a residence at Deal, by an old Westminster—who, from being a very idle well-flogged boy, had, after a course of distinguished service, been named to the command of a fine frigate in the Downs—to visit him on board his ship. The doctor accepted the invitation; and, after he had got up the ship's side, the captain piped all hands for punishment, and said to the astonished doctor, "You d—d old scoundrel, I am delighted to have the opportunity of paying you off at last. Here, boatswain, give him three dozen."

SCOTCH AND IRISH.

"AN AWFU' NICHT."

A Mrs Hughes repeated to J. C. Young several anecdotes which she had heard from the mouth of Sir Walter himself; one of Lady Johnson, sister to the late Earl of Buchan and Lord Erskine, and widow of Sir J. Johnson. When on her deathbed, a few hours prior to her dissolution, she had her notice attracted by the violence of a storm which was raging with great fury out of doors. Motioning with her hands to have the curtains thrown open, she looked earnestly at the window through which the lightning was flashing very vividly, and exclaimed to her attendants: "Gude faith, but it's an unco awfu' nicht for me to gang bleezing through the lift!"

"A WALE O' WIGS."

Another story told by Sir Walter was of a drunken old laird who fell off his pony into the water while crossing a ford in Ettrick. "Eh, Jock," he cried to his man, "there's some puir body fa'en into the water; I heard a splash; who is it, man?" "Troth, laird, I canna tell; foreby it's no yersell," said John, dragging him to the bank. The laird's wig meanwhile had fallen off into the stream, and John in putting it on again placed it inside out. This, and its being thoroughly soaked, annoyed the old gentleman, who refused to wear it:—"Deil ha' my saul, it's nae my ain wig; what for do ye no get me my ain wig, ye ne'er-do-weel?" "Eh then, laird, ye'll no get ony ither wig the nicht, sae e'en pit it on again. There's nae sic a wale o' wigs in the burnie, I jalouse."

"A PUIR BIT BODIE."

Another of Sir Walter Scott's stories was of a party of Highland gentlemen who continued drinking three whole days and nights successively without intermission. "Hech, sirs," cried one at last, "but M'Kinnon looks gash!" "What for should he no?" returned his neighbour; "has na' the chiel been dead these twa hoors?" "Dead," repeated his friend, "an ye did na' tell us before!" "Hoot, man," was the answer, "what for should I ha' spoiled gude company for sic a puir bit bodie as yon?"

A SCOTCH SHEPHERD.

Mark Boyd writes:—My late esteemed friend, Mr John Mackie, M.P. for Kirkcudbrightshire, used to describe an extensive view which one of a friend's hills commanded. This he never failed to call to the attention of his English visitors when the weather was clear. Willy the shepherd was always the guide on such occasions, as he knew precisely the weather that would suit. One forenoon an English friend was placed under Willy's charge to mount the hill, in order to enjoy the glorious view. "I am told, shepherd, you are going to show me a wonderful view." "That's quite true, sir." "What shall I see?" "*Weel*, ye'll see a *feck* (many) o' kingdoms, the best part o' *sax*, sir." "What the deuce do you mean, shepherd?" "*Weel*, sir, I mean what I say." "But tell me all about it." "I'll tell ye *naething mair*, sir, until we're at the *tap* o' the hill." The top reached, Willy found everything he could desire in regard to a clear atmosphere. "*Noo*, sir, I hope you've got *guid een*?" "Oh, my eyes are excellent." "Then that's *a' recht* (right), sir." "*Noo, div ye* see yon hills awa' yonder?" "Yes, I do." "Weel, sir, those are the hills o' Cumberland, and Cumberland's in the kingdom o' England; that's *ae* kingdom. *Noo, sir*, please keep *coont*. Then, sir, I must *noo* trouble you to look *ower* (over) yonder. *Div ye* see what I mean?" "Yes, I do." "That's *a' recht*. That's the Isle o' Man, and that was a kingdom and a sovereignty in the families o' the Earls of Derby and the Dukes o' Athol frae the days o' King David o' Scotland, if ye ken *anything* o' Scotch history." "You are quite right, shepherd." "Quite *recht, div ye* say? I *wouldna hae brocht* ye here, sir, if I *wus* to be wrang. *Weel*, that's *twa* kingdoms. Be sure, sir, to keep *coont. Noo*, turn *awee aboot. Div ye* see yon land yonder? It's a bit *farder*, but never mind that, *sae lang* as you see it." "I see it distinctly." "*Weel*, that's *a'* I care *aboot. Noo*, sir, keep *coont*, for that's Ireland, and *maks* three kingdoms; but there's nae trouble *aboot* the *niest* (next), for ye're *stannen on't*—I mean *Scoteland. Weel*, that *maks* four kingdoms; *div ye* admit that, sir?" "Yes, that makes four, and you have two more to show me." "That's true, sir, but don't be in *sic* (such) a hurry. *Weel*, sir, just look up *aboon* (above) *yer heed*, and this is by far the best of *a'* the kingdoms; that, sir, *aboon* is *Heeven*. That's five; and the saxth kingdom is that *doon* below *yer* feet, to which, sir, I hope you'll never *gang;* but that's a point on which I cannot speak with *ony* certainty!"

ANOTHER SCOTCH SHEPHERD.

There is no class of persons more truly devout (says J. C. Young) than the shepherds of Scotland. Among them the exercise of family worship is never neglected. It is always gone about with decorum; but, formality being a thing despised by them, there are no compositions so truly original, occasionally for rude eloquence, and not unfrequently for a plain and somewhat unbecoming familiarity. One of the most notable men for this sort of homely fireside eloquence was Adam Scott, of Upper Dalgleish. I had an uncle who herded with him, and from him I had many quotations from Adam Scott's prayers. Here is a short sample. "We parteeclarly thank Thee for Thy great gudeness to Meg; and that it ever cam into your head to tak' ony thought o' sic a useless bow-wow as her [alluding to a little girl of his who had been miraculously saved from drowning]. For Thy mercy's sake—for the sake o' Thy puir sinfu' creeturs now addressing Thee in their ain shilly-shally way; and, for the sake o' mair than we daur weel name to Thee, hae mercy on our Rob. Ye ken Yoursel', he's a wild mischievous callant, and thinks nae mair o' committing sin than a dog does o' licking a dish. But put Thy hook intil his nose, and Thy bridle intil his gab, and gar him come back to Thee wi' a jerk, that he'll no forget the langest day he has to live. Dinna forget puir Jamie, who's far awa frae us the night. Keep Thy arm o' power about him, and, ech, sirs, I wish Ye wad endow him wi' a little spunk and smeddum to act for his sell : for if Ye dinna, he'll be but a bauchle i' this warld, and a back-sitter i' the next. Thou hast added ane to our family. [*N.B.*—One of his sons had just married against his approbation]. So has been Thy will. It wad never hae been mine. But, if it is of Thee, do Thou bless the connection. But, if the fule hath done it out o' carnal desire, against a' reason and credit, may the cauld rain o' adversity settle in his habitation."

THE ONE FROM THE OTHER.

The following occurs in Jerdan's Autobiography:—One of the small tenants [on a Scotch estate] happened to die in the winter, when the severe weather rendered it impossible to proceed to the [cemetery] with the body for interment. Some time, therefore, elapsed before the ceremony was performed; but at length Donald was properly buried, and the clergyman of the parish, and the neighbours who had attended the funeral returned, as is usual in these parts, to the dwelling of the widow for refreshments. [The cleric] found her in great tribulation, weeping and wailing for her loss, and addressed her : "Janet, ma woman, this excessive sorrow is unbecoming and unchristian ; remember you have a family to care for, and ought not to give way to useless grief." "Ohone, ohone !" was all that the sobbing Janet could reply, and the minister went on:—"Janet, desist. The Lord giveth, and the Lord taketh away." "Oh, aye !" cried Janet, "blessed be His holy name ! Truly, sir, a' shoudna tak on sae, but he was a gude man to me. O Donald, Donald— whew !" Another reproof brought the poor woman more to her senses, and she confessed that she ought not to lament so loudly, seeing she was sure, "by this time the dear departed was in Belzebub's bosom." "Belzebub's bosom !" exclaimed the minister. "It is Abraham's bosom, ye mean. Hae ye sat sae lang under ma ministry, and no ken the difference between

Belzebub and Abraham?"   "Waes me, waes me," rejoined the widow, "I'm a puir ignorant creature! Belzebub and Abra-ham—Abra-ham and Belzebub; a' declare that in spite o' aw yer teaching, a' wadna ken the ane frae the ither gin they were baith standing afore me!"

HER DAVIE.

Moore records in his Diary:—Talked of Sir David Baird, his roughness, &c. His mother said, when she heard of his being taken prisoner at Seringapatam, and of the prisoners being chained together two and two, "God help the man that's tied to my Davie."

TAKING HER BREAKFAST.

Mark Boyd narrates this of his cook in Scotland, whom he found one night after twelve o'clock sipping her tea:—"Halloa, cook! how late you are in drinking you tea." "Na, na, sir, I am *no* at my tea, I am at my breakfast, as I *thocht* it best to *tak* mine *afore ganging* to bed, as you and the *ither* young gentlemen *hae* ordered yours to be ready at five, that ye *mae* get aff in *guid* time to the muirs."

HONEST MAN!

Frederick Locker writes:—Miss D., on her return to the Highlands of Scotland from Rome, went to see an auld Scottish wife, and said, to interest the woman, "I have been to Rome since I last saw you. I have seen all sorts of people. I have seen the Pope." The sympathetic old dame replied, with animation, "The Pope of Rome!—honest man!—haze he ony family?"

WHAT AILED HIM?

A friend tells me (says the same writer) a funny little story of Mrs —— (the grandmother of Colonel M——), who was shown a picture of Joseph and Potiphar's wife, in which, of course, the patriarch exhibited his usual desire to withdraw himself from her society. Mrs —— looked at it for a little while, and then said, "Eh, now, and what ails him at the lassie?"

AN IMPRESSIVE ADJURATION.

A Bailie of Dundee, after witnessing the Lord Justice-Clerk pass sentence of death very impressively on a criminal, happening to have a fine of eighteenpence to impose on an offender, thus solemnly addressed him:—"You must either go to jail or pay the money, and the Lord have mercy on your soul!" Jerdan tells the anecdote.

MORE CURIOUS THAN EDIFYING.

Mrs Somerville says in her Autobiography:—My mother set me in due time to learn the catechism of the Kirk of Scotland, and to attend the public examinations in the kirk. These meetings were attended by a great many old women, who came to be edified. They were an acute race, and could quote chapter and verse of Scripture as accurately as the minister himself. I remember he said to one of them, "Peggie, what lightened the world before the sun was made?" After thinking for a minute, she said, "'Deed, sir, the question is mair curious than edifying."

"WE ARE A' THAT!"

Sir James —— on one occasion had ventured (says F. Locker) to buy a cow without consulting his dairy-maid, a great authority on such matters. When the new purchase was exhibited to her, she found herself divided between her love of truth and her amiable desire not to wound the feelings of her beloved master by expressing her candid opinion. She looked meditatively at the new acquisition, and then said, "She's a bonnie beastie" (pause). "She's some hee (high) at the root o' the tail" (longer pause)—"but we're a' that."

COMPLIMENTARY.

Says Frederick Locker again:—My friend Admiral E. E., shortly after his return from a cruise, met an old acquaintance in the streets of ——, who said, after the usual salutations had passed, "They tell me, Admiral, that ye had got married?" The Admiral, hoping for a compliment, replied, "Why, Bailie, I'm getting on, I'm not so young as I was, you see, and none of the girls will have me." On which the Bailie, with perfect good faith and simplicity, replied, "'Deed, Admiral, I was na evenin' ye to a lassie, but there's mony a fine, respeckit, *half-worn* wumman wud be glad to tak ye."

GOOD ADVICE.

A Highland Donald was tried for a capital offence, and had a rather narrow escape; but the jury (says Jerdan) found him "not guilty." Whereupon the judge, in discharging, thought fit to admonish him. "Prisoner! before you leave the bar, let me give you a piece of advice. You have got off this time, but if ever you come before me again, I'll be *caution* (surety) *you'll be hanged.*" "Thank you, my lord," answered Donald; "thank you for your good advice; and as I'm na ungratefu', I beg to gie your lordship a piece of advice in return. Never be caution for ony body, for the cautioner has often to pay the penalty."

HIS LAST.

A Highland chief, being on his deathbed, was exhorted to forgive his enemies. He called his eldest son to his bedside, and thus (says Jerdan) spoke his last:—"Donald, you see what a pass I hae come to, and I am told that I must forgive my enemies, and especially the M'Tavish; and, for my soul's sake, I do forgie him accordingly. But, Donald, ma dear son, if ever ye forgie the Tavish, or ony o' his infernal name, may ma curse rest on ye for ever and ever. Amen!"

TAKING TIME BY THE FORELOCK.

My grandmother (says Mark Boyd) once awoke my grandfather in the middle of the night, and told him that she much feared their son Willie, who slept next room to them, had become deranged, as she had been listening to him for some time speaking loudly and rapidly to himself. Her husband listened, and came to the same conclusion; and they forthwith hurried to their boy's bedroom to know what was the matter. Willie's explanation was, that as they were going to the seaside next day, he wished to save time, and was saying his prayers over and over to last him during the holidays.

"ONY LASSIE COULD HAE TOLD YE THAT."

Says Archdeacon Sinclair:—I was conversing one day with Dr Williams about schools and school examinations. He said, "Let me give you a curious example of an examination at which I was present in Aberdeen. An English clergyman and a Lowland Scotsman visited one of the best parish schools in that city. They were strangers, but the master received them civilly, and inquired, 'Would you prefer that I should *speer* these boys, or that you should *speer* them yourselves?' The English clergyman having ascertained that to *speer* meant to question, desired the master to proceed. He did so with great success, and the boys answered satisfactorily numerous interrogatories as to the exodus of the Israelites from Egypt. The clergyman then said he would be glad in his turn to *speer* the boys, and at once began: 'How did Pharaoh die?' There was a dead silence. In this dilemma the Lowland gentleman interposed: 'I think, sir, the boys are not accustomed to your English accent; let me try what I can make of them.' And he inquired in broad Scotch: 'Hoo did Phawraoh dee?' Again there was a dead silence; upon which the master said: 'I think, gentlemen, you can't *speer* these boys; I'll show you how to do it!' And he proceeded: 'Fat cam to Phawraoh at his hinder end?' *i.e.*, in his latter days. The boys, with one voice, answered, 'He was drooned;' and a smart little fellow added, 'Ony lassie could hae told ye that.' The master then explained, that in the Aberdeen dialect, 'to dee' means to die a natural death, or to die in bed; hence the perplexity of the boys, who knew that Pharaoh's end was very different."

HIS PREFERENCE.

There was a Presbyterian minister (says J. C. Young) who married a couple of his rustic parishioners, and had felt exceedingly disconcerted, on his asking the bridegroom if he were willing to take the woman for his wedded wife, by his scratching his head and saying, "Ay—I'm wullin', but I'd rather hae her sister."

"SUCH A SET."

The minister of Renfrew (says Jerdan) was desired to pray for some newly-elected bailies, and thus he performed his apologetic duty: "I should ha'," said he, "to petition again for the sake of ithers; but, and —d, it is na worth while to trouble ye for such a set o' puir bodies!"

CHRISTIANS WANTED.

Sir John Malcolm was wont (says the same writer) to tell one unvarying tale at the expense of my good border name. An English traveller, benighted on a bitter night in the wilds of Liddesdale, got at last to a straggling village, in one attic, *i.e.*, second floor, of which there was a light burning. By repeated knocking on the door he at length roused the inmate, an ancient crone, who opened the casement. "Is there any Christians here," he exclaimed; "if so, pray let me in for shelter!" "Na, na," responded the old lady; "na, na, gif ye want Christians ye maun ride to the next town—we are a' Jerdans and Johnstones here!" I should state that the family name of Christian was equally predominant in the town referred to.

"DON'T BE AFRAID."

It was at Kilravock (says Lord Cockburn) that old Henry Mackenzie used to tell that a sort of household officer was kept, whose duty it was to prevent the drunk guests from choking. Mackenzie was once at a festival there, towards the close of which the exhausted topers sank gradually back and down on their chairs, till little of them was seen above the table except their noses; and at last they disappeared altogether and fell on the floor. Those who were too far gone to rise lay there from necessity; while those who, like the *Man of Feeling*, were glad of a pretence for escaping, fell into a dose from policy. While Mackenzie was in this state, he was alarmed by feeling a hand working about his throat, and called out. A voice answered, "Dinna be feared, sir, it's me." "And who are you?" "A'm the lad that louses the craavats."

SHAKESPEARE A SCOTCHMAN.

Here is one of Dean Ramsay's stories which is not in his *Reminiscences:*[1]— An Englishman was speaking one day to a Scotchman. The Scotchman said, " It is not mere national pride if I say, *what is a matter of fact*, viz., that my country is the finest in the world !" " Well," said John Bull, " if it be the finest, it is not the biggest. I suppose you'll allow that England is bigger than Scotland ?" " 'Deed, sir," answered Sandy, " I'll allow nae sic a thing ; for if oor grand hills were rolled out as flat as England is, Scotland wad be the bigger o' the twa !" " Well," retorted John Bull, " you'll acknowledge that Shakespeare was not a Scotchman ?" Discomfited at this home-thrust, but not disheartened, he once more replied, " I'll acknowledge that Shakespeare had *pairts* (parts) that would justify the inference that he was a Scotchman."

HE READ!

It is a well-known fact (says J. C. Young) that Presbyterians, with few exceptions, have an invincible repugnance to a sermon conned over and composed in the study, on the ground of its lacking spontaneity and the apparent impress of the Spirit. I have a distinct recollection, one Sunday, when I was living at Cults, and when a stranger was officiating for Dr Gillespie, observing that he had not proceeded five minutes with his " discourse," before there was a general commotion and stampede. The exodus at last became so serious, that, conceiving something to be wrong, probably a fire in the manse, I caught the infection, and eagerly inquired of the first person I encountered in the churchyard what was the matter, and was told, with an expression of sovereign scorn and disgust, " Losh keep ye, young man ; hae ye eyes and see not ? Hae ye ears and hear not ? *The man reads !*"

A USEFUL TOOTHPICK.

Tom Campbell (says Jerdan) told an amusing story of an accident that had happened to him in a small country inn when travelling in Scotland. He had been stopped by the weather in the afternoon, had dined, and indulged himself with a toothpick to wile away the idle after-hour. Enter chambermaid— " Sir, if ye please, are ye dune with the toothpick ?" " Why do you ask ? I suppose I may pick away as long as I like ?" " Oh, dear, na, sir, for it belongs to the Club, and they hae been met amaist an hour !" The disgust with which the instrument was thrown away may be more readily imagined than described.

---

[1] We make no attempt to draw upon this familiar repository of "good things."

EASILY FRIGHTENED.

Quaint terms (says Jerdan) often baffle the skill of the lawyer. On a trial for murder of an excise officer, an old rogue of a town carrier was giving evidence in favour of the smugglers where the affray ended so fatally. He swore that "a wee bit of a pistol was held up merely to frighten the officer," when [Henry] Erskine produced a huge horse pistol, to overwhelm the witness, and triumphantly asked him if that was the sort of engine merely to frighten people. "I dinna ken," was the answer; "some folks, like you, are easily frightened."

OVER-PAID.

Luttrell (says Moore) once told of an Irishman who, having jumped into the water to save a man from drowning, upon receiving sixpence from the person as a reward for the service, looked first at the sixpence, then at him, and at last exclaimed, "By Jasus, I'm over-paid for the job."

AT THEIR EASE.

Luttrell also told a story of some Irish lady who had been travelling with her family, and on being asked whether they had seen *Aix,* answered, "Oh, yes! indeed; very much at our *ase* everywhere."

RINGING THE CHANGES.

Dawson (says Moore) told a good story about the Irish landlord counting out the change of a guinea. "12, 13, 14" (a shot heard); "Bob, go and see who's that that's killed; 15, 16, 17" (enter Bob). "It's Kelly, sir." "Poor Captain Kelly, a very good customer of mine; 18, 19, 20—there's your change, sir."

FOR HIS DIVERSION.

Some of Luttrell's Irish stories (says Sydney Smith) were most amusing. One: "Is your master at home, Paddy?" "*No,* your honour." "Why, I saw him go in five minutes ago." "Faith, your honour, he's not exactly at home, he's only there in the backyard a-shooting rats with cannon, your honour, for his devarsion."

A PLEASANT FEMALE.

They do nothing in Ireland (says Sydney Smith) as they would do elsewhere. When the Dublin mail was stopped and robbed, my brother declares that a sweet female voice was heard behind the hedge, exclaiming, "Shoot the gintleman, then, Patrick, dear!"

BARRING THE BEEF.

Moore writes in his Diary :—Abundance of Irish stories from Lattin ; some of them very good. A man asked another man to come and dine off boiled beef and potatoes with him. "That I will," says the other ; "and it's rather odd it should be exactly the same dinner I had at home for myself, barring the beef."

OPEN TO JUDGMENT.

When O'Connell, in his last speech [1831], said, "I am open to conviction," some one in the crowd said, "and to judgment, I hope." Moore tells the tale.

BLACK ALREADY.

Greville writes on one occasion :—Moore told several stories which I don't recollect. And this amused us :—Some Irish had emigrated to some West Indian colony ; the negroes soon learnt their brogue, and when another ship-load of Irish came soon after, the negroes, as they sailed in, said, "Ah, Paddy, how are you?" "What," said one of them, "y're become black already!"

HE WANTED HIS SPECTACLES.

Party spirit in Dublin (says Jerdan) was at one time attended by continual duels. It was upon one of these occasions that Giffard, the editor of the *Dublin Journal*, being called out, appeared on the ground with his spectacles on. This was objected to by his adversary's second, and he was desired to take them off, which he did, exclaiming, "By my soul, this is too bad. I could not see to shoot my own father without them!"

OUT OF THE WAY.

Morgan John O'Connell, nephew of the agitator had (says Harrison) the ready wit of his country in a remarkable degree. We were walking by the *Wey* one day when an Oxford graduate, a Mr White, who had a taste for botany, plucked a flower (*Balsamum impatiens*) from the river, remarking that "it was a very rare plant." "It is an out-of-the-*Wey* one, at any rate," was the instantaneous reply.

IT BEAT EVERYTHING.

Charles Kemble told the story of how, one day, he was followed up Sack-ville Street, Dublin, by two beggar women, between whom the following dialogue passed, evidently with a veiw to his edification :—"Och, but he's an illgant man, is Misther Charles Kemble!" "An', 'deed, so was his brudher,

Misther John, thin—a moighty foine man ! and to see his *demanour*, puttin' his hand in his pocket and givin' me sixpence, bate all the world ! "

NO EXAGGERATION.

A person, who shall be nameless, goes to purchase a horse of an Irish dealer. *Buyer:* "Have you got a clever horse to show me?" *Seller:* "I have that, sir." *Buyer* (looking at a horse that is brought out for inspection): "Is he a good hunter?" *Seller:* "Is it a hunter, sir? Why, then, sir, I'll be open with ye. He's a craving oss, but he's what I call a flippant lepper (leaper). I might say he's the most *intrickate*-left oss in the north of Ireland." *Buyer:* "Is he a good hack?" *Seller:* "Is it a hack you mane, sir? Well, sir, I'll be fair with ye. He could not, convaniently to himself, trot under sixteen miles the hour." *Buyer:* "And whereabouts is the figure?" *Seller:* "And is it the figure, sir? Then, I'll tell you, by the virtue of my oath, I should consider it my duty to go a hundred miles to call *anny* man out who would preshume to offer me less than £80 for him." *Buyer:* "Is he good at water?" *Seller:* "Is it wather, bedad?" (looking round, and standing up in his stirrups, and surveying the country, as if he were a stranger in these parts)—"Boys, is there anny canals about?" This story is narrated by J. C. Young.

PARADOXES EVEN.

Planché writes in one place:—A nobleman I met at dinner some time ago told us he had been shooting at a friend's place on the west coast of Ireland, and that the gamekeeper had indulged in the most exaggerated accounts of the quantity of every description of game upon his master's estate. Nothing that ever ran or flew that his lordship inquired about but was asserted by the man could be found there by hundreds and thousands. Having, for amusement's sake, exhausted the catalogue of "fur and feather," probable or improbable, and received the most positive assurance of the existence of every beast and bird in abundance, he asked, "Are there any paradoxes?" This was rather a poser; but, after a moment's hesitation, the keeper answered undauntedly, "Bedad, then, your lordship may find two or three of *them* sometimes on the sand when the tide's out."

"BUONO MANO."

When I was in Italy (says Mark Boyd) a quarter of a century back, it used to be alleged that, pay an Italian postboy as liberally as you liked, he would still ask you for a "buono mano." The Irish Dublin carman is said to belong to the Italian school in this respect. The peculiarity came on the *tapis* at a dinner party at Morrison's Hotel in Dublin, when one of the party present defended Paddy from what he considered an unjust imputation; and, in support of his opinion, offered to bet his friends £10 that he would drive from their hotel to the Rotunda, at the top of Sackville Street, and back without any such importunity, one of the party to accompany him, as a guarantee that nothing *ex curia* was said to Paddy *en route.* Accordingly, an outside car was sent for, and started for the Rotunda, the rest of the party awaiting its return outside the hotel. Paddy set down his two **passengers, and** was presented with three half-crowns, being more than three times his fare. He turned **them** over in his hand, and then said, " Och, yer honour, can't **you** *jist* make it the *nate* half-sovereign ?"

HIS WIFE A WIDOW.

Planché writes in another place:—My old fellow-traveller in **Germany, him-self an Irishman,** being on **the box of an Irish mail-coach on a very cold day, and observing the driver enveloping his neck in the voluminous folds of** an ample "comforter," remarked, "You seem to be taking very good care of yourself, my friend ?" " Oh, to be sure I am, sir," answered the driver; " what's all the world to a man when his wife's a widdy ?"

NO STRANGER THERE.

Planché writes elsewhere:—An acquaintance **of mine who frequently** visited **Ireland, and** generally stopped and dined at the same hotel in Dublin, on his arrival one day, perceived **a** paper wafered on the looking-glass **in the** coffee-room, with the following written notice:—" Strangers are particularly requested not to give any money to the waiters, as attendance is charged **for in** the bill." The man who had waited on him at dinner, seeing **him reading this notice,** said, " Oh, Misther ——! sure that doesn't **concern you in any way. Your** honour was niver made a stranger of in this house."

QUITE SUFFICIENT.

Raikes diarizes:—Glengall, talking at dinner to-day of his countrymen, **and the ready wit of the lower** orders in Ireland, said, " Old Lord Castlemaine was **extremely rich, but a miser.** One day he was stopping in his carriage to change horses at the inn at Athlone, when the **carriage was surrounded** by paupers imploring alms, to whom he turned a deaf ear, and drew up the glass. A ragged old woman in the crowd cried out, ' **Faith, an'** it's no use;' but, going **round to the other side of the** carriage, she bawled out, in the old peer's hearing, ' **Plase** you, my lord, just chuck **one** tinpenny **out of** your coach, and I'll answer it will trate all your friends in Athlone.'"

TOO BAD.

"The mercy of God follow you!" exclaimed a beggar-woman in Dublin to a passing stranger; "give a poor soul a halfpenny." "I haven't got one." "Oh, the mercy of God follow—" "Go away, woman!" "And" (changing her tone and shaking her fist at him) "*niver overtake you!*" This is one of Planché's stories.

CONCLUSIVE.

A Mrs Moll Harding kept the *natest* inn at Ballyroan, close to my father's house. I recollect (says Barington) to have heard a passenger (they are very scarce there) telling her "that his sheets had not been aired." With great civility Moll Harding begged his honour's pardon, and said: "They certainly were and *must* have been *well* aired, for there was not a gentleman came to the house this last fortnight that had not slept in them!"

HIS FAVOURITE GUNS.

When (says Lord Wm. Lennox) my father was Lord-Lieutenant of Ireland, among those who were on the most intimate terms with my family, were Mr Gun and his two daughters. These young ladies were as beautiful as they were talented, and of course were the objects of ill nature and spite to their less-favoured sex. The slightest attention paid to them by my father was severely commented upon by many a prim, stiff-necked old lady, and by many an antiquated spinster, who shook their heads, and exclaimed—"Dreadful! how shocking! the poor Duchess! who'd have thought it!" with other pious and charitable ejaculations which such people usually indulge in. One night at the theatre, when a play, founded on Defoe's beautiful romance of "Robinson Crusoe" was being performed, and the Viceroy, surrounded by his wife, sons, and daughters, was all intent upon the drama, the hero of the piece made his appearance in his savage dress, with two fowling-pieces under his arms, supposed to have been saved from the wreck. No sooner did the actor come forward, and was seen tracking the footsteps which he afterwards found to be those of his man Friday, than, amidst a breathless silence, a man called out from the upper regions—"Why, sure enough, if it an't the Lord-Lieutenant himself, with his two favourite *guns* under his arms."

MORE POINTED THAN POLITE.

An anecdote connected with the Duke of Rutland, who, in 1784, was Lord-Lieutenant of Ireland, relates to a state visit paid by His Excellency to the Royal Theatre in Crow Street, now no longer in existence, when a man in the gallery shouted out:—"Who was seen last evening coming out of Poll Flana-

P

gan's house ?" meaning a female of rather unenviable notoriety in Dublin, and with whose charms the scandalmongers falsely hinted the Viceroy was captivated. The reply—"Manners, you blackguard !" Quick as it was (says Lord Wm. Lennox), it was more pointed than polite.

FOREIGNERS.

HIS TWENTIETH OF MARCH.

Louis XVIII. (says Lady Davies) did not like Talleyrand,[1] and none the more so because he felt that his own somewhat pedantic conversation was overpowered by the Prince's brilliant intelligence. Sometimes a sharp though short encounter of words would take place between His Majesty and the great diplomatist ; and one of these encounters I remember to have occurred on a court day at the Tuileries when I was present. The King and the Duchess d'Angoulême were both receiving that day ; the rooms were almost full, and His Majesty appeared to be in most excellent spirits. Presently Prince de Talleyrand came in, and it was soon rumoured that he had asked for leave of absence from the King. Now everybody in Paris at that time knew that Talleyrand, though separated from his wife, was often threatened by her with the assurance that she would insist on taking up her abode with him, if he did not at once send whatever sums of money she happened to require. So the King being in a merry mood, said, quite aloud, to the Prince, as the latter approached His Majesty,—"Why, Prince, I hear that, as Madame de Talleyrand has just arrived in Paris, you wish to leave ;" and as Lous XVIII. said this he laughed, his laugh being of course echoed instantly by the numerous courtiers present who had heard his words. But Talleyrand only bowed, and in a clear sonorous voice replied,—"Yes, your Majesty, it is my 20th of March." It was then the King's turn to get up a laugh at his own expense, but he merely coloured and looked annoyed, for few things galled him more than an allusion to his flight on the date just named—a flight caricatured at the time in Paris by a flock of geese waddling out from the Tuileries, while eagles were flying in.

A ROYAL PUN.

Louis XVIII. (says Raikes) always professed himself an *esprit fort.* My friend General Clari told me that, on the Sunday preceding his dissolution,

---

[1] The famous French diplomatist; b. 1754, d. 1838.

the officer on guard at the Tuileries came to him as usual in the evening to receive the parole and the countersign to be given to the troops. It is customary on these occasions to give the name of a saint for the one and of a fortified town for the other. Louis, with a significant look, gave "St Denis and *Gyvet*" (J'y vais). He might be said to have died with a *calembourg* in his mouth.

"ALREADY?"

Nobody's wit (says Sydney Smith) was of so high an order as Talleyrand's, or has so well stood the test of time. You remember when his friend Montrond was taken ill, and exclaimed, "Mon ami, je sens les tourmens de l'enfer." "Quoi! déjà?" was his reply.[1]

A DOWNWARD TENDENCY.

Talleyrand's *bons mots* (says Raikes) always fly about. His friend Montrond has been subject of late to epileptic fits, one of which attacked him lately after dinner at Talleyrand's. While he lay on the floor in convulsions, scratching the carpet with his hands, his benign host remarked with a sneer—"C'est qu'il me paraît, qu'il veut absolument descendre."

"YOU CAN SWIM!"

When Talleyrand sat at dinner between Madame de Stael and Madame Récamier, the celebrated beauty, Madame de Stael, whose beauties (says Sydney Smith) were certainly not those of the person, jealous of his attentions to her rival, insisted upon knowing which he would save if they were both drowning. After seeking in vain to evade her, he at last turned towards her and said, with his usual shrug, "Ah, madam, *vous savez nager.*"

NEITHER ONE NOR THE OTHER.

When some one exclaimed, "Me voilà entre l'esprit et la beauté," Talleyrand answered, "Oui, et sans posséder ni l'un, ni l'autre."

BEGINS TOO SOON AND ENDS TOO LATE.

Talleyrand said of a certain lady, "Oui, elle est belle, très belle ; mais, pour la toilette, cela commence trop tard and finit trop tôt."

---

[1] "I find," says Lady Holland, "that Talleyrand used to tell this story as having passed between Cardinal De la Roche-Guyon, a celebrated epicure, and his confessor."

AGGRESSIVE BENEVOLENCE.

Of Lord Holland, Talleyrand said, "C'est la bienveillance même, mais la bienveillance la plus perturbative que j'ai jamais connu."

A MOT.

According to Raikes, Talleyrand said of Lady Holland, "Elle est toute assertion, mais quand on demande la preuve, c'est là son sécret."

AN ENORMOUS LATITUDE.

Talking in Talleyrand's presence (says Sydney Smith) to my brother Bobus,[1] who was just then beginning his career at the bar, I said, "Mind, Bobus, when you are Chancellor I shall expect one of your best livings." "Oui, mon ami," said Bobus, "mais d'abord je vous ferai commettre toutes les bassesses dont les prêtres sont capables." On which Talleyrand, throwing up his hands and eyes, exclaimed with a shrug, "Mais quelle latitude enorme !"

VERY CURIOUS.

For several days (says Lord Dalling and Bulwer) M. de Talleyrand saw, without recognizing, a well-dressed individual, with his hat in his hand, and bowing very low as he mounted the steps of his coach. "Et qui êtes vous, mon ami ?" he said at last. "Je suis votre cariossier, Monseigneur." "Ah ! vous êtes, mon cariossier ; et que voulez vous, mon cariossier ?" "Je veux être payé, Monseigneur," said the coachmaker, humbly. "Ah, vous êtes mon cariossier, et vous voulez être payé ; vous serez payé, mon cariossier." "Et quand, Monseigneur ?" "Hum !" muttered the bishop, looking at the coach-maker very attentively, and at the same time settling himself in his new carriage ; "vous êtes bien curieux !"

WHEN WILL IT END?

Talleyrand's (says the same authority) was the saying, cited by Chamfort, à propos of Rulhiéres,[2] who, on observing that he did not know why he was called ill-natured, for in all his life he had never done but one ill-natured action, was replied to by M. de Talleyrand's drily observing, "*Et quand finira-t-il ?*"—"When will it end ?"[3]

---

[1] Robert. See p. 34.

[2] "Le confident du Marechal de Richelieu, le poéte de la duchesse d'Egmont," etc.

[3] Recorded also by Raikes.

AT NINE.

One evening, playing at long whist, the conversation turned on an old lady who had married her footman ; some people expressed their surprise, when M. de Talleyrand, counting his points, drawled out in a slow voice, "At nine, one does not count honours."

EVERYTHING USEFUL.

Talleyrand, speaking of the members of the French Academy, observed— "After all, it is possible they may one day or other do something remarkable. A flock of geese once saved the capital of Rome."

A PREGNANT POSTSCRIPT.

Talleyrand had a confidential servant excessively devoted to his interests, but withal superlatively inquisitive. Having one day entrusted him with a letter, the prince watched his faithful valet from the window of his apartment, and with some surprise saw him reading the letter *en route*. On the next day a similar commission was confided to the servant, and to the second letter was added a postscript, couched in the following terms:—"You may send a verbal answer by the bearer; he is perfectly acquainted with the whole affair, having taken the precaution to read this previous to its delivery."

WHAT HAD PASSED.

A council of the ministry having sat three hours upon some important question, an eminent nobleman met Talleyrand as he came from the meeting, and asked, "Qui s'est il passé, dans ce conseil ?" to which the witty diplomatist answered, "Trois heures !"

LIKE THE BOOK.

M. de Chateaubriand was no favourite with M. de Talleyrand. When the "Martyrs" first appeared, it was run after by the public with an appetite which the booksellers could not satisfy. M. de Fontanges, after speaking of it with an exaggerated eulogium, finished his explanation of the narrative by saying that Eudore and Cymodocée were thrown into the circus and devoured "par les bêtes." "Comme l'ouvrage," said M. de Talleyrand.

TWO OF THEM.

A distinguished personage (says the same authority) once remarked to Talleyrand, "In the Upper Chamber at least are to be found men possessed of consciences." "Consciences," replied Talleyrand, "to be sure; I know many a peer who has got two."

HE HAS STUDIED HIMSELF.

Some persons saying that Fouché had a great contempt for mankind, " C'est vrai," said M. de Talleyrand; "cet homme s'est beaucoup étudié."

BITTER.

On a certain occasion (says the *Foreign Literary Gazette*) a friend was conversing with Talleyrand on the subject of Mademoiselle Duchenois, the French actress, and another lady, neither of them remarkable for beauty. The first happens to have peculiarly bad teeth, the latter none at all. "If Madame S——," said Talleyrand, "only had teeth she would be as ugly as Mademoiselle Duchenois."

OH! AND AH!

Dedel told in Moore's presence of the Duchesse de Grammont, sister of the Duc de Choiseul, coming to dinner, and on her passing the ante-room where Talleyrand was standing, he looked up and exclaimed significantly, "Ah!" In the course of the dinner, the lady having asked him across the table why he had uttered the exclamation of "Oh!" on her entrance, Talleyrand, with a grave, self-vindicatory look, answered, "Madame, je n'ai pas dit, *oh* / j'ai dit *ah* /" Comical, very (adds Moore) without once being able to define *why* it is so.

CIVIL *V.* MILITARY.

Moore narrates the remark of the French military coxcomb to Talleyrand: "Nous appelons péquin tout ce qui n'est pas militaire." Also, Talleyrand's answer: "Et nous, nous appelons militaire tout ce qui n'est pas civil."

IT WAS HIS FATHER.

Lord John Russell told Moore that Bobus Smith one day, in conversation with Talleyrand, having brought in somehow the beauty of his mother, T. said, "C' était donc votre père qui n' était pas bien ?"

HELAS AND OH! OH!

In Moore's Diary also we read the story of the lady who wrote to Talleyrand, informing him, in high-flown terms of grief, of the death of her husband, and expecting an eloquent letter of condolence in return. His answer only, "Hélas, Madame, votre affectionné, etc., Talleyrand." In less than a year, another letter from the same lady informed him of her having married again, to which he returned an answer in the same laconic style :—"Oh! Oh! Madame! votre affectionné, etc., Talleyrand."

HIS DEAFNESS EXPLAINED.

In talking of Chateaubriand, and of his having got deaf lately, Lord Lansdowne quoted in Moore's hearing Talleyrand's saying of him that "Il se croit sourd parcequ' il n' entend plus parler de lui."

TWO FEMALES.

Crabb Robinson says that Professor Scott once related a *mot* of Talleyrand to Madame de Stael on occasion of her "Delphine," which was thought to contain a representation of Talleyrand in the character of an old woman. On her pressing for his opinion of that work, he said: "That is the work, is it not, in which you and I are exhibited in the guise of females?"

THE POST-CHAISE.

Crabb Robinson also relates this :—"There is no middle course," said Charles X. to Talleyrand, "between the Throne and the Scaffold." "Your Majesty forgets the Post-chaise."

AS YOU SEE.

One of the readiest retorts by Talleyrand was made by him (says Harrison) at a time when Paris was in a very disturbed state, and everything there was going wrong. A person of some position who squinted horribly, addressed him one day with, "Ah, Monsieur le Prince! comment vont les affaires?" "Comme vous voyez, Monsieur," was the reply.[1]

IT DID NOT MATTER.

The same authority says that Talleyrand once, in despatching two letters, put them into wrong envelopes, so that the letter intended for one correspondent went to the other. He discovered his mistake too late, but only remarked, "N' importe! neither of them will believe me."

SOMETHING RARE.

General Flahault, who when young was bald, had received (says Gronow)[2] an invitation to dine with the Prince de Talleyrand. In the course of conversation, he expressed to the Prince a desire to present something rare to a great lady as a mark of his esteem. Talleyrand replied—"Then present her with a lock of your hair."

---

[1] This is told by Jerdan also, but not so successfully.
[2] Gronow also tells this story of Montrond.

THE CHARLATAN.

Fontaine, the architect who built the triumphal arch in the Carrousel, placed upon it (says Gronow) an empty car, drawn by the famous bronze Venetian horses. Talleyrand asked him—"Qui avez vous l'intention de mettre dans le char?" The answer was—"L'Empereur Napoléon, comme de raison." Upon which Talleyrand said—"Le char l'attend."

NOT "PARVENU"—"ARRIVE."

Some one (says Raikes) observed before Prince Talleyrand, that Thiers was a *parvenu*. His reply was: "Vous avez tort, il n'est pas parvenu, il est arrivé."

EXCEPT.

Raikes records what he calls Talleyrand's severe remark on Maret, when he received his title under the empire :—"Il ne connais pas de plus grande bête au monde que M. Maret, excepté le Duc de Bassano."

SOME BONS-MOTS.

The following (says Gronow) are some of Montrond's best sayings; the two first have been falsely attributed to Talleyrand: "La parole a été donnée à l'homme pour l'aider à cacher sa pensée." "Défiez-vous des premiers mouvements ; ils sont presque toujours bons." "S'il vous arrive quelque-chose d'heureux, ne manquez pas d' aller le dire à vos amis, afin de leur faire de la peine."

A GOOD REASON.

According to the same authority, Emile de Girardin, the famous political writer, a natural son of Alexandre de Girardin, becoming celebrated, Montrond said to the father, "Dépêchez-vous de la reconnaître, ou bientôt il ne vous reconnaitra pas."

SUPER-NATURAL.

A friend, who was about to marry the natural daughter of the Duke de ——, was expatiating at great length on the virtues, good qualities, and talents of his future wife, but without making (says Gronow) any allusion to her birth. "A t'entendre," observed Montrond, "on dirait que tu épouses une fille *sur*naturelle."

A PLAIN COUNTRY.

A very thin lady, with whom he had a violent quarrel, saying, "Qu'elle lui ferait voir du pays," Montrond, calmly surveying her from head to foot, replied, "Madame, ce serait du plat pays." This is also told by Gronow.

QUERY.

The Bailli de Ferrette was always dressed in knee-breeches, with a cocked hat and court sword, the slender proportions of which (says Gronow) greatly resembled those of his legs. "Do tell me, my dear Bailli," said Montrond, one day, "have you got three legs or three swords?"

FULL OF ATTACHMENT.

Montrond's death (says Gronow) was a very wretched one. Left alone to the tender mercies of a well-known "lorette" of those days, Desirée R——, as he lay upon his bed, between fits of pain and drowsiness, he could see his fair friend picking from his shelves the choicest specimens of his old Sèvres china, or other articles of "virtu." Turning to his doctor, he said, with a gleam of his old fun, "Qu'elle est attachante, cette femme là !"

BUSH AND ALLEN.

Lord Allen (says Gronow) being rather the worse for drinking too much wine at dinner, teased Count D'Orsay,[1] and said some very disagreeable things, which irritated him; when suddenly John Bush entered the club and shook hands with the Count, who exclaimed, "Voilà la différence entre une bonne bouche et une mauvaise haléine."

PEER AND PÈRE.

The following bon mot (says the same authority) was also attributed to the Count. General Ornano, observing a certain nobleman, who, by some misfortune in his youth, lost the use of his legs, in a Bath chair, which he wheeled about, inquired the name of the English peer. D'Orsay answered, "Père la Chaise."

TO PARDON HIM.

Walpole says in one of his letters:—The Comte d'Artois, forgetting that his brother is king, treats him with all the familiarity of their nursery. It was thought necessary to correct this, and M. de Maurepas was commissioned to

---

[1] See pp. 37, 38.

give the hint. Being urged, he said the king would grow offended. "Well," said the prince, "and, if he is, que peut il me faire?" "Vous pardonner, monsigneur," replied the minister.[1]

THE PRECURSOR.

Walpole says again:—One of the ladies to the Queen of France announced to her that the Comtesse d'Artois was *enceinte*. The Queen was a little piqued and envious, and, to conceal it, said, "I wonder what the child will be called?" The lady answered, "I hope, madam, *le Precurseur*."

NOTHING BURNS LIKE DRY LAURELS.

Madame de Coigny (says Walpole), on hearing that the mob at Paris had burnt the bust of their late favourite, Monsieur l'Epremenil, said, "Il n'y a rien qui brule si tôt que les lauriers secs."

ALL IN HER HAIR.

Moore relates another good *mot* of Madame de Coigny's, about some woman who had red hair and all its attendant ill consequences, and of whom some one said that she was very virtuous: "Oui, elle est comme Samson ; elle a toutes ses forces dans ses cheveux."

IT WAS SO LIKE HIM.

Moore gives the following anecdote, told by Croker, as one of the happiest things he ever heard. Fenelon, who had teased Richelieu (and ineffectually it would seem) for subscriptions to charitable undertakings, was one day telling him that he had just seen his picture. "And did you ask it for a subscription," said Richelieu, sneeringly. "No, I saw there was no chance," replied the other; "it was so like you."

·IT WAS HE!

It is in Moore's Diary that we read the story of an Englishman giving a *carte* of a restaurateur (which he happened to have in his pocket), instead of his passport, and the *gen d'arme*, maliciously reading it and looking at him : "Tête de veau; pied de cochon! ça suffit, Monsieur, c'est vous."

---

[1] Writing to the Countess of Ossory, Walpole adds:—" If you don't admire this more than any reply in your Diogenes Laertius, or ancient authors, I will never tell your ladyship another modern story."

IN MUTTON AND VEAL.

A French bookseller told Benson, speaking of two books that he had in his hand, "This is bound in mutton, sir, and this in veal."

FACTS.

Benjamin Constant (says Moore), on some one asking him (with reference to his book on religion) how he managed to reconcile the statements of his latter volumes with those of his first, published so long ago, answered, "Il n'y a rien qui s'arrange aussi facilement que les faits."

A VICIOUS CIRCLE.

Lord L—— said to Moore he had been told by Maury that, one time when Mirabeau was answering a speech of his, he put himself into a reasoning attitude, and said, "Je m' en vais renfermer M. Maury dans un cercle vicieux;" upon which Maury started up and exclaimed, "Comment! veux-tu m' embrasser?" which had the effect of entirely disconcerting Mirabeau.

TRANSLATING.

Miss N—— mentioned, in Moore's hearing, a French lady, of whom she inquired, by way of compliment, "in what manner she had contrived to speak English so well?" and the answer was, "I began by *traducing.*"

YAWNING AND HISSING.

Moore records:—D—— mentioned Piron's reply to Voltaire, on his boasting that he did not hiss his tragedy: "Quand on baille, on ne siffle pas."

A PRINCE OF PEAS.

Moore gives this as one of Fox's stories:—The Prince de Poix, stopped by a sentry, announced his name. "Prince de Poix!" answered the sentry; "quand nous seriez le Roi des Haricots, vous ne passeriez pas par ici."

POOR LITTLE BEAST!

You remember (says Sydney Smith) the story of the French marquise, who, when her pet lap-dog bit a piece out of her footman's leg, exclaimed, "Ah, poor little beast! I hope it won't make him sick."

TO-DAY, FOR EXAMPLE.

Denon told Moore an anecdote of a man, who, having been asked repeatedly to dinner by a person whom he knew to be but a shabby amphitryon, went at last, and found the dinner so meagre and bad that he did not get a bit to eat. When the dishes were removing, the host said, "Well, now the ice is broken, I suppose you will ask me to dine with you some day?" "Most willingly." "Name your day, then." "Aujourd'hui, par exemple," answered the dinnerless guest.

HIS POOR MASTER.

Such (says Sydney Smith) is the horror the French have of our *cuisine*, that, at the dinner given in honour of Guizot at the Athenæum, they say his cook was heard to exclaim, "Ah, mon pauvre maitre ! je ne le reverrai plus."

BREVITY ITSELF.

The letter of a celebrated Frenchwoman to her husband is (says Hayward) a model of conciseness: "Je commence, parce que je n'ai rien à faire : je finis, parce que je n'ai rien à dire."

THE LEAST CHRISTIAN POSSIBLE.

It being asked at Paris (says Haydon) whom they would have as godfather for Rothschild's baby, "Talleyrand," said a Frenchman. "Pourquoi, Monsieur?" "Parce qu'il est le moins chrétien possible."

ENOUGH ! ENOUGH !

One day (says Lady Davies) Prince Talleyrand and my father went to the Colisée. This was a promenade where the nobility and persons of position only were admitted, and without an introduction no one could go in. The gate-keeper did not hold Prince Talleyrand in anything like the respect due to the future great diplomatist of Europe, and my father was so young and so fair that, notwithstanding his uniform, he thought Prince Talleyrand's companion was a young lady in disguise, and cried out—"Vous ne pouvez pas passer, Mademoiselle," and held the gate closed. Talleyrand, thinking it an excellent joke, with a most serious expression turned to my father, saying— "Tu vois, ma mie, tu ne peux pas entrer." Upon this the gate-keeper came boldly forward to my father, to interpose his stern authority, when my father, taking his sword, gave him such a thrashing with the flat side of it, that, capering about in pain, he cried out—"C'est assez, c'est assez—ah passez, Monsieur, ah passez, Monsieur." Talleyrand was perfectly delighted, although I was told he did not even smile.

A KNOTTY QUESTION.

Lady Davies writes :—My grandmother and my aunt, Lady Emilia Drummond, were one day in attendance upon Her Majesty, being, like the rest of the more demure members of the Court, in open carriages. But the Queen was riding on a donkey, as indeed were various of her younger favourites. Suddenly, however, the whole cavalcade was stopped, for Marie Antoinette's donkey, having felt a sudden inclination to roll on the green turf, had thrown its royal rider, and she, being quite unhurt, remained seated on the ground, laughing immoderately. As soon, however, as she could command her countenance, she assumed a mock gravity, and, without attempting to rise from her lowly position, commanded that the Grand Mistress of the Ceremonies should at once be brought to her side. Nobody could imagine what Her Majesty was about either to say or do ; but when the lady thus suddenly summoned to her presence, stood, in no good temper and with dignified aspect before her, she looked up and said—"Madam, I have sent for you that you may inform me as to the etiquette to be observed when a Queen of France and her donkey have both fallen—which of them is to get up first ?"

THE CHIEF "GANACHE."

One day (says Lady Davies) Napoleon, having been provoked by her father, the Emperor of Austria, declared to Marie Louise that he was "an old *ganache*" (blockhead). Her Majesty asked one of her ladies-in-waiting, as she said the Emperor had called her father by that name, the meaning of the word *ganache*, and the lady, not knowing what to say in reference to the Empress's own father, answered that it meant "a venerable old man." Marie Louise believed this, and afterwards, when Cambacérès came to pay his respects to her, she, wishing to be very complimentary to him, said, "Sir, I have always regarded you as the chief *ganache* of France."

UP A CHIMNEY.

An Englishman and a Frenchman had to fight a duel. That they might have the better chance of missing one another, they were to fight in a dark room. The Englishman fired up the chimney, and, by Jove! he brought down the Frenchman ![1]

[1] Rogers used to add : "When I tell this story in Paris, I put the Englishman up the chimney !"

A UNIQUE EPISTLE.

The [following] letter will tell its own tale. It has not the date of the year in which it was written; but the original, which was sent (says J. C. Young) to a friend of my father's, was given him by the proper owner as a curiosity. "C—— D——s Priory, Aug. 27, till Sept. 10, that I shall go at Lady E. F——. My dear E——,—I am shameful to have not had the pleasure to entertain you since you have with disdain abandon London; but the respect to which I am indebted for your eldest sister had oblige me to think of her Ladyship before you. i hope that you have a better weather during your excursion on the lacs than that we have here; for almost every day the tunder is rolling upon our head with noise that should faint you, being as coward as a turkey; but what is more tiresome is the lamentations of peoples, which seeing the rains fall all the days, predict us with famine, plage, and civil wars, by the scarcity of bread, but it is a great error, for the harvest look very well. Be not surpriz'd i write so perfectly well in English, but once i am here, i speak and hear speaking all the day English; and during the nights, if some rats or mouses trouble me, i tell them go lon, and they obey, understanding perfectly my English. Sir G——e is suffering with a rheumatism. Lady H——e O—— who have the pretension to be a very good Physitien, but who is very ignorant, after that he have yesterday well breakfast, has given him a physic, and after he have dined she gave him another, and she desire that he take a walk, *au clair de la lune*, in place of to be near good fire. No: a dog or cat would be more prudent. Before yesterday, the brother having eat and drank too much, and being tormented with a strong indigestion, my lady gave him 8 grains of James Powder. the unhappy brother was near to die, and one was obliged to send to a physitien at Shelford, who arriving, found him so well, that he judged it best to wait if the nature would save him or not; but happily, being a strong nature, he was restored. Lady H——e, the best of women, is the worst of Physitien. She had killed some year ago a superb ox with James powder; and, on another occasion, having received 24 turkeys very fatigued to have walked to foot a too long journey, she contrive to refresh them to give them some *huile de castor;* but 12 of that number died, and the rest did look melancholy, so long as they did live. i have receive at this moment a letter from Lady S——n. i put my thanks at her feet. As the post go at 2 o'clock, i have not time to write to her ladyship, but I will comply soon with the liberty she gave me. Be sure that I have not forgot Lady S——n in my prayers, though not so good as I could wish indeed. Believe the faithful friendship that I feel for you, my dear sister-in-law, since that you were so much high than my finger. Write me often and my old wife. Believe me that I love a friendly letter more than a purse of guineas. Yours, Comte De C——z."

THE LIBERTY OF THE PRESS.

Some of the last masquerades at private houses were given (says Lady Chatterton) by my aunt, in Arlington Street, before I was born there. At the last of these, Madame de Stael was present. She had just arrived in England to escape from Parisian censorship, and publish her works out of the protecting shade of a gendarme's cocked hat. At one moment, the crowd being excessive, Madame de Stael remarked to my mother, "Il paraît qu' on souffre même ici de la liberté de la presse."

A MAN OF THE CENTURY.

C. de M——, one of the most fashionable at the same time, one of the cleverest, young men of the Restoration, had a singular taste of being in love with two ladies, each old enough to be his mother—the one a Duchess, the other a celebrated actress. When the Duchesse de Berrie asked him whether it was really true that his taste was for old women, he replied, "Oui Madame, je suis l'homme du siècle."

LES DIABLES ANGLAIS.

Gronow writes:—One of our countrymen, having been introduced by M. de la Rochefoucauld to Mademoiselle Bigottini, the beautiful and graceful dancer, in the course of conversation with this gentleman, asked him in what part of the theatre he was placed; upon which he replied, "Mademoiselle, *dans une loge rôtie*," instead of "grillée." The lady could not understand what he meant, until his introducer explained the mistake, observing, "Ces diables d' Anglais pensent toujours à leur Rosbif."

AN EPIGRAM.

The original of Tartuffe (says Raikes) was one Roquette, who was much more of a polisson than a priest, and who belonged to the diocese of Autun. This circumstance has suggested the following epigram on Talleyrand:—

> " Roquette dans son tems,
> Talleyrand dans le nôtre,
> Furent évêques d' Autun ;
> Tartuffe est le surnom de l' un—
> Ah ! si Molière eut connu l'autre."

FOR QUIETNESS' SAKE.

Raikes says in his Diary :—The Princess de T—— died yesterday, aged seventy-four; she was formerly Madame Grand, a Créole, very handsome, but very stupid ; her witty husband said that he took her *pour se reposer l'esprit*.

SIMPLY PICKPOCKETS.

Jordan writes:—I had dropt in at the Strand about two o'clock, about something or other, when Mr A. insisted on my staying to eat "suberb saur prout" with a fine German boy, the son of a nobleman, just imported. I consented, and we chatted together till long past the dinner hour, for which Ackermann and his stomach were particularly punctual. His nephew (?) and the young noble had gone out in the morning to see lions, and had not returned. We waited, and waited, till near three o'clock (an hour over time), when my host, unable to contain his anger and hunger any longer, ordered dinner, and we sat down to excellent rotten cabbage, but washed down with sensible muzzle and schnaps. About the middle of the repast, the young gentlemen made their appearance, and were told to sit down and feed, with the politeness, and in the tone which might become an incensed bear. However, as our host's appetite got appeased, his temper improved, and by the time the cloth was removed, the bumpers of muzzle had converted frowns into smiles, and at length I heard his cavernous issue of the question, "Vell, boisse (boys), vere ave you been, and vat ave you see?" The youngsters, delighted by this condescension, burst out in answer, the lead being taken by the nephew, who spoke as follows:—"Oh, mine oncle! after ve ave see two mans ahenging at Old Belly—vat a crowds!—ve go to de riveri to dox at Voolvitch to see de launch of de great sheep—vat a crowds!—and oh, mine oncle, vat a many billa box." "Billa box," repeated Ackermann, "vat you mean by billa box?" "Oh, sare," broke in the stranger, "so I ave been only a veeks in Engleland, I thinks I gan spake de langidge better as he. He means Bocca bills!" "Billa box, Bocca bills," muttered Ackermann. "Vat de divels does you mean? Say it in Yarman!" which they immediately did; and thus informed, he turned laughing loudly to me, and exclaimed "O, mine Kodds, vat you tink dey means?" I had not heard, and could not tell; and their interpreter, still convulsed with laughter, sputtered out, "Vy, dey means big boggets!" Not to lengthen the story, for some time longer unintelligible to me, I at last discovered that billa box, and bocca bills, and bigg boggets, all and sundry, meant simply pickpockets!

A RARITY.

Mark Boyd records the answer the German innkeeper gave to a former Duke of Brunswick, who, while travelling, had stopped his suite to breakfast at his auberge. When the duke called for his bill, he observed an enormous charge for eggs, and sent for the landlord, holding the bill in his hand. "Why, eggs must be very scarce in this country?" "Oh no, your Serene Highness, eggs are not at all scarce, but grand dukes are!"

THEIR EXCELLENCIES.

Charles Mayne Young, the actor, says:—A magistrate of the canton of Berne, seeing Voltaire for the first time, keeps his seat, fixes his spectacles firmly on his nose, and says, "Ah! ah! c'est a donk fous [*sic*] Mons. de Voltaire qui se permettra de dire tout des mauvaises choses du bon Dieu. Je ne vous conseille pas d'en dire de leurs excellences de Berne."

PRAYER IN DETAIL.

The same authority declares:—A Genevese, fishing in a tub close to the shore, finds himself unexpectedly driven some distance from the land by a sudden gust of wind, and, fearing the frailty of his vessel, he says, "Seigneur Dieu, Père Eternel, ayez pitiè de ton serviteur Jean Douron q's 'trouve dans la plus grand infortune. Ce n'est pas c'lui là, derrière la Rhone, c'est lui là qui demeure rue du temple, t'entends-tu ?"

A RISE.

The Italian who had the honour of teaching Geerge III. the violin, on being asked (says Hayward) by his royal pupil what progress he was making, observed:—"Please your Majesty, there are three classes of players—1, those who cannot play at all; 2, those who play badly; 3, those who play well. Your Majesty is just rising into the second class."

HE HAD A START.

When Macleane, the principal of Brighton College, was at Trinity College, Cambridge, he one day met the Marquis Spolêto, a teacher of Italian, and a refugee, and th's accosted him,—"Have you many pupils this term?" "Vel, I 'ave vone in Hebrew." "Dear me," said Macleane, "I had no idea you knew Hebrew." "Vel, no; not exactly. But then, you see, we do not begin for vone five veek." The story is told by J. C. Young.

"NOT SO THE RESPECT," &c.

Lord L. mentioned in Moore's presence the conclusion of a letter from a Dutch commercial house, as follows:—"Sugars are falling more and more every day; not so the respect and esteem with which we are," &c., &c.

SOME OF HER EYES.

We read in Young's Diary:—Dined with Count Danniskiold. The Count is a Dane of high rank, an accomplished man, and one of the most elegant dancers in Europe. He speaks English admirably, and rarely makes a blunder

Q

However, he made an amusing one [one] night. He was being bantered on having paid marked attention to one of the Miss C——'s, a young lady in the neighbourhood, reputed rich, but rather plain. On some one saying, " You can't admire her looks, Count!" he replied in a deprecating tone, " Come, come—you are a leetle hard upon me. She may not be beautiful, but, I must say, I tink she has a sweet expression in some of her eyes."

IT WAS SAFER.

Moore relates in his Diary:—During breakfast arrived Count Krasinksi, an intelligent Polish refugee, and man of letters. Remarked that there was a strong similarity between the Poles and the Irish, and mentioned as an instance of this, a countryman of his, who having, on some occasion, knocked a man down for being, as he thought, insolent to him, was expostulated with for having done so by some friend, who remarked that, after all, what the man had said to him was not so very offensive. " No, it was not," answered the other; " but still it was safer to knock him down."

A COMPARISON.

A distinguished diplomatist from the United States of America, a very genial and social being, soon after his arrival in London (says F. Locker), made the round of the sights, Madame Tussaud's among the number. "And what do you think of our waxwork?" said a friend. "Well," replied the General, "it struck me as being very like an ordinary English party."

WHAT THEY WANTED.

Moore recounts the anecdote of a Swiss and a Brabanter talking together, and the latter reproaching the Swiss with fighting for money, while he (the Brabanter) fought for honour. "The fact is," answered the Swiss dryly, "we each of us fight for what each most wants."[1]

A CRUEL DECEIVER.

An extract from Moore's Diary :—Clutterbuck's story of the old lady (his aunt) is excellent. Being very nervous, she told Sir W. Farquhar she thought Bath would do her good. "It's very odd," says Sir W.; "but that's the very thing I was going to recommend to you. I will write the particulars of your case to a very clever man there, in whose hands you will be well taken care of." The lady, furnished with the letter, sets off, and on arriving at

---

[1] Moore adds, "An old story this."

Newbury, feeling as usual very nervous, she said to her confident :—"Long as Sir Walter has attended me, he has never explained to me what ails me. I have a great mind to open his letter and see what he has stated of my case to the Bath physician." In vain her friend represented to her the breach of confidence this would be. She opened the letter, and read, "Dear Davis, keep the old lady three weeks, and send her back again."

THE VERY FIRST.

Another extract from Moore's Diary :—When Gally Knight was first introduced to old Dr Denman, the doctor said, "I have had the pleasure of seeing Mr Knight before." "I do not remember," rejoined Gally, "having ever had the honour of meeting you." "The truth is, young gentleman," said Denman, "I was the first person that *ever* saw you."

GENUINELY GRATIFIED.

Yet another extract from Moore's Diary :—Story of a sick man telling his symptoms (which appeared to himself, of course, dreadful) to a medical friend, who, at each new item of the disorder, exclaimed "Charming!" "Delightful!" "Pray go on!" and when he had finished, said with the utmost pleasure—"Do you know, my dear sir, you have got a complaint which has been for sometime supposed to be extinct?"

HE LIKED PUTTY.

Mr Lee, the artist, told J. C. Young a delicious story of Constable, the artist. On one of the days previous to the opening of the Royal Academy, when Academicians have the privilege of touching up their pictures, Constable went to look at what Stanfield was doing. He praised the picture on which he happened to be engaged, and took particular notice of the sky as boldly and originally treated. Shortly after, he went up to Reinagle and asked him what he thought of Stanfield's picture. "I have not seen it," said Reinagle. "Then go and see it, I beg of you!" continued Constable; "you never saw such a thing. Pray take notice of the sky, it is just like putty." Presently Reinagle walked up in front of Stanfield's picture, and, as he looked at it, quite taken by surprise, exclaimed aloud, "Why! *I* like the sky." "What do you mean," asked Stanfield, "by expressing yourself in that tone? Why should you not like the sky?" "Oh! I was off my guard when I spoke in that way," replied Reinagle, "but the fact is that I was told it was like putty." "Who told you so?" said the wounded painter. "Constable," was the answer. Stanfield, stung to the quick by hearing of this depreciatory criticism from such a quarter, goes up to the author of it, and says, "Constable, you are a humbug ! you came up to my picture just now and praised it.   I never asked your opinion about it ; but you said, particularly, that you *liked* the sky ; and then you go off to Reinagle and tell him that it is like putty !"   "Well," was the reply, "what of it ?   I like putty ! "

"WHAT A DONKEY!"

There are degrees of immortality (says Haydon).   On leaving Petworth, and when waiting for the coach to return to Brighton, a man of the village came up, looked hard at me, and said, "I beg your pardon, sir, but are you the great painter?"   "Well, I don't know about that exactly."   "But, sir, did you paint the picture of Christ entering into Jerusalem?"   "Yes, my friend, I did."   "Ah, sir, that was a picture—that was a picture—and— *what a donkey!*"

A DRAWBACK.

W. H. Harrison says :—The father of L——, a distinguished artist, was complimented by a friend on the talents and reputation of his son, and on the comfort he must be to his father.   "Yes," was the reply, "he is a very good son—a very good son, if he did not swear at his mother so."

WHY?

Barham tells of Dignum, the vocalist, an anecdote which he first heard from Neild, the lay vicar of St Paul's.   Dignum, it seems, was complaining one morning to old Knyvett, the king's composer, that his health was much impaired, and what was very extraordinary, that so strong a degree of sympathy existed between him and his brother, that one was no sooner taken ill than the other felt symptoms of the same indisposition, whatever it might be.   "We are both of us very unwell now," added Dignum, "and as our complaint is supposed to be an affection of the lungs, we are ordered to take asses' milk ; but unfortunately we have not been able to get any, though we have tried all over London ; can you tell us what we had better do ?"   "Do," answered Knyvett, "why the deuce don't you suck one another ?"

WHOSE WAS IT?

At a musical *soirée* in Paris, at which Rossini was present, a lady possessing a magnificent soprano voice and remarkable facility of execution, sang the great maestro's well-known aira, "Una voce," with great effect, but overladen with *fioriture* of the most elaborate description.   Rossini, at its conclusion, advanced to the piano and complimented the lady most highly upon her vocal powers, terminating his encomiums (says Planchè) with the cruel inquiry: "Mais de qui est la musique?"

HAPPY CEILING?

On another occasion (says Planchè) at a concert, a very indifferent tenor, who sang repeatedly out of tune, was indiscreet enough to express his regret to Rossini that he should have heard him for the first time in that room, as he complained: "Le plafond est si sourd." Rossini raised his eyes to the abused ceiling, and simply ejaculated : "Heureux plafond!"

SURELY AND CHORLEY.

Chorley, writing of Mendelssohn, gives the following illustration of the composer's *gaieté de cœur*—trifling enough in itself, but yet characteristic of the man. While spending an evening at his house, a note with a ticket enclosed was put into Chorley's hand. The note ran thus:—"The Directors of the Leipzig Concerts beg leave to present to Mr *Shurely* a ticket of the concert of to-morrow." Whereupon, writes Chorley, Mendelssohn ran to the pianoforte, and began to play the subject from the chorus of the "Messiah," "*Surely* he hath borne," &c.

JUSTLY INDIGNANT.

I once presided (Jerdan represents a man as saying) over a jolly company, when it was more customary than it now is—and the more's the pity—to call upon every guest in turn for a song or a tale, under the penalty, in case of refusal or non-compliance, of a strong tumbler of salt and water. I, at last, came to a contumacious chap, who protested that he could neither sing a song nor tell a tale. This would not pass with me, and especially as I had my eye upon this Billy for some time, and did not at all like his jeering leers and scoffing manners. So I said to him peremptorily, "Well, sir, if ye can do neither the one nor the other, you must oblige me by tossing off the tumbler I will now order to be brought to you." "Stop," he cried hastily, "let me try first." Silence ensued, and he proceeded:—"There was once a thief who chanced to find a church door open, of which carelessness he took advantage and stepped in, not to worship, but to carry off whatever of portable he could find. He put the cushions under his arms, hid as much as he could, and impudently wrapt the pulpit cloth about him like a plaid. But, lo and behold, whilst he was thus employed the sexton happened to pass by, and seeing the church door open, got the key and locked it ; so that when our sacrilegious friend thought he had nothing to do but to slip out as he slipt in, he discovered that he was a close prisoner and all egress stopped. What to do he knew not; but at last it struck him that he might succeed in letting himself down to the ground by the bell-rope. Accordingly, with it in hand, he swung gently off; and you may be certified set up a ringing that alarmed the neighbourhood. In short, he was captured with his booty upon him as soon as he reached mother earth ; upon which, looking up to the bell, as I now look up to your lordship, he remonstrated, 'Had it not been for your long tongue and empty head, I might have escaped!'"

ESPECIALLY POTATOES.

There is no doubt bulls are occasionally perpetrated by others than natives of Ireland, as in the case of the English viceroy, who advised that "the greatest economy was necessary in the consumption of all species of grain, especially of potatoes."

AN UGLY FAMILY.

I recollect, when a boy (says Captain Gronow), seeing a strange couple, a Mr and Mrs Turbeville, who were famed for their eccentricities. Mr Turbeville was related to Sir Thomas Picton, but did not possess the talent or discretion of the gallant General. Upon one occasion, at a dinner at Dunraven Castle, after the ladies had retired, Mr Turbeville observed to a gentleman present, that the woman who had sat at his right was the ugliest he had ever seen; upon which the gentleman said, "I am sorry to hear that you think my wife so ill-looking." "Oh, no, sir, I have made a mistake ; I meant the lady who sat on my left." "Well, sir, she is my sister." "It can't be helped, sir, then; for, if what you have said is true, I must confess I never saw such an ugly family during the course of my life."

A CULTIVATOR OF RELIGION.

To Justice Park's brother, who was a great church goer, some one (says Moore) applied the words, "*Parcus* deorum cultor."[1]

"LONG MAY SHE REMAIN SO."

I have heard (says Lord William Lennox) of a post-prandial speaker who, wishing to pay a compliment to the land of his birth, shouted out, "England is an island—England is an island;" then, forgetting the fervent eulogium he was about to make, abruptly concluded by saying, "and long may she remain so."

---

[1] Horace, *Odes*, I., xxxiv.

ACCOMMODATING.

Colley Cibber's brother told Dr Sim. Burton on a visit, "that he did not know any sin he had not been guilty of but one, which was avarice; and if the doctor would give him a guinea, he would do his utmost to be guilty of of that too."

ONE FOR THE FRENCHMAN.

Mr Hayward tells how a Frenchman, dining with an Englishman, let drop the remark, "I eat a great deal of bread with my meat." "Yes," was the reply, "and a great deal of meat with your bread."

DE OYLEY AND DE-UMPLING.

A conceited man, of the name of D'Oyley, having said that he wished to be called De Oyley, somebody at dinner (says Moore) addressed him thus: "Mr De Oyley, will you have some De-umpling?"

A DEUCED ODD PLAY.

I wish (says Fanny Kemble) to preserve a charming instance of *naïve* ignorance in a young guardsman, seduced by the enthusiasm of the gay society of London into going, for once, to see a play of Shakespeare's. After sitting dutifully through some scenes in silence, he turned to a fellow guardsman, who was painfully looking and listening by his side, with the grave remark, "I say, George, *dooced* odd play this; it's all full of quotations."

NOT COME AGAIN.

An Englishman of letters and politics, at his solitary dinner in an Old Bailey beef-shop, ate seven pounds and a half of solid meat, sliced from a round of boiled beef. As his customer ate (says Lord William Lennox), the keeper of the shop regarded him with increasing anger, for diners at the establishment were at liberty to eat as much as they pleased for a stated sum. "Excellent beef!" said the gourmand, graciously, when he at length rose from his seat; "a man may cut and come again here." "You may *cut*, sir," responded the purveyor of dinners, "but I'll be blowed if you shall *come* again."

A PARTY OF TWO.

A story I once heard (says the same writer), the scene of which was at Avignon in France:—"By my faith," said the President of the Tribunal to an interested auditor, "we have just had a superb turkey, tender as a chicken, fat as an ortolan, aromatic as a thrush. By my faith we left nothing but its bones." "And how many were there of you?" inquired the curious hearer. "Only two," answered the *gourmet*, with a self-complacent smile. "Only two!" ejaculated the simple auditor with amazement. "Precisely so," the lawyer answered. "Only two. There was myself, and there was—the turkey."

A PLAINTIVE INQUIRY.

Scott told Moore of a Jew in some small theatre, saying at the very moment when the whole audience was in still and breathless attention to the sorrows of Mrs Beverley,[1] "I should like mosh to know who dat was dat spat in my eye."

AN EPIGRAM.

I do not know (says J. C. Young) who is the author of the following lines, but they were sent to me by a very charming person, who, for aught I know to the contrary, may have been the author of them. They were written, I need hardly say, in allusion to the case of "The Plaintiff," Sir Roger Tichborne:—

> "The firm of Baxter, Rose, and Norton,
> Deny the plaintiff's Arthur Orton;
> But can't deny, what's more important,
> That he has done what Arthur oughtn't."

THE THREE PER CENT. CONSOLS.

At a city dinner (says Jerdan), so political that "the Three Consuls" of France were drunk, the toast-master, quite unacquainted with Buonaparte, Cambacères, and Lebrun, holloaed out from behind the chair—"Gentlemen, fill bumpers! the chairman gives 'The Three Per Cent. Consols!'"

THE DUTY OFF.

A young friend of mine (says Harrison) had an appointment with Christal, the artist. His father, however, wanted him to accompany him elsewhere. "But," remonstrated the son, "it is a sort of duty to Christal to go to him." "Nonsense," rejoined the elder, "there is no duty in the case; it was taken off *glass* by the late Act."

---

[1] In the

HE WOULD NOT DINE.

At the end of the last and beginning of the present century, few of the great London merchants (says Boyd) had their private residences in the West End. They lived chiefly in the city, or in the suburbs. There was, however, an exception, one whose exercise for six days in the week was his walk into and out of the city. Moreover, he dined in the city, immediately on 'Change closing, returning for an hour afterwards to his counting-house to sign his letters, and see the transactions of the day complete. He was a stately and methodical personage in all he said and did. He had for years dined at a coffee-house in St Paul's, and his habit was in the morning, on his way eastward, to enter the coffee-room and address the head waiter thus, from which he was only once known to make a deviation :—"Well, John, and what have you got for dinner to-day?" "A nice slice of Thames salmon, sir; soup as always, and haunch o' mutton, sir." "Then, John, I shall dine with you to-day, you may depend upon it." These questions and the answers were almost as well known to the frequenters of the coffee-house as the establishment itself. One July morning, under a broiling sun, the great merchant entered as usual. "Well, John, and what have you got for dinner to-day?" "Werry nice dinner indeed, sir, to-day; ain't it vonderful hot, sir?" the perspiration pouring down John's face. "Sir, there's a beautiful salmon, sir, two kinds o' soup, sirloin o' beef, turkey and sausages; the burial people, sir, dine with us to-day." "The burial people, John?" "Yes, sir, the poor gemman vat died in the room over this of putrid fever on Tuesday is to be buried to-day, as ve fears 'e von't keep no longer." "Then (hurrying to the door), John, I shall *not* dine with you to-day, you may depend upon it."

EATING HIS DEEDS.

Barham records this story of Edward Walpole, who, being told one day at the Garrick that the confectioners had a way of discharging the ink from old parchments by a chemical process, and then making the parchment into isinglass for their jellies, said, "Then I find a man may now eat his deeds as well as his words." "This," adds Barham, "has been very unfairly attributed to James Smith."

A BAD CONUNDRUM.

At a gathering at which Moore was present, they talked of Sir Alexander M—— and his son, on whom the following conundrum was made :—"Why is Sir A. like a Lapland winter?" "Because he is a long night (knight), and his sun (son) never *shines*."

SOME OF THEM, THAT WAY!

Mr Nightingale walked one day into the shop of Saunders & Otley, and began to tell one of the persons behind the counter that he considered himself very ill-used; **for** that he had subscribed for years to their library, and yet never could get any of the new **works that came** out : whereas, friends of his who had **not** subscribed twelve months, were accommodated with all the best **books of the season.** On hearing the angry tone and language of Mr N., a highly respectable gentleman came from the inner shop, and said that "if Mr N. were dissatisfied, he had his redress in his own hands; he had better withdraw his name from the list of subscribers." On this the old gentleman became exceeding **wroth**, winding up a somewhat intemperate **speech** with these words :—"There, **sir !** now you know my mind as to your **conduct.** I think I have spoken pretty freely, but in case I have not—I don't know who you are—but, if **you are Saunders, hang Otley !** and if **you are Otley, hang Saunders !**"

A PLEASURE THAT NEVER PALLS.

The **other day** (says Frederick Locker) I heard that whimsical fellow, G——, **make a rather foolish remark, to the** effect that the pleasure of *not* going to church was a pleasure that *never* palled.

"A BIRD, BY JOVE !"

Talking of practical jokes, Moore records Rogers's story of somebody who, when tipsy, **was** first rolled in currant jelly, and then covered with feathers : his exclaiming, when he looked at himself in a glass, "A bird, by Jove !"

A LUKEWARM CHRISTIAN.

Evanson, in his *Dissonance of the Gospels*, thinks Luke most worthy of credence. P—— (remarks Crabb Robinson) said that Evanson was a *lukewarm Christian.*

"I'LL BE BOUND."

Campbell, talking of dog-Latin, gave specimens of a conversation he had heard (or heard *of*) between an Irish priest and a foreigner in Latin. One of them, speaking of a friend he had dined with, called him a "*Diabolicus bonus socius*," and the other said, "*Vinciar habebatis bonum vinum.*" Campbell defied us to find out what he meant, but I (says Moore) saw it immediately : "I'll be *bound* you had good wine."

MALAPROPOS.

When, on one occasion, the Queen and the Prince Consort were going over the British Museum, their attention was directed to an icthyosaurus. Just at that moment (says Harrison), Mr König entered the room, when Sir Henry [Ellis] presented him, as the then head of the department, to the Queen and the Prince. The latter, whose ear was struck by the German name, desired to know from whence in Germany he came, and asked, "From what part?" König, supposing the inquiry to refer, not to himself, but to the fossil, replied, "From the blue lias at Lyme Regis, in Dorsetshire, your Royal Highness." Sir Henry said that the Queen was especially diverted by the *malapropos* reply.

THE TRAVELLER AND HIS DOG.

Dr Taylor read to Barham the following extract from a letter addressed to him by Archbishop Whately :—"O'Connell has spoilt the dog. The story is of a traveller who, finding himself and his dog in a wild country, and destitute of provisions, cut off his dog's tail, and boiled it for *his own* supper, giving the 'dog *the bone.*'"

NOT A HELPMEET FOR HIM.

We read in the *Literary Gazette* this story :—"I will never marry a woman that can't carve," said M——. "Why?" "Because she would not be a help-meat for me."

A GREAT DISAPPOINTMENT.

A friend of W. H. Harrison's told him he was dining at the British Embassy in a foreign city, when the minister's lady inquired of a gentleman from Manchester if she had been rightly informed that things were so much cheaper in England than they had been. "Yes, your ladyship, was the reply; "for instance, my father died last year, and I buried him for fifty pounds, and now I could have done it for twenty."

A "DISGOUSTING" STOMACH.

The Duke of Gloucester told the following anecdote of a Mayor of Liverpool :— He was seated at the chief magistrate's right hand. When the fish was produced, it was speedily discovered by all whose olfactory organs were in the least sensitive, to be in such a progressive state that His Royal Highness, with the guests on both sides the table, lost no time in sending away their plates. Still the mayor went on with his fish. "Mayor, mayor," said the Duke, "do send away your plate—the fish is quite tainted." The mayor, at the moment he was addressed by royalty, was in the act of taking another mouthful. "I thank your Royal Highness, but I have a stomach that will *disgoust* anything." The anecdote is recorded by Mark Boyd.

APPROPRIATE.

A wealthy farmer, whom I knew (says Jerdan), was induced to embark in a parochial contest at considerable expense, and in acknowledgment was fêted with a public dinner at Kensington. On his health being drunk with all the honours, the singer on the *rota* sang "The Wealthy Fool with Gold in Store," amid great applause.

NOT SO PLAIN.

James Fenimore Cooper, the novelist, told Moore the following anecdote of a disputatious man :—"Why, it is as plain as that two and two make four." "But I deny *that*, too; for 2 and 2 make twenty-two."

N.B.

A curious specimen of elegant letter-writing has been printed by J. C. Young. It is a note written to the late Bishop of Norwich, Dr S——, in answer to an invitation given by him :—"Mr O ——'s private affairs turn out so sadly that he cannot have the pleasure of waiting upon his lordship at his agreeable house on Monday next.—N.B., his wife is dead."

NATURALLY.

In a conversation which happened to turn on railway accidents and the variety of human sufferings, a bank director (says Jerdan) observed that he always felt great interest in the case of a broken limb. "Then, I suppose," said ——, "for a compound fracture you feel compound interest."

MEN'S AND WOMEN'S.

Moore gives a place to this anecdote of the rival shoemakers; one of them putting up over his door "Mens conscia recti;" and the other instantly mounting "Men's and women's conscia recti."

OVER THE REPUBLIC.

Talking of Switzerland, "Well," said Sydney Smith, "what are they doing now in that irritable little republic? You remember ——'s answer, when they sent him a decree that he could not be permitted to fire *in* the republic? 'Very well,' said he, 'it makes no sort of difference to me; I can very easily fire *over* the republic!'"

TRUE FRIENDSHIP.

The attachment of perfect friendship was exhibited (says Jerdan) by Coleman in the instance of a loving pair of cronies staggering home from the tavern, when one tumbled into the kennel and besought his comrade to help him up. "Ah, no," hiccuped the true friend, "I am too drunk to do that, but, my dear boy, I will lie down by you," which was no sooner said than done.

TOO FAT.

Says Planché, on one occasion :—Our Amphitryon, John Andrews, was exceedingly corpulent, and upon one occasion had a severe attack of illness, which nearly proved fatal. On his recovery he received, by post, the following lines:—

> "By an illness, much worse than he'd e'er had before,
> Poor Andrews, they say, has been brought to Death's door,
> But danger there's none, unless he should grow thin,
> For Death hasn't a door that would now let him in."

NOT TWENTY-THREE.

H—— tells me (says F. Locker) that his cook has lately won a good deal of money in a lottery, with the number *twenty-three.* H—— asked her how it was she had happened to tumble on such a lucky number, and she replied, "Oh, sir, I had a dream; I dreamt of number seven, and I dreamt it three times, and as three times seven is twenty-three, I chose that number, sir." This proves that an ignorance of the multiplication table is not always a calamity. I was relating this anecdote to a distinguished friend, who holds a rather responsible position, and is usually anything but slow in apprehending a joke. When I had concluded, I observed a wistful expression on his countenance as if he were ready, nay anxious, to be amused, but could not for the life of him quite manage it. Then suddenly his face brightened, and he said, but with a tinge of dejection in his manner, "Ah, yes, I see—yes—I suppose three times seven is not twenty-three."

WHAT IT WAS ABOUT.

Moore gives this anecdote of Dr Barnes :—Being sometimes inclined to sleep a little during the sermon, a friend who was with him in his pew one Sunday, having joked with him on his having nodded now and then, Barnes insisted he had been awake all the time. "Well, then," said his friend, "can you tell me what the sermon was about?" "Yes, I can," he answered, "it was about half-an-hour too long."

TAKING TIMBER.

A good story is told by Moore of a man selling a horse. The would-be purchaser, inquiring as to his leaping powers, asks, " Would he take timber?" "He'd jump over your head," answered the other; "I don't know what you call *that.*"

A RHYME.

Lord H. mentioned to Moore some one being defied to find a rhyme for Carysfort, and writing—"I'm writing a note to my uncle Carysfort; he has got the gout, and is gone to Paris for't."

A PARODY.

Moore writes in his Diary :—Forgot to mention that Casey mentioned to me a parody of his on those two lines in the "Veiled Prophet :"—

> "He knew no more of fear than one who dwells
> Beneath the tropics, knows of icicles."

The following is his parody, which, bless my stars, none of my critics were lively enough to hit upon, for it would have stuck by me :—

> "He knew no more of fear than one who dwells
> On Scotia's mountains, knows of shoe-buckles."

"SUCH AS IT IS."

A literary character—I need not mention names (says Jerdan)—on a visit to Bath, was pressed into a hospitable engagement with a resident gentleman, who had a penchant for cultivating the acquaintance of such celebrities. He had also the peculiarity of using the above expression in and out of season, and often with ludicrous effect. His guest being seated at an excellent plain dinner, the Amphytrion most unnecessarily would apologise for its deficiencies. Bath, to be sure, was one of the best markets in England, and he endeavoured to get everything good ; but the fish, he feared, was not that most fashionable in town at present ; and the roast mutton was a very homely joint, &c., &c.; but he hoped Mr ——— would excuse the deficiencies, for he is most welcome to the fare, "such as it is !" A smile rewarded this first ebullition, which was almost converted into a burst of laughter when the wines came within a similar category. "This sherry is direct from Cadiz, but not, I am afraid, of the highest quality ; and the other was only humble port, a kitchen wine with high people ; but I have had it in bottle nine years, and I hope you will be able to drink it, sir, such as it is !" Everything went on in the same manner till Mr ———, unable to keep his countenance much longer, pretended an urgent engagement in order to get away early in the evening. His host regretted this exceedingly, and said, "I am indeed very sorry that you are obliged to leave us so soon, and the more so as I can assure you I have been much entertained by your conversation, *such as it is !*"

A WEARY NIGHT.

Moore relates what he calls the good story of the fellow in the Marshal-sea having heard his companion brushing his teeth the last thing at night, and, then upon waking, at the same work in the morning : "Ugh, a weary night you must have had of it, Mr Fitzgerald."

HE KNEW HIM.

Writes Frederick Locker :—In recent hill warfare with the Afreedees, who are human beings not a whit more degraded than the aborigines of West-minster, some of the native population zealously took our side. On one occasion an officer on duty pointed out to a native sentry a certain black fellow whom he had observed skulking with others round the fort, evidently with sinister intentions. "I see him, sar," said the sentry—"had two shots at him a'ready, him dam hard to hit, he hardest man to hit I know." "Oh you know him, do you?" said the officer. "Oh yes, sar, I know de dam rascal. I been tryin' to shoot him all de week." "Well, who is he ? What's his name ?" "Oh, de dam rascal—he my father."

A LEVER AND A PULLEY.

Poole told Moore of a man who said "I can only offer you for dinner what the French call a *lever* (lièvre) and a *pulley* (poulet)."

HE NEVER LOOKED AT THEM.

Lord Holland told in Moore's hearing the story of a man who professed to have studied "Euclid" all through, and upon some one saying to him, "Well, solve me that problem," answered, "Oh, I never looked at the cuts."

A SARCASTIC BOOTMAKER.

I remember (says Gronow) Horace Churchill (afterwards killed in India, with the rank of major-general), who was then an ensign in the guards, entering Hoby's shop in a great passion, saying that his boots were so ill made that he should never employ Hoby for the future. Hoby, putting on a pathetic cast of countenance, called to his shopman, "John, close the shutters. It is all over with us; I must shut up shop : Ensign Churchill withdraws his custom from me." Churchill's fury can be better imagined than described.

FOR RIDING.

On another occasion (says the same authority) the late Sir John Shelly came into Hoby's shop to complain that his top-boots had split in several places. Hoby quietly said, "How did that happen, Sir John?" "Why, in walking to my stable." "Walking to your stable!" said Hoby with a sneer; "I made the boots for riding, not walking."

STEWED IN ONIONS.

Mrs Wordsworth and a lady were walking once in a wood when the stock-dove was cooing. A farmer's wife coming by, said, "Oh, I do like stock-doves!" Mrs Wordsworth (says Haydon), in all her enthusiasm for Wordsworth's beautiful address to the stock-dove, took the old woman to her heart. "But," continued the old woman, "some like 'em in a pie; for my part there's nothing like 'em **stewed in onions!**"

ONE OVER.

Walpole writes :—After the execution of the eighteen malefactors [1787], a female was bawling an account of them, but called them nineteen. A gentleman said to her, "Why do you say nineteen? There were but eighteen hanged." She replied, "Sir, I did not know you had been reprieved."

A FILLET OF VEAL.

Mrs R. A. mentioned to Moore a good *bon mot* of a friend of hers, a lady, who was at a fancy ball, dressed with a band round her forehead, and a veil hanging from it. "Is that a veal?" said a vulgar man, addressing her, and mincing the word as I have spelt it. "Yes," she answered, pointing to the band, "a *fillet.*"

NOT SO BAD AS THAT.

One day Theodore Hook was travelling in a coach. There were (says Young) but two inside passengers—a very pretty, but very delicate-looking young lady, attended by a very homely-looking maid. The coach stopped twenty minutes to allow of dinner. Hook returned first to his place; the maid next. During the absence of her young mistress, Hook said to her, in a tone of great sympathy—"Your young lady seems very unwell." "Yes, sir; she suffers sadly." "Consumption, I should fear?" "No, sir; I am sorry to say it is the heart." "Dear me! Aneurism?" "O no, sir! it is only a lieutenant in the navy."

THE MYSTERY EXPLAINED.

A certain noble housewife—Cannon used to say—had observed that her stock of pickled cockles was running remarkably low, and she spoke to the cook in consequence, who alone had access to them. The cook had noticed the same serious deficiency : "she couldn't tell how, but they certainly *had* disappeared much too fast!"· A degree of coolness, approaching to estrangement, ensued between these worthy individuals, which the rapid consumption of the pickled cockles by no means contributed to remove. The lady became more distant than ever, spoke pointedly and before company of "some people's unaccountable partiality to pickled cockles," etc. The cook's character was at stake : unwilling to give warning, with such an imputation upon her self-denial, not to say honesty, she, nevertheless, felt that all confidence between her mistress and herself was at an end. One day, the jar containing the evanescent condiment being placed as usual on the dresser, while she was busily engaged in basting a joint before the fire, she happened to turn suddenly round, and beheld, to her great indignation, a favourite magpie, remarkable for his conversational powers and general intelligence, perched by its side, and dipping his beak down the open neck with every symptom of gratification. The mystery was explained—the thief detected ! Grasping the ladle of scalded grease which she held in her hand, the exasperated lady dashed the whole contents over the hapless pet, accompanied by the exclamation—"Oh, d— me, you've been at the pickled cockles, have ye ?" Poor Mag, of course, was dreadfully burnt ; most of his feathers came off, leaving his little round pate, which had caught the principal part of the volley, entirely bare. The poor bird moped about, lost all his spirit, and never spoke for a whole year. At length, when he had pretty well recovered, and was beginning to chatter again, a gentleman called at the house, who, on taking off his hat, discovered a very bald head ! The magpie, who happened to be in the room, appeared evidently struck by the circumstance : his reminiscences were at once powerfully excited by the naked appearance of the gentleman's skull. Hopping upon the back of his chair, and looking him hastily over, he suddenly exclaimed in the ear of the astounded visitor—"Oh, d— me, *you've* been at the pickled cockles, have ye ?"

OUT AND IN.

J. C. Young says :—Colonel ——, dining with Mrs R——, and finding that she, like himself, was suffering from a bad cold, expressed warm sympathy for her. She thanked him, and asked him how he had caught his ? "Oh," said he, "I just got it by lying out. And you, madam, how did you catch yours ?" "Oh !" was the reply, "I just got it by lying *in*."

R

METAPHYSICS.

According to L'Estrange, Mrs **Charles Kemble's** description of metaphysics was—" When **A** calls to B and C, and B and C don't understand him, and A does not understand himself—that is metaphysics."

AS THEY WERE.

Dined at Birmingham (writes Moore). . . One of my companions mentioned that an old woman said, upon the regiment of the Inniskilleners lately entering that town, "Well, boys, you look mighty well, considering **it** is now a hundred and nine years since you were here before."

THEIR NASTY SINS.

A clergyman (says Young) was exceedingly annoyed by **the intemperate** freaks and excesses of certain Baptists who invaded his parish, and estranged many of his flock from him. He was **surprised and** hurt **to** find an **old** lady, a farmer's wife, had allowed **them** to **dip their converts in her** pond. On his remonstrating with her, **she declared that they had** done **it** entirely without her consent, **or** even her **knowledge,** but vowed they **should** never do so again. **"I ain't no** idea **of their coming and** leaving all **their** nasty sins behind them in my** water."

SO WARM AND COMFORTABLE.

Young writes again:—Mrs Young and I **dined with the Rector of** Wootton **Basset. His** wife is lovely in person, amiable **in manner,** essentially feminine, **but** lamentably deaf. Owing **to** this infirmity, **a ludicrous** mistake **arose.** The ladies were in the drawing-room, and my wife **was sitting** with **her** back **to the door.** A gentleman, whom we had met for the first **time,** had **left** the dining-room before the others, and had entered so silently, **that Mrs Young, unconscious of** his being behind her, made the following **remark to the** lady of the house :—"What a **very** agreeable man Mr Hare is" **(the** very man at the back of her chair). "Oh, yes," said the deaf lady; **"and so** warm and comfortable of **a winter's** night." The hostess **had** thought Mrs Young was **praising her rooms, not her** friend.

A GOOD DEFINITION.

Says the same **writer:—A Mrs** Tomkinson was staying at Putney with Mr **Leader, the father of** the ex-member for Westminster, when one day, after a **dinner** party, **while** sitting in the drawing-room with the ladies, who were **dissecting** the characters of the gentlemen they had **just** left at the dining-**table,** the name of one individual came on the *tapis* who had made himself particularly disagreeable, not so much by anything he had said or done as by what he had left unsaid and undone, and by his exclusiveness, arrogance, and sullen taciturnity. Each lady present, with the exception of Mrs Tomkinson, having expressed her sentiments pretty freely about the noxious "party," her opinion was challenged. "Well," she said, in her passive way, "he seems to me to be an anomaly in natural philosophy: he is 'gravity without attraction.'"

SOMETHING IN THE HOUSE.

Mathews, sen., gave a very entertaining account of his having been recommended by Mr Lowdham, a member of the club, to stop at a particular inn in Nottingham, when upon his last theatrical tour. He found it, however, quite a third-rate inn, and could get no attendance. Half-a-dozen different people successively answered the bell when he rang, stared at him, said "Yes, sir!" and went away; nor could he get anyone to show him into a private room, though he had bespoken one. At last a great lubberly boy came blubbering into the room, when Mathews addressed him very angrily:—M.—"When am I to have my private room?" Boy.—"We han't got none but one, and that's bespoke for Mathews the player." M.—"Well, I am Mathews the player, as you call him." Boy.—"Oh, then you may come this way!" He was ushered, at length, into a room with a fire just lighted, and full of smoke; still there was nothing to be got to eat, while Mathews, who had travelled between forty and fifty miles that day, was very hungry. M.—"Send me up the master of the house! Where is the master?" Boy.—"He's dead, sir!" M.—"Then send the mistress." Boy.—"Mother's gone out!" M.—"Well, do let me have something to eat, at all events; can you get me a mutton chop?" Boy.—"Not till mother comes home." M.—"Well, then, some cold meat—anything, confound it! boy; have you got nothing in the house?" Boy.—"Yes, sir." M.—"Well, what is it then?" Here the poor boy burst into a flood of tears and blubbered out, "An execution, sir!"

A LUCKY BOY.

Mark Boyd relates an anecdote which the late Mr Coates used to tell. He had, he said, never known a request so ably and so judiciously put, inasmuch as it was complied with four-fold. A boy, on a hot summer morning, was passing down St James's Street, or along Pall Mall, when he observed two gentlemen agreeably occupied at breakfast at their club window, which was open. Adopting as rapidly as possible a supplicatory attitude and tone, he addressed one of the gentlemen thus: "Please, sir, will you kindly give me a little salt?   Oh, sir, please do ; for, if you give me a little salt, perhaps this gentleman will give me an egg."   Not only was an egg forthcoming, and salt, but a good sized cup of coffee, in addition to a muffin.

A VERY BAD BARGAIN.

Sir Patrick Hamilton, Mayor of Dublin, had, according to Walpole, a parsimonious wife.   In his mayoralty, he could not persuade her to buy a new gown.   The pride of the Hamiltons surmounted the penury of the Highlands. He bought a silk that cost five-and-fifty shillings a yard, but told his wife it cost but forty.   In the evening she displayed it to some of her female acquaintances.   "Forty shillings a yard !   Lord, madam," said one of them, "I would give five-and-forty myself."   "Would you, madam ?   You shall have it at that price."   Judge how Sir Patrick was transported when he returned at night, and she bragged of the good bargain she had made !

WHAT A PROPHET IS.

Examining one of the Sunday School boys at Addington, I asked him (says Barham) what a prophet was.   He did not know.   "If I were to tell you what would happen to you this day twelvemonth, and it should come to pass, what would you call me then, my little man?"   "A fortune-teller, sir," said the little boy.   There was an end of the examination for the day.

AN ENFANT TERRIBLE.

Hicks told J. C. Young that the children of the National Infant School at Swansea were taught very much by sign : the hand of the teacher sloped signifying "oblique," the hand held flat, "horizontal," the hand upright, "perpendicular."   One of the Welsh bishops was preaching one day in behalf of the school, when, observing several children whispering together, he held his hand upright in a warning manner, meaning thereby to impose silence, on which almost all the school, in the midst of his sermon, holloed out, "Perpendicular!"

A YOUTHFUL PREFERENCE.

Young speaks of hearing a charming story of one of the royal children, which he hopes is true.   When last the Queen was about to be confined, the Prince Consort said to one of his little boys, "I think it very likely, my dear, that the Queen will soon present you with a little brother or sister; which of the two would you prefer ?"   The child, pausing—"Well, I think, if it is the same to Mamma, I should prefer a pony."

BRAVO, WORM !

I had (says Jerdan) a pleasing correspondence with Lord Erskine, when he printed his humane appeal in favour of the rooks, and contended that by their destruction of insects they much overpaid the loss of any injury done to the farmers' crops. There was nobody, to be sure, to take up the case of the suffering insects. The only word I ever heard uttered in favour of the tribe was the reply of the lazy fellow in Dublin, when reproached with his sluggard habits. "Ah, Dick, Dick, thou wilt never come to good, lying in bed till noon ! It is the early bird, Dick, that picks up the worm." "Ay, but," said Dick, "the worm was up first !"

A PERTINENT QUERY.

Moore writes:—Sheridan, the first time he met Tom, his son, after the marriage of the latter, seriously angry with him, told him he had made his will, and had cut him off with a shilling. Tom said he was, indeed, very sorry, and immediately added : "You don't happen to have the shilling about you now, sir, do you?" Old S. burst out laughing, and they became friends again.

A SIN AND A SHAME.

A story of Barham on a steamboat trip :—An old woman on board told some of her friends who were very merry, that while she was at Margate in the course of the summer, the friend at whose house she had been staying had gone into the market for the purpose of purchasing a goose. There were but two in the whole place, offered for sale by a girl of fourteen, who refused to part with one without the other, assigning no other reason for her obstinacy than that it was her mother's order. Not wishing for two geese, the lady at first declined the purchase, but at last finding no other was to be had, and recollecting that a neighbour might be prevailed upon to take one off her hands, she concluded the bargain. Having paid for and secured the pair, she asked the girl at parting if she knew her mother's reason for the directions she had given. "O yes! mistress," answered the young poultry merchant readily; "mother said that they had lived together *eleven years,* and it would be a sin and a shame to part them now!"

SO CLEANLY.

A story has been told (says Lord Wm. Lennox) of a noble lord, still flourishing (1876), who upon saying to a keeper, "I suppose you've scarcely ever met with a worse shot than I am?" "Oh yes, my lord," responded the other, "I've met with many a worse, for you misses them so cleanly."

IS THAT ALL?

J. C. Young writes :—At the Duke of Wellington's funeral the little child of a friend of mine was standing with her mother at Lord Ashburton's window to see the mournful pageant. During the passage of the procession, she made no remark until the duke's horse was led by, its saddle empty, and his boots reversed in the stirrups, when she looked up into her mother's face, and said, "Mamma, when we die, will there be nothing left of us but boots?"

DYING AND DYEING.

Captain Gronow writes:—The Duke of Gloucester frequently visited Cheltenham during the season. Upon one occasion he called upon Colonel Higgins, brother to the equerry of His Royal Highness the Prince Regent, and on inquiring of the servant if his master was at home, received for answer, "My master is dyeing." "Dying!" repeated the Duke, "have you sent for a doctor?" "No, sir." His Royal Highness immediately ran back into the street, and having the good fortune to find a medical man, he requested him to come at once to Colonel Higgins, as he was at the point of death. The Duke and the doctor soon reached the Colonel's house, and after again asking the servant how his master was, that functionary replied, "I told you, sir, that he was dyeing." They mounted the staircase, and were rather amused to find the reported invalid busily occupied in dyeing his hair.

OUT TOO.

Moore gives the story of a man asking a servant, "Is your master at home?" "No sir, he's out." "Your mistress?" "No sir, she's out." "Well, I'll just go in and take an air of the fire till they come." "Faith, sir, that's out too."

SO DARK-LIKE YOURSELF.

Frederick Locker writes:—A lady of my acquaintance, a brunette, happened to show her maid one of those little sticking-plaster profiles which they used to call *silhouettes*. It was the portrait of the lady's aunt, whom the girl had never seen, and she said quite innocently, "La, ma'am, I always thought as how you had some black relations, you are so dark-like yourself, you know."

SLIGHTLY DIFFERENT.

"Monk" Lewis (says Gronow) had a black servant, affectionately attached to his master; but so ridiculously did this servant repeat his master's expressions, that he became the laughing-stock of all his master's friends.

Brummell used often to raise a hearty laugh at Carlton House by repeating witticisms which he pretended to have heard from Lewis's servant; some of these were very stale, yet they were considered so good as to be repeated at the clubs, and greatly added to the reputation of the Beau as a teller of good things. "On one occasion," said Brummell, "I called to inquire after a young lady who had sprained her ankle." Lewis, on being asked how she was, had said in the black's presence, "The doctor has seen her, put her legs straight, and the poor chicken is doing well." The servant, therefore, told me, with a mysterious and knowing look, "Oh, sir, the doctor has been here; she has laid eggs, and she and the chickens are doing well."

A MODEL WAITER.

Charles Mathews, jun., once told me (says J. C. Young) that he went into an eating-house to have lunch, and found the orders given by the visitors on the first floor were conveyed below to the kitchen through a tube. A gentleman came in and ordered a basin of ox-tail soup; two, mock-turtle; three others asked for pea-soup; and one more, for bonilli. The waiter, too busy to give the orders for each separately, gave them altogether, with great rapidity, in this concentrated form, at the mouth of the tube:—"One ox—two mocks—three peas—and a bully!"

HE WAS DRUNK.

Mr Tenant (says Lady Holland) lived in a small lodging, and his establishment consisted solely of an old black servant, who tyrannized over him in no small degree, called Dominique. He was overheard one morning calling from his bed, "Dominique! Dominique!" but no Dominique appeared. "Why don't you bring me my stockings, Dominique?" "Can't come, massa." "Why can't you come, Dominique?" "Can't come, massa; I'm dronke."

A SMALL GROOM.

This is one of Dickens's stories[1]:—A very small groom, with fiery-red hair, has looked very hard at me, and fluttered about me at the same time like a giant butterfly. After a pause, he says, in a Sam-Wellerish kind of way, "I went to the club this mornin', sir. There vorn't no letters, sir." "Very good, Topping." "How's missis, sir?" "Pretty well, Topping." "Glad to hear it, sir. *My* missis ain't very well, sir." "No!" "No, sir; she's agoin', sir, to have a hincrease very soon, and it makes her rather nervous, sir; and ven a young voman gets at all down at sich a time, sir, she goes

1 Field's *Yesterdays with Authors.*

down werry deep, sir." To this sentiment I reply affirmatively, and then he adds, as he stirs the fire (as if he were thinking out aloud), "Wot a mystery it is! Wot a go is natur'!" With which scrap of philosophy he gradually gets nearer to the door, and so fades out of the room.

N O W !

One of Hook's stories was of Sir George Warrender, who was once obliged to put off a dinner-party in consequence of the death of a relative, and sat down to a haunch of venison by himself. While eating, he said to his butler, "John, this will make a capital hash to-morrow." "Yes, Sir George, if you leave off *now!*"

THE SAME.

This same man (adds Dickens) asked me one day, soon after I came home [from America], what Sir John Wilson was. This is a friend of mine, who took our house and servants and everything as it stood, during our absence in America. I told him an officer. "A wot, sir?" "An officer." And then, for fear he should think I meant a police officer, I added, "An officer in the army." "I beg your pardon, sir," he said, touching his hat, "but the club as I always drove him to wos the United Servants." The real name of this club is the United Service, but I have no doubt he thought it was a high-life-below-stairs kind of resort, and that this gentleman was a retired butler or superannuated footman.

THEY WILL DO IT.

A friend of mine (says Frederick Locker) had a gamekeeper who was an original, and often expressed himself very incisively. One day he was in the cover with a neighbour who invariably missed everything he aimed at. A pheasant got up, the neighbour blazed away, some feathers flew, and he exclaimed in a voice of natural exultation, "I hit him that time, Cox, and no mistake." The man's reply was characteristic: "Ah, sir, they *will* fly into it sometimes."

A THOUGHTFUL SERVANT.

Nearly one hundred years ago (says the same writer) my grandfather, Captain William Locker, was at dinner, and a servant boy, lately engaged, was handing him a tray of liqueurs, in different-sized glasses. Being in the middle of an anecdote to his neighbour, he mechanically held out his hand towards the tray, but, as people often do when they are thinking of something else, he did not take a glass. The boy thought he was hesitating which liqueur he would have, and like a good fellow, wishing to help his master, he pointed to one particular glass, and whispered, "That's the biggest, sir."

A JACK-ASS HURRY.

[When George Young, uncle of the Rev. J. C. Young], was taking the waters at Carlsbad, he was favourably impressed by the looks and manners of a young man, attached to the hotel in which he was living. Leopold Kiefer (says J. C. Young) was an intelligent, honest, sober, well-principled creature; but he laboured under one besetting infirmity, which he never could get the better of. His utterance was so rapid, and his articulation so indistinct, that —what with his broken English and his German dialect, and his nervous anxiety to satisfy his benefactor—he made himself perfectly unintelligible. My uncle was so indisposed to find fault, that he usually contented himself with giving the erring one a look of eloquent reproof. But on one particular occasion, when he was rattling off his messages in his usual style, he was interrupted in his wild career with this admonition, "Leopold, don't be in one of your jack-ass hurries." These words, and the tone in which they were spoken, sank so deep into the poor fellow's soul, that he generally, ever after, preluded anything he had to say with the assurance that he "was not in a jack-ass hurry." I recall, with much amusement, being at dinner with my two uncles on one occasion, when a thundering knock at the front door, and a violent ring at the bell, caused my uncle George to drop his knife and fork on his plate. The din which unnerved the master only excited the man; a torpedo could not have affected his sympathetic nature more powerfully. In one instant he had darted out of the room; in another, he had darted in again, and delivered himself of the following statement, with the volubility peculiar to Charles Mathews and the incoherency peculiar to himself, and with all the words strung together:—" Eef—you—bleaze—shur —here—ees—a—shentleman—on—a—door—at—a—hoarse—mit—a—groom —vich—vould—speak—mit—you—on—a—door." He was received with a look of sad reproof by my uncle, who had risen from table, napkin in hand, fearing that something serious was the matter. This at once brought the culprit to his bearings. Conscious that he had transgressed, he suddenly *drew himself up*, and, in a manner as stiff and constrained as that of a private when told at drill to "stand at ease," and taking care to enunciate his words with a suitable interval between each, he thus corrected himself:—" Eef—you —bleaze—shur—I—ham—not—in—a—shack—hass—horry—bot—dere—ees a—shentleman—on—he's—groom—mit—he's—horse—on—de—door."

A PIOUS HOPE.

When one day visiting a prison chaplain, the Rev. W. Harness[1] asked him whether his ministry had been attended with success. "With very little, I grieve to say," was the reply. "A short time since I thought I had brought to a better state of mind a man who had attempted to murder a woman and had been condemned to death. He showed great signs of contrition after the sentence was passed upon him, and I thought I could observe the dawnings of grace upon the soul. I gave him a Bible, and he was most assiduous in the study of it, frequently quoting passages from it which he said convinced him of the heinousness of his offence. The man gave altogether such a promise of reformation, and of a change of heart and life, that I exerted myself to the utmost, and obtained for him such a commutation of his sentence as would enable him soon to begin the world again, and, as I hoped, with a happier result. I called to inform him of my success. His gratitude knew no bounds ; he said I was his preserver, his deliverer. "And here," he added, as he grasped my hand in parting, " here is your Bible. I may as well return it to you, for I hope that I shall never want it again."

IN DANGER OF HIS LIFE.

Sir Nicholas Bacon (says Lord Campbell) used to tell a story which he was supposed to have invented or embellished—that at [an] assize town a notorious rogue, knowing there was a clear case against him, and hoping that he might have some chance from my Lord Judge's tone of humour, instead of pleading, took to himself the liberty of jesting ; and, as if the Judge having some evil design, he had been to sware the peace against him, exclaimed, " I charge you in the Queen's name to seize and take away that man in the red gown there, for I go in danger of my life because of him."

V. AND W.

The grand Vittoria Festival in Vauxhall Gardens was (says Jerdan) an enjoyment in its way. The illuminated V's and W's were very brilliant, and the jest was made of one Cockney asking another what the letters meant, and receiving for answer, " Vy, the V's stand for Vellington, and the W's for Wictory, to be sure."

A DOUBLE-BREASTED GUN.

Jones, the tailor, was asked by a customer who thought much of his cut, to go down and have some shooting with him in the country. Among the party

---

[1] See the *Life and Letters* by L'Estrange.

(says **L'Estrange**) **was** the Duke of Northumberland. "Well, Mr Jones," observed his Grace, "**I'm glad to see** you are becoming a sportsman. **What** sort of gun **do you shoot with?**" "Oh, **with** a double-breasted one, your Grace," **was the reply.**

A REMARKABLE CLERK.

The following letter (says J. C. Young) was sent from a clerk to his rector. It would appear that the clerk had complained of the insignificant remuneration he had received **for his services, and** finding that there was no idea on the part of the rector or the churchwardens of raising his fees, he threw up his office in disgust. **Subsequent reflection convinced him he had made a mis-**take. **It was, therefore, in the spirit of penitence that he wrote the following** extraordinary production to **his rector :--"Dear and Rev. Sir,—I avail my-**self of the opportunity of troubling **your honour with these blundered-up** lines, which I hope you will excuse, and which is the very sentiments of your humble servant's heart. I, ignorantly, rashly, but reluctantly, gave warning to leave your highly-respected office, and most amiable duty, as being your servant and clerk of this your most well-worked parish, and place of my succour and **support.** But, dear sir, I well know it was no fault of yours, nor **any of** my most worthy parishioners. It was because I thought I were not sufficiently paid for the interment of the silent dead. **But,** will I be a Judas, and leave the house of my God, the place where His honour dwelleth, for a few pieces **of silver?** No! Will I be a Peter, and deny myself of **an office** in His **sanctuary,** and cause myself to weep bitterly? **No! Can I be so** **unreasonable as** to deny, if **I live and am well, the pleasure to ring that** solemn toll that speaks **the departure of a soul?** No! **Can I leave off** digging the tombs of my neighbours and acquaintance, which **have many a** **time made me shudder and think of my** mortality, **especially when I have** dug up **the mortal remains of some one as I perhaps very well** knew? **No!** Can I so **abruptly forsake the services of my beloved** church, which I have not failed **to attend** of every Sunday, for **this seven** year and **a** half? No! Can I **leave** waiting upon you, **a** minister of that Being 'that sitteth between the **cherubims, and** flieth upon the wings of **the wind?'** No! **Can I leave** the place where our most holy service calls forth, and says—'Those whom God hath joined together (and being, as I **am, a married man), let no man** put asunder?' No! **Can I** leave that ordinance, where you say, 'Thus and thus, I baptize thee in the name of,' etc., etc., etc.; and he becomes 'regene-rate and grafted into the body of Christ's church?' No! Can I think of leaving off cleaning, at Easter, the house of God, in whom I take such delight, in looking down her aisles, **and beholding her sanctuary and the** table of the Lord? No! **Can I forsake** taking a part in the service of thanksgiving of women after childbirth, when mine own wife has been delivered these ten times ? No ! Can I leave off waiting on the congregation of the Lord, which you well know, sir, is my delight ? No ! Can I leave the table of the Lord, at which I have feasted a matter of, I dare say, full thirty times ? No ! And, dear sir, can I ever forsake you, who has ever been kind to me ? No ! And I well know 'you will entreat me not to leave you, neither to return from following after you : for where you pray, there will I pray ; where you worship, will I worship ; your church shall be my church ; your people shall be my people ; and your God shall be my God.' By the waters of Babylon am I to sit down and weep, and leave thee, O my church, and hang my harp upon the trees that grow in the yard ? No ! One thing have I desired of the Lord all the days of my life—'to behold the fair beauty of the Lord, and to visit His temple.' 'More to be desired art thou, O my church, than gold, yea, than much fine gold: sweeter to me than honey and the honeycomb.' Now, think, sir, this is the very desire of my heart, still to wait upon you, which I hope you will find to be my delight as hitherto ; but I, unthinkingly and rashly, said I would no longer ; for which ' I have roared for the very disquietness of my heart.' Now, if you think me worthy to wait upon you, please to tell the churchwardens that all is reconciled ; and, if not, ' I will get me away into the wilderness, and hide me in the desert, in the clefts of the rocks ;' but I hope still to be your Gehazi, and when I meet my Shunamite, to be able to say—' All, all, is well.' I will conclude my blunders with my oft-repeated prayer, that it may be ' As it was in the beginning, is now, and ever shall be, world without end—Amen.' Now, sir, I shall go on with my fees a same as I found them, and will make no more trouble about them ; but I *will not,* I *cannot,* I *must not,* leave you nor my delightful duties. Your most obedient servant, —— —— "

INDEX.

NOTE.—In part of this edition, "Oxford," in the footnote on page 44, is a misprint for "Orford ;" and on page 95, "Maywood" **should be** read "Maynard."

THE END.

COMMERCIAL PRINTING COMPANY, EDINBURGH.

www.ingramcontent.com/pod-product-compliance
Lightning Source LLC
Chambersburg PA
CBHW031347070726
47496CB00017B/1812